KATHLEEN E. WOODIWISS

and

CATHERINE ANDERSON
LORETTA CHASE · LISA KLEYPAS

Three Weddings And A Kiss

AVON BOOKS ◆ NEW YORK

THREE WEDDINGS AND A KISS is an original publication of Avon Books. This work, as well as each individual story, has never before appeared in print. This work is a collection of fiction. Any similarity to actual persons or events is purely coincidental.

AVON BOOKS
A division of
The Hearst Corporation
1350 Avenue of the Americas
New York, New York 10019

Copyright © 1995 by Avon Books
Fancy Free copyright © 1995 by Adeline Catherine Anderson
The Mad Earl's Bride copyright © 1995 by Loretta Chekani
Promises copyright © 1995 by Lisa Kleypas
The Kiss copyright © 1995 by Kathleen E. Woodiwiss

Published by arrangement with the authors
Library of Congress Catalog Card Number: 95-94144
ISBN: 0-380-78122-0

First Avon Books Printing: September 1995

AVON TRADEMARK REG. U.S. PAT. OFF. AND IN OTHER COUNTRIES, MARCA REGISTRADA, HECHO EN U.S.A.

Printed in the U.S.A.

RA 10 9 8 7 6 5 4 3 2 1

A magnificent collection of NEW love stories—a glorious celebration of the tender enchantment of a kiss . . . and the powerful magic of two hearts uniting for all time.

Featuring—

KATHLEEN E. WOODIWISS, the grande nb dame of romantic fiction, author of eight consecutive *New York Times* bestsellers. There are over 32 million copies of her books in print, beginning with *The Flame and the Flower* through to her latest, *Forever in Your Embrace.*

❦

CATHERINE ANDERSON is a past winner of the Romance Writers of America JANET DAILY Award, as well as CAREER ACHIEVEMENT, REVIEWER'S CHOICE, and six consecutive KISS awards from *Romantic Times.*

❦

LORETTA CHASE is a winner of the Romance Writers of America RITA Award.

"A true treasure"
Romantic Times

❦

LISA KLEYPAS is one of the most popular and fastest-rising stars in the romantic firmament.

"More than just a fine writer . . .
She's a genuine phenomenon."
Heart to Heart

❦

*Don't Miss These Romantic Anthologies
from Avon Books*

AVON BOOKS PRESENTS:
HAUNTING LOVE STORIES

AVON BOOKS PRESENTS:
LOVE BEYOND TIME

AVON BOOKS PRESENTS:
NIGHT MAGIC

AVON BOOKS PRESENTS:
STARDUST

AVON BOOKS PRESENTS:
TO HAVE AND TO HOLD

AVON BOOKS PRESENTS:
TO LOVE AND TO HONOR

AVON BOOKS PRESENTS:
UNDER THE MISTLETOE

Contents

Fancy Free
Catherine Anderson

1

The Mad Earl's Bride
Loretta Chase

121

Promises
Lisa Kleypas

255

The Kiss
Kathleen ER. Woodiwiss

359

Three Weddings And A Kiss

Fancy Free

Catherine Anderson

Prologue

~⚡~

Clint Rafferty strode across the worn board-walk in front of the Golden Goose Saloon and shoved open the bat-wing doors. It was hot and noisy inside, reminding him of the bowels of hell that Preacher Wells thundered about on Sunday. As he'd expected, the place was full, a usual oc-currence at half past ten Saturday night, and the hazy, lantern-lit interior reeked of tobacco smoke, unwashed bodies, and cheap perfume.

A girl in a blue gown stood nearby, as though placed there to greet patrons. As soon as she spied Clint, her painted mouth curved into a smile and her glittering blue eyes narrowed. "Looking for company, cowboy?" she asked, sidling his way.

Clint inclined his head politely, his mother's teachings still strong in him even at the age of twenty-seven. "No, ma'am," he drawled. "I'm lookin' for my brother."

"Is that a fact?"

Clint reined in his impatience. Though he had no quarrel with how this soiled dove or any other made her living, he'd never felt the need to pay for a woman's attention—especially when he was tired

3

and hungry and had a good two hours of chores awaiting him at home. "That is a fact."

He glanced past her toward the bar. Sure enough, there stood Matthew leaning against the polished top as if for support, his thick ebony hair lying in sweat-damp waves over his high forehead. From the looks of the kid, he was already sloppy drunk.

Clint muttered an oath under his breath.

"Are you two twins or something?" she asked, glancing back and forth between the two Rafferty men.

Folks had claimed for years that he and Matt were dead ringers for each other, and Clint guessed there were similarities. They shared the same square chin, high cheekbones, smoky eyes and black hair. But there the similarities ended. When Clint smiled, which wasn't often, no one seemed to care. But when Matt flashed that lopsided, lazy grin of his, the whole world seemed to smile with him, especially the female half, many of whom tended to go weak at the knees as well. Even now there was a woman hanging on Matt's opposite arm—a cute little redhead with big green eyes. She went by the name of Dora Faye, if Clint recollected right.

"I've got seven years on him," he explained to the soiled dove, a fact that seemed to surprise her. No sense adding that he'd spent those seven years trying to be both mother and father to Matthew and all his other brothers.

"Then this is your lucky night, sugar," she muttered, "because I just happen to be extra partial to older men."

"Thanks for the offer, but I've got hungry horses to feed and a ledger to balance yet tonight," Clint cut in before she could suggest he buy them both a drink.

She gave him a look of disappointment before

shrugging one bare white shoulder. "The offer's always open. Just ask for Maydeen."

"I just might do that sometime."

Picking his way through the milling bodies, Clint headed in Matthew's direction. Here lately, Matt's drinking sprees had become a weekly occurrence. Damn the kid's hide. He knew about the Rafferty weakness for alcohol. Hadn't he stood at Clint's side when they'd lowered their pa into his grave five years past? The old man had drunk himself to death, for Christ's sake, not to mention that his drinking had left his sons penniless. Unable to make the mortgage payments, they had lost the old home place back in Ohio and wouldn't have had a roof over their heads if not for their moving west to find land they could homestead. By the sweat of all their brows, they were finally starting to get ahead, no thanks to their father, and now here was Matt following in the old man's footsteps.

Clint's first impulse was to grab his brother by the collar and shake him. Instead he elbowed his way in beside him and propped a heel on the boot rail. "Matt, the cattlemen's meetin' is over. I reckon it's about time we thought about headin' home."

Matt turned slowly, his gray blue eyes slightly out of focus, his usually firm mouth lax at the corners. "Clint?" he asked, his tone indicating that he was none too sure.

"Who else?" Clint couldn't stifle a smile as he slowly waved a hand in front of his brother's nose. "You in there, Matthew?"

"Last time I checked, I was." Matt hiccupped, then grinned down at the woman on his other side. "This here pretty lady has been kind enough to buy me a drink, haven't you, darlin'?"

Dora Faye darted a look at Clint's face. "Evenin', Mr. Rafferty," she said in a surprisingly subdued tone. "I didn't realize that you were in town, too."

"Old Clint here, he came in for a meeting with

the other big boys," Matt joked, his voice slurring. "Ain't that right, Brother?"

"Right."

Matt licked his lips, then frowned. "I di'n't think you frequented places like this."

"I don't usually. That doesn't mean I never do." Clint glanced at the glass of whiskey in front of his brother. Not a jigger but a tumbler, for Christ's sake, and half full at that. The last thing Matt needed was more liquor.

Moving quickly so his brother wouldn't anticipate what he meant to do, he reached for the glass. "You don't mind sharin', do you? The old whistle's a little dry."

As Clint curled his hand around the tumbler, Dora Faye caught hold of his wrist. "Say, there, Mr. Rafferty." She inclined her head at the whiskey jug. "Let me pour you your own drink. We've got plenty, and more where this came from."

Wasn't that just the problem? Casting a jaundiced eye at the whiskey jug, Clint saw that the container was three-quarters empty. Little wonder Matt was drunk.

"I don't mind drinking after my brother," he informed the soiled dove, forcing a grin. "Besides, it looks to me like he's had about enough."

For just an instant, her grip seemed to tighten on his wrist. Then, with a nervous smile and a flash of her green eyes, she released him, muttering something under her breath that he couldn't quite catch. Tipping the glass to her in a mock toast, Clint tossed down the liquor, then clenched his teeth at the burn. "Not bad."

Grabbing the bottle, Matt poured another measure of whiskey, some of which sloshed over the edge of the glass onto the bar. "Go ahead, Clint. Enjoy. Like Dora Faye says, there's always more where this came from."

Though Clint could have done without another

drink, he didn't want his brother to consume what remained in the bottle, either. Making no objection, he drained the glass a second time and said nothing when Matt filled it with liquor yet again. Unfortunately, as he set the tumbler down for the third time, Matt signaled the bartender for a new jug.

"Forget it, Matt—you've had enough," Clint suggested softly. "Let's just call it a night, pard, and head on home."

"Don't go tryin' to play mama, big brother. I'm a little old for coddlin'."

"Coddlin' is the last thing on my mind." Clint clamped a hand over his brother's shoulder and gave him a jostle. "It's late, and we've both had a full day. It's best we go home now, okay? Build us a fire, brew us some coffee. It'll be nice for a change."

"You go ahead." Matt slipped an arm around Dora Faye's waist. "As the old sayin' goes, the night is still young." The slightly built barmaid caught him from stumbling as he shifted his weight toward her and released his hold on the bar. "I'll be home in the mornin', Clint. Bright 'n' early, and none the worse for wear, I promise."

Clint knew better. After a few more drinks, Matt would pass out and sleep until late tomorrow, whereupon he would awaken sick to his stomach and with a terrible headache.

"I guess I was just hopin' to have some company on the ride home," Clint tried. "We hardly ever get any time together when we're not working anymore."

"Maybe next time," Matt suggested. With that, he bent to nuzzle Dora Faye's ear. To keep them both from falling, she leaned into him with all her weight. "Hey, honeybee," he said. "How's about we go upstairs?"

Clint drew his hand from his brother's shoulder. "Well, I guess I'll be moseyin'."

Matt, who had abandoned Dora Faye's ear to nibble on her neck, didn't bother to respond. Heavy of heart, Clint stood there, reluctant to leave, yet knowing Matt was old enough to make his own choices. He finally turned away when he saw his brother signal the barkeep for another jug. For better or worse, Matt was on his own.

Pushing the bat-wing doors open with one shoulder, Clint spilled out onto the boardwalk and took a bracing breath. Instead of clearing, however, his head seemed to fog over even more, a result of the whiskey he rarely consumed, he decided sourly.

Letting the doors swing shut behind him, he turned left along the boardwalk, his heels tapping out a hollow-sounding tattoo on the weathered wood. From between the buildings, stripes of silvery moonlight spilled across the walkway, marking his progress.

Glancing up Main, he saw lights at only a few windows. It was almost midnight. Most families had settled in for the night. The thought made him feel sad and hollow inside. Not long ago, all the Raffertys would have been home in bed as well.

Not long ago? He squeezed his eyes closed, remembering what it had been like when his folks were alive. Wonderful, home-cooked meals. Lace curtains at the windows. The sound of laughter. Six years had passed since his ma's death, five since his da had joined her. In actuality, it wasn't so very long a time, yet to Clint, who'd shouldered the responsibility for his younger brothers, it seemed an eternity.

Pausing in front of the mercantile, he gazed with an ache of yearning at the window display, illuminated by the moon. Bess Harrison, the proprietor's wife, who was very talented with her hands, had fashioned a miniature kitchen on the opposite side of the glass. The cheery scene made him think of the drab, austere atmosphere awaiting him at home. No cheery kitchen, no place settings, no flowers, no lace curtains. It took a woman's touch to make a house cozy, and that the Raffertys sorely lacked.

Not for the first time, Clint found himself wondering if he shouldn't get married. Maybe Matt wouldn't find it necessary to stay in town so much if his home were more pleasant. Since moving to Shady Corners, Clint had accomplished a lot, but most of the improvements he'd made were on the land. The house needed fixing, and six-year-old Cody needed a mother. Even Daniel, next youngest at fourteen, was showing signs of growing up uncivilized, a result, Clint figured, of his own inadequate parenting skills.

But damn! He was a rancher, not a nursemaid. He knew cows and horses, and on occasion, how to prod his lazy brothers into pulling their own weight. But Cody and Daniel still had bad dreams about their parents' deaths that Clint didn't know how to soothe and temper tantrums he didn't understand. Worst of all were the nights Cody cried himself to sleep from sheer misery because Clint didn't know how to comfort him.

That was one of the main reasons Clint had written to his great-aunt Hester a few months back. She was a kindly woman who'd never been blessed with children of her own. Now that she was widowed, he was hoping she'd be interested in leaving Ohio and starting a new life with them here in Oregon. So far, though, she hadn't answered his letter, and now so much time had gone by that he was beginning to doubt she ever would. Which led him right back to his original thought, that maybe he should get married.

Resuming his pace along the boardwalk, he tried to imagine what it would be like to have a female in the house again. Better, he guessed. Probably a lot better. It would definitely be nice to come in of an evening to a hot, home-cooked meal, and it sure couldn't hurt to have someone around to keep up with the laundry. With eight people contributing, the pile of unwashed clothes seemed mountainous. Yep. No question about it; having a woman around the house would be a big improvement.

The way his luck had been running lately, however, none of the pretty, sought-after young ladies hereabouts would be interested in taking on such a large, ready-made, and admittedly rowdy family of males, and he'd be forced to settle for some homely girl no one else wanted.

It was a singularly unappealing thought.

1

Heart pounding in her throat, Rachel Constantine stared at her intended victim as he drew abreast of her on the opposite boardwalk. She would have been pleased to see him stagger just a little, anything to assure her he had indeed been drugged. As it was, it was difficult to tell he'd even had anything to drink.

With a sigh, she plucked her wire-framed spectacles from her nose and stashed them in her skirt pocket. From here on, she would have to settle for looking at Rafferty through a blur. Better that than risk being seen wearing eyeglasses. Most men didn't find ladies with poor eyesight attractive, and for tonight, at least, it was vitally important that Rachel be a femme fatale. *Drat!* Why did he look so sober? Had something gone wrong inside the saloon? Maybe he wasn't drugged, after all. Just the thought made her pulse race even faster and her knees go weak.

Biting her lip, she cast a glance at the saloon. To her relief, she saw Dora Faye standing inside the doors, signaling just as they had planned, to let her know everything had gone smoothly. Unless Matt

Rafferty had the constitution of an ox, he would be unconscious in a few minutes. Rachel smiled into the darkness. From her hiding place in the shadows, it would do no good to wave back at her friend, so she made a mental note to stop by the saloon tomorrow to thank Dora Faye profusely. None of this would have been possible without her help.

As Rafferty moved past the mercantile, he slowed to a stop, standing in silhouette against the moon-washed glass. Rachel squinted to see him better, then wished she hadn't. He seemed taller than she remembered, maybe a little broader across the chest and shoulders as well. *Just a trick of moonlight and shadow,* she assured herself. *Don't go letting your nerves get the best of you.*

Unfortunately, it wasn't that simple. Matt Rafferty was walking, talking trouble, definitely not the type a decent young woman approached without some measure of trepidation. Nevertheless, the man couldn't be allowed to go around humiliating young girls and breaking their hearts. At the very least, he deserved to be taken to task. Because her fourteen-year-old sister Molly was his latest victim, Rachel felt that it was her job to do just that. Hence, the plan she'd concocted with Dora Faye's assistance.

As surefooted as a prospector's mule, Rafferty stepped off the boardwalk to cross the street. Watching him come toward her, Rachel felt her mouth go dry. This was it. Going down the list of dos and don'ts Dora Faye had given her, she stepped out from the shadow of the general store. "Well, hello, Mr. Rafferty!" she called, trying for a flirtatious twitter. "What a pleasant surprise!"

Evidently taken off guard, he broke stride and came to a slow stop. Without her eyeglasses, Rachel knew she tended to look a bit owlish, so she tried not to open her eyes too wide. As she closed the distance between them, his blurry edges took on better definition. No doubt about it, the man was bigger than she cared to admit.

"Rachel Constantine? Rachel Constantine, the marshal's daughter?"

Giving a throaty laugh, just as Dora Faye had taught her, she said, "How many Rachel Constantines do you think there are in Shady Corners, a baker's dozen?"

He seemed baffled by the question. Clearly, his thought processes were muddled, a sign the valerian Dora Faye had put in his whiskey was taking effect.

She drew up a few feet shy of him and struck a seductive pose. It was hard to remember all that Dora Faye had taught her—how to move, stand, and smile.

"Trust me, sir," she informed him in a twittery little voice, "there is only *one* Rachel Constantine. My pa says that after me, they broke the mold."

She immediately wanted to call back the words. Irresistible temptresses did *not* talk about their fathers. Even she knew that.

Though the eight Rafferty brothers had been living in the area for nearly a year now, her eyesight was such that she'd never gotten close enough to get a good look at any of them. It seemed to her that tongues had been buzzing forever about how handsome they all were. She was absolutely dying to see what all the fuss was about.

Not that she was personally interested. Goodness, no. She had her eye on Lawson Wells, the minister's son. Tall, painfully thin, and nearly as blind as she, he was about as far from handsome as a body could get. Consequently, he was sweet and thoughtful and caring, all the things Matt Rafferty obviously wasn't, no doubt because he was so handsome he felt he had no need to be. A pox on handsome men: that was Rachel's motto.

Even so, she was curious. At the risk of appearing myopic, she leaned closer so she could see his face more clearly and judge his looks for herself. No question about it, he *was* handsome. A bit older looking than expected, but she imagined working outdoors and drinking heavily would make anyone look older than he actually was.

Even shaded by his hat, his smoky blue eyes glistened in the moonlight like raindrops shot through with lightning. Thick waves of ebony hair fell lazily across his forehead, and whether it was a trick of light or an actual cast to his skin, he looked to be deeply tanned. Oh, yes, he was handsome, but not in the usual way. There was something about him, a lethal edge, that made her wary. *Dangerous.* Matt Rafferty wasn't merely dreamy, as rumor painted him, but dangerous. Little wonder poor Molly had come away lacerated and heartsick.

Rachel didn't like the way he studied her—a lazy appraisal, his eyes glinting as if at some private joke. It seemed at odds with the stories she'd heard, namely that he was a charmer. Instead, he was making her feel awkward and more than a little frightened, which seemed more in keeping with the stories she had heard about his older brother, Clint. Now *there* was a man to avoid, always serious, never smiling. His gray-blue eyes could sear right through a woman, according to her friends.

After completing the slow appraisal of her person, Matt flicked his gaze to hers and said in a deep, silken voice, "That must've been quite some mold, sweetheart."

Mentally, Rachel stumbled about, trying to make sense of his comment. In her bewilderment, she forgot all about looking owlish. Lands, he was attractive. No wonder poor little Molly had gotten a crush on him. "Pardon?"

A smile flickered across his firm mouth. "The mold that got broke after they made you? Judging by the results, it must've been quite some mold.''

"Oh!" Rachel gave a horrified little laugh. "*That* mold. So much time passed that—well, I totally forgot—" She realized she was babbling and waving her hands like a lunatic. She punctuated the inanity with another shrill laugh.

"What are you doing out at this time of night? Good little girls like you should be home in bed with the covers tucked up to their chins."

Coming from any other man, the appellation "little girl" would have infuriated her. At eighteen, she was still new enough to womanhood to be easily offended if someone insinuated she wasn't yet an adult. Not so with Matt Rafferty. Compared to him, she'd be a child at ninety. In the silvery gloom, his features, sharp, uncompromising, and blatantly male, looked as if they had been carved from polished mahogany, giving his face a hardness that made her pulse skitter.

"Maybe I'm not the good little girl you think I am."

Touching a fingertip to the edge of his hat, he nudged back the brim and arched one black eyebrow. "Is that so?"

Shoving her hand into her skirt pocket, she curled her fingers around her spectacles and raised her chin a notch. Swamped with old resentments, she glared at him through the gloom, remembering another man who had laughed at her.

"It's been my observation that good little girls don't have very much fun."

"True," he agreed with a slow grin, "but, then, most good little girls don't realize what they're missing."

"Well, I do."

Judging by the way one corner of his mouth twitched, that proclamation amused him. "Oh, really? And who was the lucky fellow?"

Rachel couldn't see how any one fellow played into it. "Pardon?"

He chuckled, the sound a low murmur from deep in his chest.

"Is it a private joke, Mr. Rafferty, or will you share it with me?"

"It's nothing, really. Just that you answered my question."

"What question?"

"As to whether or not you realize what you're missing. I have a hunch you don't."

Rachel's chin went up another notch. "If not, why would I be here?"

"Good point. Care to enlighten me?"

"Because I'm tired of living a dull existence, that's why."

His full but firm mouth tipped up at one corner again. The grin had scarcely left his lips when he yawned. He pinched the bridge of his nose and shook his head. When he looked at her again, his eyes were a little unfocused. "So you're tired of a dull existence, are you? Why do I have this feelin' you're hopin' I'll remedy that?"

"Possibly because I am." Rachel affected a sultry smile and tried not to think about the seconds that were racing by. "Who better than you when a girl's lookin' for an exciting experience? I hear tell you're a carefree fellow and always game."

"You must have me confused with someone else, darlin'. Carefree isn't in my vocabulary, especially not when it comes to you. I have an aversion to bein' locked up, you see. A man'd have to be crazy to mess with Big Jim Constantine's daughter."

"Don't tell me you're scared of my pa?"

"Damned straight." His mouth tipped into another teasing grin that flashed perfectly straight white teeth. "And scared I'll stay as long as he's wearin' that badge."

"But, Mr. Rafferty, my pa's never gonna know about this. You have my word."

"He ain't gonna know because there ain't gonna be a *this*," he said with a laugh.

Driven to brazenness by sheer desperation, Rachel stepped closer to him. Recalling Dora's instructions, she hooked a finger under the front placket of his shirt. She couldn't help but notice how iron hard his flat belly felt against her knuckles.

Trying to remember all that her friend had told her to say, she crooned, "I know this is going to sound terribly forward, but I can't help myself, Mr. Rafferty. I want you."

His smile deepened. "Say what?"

Rachel wiggled closer, not at all sure she liked the tingling sensation in her nipples as she grazed his shirt with her bodice. "I want you." She paused, trying to remember the other things Dora had suggested she say. "I'll do whatever I have to. Deep and slow, or hard and fast, however suits you, I'm yours for the taking."

He gave another low laugh. "All right. I'll bite. Why?"

His response was so unexpected that Rachel's heart leaped. "What?"

Stressing each word as if she were an imbecile, he said, "Why do you want me?"

Of all the questions she and Dora had anticipated he might ask, this wasn't one of them. The truth was, Rachel didn't have a clue why any female would be attracted to him. Oh, he was handsome, she'd give him that, but he was also a little terrifying.

"Because you fascinate me," she blurted, which was the unvarnished truth. She *was* fascinated by him—in a morbid sort of way.

"Why are you fascinated?"

"Because you're exciting."

Even in the moonlight, she saw his eyes twinkling. He chucked her under the chin. "More exciting than you can handle. Go home, honey. If you want to cut your teeth on some poor fellow, go gnaw on your little friend Lowry, the minister's son. He won't bite back. I just might."

"Lawson, his name is Lawson. And he's not the one I'm interested in."

He touched the brim of his hat. "G'night, sweet cheeks. I appreciate the offer. It's mighty generous and about as sweet a proposition as I've ever had. But, unfortunately, I'm going to have to pass."

With that, he started to walk away. Rachel saw him sway slightly before he caught himself. Filled with a sense of urgency, knowing that this chance would be forever lost unless she acted fast, she grabbed his arm. "Please, don't go! Please?"

He swung back around. In a tone that was suddenly serious, he said, "Rachel, I told you to go home." He paused for a moment as if to let that sink in. "If you're smart, you'll run, not walk. From the way I'm startin' to feel, I'd say I've had a little too much to drink, and you're too tempting by half. My head isn't real clear. When a man can't think straight, he doesn't have as much willpower as he ought. Keep on, and I'm liable to accept your offer. We'll both regret it come morning, you more so than me."

Rachel had news for him: he would be the one with regrets. "What can I do to make you change your mind?" She pressed her body against his. "I've already thrown myself at your feet. Don't humiliate me more by walking away."

"Christ!" Teeth clenched, jaw muscle twitching, he squeezed his eyes shut.

Rachel rubbed herself against him more insistently. "Please?"

"Damn it, girl," he said in a gravelly voice, "go

home. Play with fire and you're bound to get burned."

"Oh, yes, if you're the fire, I *want* to be burned. Please, I wan—"

He vised an arm around her waist and settled his mouth over hers. For an instant, she wasn't sure what had happened. Slowly, measure by measure, her stunned mind began to register sensations: his mouth, hot and silken, pressed firmly against hers; his arm cinched around her waist; his hand splayed over her back; his fingertips curled over her side; his steely thighs bracing hers. Fire didn't describe Matt Rafferty. A blazing inferno, more like. She felt as though she were being consumed.

Just last week, she'd finally permitted Lawson to kiss her. The techniques of the two men were about as much alike as warm milk and jalapeño juice. In Lawson's arms, Rachel had felt safe and faintly bored. In Matt's, she felt as if she were dangling from a cliff, he her only anchor. His kiss was hard and demanding. There was no shyness in him, no hesitation, only steely determination. Beneath her hands, which she'd instinctively brought up to push him away, his chest was roped with muscle that lay rigid under a layer of firm yet resilient male flesh. His torso was like an unyielding wall of granite, crushing her breasts, making her intensely aware that her body was far more sensitive and vulnerable than his.

When he finally drew back, Rachel gasped for breath, her gaze startled. "Are you still sure you want to be burned?" he demanded gruffly. "I'm warnin' you—think carefully before you answer. There comes a point where there is no turnin' back, you know, and I've about reached it."

It occurred to Rachel in that moment that he had deliberately kissed her roughly to frighten her away and that now he expected her to bolt. Well, she didn't scare quite that easily. He burned hot, all right, but thanks to some whiskey laced with valerian, his flame would soon flicker out. The most he could do in the time he had left was singe her edges a bit.

"Oh, yes," she whispered, "I still want to be burned."

For just an instant, he hesitated, his gaze delving deeply into hers as if he searched for answers. Then, as if he'd found them, he bent his head and settled his mouth over hers again, more gently this time, but with even more devastating impact.

2

Wet silk. Cool fire. Icy flames licked Rachel's skin, making her burn and shiver.

"Part your lips, sweetheart," Matt Rafferty whispered urgently against her mouth.

Afraid to deny him for fear he'd guess that her seductive act was all a ruse, she did as he told her. The next thing she knew, his tongue slipped past her teeth. Shock snapped her body taut. She made fists on his shirt front. As if he sensed her startlement, he drew back to nibble lightly at her lower lip. "It's all right. Just trust me."

Rachel would have sooner trusted a snake, but deep within her, everything that was feminine responded to the husky timber of his voice. When he kissed her again, she parted her lips, allowing him to taste her mouth. He plundered the sensitive flesh, tickling the roof of her mouth and drawing sharply on her tongue, forcing it to dance with his in a rhythmic thrust that made her belly tighten and tingle in a strange way.

The unfamiliar sensation frightened her, but when she tried to end the kiss, she discovered that he'd curled a hand over the back of her head. She remembered his warning, that after a certain point, there was no turning back. Fighting down panic, she reminded herself he'd lose consciousness soon. But somehow that wasn't very reassuring. A flash fire could cover a lot of ground in a few short minutes.

His breathing was uneven with need, and when she writhed to disengage herself from his embrace, he moaned, the sound catching and quivering at the base of his throat. Another wave of panic surged within her when he slid his hand from her back to her side, his fingertips searching out the shape of her breast and homing in on its peak. She jerked at the contact and managed, finally, to draw her mouth from under his.

"Christ," he whispered against her cheek, each huff of his breath as hot and moist against her skin as the steam from coffee. Through the layers of her clothing, he staked claim to the hardened tip of her nipple, tugging and rolling the sensitive flesh. Rachel was so stunned by the feelings that rocked her, she couldn't breathe, let alone protest. "Ah, sweetheart," he rasped against her temple. "I want that in my mouth."

Given the location of his hand, there was little doubt in Rachel's mind what part of her anatomy he referred to. The very thought appalled her.

"I bet you're as sweet there as sun-warmed honey."

The picture that had begun to form in Rachel's mind was so indecent she nearly kicked him. How dare he even suggest—well, no woman, lady or otherwise, would engage in such outrageous conduct. She jerked his hand from her breast. Because she didn't dare reveal what was actually on her mind, she settled for saying, "Mr. Rafferty, we are standing in the middle of the street where anyone might see us."

"Then let's find someplace private," he murmured near her ear. "It's not every day I have Rachel Constantine beggin' me to make love to her."

He had that much correct, at least. With careful maneuvering, she managed to get some space between their bodies. Cheeks afire, she found it difficult to meet his gaze, so instead she focused on his nose. Even in the dim light, she noticed that there was a knot along its bridge. She wondered if he'd broken it in a fight. Given his reputation as a scrapper, he probably had.

"How about if we go to the church?" she suggested shakily.

"Where?"

By his shocked tone, she guessed he had understood her perfectly. "The church," she repeated. "It's as private a place as we're likely to find."

"The church?" He gave a sharp laugh. "I'm not usually what you'd call a finicky man, but that's not exactly my idea of a suitable spot, darlin'."

"Of course it's suitable. One might even say perfect! Just think. Who ever goes there at this hour on a Saturday night? Even Preacher Wells is home in bed."

"That's true, but—"

"Just think of all those pews, those lovely pews, empty and waiting. It'll be dark in there. We can have hours and hours of uninterrupted privacy." On that last word, Rachel squeezed her eyes closed for a second and sent up a quick, frantic prayer that he wasn't going to be difficult. "It'll be wonderful, just wait and see."

He traced the shape of her ear with the tip of his

tongue. "It just doesn't seem right somehow, fornicating in a holy place."

Of all the things she had planned on, Matt Rafferty having scruples wasn't one of them. Thinking quickly, she said, "Oh, pshaw. Paint and wood, that's all. It's the folks gathering inside the building that makes it holy, not the structure itself. A barn would be just as sacred if people gathered there to worship."

"A barn?"

"Or any other building. Trust me, if we use the church, God won't mind a bit."

He laughed again, more mellowly. "Why do I have this feelin' you're bent on doin' it on a church pew?"

Rachel assumed an impish smile and leaned back. "It's a wonderfully wicked idea, isn't it? And, oh, I do so want to be wicked. Deliciously wicked . . . with you."

It seemed to her that he was beginning to lean his weight more heavily against her. "Then let's go," he said. "Oh, and by the way, hard and fast."

"What?"

"Hard and fast," he repeated, bringing his face closer to hers as he spoke. "You gave me a choice, remember? Deep and slow or hard and fast. I'll take hard and fast."

Rachel shoved against his shoulders, but it was like trying to hold back a mountain. "Um . . . Mr. Rafferty?" She twisted her face to one side so that his hot, silken lips landed harmlessly on her ear again. Or maybe not so harmlessly. He caught her lobe between his teeth and— Rachel gulped. Oh, dear God. He was *sucking* on her earlobe. "Mr. Rafferty?" she tried again, fighting off panic. "Not out here. We have to go to the church, remember?"

"Oh, yeah . . ."

He straightened so abruptly that he staggered, carrying her along with him. She hugged his waist and struggled to regain her balance, terrified he might fall. If he landed on top of her—well, she'd be in a pickle, and no mistake. He was well over six feet tall, and probably outweighed her by close to a hundred pounds.

"Lead the way, ma'am." He stepped aside and swept his hat from his head in an unsteady bow. "Believe me, makin' love to such a pretty lady will be my pleasure."

Rachel grabbed his arm, helped him get his hat back on, and then struck off for the church, an endeavor she quickly learned was going to take far longer than she had estimated. For every step Matt Rafferty took forward, he executed anywhere from two to a dozen in either direction sideways, dragging Rachel with him.

The possibility that he might collapse in the street became more of a threat with each passing moment. If that happened, she could still steal his trousers and leave him where he lay to sleep it off, but it wouldn't be nearly as satisfying as having him wake up in church. After his public rejection of Molly, he deserved to be repaid with the ultimate humiliation. On that thought, Rachel felt him sway again. She was a little amazed at how suddenly the sedative seemed to be hitting him now.

He draped his arm over her shoulders for support. "I think I'm drunk. Not just a little, but real drunk."

"Really?" she asked, feigning incredulity.

"My senti—sendimun—well, shit. I can't even talk straight."

"Sentiments?" she supplied.

He snapped his fingers, nearly taking off the end of her nose in the process, and then started to laugh. "Sent—uh—ments. My sent—uh—ments exack-ly. Only now I can't remember what I was sent-uh-mentin' about."

Looking up at him, Rachel smiled in spite of herself. For a low-down, dangerous, heartless scoundrel, he had a way about him. She decided it was partly that lopsided grin of his, so boyishly disarming in contrast to his harshly planed features. Then, of course, there were his eyes, which always seemed to be twinkling.

"You were just making the observation you might be drunk," she reminded him.

"Boy, howdy." He snapped his fingers again. "On three measly drinks."

"You must have lost count and had more than that."

"Nope. Never have more'n that."

That came as a surprise. Unless the stories she'd heard were totally false, Matt Rafferty frequented the Golden Goose every Saturday night and drank all evening, playing cards and cavorting shamelessly. A man of moderation, he definitely wasn't.

"Oh, come on, you can tell me. You drink the well dry, right?"

He shook his head. "Nope. I don't cotton much to drinkin'."

"Since when?" she asked, curious in spite of herself.

"Since forever. Outa respe—respect for my ma. She didn't cotton to drunkenness, not in her boys. Claimed liquor 'n' Irish was a bad mix. I reckon she was right, 'cause whiskey killed my da."

"Then why drink at all?"

He started to laugh. "Now there's a plan."

She couldn't see what he found so humorous. "I take it you've considered that."

He held up a finger. "But, as you can see, plans have a way of not always working out." He reeled to a sudden stop, focused blearily on something ahead of them in the darkness, and said, "I can't hold the damned things still long enough to get a good count, but they look like too many."

She realized they had reached the church and that he was referring to the front steps. Like him, she had to squint to see them, albeit for different reasons. "Too many for what?"

"To climb." As if he found that hysterically funny, he began to laugh again. Then, with no warning, he leaned down, thumping his forehead sharply against hers. "Jesus . . ." He exhaled in a great rush. "I don't know, honey. I hate to disappoint a lady, but this is one time my good friend Henry may fail to rise to the occasion."

Thinking that he might have made arrangements to meet with his friend Henry after leaving the saloon, Rachel glanced worriedly over her shoulder. "Who's that?"

"Who's what?"

"Henry. Who is he?"

"Henry is—" He broke off and started to laugh again. When he caught his breath, he said, "Dear God, you are sweet. Honest to goodness, pure as an angel, genuine sweet. It's been so long, I'd forgotten girls like you exist."

Rachel couldn't see what her disposition had to do with anything. "Thank you," she said distractedly. "But you didn't answer my question. Who is Henry? You didn't mention that he was going to come."

His shoulders jerked with mirth again. "He isn't. That's the whole damned problem. Ain't that a hell of a note?"

Growing impatient with his nonsensical responses, Rachel steered him toward the steps. "We shall do quite well without him, I assure you."

"Lord, help me."

A chance for revenge beckoning sweetly, she endeavored to help him up the flight of steps. So what if Matt Rafferty seemed kind of nice? She knew he wasn't, that he couldn't possibly be. If he were, he wouldn't have done something so reprehensible to her sister. Why should she show him any mercy when he'd shown Molly none?

All of a sudden, Matt reeled backward. Taken off guard, Rachel tumbled with him. Luckily, they had scaled only a few levels. Dust mushrooming around them, they landed in an ungainly heap at the bottom of the steps, Rachel's skirts and petticoats around her waist, Matt's long legs crisscrossing hers.

"Damn." After taking one look at her, he sat up and brushed at her clothing. "I apologize. There seems to be a slight hitch in my get along. Are you all right?"

With her skirts tossed up as they were, Rachel was too flustered to feel any pain, if indeed she was injured somewhere. He flashed one of those disarming grins at her. "Lucky for you, no one but me is here to see."

She shoved at his shoulder. "I'd prefer that no one see, you included."

"I'm gonna see more'n that before all is said and done."

He attempted to get up, but only made it as far as his knees before losing his balance again. He waved away another plume of dust. "Well, hell."

Rachel read the defeat in his expression and was determined to have none of it. She would get him inside that church, she vowed, even if she had to carry him every inch of the way. "You can do it," she said in an encouraging voice.

"It doesn't look like it to me."

"Yes, well, you're drunk and therefore no judge." She pushed to her feet, grabbed him under the arms, and strained to lift him. "Get up, Mr. Rafferty."

"I'm tryin'."

"Try harder!" Her throat burning from the dirt particles she had inhaled, Rachel groaned with frustration when, after utilizing nearly all her strength, he still hadn't gained his feet. "You have to make it. After getting you this far, I can't quit now."

He jerked his arms from her grasp. "Stop strainin' to lift me," he ordered gruffly. "You're gonna keep on until you hurt yourself."

After making that assessment, he just sat there. Rachel bent over him, hands braced on her knees. "Well, then? Are you going to try or not?"

He smiled blearily up at her. "You know, darlin', I don't believe I've ever run across such an eager little swatch of calico."

Rachel felt like jerking him up by his ears. "Please, Mr. Rafferty, at least try."

"Mr. Rafferty? If we're gonna get cozy"—he rose to his knees again—"then you oughta at least call me by my first name." With a great heave, he stood and started up the steps again, this time with no assistance, calling back over his shoulder, "You better get your little fanny up here and make hay while the sun's shinin'. I feel a little sick."

Rachel hurried after him. Once at the landing, she caught his arm so he wouldn't fall again. Drawing him toward the doors, she said, "Just a few more steps."

"I hate to tell you this, but gettin' there may prove to be the easy part." He chuckled as though he'd said something hysterically funny.

She wrenched one of the double doors open and entered the church rump first, his hands clasped in hers so she could tug him along after her. When the door swung shut, an intense blackness swooped over them. The smell of varnish and beeswax assailed her nostrils. Groping blindly, she located the last row of seats and maneuvered Matt around until she could prop him up against the back of the pew.

Now all she had to do was wait for him to pass out.

That thought no sooner crossed Rachel's mind than his hands settled at her waist. With a gentle strength that, given his condition, surprised her, he drew her toward him. Even in the darkness, she had no difficulty determining that he'd parted his booted feet to pull her between his legs. No more than a black outline, he seemed to loom over her, a threatening wall of masculinity. The brim of his Stetson bumped her forehead. The next instant, his hot, oh-so-soft mouth had taken command of hers and his hands were busily unfastening her bodice.

Rachel tried to scream, but her breath was stolen by his kisses and any sound she might have made was muffled by his mouth. Grabbing his wrists, she arched away from him. Panic welled within her when she felt cool air touch her breasts. Just that quickly, he had opened her bodice. Now only the thin cloth of her chemise shielded her nipples from his searching fingers. His hard palms cupped her fullness, the contact snatching the oxygen from her lungs in a whining rush. A heartbeat later, he firmly captured the peaks of her nipples between thumb and forefinger. Rivulets of fire ran through Rachel, warming her deep within, making her pulse escalate, kindling a need for something indefinable that soon grew to an ache.

Dimly she realized she had completely lost control, that Matt had taken over. He knew his way around a woman's body, that much was clear, and he was pummeling her senses with an onslaught of feelings she'd never dreamed existed.

Struggling to clear her head, Rachel knew she had to get away from him. For some reason, he hadn't passed out on schedule, and now it was anybody's guess when he might. Even so, she had no intention of abandoning her plan, not after having gone through so much to get him here.

Before she left, she had to get his trousers off him.

Trying not to feel what he was doing to her breasts—and failing—she fumbled with his gun belt. When the buckle finally came loose, one hol-

ster swung free and the butt of the revolver
smacked the pew. She winced and bent at the knees
to lower the weapons to the floor before turning
her attention to his trouser belt. Luckily, it was easier to unfasten. She groped for the brass buttons of
his fly. At her touch in so private a place, he stiffened and sucked in his breath.

"Jesus . . ." he whispered raggedly. "Slow down,
sweetheart; you're gettin' ahead of me here."

There was no way that Rachel intended to slow
down. She jerked frenziedly at his trousers, her face
beading with sweat, her heart thudding wildly, her
breasts electrified with unfamiliar sensations where
his masterful fingers toyed with her.

To her relief, he finally abandoned her breasts. A
heartbeat later, however, she felt his hands at the
fastenings of her skirt. She jerked more urgently at
his pants, determined to see this through. Once she
got away from him, she could refasten her own
clothing. He was so sozzled, he wouldn't remember anything that was happening. It would be her
guilty secret that he'd touched her so intimately.

Suddenly he leaned forward to press his forehead against her shoulder. "Whoa," he said in a
slurred, rather faint voice. "I don't feel so good."

Still intent on getting his trousers down, Rachel
strained to bear his weight.

"Oh, Christ," he whispered raggedly.

With that, he slumped toward her. Before Rachel
could react, the breadth of his shoulders struck her
squarely, the full force of his considerable weight
knocking her backward. She screamed, the sound
echoing in the darkness as she fell. Pain exploded
at the base of her skull, and a brilliant white light
flashed inside her head. Then, as though severed
by a sharp knife, all sensation stopped and she
spun away into nothingness.

3

Beeswax and varnish. Sun-dried cotton and leather. As she came awake, Rachel only vaguely registered the scents. When she started to stretch and yawn, however, she realized something was wrong. A massive weight was pressing upon her body. Not only was she unable to move, but she found it difficult to breathe.

Confused and disoriented, she fluttered her lashes, becoming more aware with each passing second that her head ached. Not just a teeny-weeny ache, but a giant, skull-crushing pain that radiated up from the back of her neck.

"For shame!" a woman whispered from somewhere close by. The unexpected sound made Rachel jerk. Before she could move or get her eyes open, another feminine voice said, "I'm telling you, Clara, the young people today have no respect."

Still trapped in a sleepy fog, Rachel frowned in total bewilderment. She didn't recognize the voices as belonging to her sister Molly or to Mrs. Radcliff, the housekeeper. What on earth were strange people doing in her bedroom?

She passed a hand over her face. A blur of multicolored light swam before her eyes. Without her spectacles, she was pretty much accustomed to everything beyond the end of her nose being indistinct, but for some reason, this morning it seemed worse than usual. Determined to clear away the cobwebs, she blinked, but her brain refused to cooperate. Objects around her went in and out of focus, rushing at her as they took on clarity, then receding a bit. Gleaming oak pews? People's faces and stained glass windows? She wasn't in her bedroom at home, that was a certainty.

"This is an abomination," some other woman cried.

"A sin against all that is holy, that's what it is!" another exclaimed.

All that was holy? Rachel had already determined she must be in the church. The question was, what was she doing there? She squeezed her eyes closed again to keep from being sick. Her head . . . Oh, God, her head felt as if it had been split by a sledge. Had she been stricken with a sudden illness? Maybe she had fainted. That would explain the oppressive weight that seemed to be holding her down. Olivia Harrington, a local matron, claimed that a lady's limbs felt heavy and useless immediately after she regained consciousness from a swoon.

Forcing her eyes back open, Rachel tried to ignore the pain and concentrate on her surroundings. Yes, she was definitely inside the church. A vague sense of alarm coursed through her. She remembered something about the church—something important—but for the life of her, she couldn't think what. She only knew she had an awful feeling that something was dreadfully wrong.

The weight that held her anchored to the floor shifted suddenly. The movement was followed by a moan, unmistakably that of a man. The sound, deep and raspy, vibrated through her torso, transforming her sense of alarm into full-blown panic. Someone was lying on her? A male someone? Oh, God. Now that she was coming more awake, she could feel his hand, large and warm, cupped over her breast. It felt as if there was next to nothing by way of clothing between his fingers and her skin.

Forgetting the pain in her head, Rachel gave a thin cry and pushed at the man's shoulders. Despite all her shoving, he didn't so much as budge. Tucking in her chin, she glimpsed wavy black hair and darkly bronzed skin. In a twinkling, her memory of the previous night came rushing back to her.

Matt Rafferty! She threw a horrified look at the sunlight streaming through the stained glass windows.

So close to her ear that his voice seemed a part of her thoughts, he whispered, "What the hell am I doing here?"

That was Rachel's question. "Off," she croaked. "Get *off* me!"

Not nearly as fast as she would have liked, he rose on one elbow. "What the—" When he glanced around them, his body snapped taut. "Oh, Christ!"

She followed his gaze and saw that a crowd of people had entered the church. She had planned for this to happen—for him to awaken, surrounded by onlookers, and feel so humiliated he wanted to die. Only she wasn't supposed to be here with him!

So many people . . . Without her spectacles, she couldn't see their faces very clearly, but even so, she couldn't shake the feeling that they were all staring at her. A prickly sensation crawled over her skin. Like vultures waiting to feed on carrion, they pressed in around her, the different shades of their clothing a kaleidoscopic blur of color beneath the pale ovals of their faces. Filled with a mounting sense of dread, she touched a tremulous hand to her throat. Her *bare* throat?

Startled, she looked down. To her dismay, she saw that the only thing covering her breasts was the thin cotton of her chemise. She gasped and brought up both hands to hide herself.

When Matt noticed the state of her clothing, he glanced down at himself. Judging by the look that crossed his face when he saw that his gun belt was gone and that his trousers had been unfastened, he remembered little of what had happened.

In a voice gone gravelly with sleep, he said, "What the hell?" As he scrambled off her, he began buttoning his blue jeans. "How did I—when did we—?"

Before he could finish, one of the church doors swung open and struck the interior wall. The bang was almost deafening. "Where is she? Rachel Marie!" Clothing rustled and shoe leather creaked as the crowd moved aside to clear a path. "Get back, folks. Out of my way!"

Even in a nearsighted blur, Rachel recognized the buckskin vest, white shirt, and shiny star that were her father's trademarks. His voice, pitched to a loud roar, was unmistakable as well. It didn't take a genius to determine that someone had gone to fetch him when she and Matt were found inside the church.

She rushed to finish fastening the buttons of her bodice before he saw her. She was only about halfway done when Big Jim Constantine finally managed to fight his way to the front of the crowd. He took one look at her and said, "Oh, Rachel . . ."

"It's not the way it looks, Daddy. Truly! Just give me a chance to explain!"

Rachel had every reason to believe her father would do exactly that. He was an easygoing and fair-minded man who always asked plenty of questions and listened to the answers before he passed judgement.

She reached up a hand. Instead of helping her up, though, her father took one look at her partially unbuttoned shirtwaist and lunged at Matt Rafferty. "You low-down miserable son of a—!"

"Daddy!" Rachel shrieked. "What are you—oh, my God! Stop it!"

Rachel may as well have saved her breath, for her father seemed not to hear her. A tall individual of considerable breadth and girth, he landed on the younger man like a diver doing a belly flop. Matt, evidently still feeling the effects of the valerian, fell back under the onslaught, his breath rushing from his lungs in a loud *whoosh*. Before he could even start to defend himself, Big Jim wrapped both hands around his throat.

"You miserable little worm! You conscienceless son of a bitch! I'll kill you for this. I'll kill you with my bare hands!"

From that point on, everything took on a nightmarish quality for Rachel. She had the oddest feeling she was hovering somewhere above herself, that she watched everything through a plate of breath-fogged glass.

"Daddy, stop this!" She clung futilely to her father's arm. "You have to stop this. He's been drugged and can't defend himself. Oh, dear God, you'll kill him!"

Her father tried to shake her off. "Let go, girl. Dammit, let go!"

Nothing could have induced Rachel to do that. This was her fault. All her fault. Nearsighted though she was, she could tell Matt's face was turning crimson. As bitter as her feelings toward him had been last night, she didn't want him dead.

"Daddy, for heaven's sake! Look what you're doing!"

Rachel nearly wept with relief when three men rushed forward to assist her. After several attempts, the trio managed to drag Big Jim off. Judging by the way Matt choked and gasped for air afterward, he hadn't been released a second too soon.

The instant the three men turned her father loose, Rachel flung herself against him. "Daddy, you have to listen to me. This isn't his fault. I swear it. Please, you have to give me a chance to explain."

His chest heaving with exertion, her father

shrugged to straighten his shirt. "All right, so explain."

Before Rachel could speak, the church doors banged open again, indicating that yet another person had entered. Bodies shuffled. The next instant, Rachel heard a horrified gasp. There was no mistaking Molly's voice, even when the noises she made were inarticulate. Rachel's heart caught. She had meant to avenge her sister, not force her to endure yet more heartbreak.

"Rachel?" Molly whispered, clearly aghast. "Oh, lands, what've you gone and done?"

Rachel thought the answer to that was fairly obvious. She'd brought Matt Rafferty down a few notches, never mind the fact that she was going down with him.

"Oh, Molly." Rachel bit her lip, wishing with all her might that her sister hadn't come into the church.

Molly shook her head. "Oh, Rachel! You did this for me. I know you did!" She pressed her hands over her cheeks. "Oh, this is awful! You got the wrong one!"

Rachel couldn't imagine what Molly meant by that, and before she had time to think about it, her father interrupted with a sharp command to explain herself. As briefly as she could, Rachel recounted the events that had led to this moment, trying her best to leave nothing out, no matter how bad it made her look. The only concession she made to that was by neglecting to mention Dora Faye. Her father could assume whatever he wished, that she had bribed one of the saloon's regular patrons to drug Matt Rafferty's whiskey or that one of the upstairs girls had done it as a favor to Rachel. It really didn't matter as long as Dora Faye didn't get into trouble.

As Rachel wound down, she watched Big Jim closely, trying without success to read his expres-

sion. "So, you see, Daddy, it really wasn't his fault.
I tricked Mr. Rafferty into coming here. I would
have been long gone this morning if I hadn't fallen
and hit my head."

Molly wailed forlornly, which prompted Big Jim
to cast her a glare. "Enough out of you, young
lady! If not for your theatrics, your sister wouldn't
be in this pickle."

Rachel, always Molly's champion, leaped to her
defense. "Now, Daddy, that isn't fair. Molly can't
be blamed—"

"You be quiet!" Big Jim cried, cutting her off
short. He pinched the bridge of his nose and
squeezed his eyes closed for an instant. "All right,
Rachel Marie, run all of that by me again. A little
slower this time."

Resisting the urge to remind him he'd just ordered her to be quiet, Rachel cautiously asked,
"Which part?"

"All of it!" her father ground out.

"All of it? Daddy, didn't you—"

Her father cut her off again, this time with a
sharp jab of his finger. "All of it! And don't give
me any of your sass, dammit. I'm in no mood for
it!"

Rachel could see that he was perilously close to
losing his temper. Forcing herself to speak more
slowly this time, she once again explained how
she'd come to be in the church this morning with
Matt Rafferty. When she had given her father a full
explanation for the second time and he still looked
confused, she raised her hands in helpless bewilderment. "Which part aren't you clear on, Daddy?
He callously broke Molly's heart, and I wanted to
get even. With that end in mind, I had him
drugged and lured him to the church, my plan being that he'd wake up this morning wearing no
trousers in a packed church." When her father still
looked befuddled, Rachel cried, "He humiliated

my sister!'' At that, Molly wailed again, more
loudly this time. To be heard over the din, Rachel
increased her own volume. ''Is it so difficult to understand why I wanted to give him a taste of his
own medicine? That's it, end of story.''

"Rachel, if, as you say, all of this is about Molly
and that silly crush she got on Matt Rafferty, then
what the hell''—he pointed a finger at the man on
the floor—"is *he* doing here?''

"I told you, I—'' An awful prickly feeling
crawled over Rachel's skin. She glanced uneasily
toward Molly, who was still moaning and wailing,
and then at the man sprawled near her feet. ''Oh,
God. This isn't Matt Rafferty?'' It wasn't really a
question. Rachel knew by Molly's behavior and the
tone of her father's voice that she had guessed correctly. ''Oh, dear,'' she whispered. ''Oh,
dear . . . oh, dear.''

"Oh, dear?'' her father repeated. ''Is that all you
can say for yourself, Rachel Marie? Oh, dear?''
With each word he spoke, his voice seemed to go
up another octave. ''You've shanghaied the wrong
man, and all you can say is 'oh, dear'?''

As the ramifications of what she'd done began
to sink in, Rachel threw another look at her victim.
"If not Matt Rafferty, then who is he?'' she asked
in a quavery voice.

"Who is he? I almost kill the man, and you're
standin' there, askin' me who he is? I'm tellin' you,
girl, this is one time I could wear the hide off your
behind with my razor strop and never feel a second's regret.''

"Big Jim, let's try to stay calm,'' the man on the
floor inserted. Though his voice still sounded a little groggy, Rachel could tell by the way he spoke
that he was fast coming awake.

"Calm? I haven't known a moment's calm since
the day she was born, I swear to God. I'm sorry
about this, Rafferty. I truly am.''

Rachel couldn't tear her gaze from the man she

had believed to be Matt Rafferty until only a few seconds ago. Without her spectacles, which she never wore in public, he was little more than a blur to her. Rafferty, her father had called him. That had to mean he was one of Matt's brothers. Long, denim-clad legs, ebony hair, gray-blue eyes. Given her poor eyesight, she supposed she could have made a mistake. All the Rafferty brothers were tall, raven-haired and dark-skinned.

Recalling the nonsensical observation that Molly had made earlier, Rachel nearly cringed. *You got the wrong one!* her sister had cried. A few minutes ago that had made no sense. Now Rachel understood all too clearly.

"If you're not Matt, then which brother are you?" she asked her victim shakily.

"Clint."

For an awful moment, Rachel felt as if her heart stopped beating. Since Clint Rafferty, the eldest of the brothers, seldom even came to town, let alone patronized the saloon, she thought she must have misunderstood him. "Pardon?"

"Clint!" he repeated a little more loudly, his voice still slightly hoarse with sleep.

4

Clint Rafferty? Feeling suddenly faint, Rachel pressed a hand to her waist. Of all the Rafferty brothers she might have chosen to cross, Clint had to be the most intimidating. Even the other men in town gave him a wide berth.

"Clint . . . ?" she said inanely. "But you never go to the Golden Goose. There must be some mistake!"

"Oh, there was a mistake made, all right," he agreed in the same hoarse voice. "It just wasn't me who made it."

A thought suddenly occurred to Rachel. "Wait a minute! You have to be Matt Rafferty. Otherwise, why did Dora Faye—" Catching herself at the last possible second, Rachel stood there, mentally swinging her arms to keep from falling in. The last thing she wanted was to get her friend in trouble.

Clint flashed her a slow, knowing smile. "Dora Faye did try to keep me from drinking the drugged whiskey, if that was your question. At the time, I wondered why. Now I know." With that, he rolled to one knee and reached for his hat. "The only mystery, as far as I'm concerned, is why she didn't step to the saloon doors and signal to you that she'd drugged the wrong man. It would've saved us both a lot of trouble."

In Rachel's mind's eye, she saw Dora Faye as she'd been last night, blurry and indistinct, standing just inside the saloon and waving her arms. Without benefit of her spectacles, Rachel had believed her friend was signaling that all was well. Instead, she'd been signaling that nothing had gone according to plan? That Rachel should retreat? If it hadn't been so awful, it might have been funny.

Gaining his feet, Rafferty said, "I hope you folks'll forgive me, but I think I'll be moseyin' along. As entertainin' as all of this has been, I've got a little brother at home to take care of and a ranch to run."

Rachel certainly had no objection to his leaving. The sooner the better, as far as she was concerned.

But her father seemed to have other ideas. "Hold up there just one minute, son."

Clint dusted his hat on his pant leg. "Hold up? Don't tell me you're arrestin' me. If so, what for? Bein' in the wrong place at the right time?"

Considering the fact that her father had almost choked him to death, Rachel couldn't blame Clint Rafferty for feeling a little less than charitable.

"I wouldn't go so far as to arrest you," Big Jim said, "but there is one small wrinkle we need to iron out."

"Wrinkle?"

Big Jim inclined his head toward Rachel. "My little girl spent the night here with you unchaperoned. It don't look good. Don't look good at all."

Rachel's heart caught. "Daddy?"

Big Jim seemed not to hear her. "The way I see it—"

"Daddy!"

"Shut up, Rachel Marie," her father said with a wave of his hand, his gaze fixed on Clint. "The way I see it, Rafferty, my little girl's good name has been ruined. Plumb ruined. And only you can set things right."

"Right?" Rachel echoed. "Whatever do you mean?"

"Yeah, what exactly do you mean?" Clint asked.

Rachel didn't need to see Rafferty's face all that clearly to know he was fast regaining his senses. Unless she missed her guess, he was only inches away from losing his temper. The heels of his boots hit the floor in a sharp stacatto as he stepped over to retrieve his Colt revolvers. She watched in horrified silence as he strapped the crisscrossed gun belt around his hips and tied the holsters down to his lean, muscular thighs. In that moment, it began to occur to her that it might end up being her father, not Clint Rafferty, who was in danger of losing his life during this confrontation. The younger man had the devil's own reputation as being fast with those guns.

Without consciously making the decision to do so, Rachel inched closer to her sire. "Daddy, this entire situation should be simple enough to resolve. I mean, as I've just explained, none of this was Mr. Rafferty's fault. The way I see it, we should all just go home and forget it happened."

"Be quiet, Rachel."

Afraid for her father, Rachel turned an imploring gaze on Clint. "Don't you agree? That we should just forget any of this happened, I mean?" With a nervous little laugh, she added, "Big uh-oh, end of story. Right?"

"Rachel Marie," her father said with exaggerated patience, "this is a far sight more serious than that. Your reputation is destroyed. Mr. Rafferty understands the implications, even if you don't."

Rachel understood far more than her father gave her credit for, and she, for one, had an awful feeling this situation was getting out of control. Gesturing toward the church members, she said, "But, Daddy, everyone here heard my explanation. They all know now that nothing untoward happened."

"It's not that simple, Rachel. When a young lady spends the night with a man unchaperoned, there's only one thing that can save her good name, and that's marriage. It don't matter if anything actually happened or not. All that counts is how it looks."

"Marriage?" Molly cried. "You can't mean it!"

"Marriage?" Rachel echoed weakly. "Did you say marriage?"

"Marriage," Big Jim affirmed.

With that proclamation still ringing in the air, Big Jim caught both Clint and Rachel by the arms and, ignoring Rachel's shrill protests, hauled them to the front of the church. Once there, he immediately began hollering for the preacher. Meanwhile, Rachel tried to talk sense to him, a task that proved impossible. Her father wasn't just big and tall; he was mule-headed. When he got it into his head to do something, no one, not even his daughters were going to stop him.

Reverend Wells, a tall, rawboned man with thinning gray hair, kindly brown eyes, and a beak nose, fought his way free of the throng and rushed to his pulpit, prayer book in hand. "Big Jim, this is highly irregular. We haven't even posted any banns."

"To hell with banns: just get them married."

The minister gave an eloquent shrug. "I was just making an observation."

"Daddy, have you lost your mind? I can't marry this man!" Rachel turned on Clint. "Don't just stand there! Do something!"

Apparently unperturbed, he shrugged a muscular shoulder. "Like what? Shoot him? Sorry, darlin', but I'm not that adverse to the idea of gettin' married."

"Not adverse? How can you say that? We're talking about marriage here!"

"The way I see it, I was thinkin' along these lines, anyway."

She couldn't believe he was being so cavalier. "You're as crazy as my father is."

Big Jim motioned to the minister. "Forget all the fancy stuff, Reverend. All we care about is that it's legal."

Rachel caught her father's arm. "Daddy, stop this! It's absolute madness! Whatever are you thinking?"

"This is all my fault!" Molly cried somewhere behind them. "All my fault."

The preacher chose that moment to say in a booming voice, "Dearly beloved, we are gathered here today . . ."

Shaking his arm free, Big Jim grasped the chancel rail and leaned toward the pulpit. "Dammit, William, I said to skip all the folderol. Just get to the important parts."

Wells coughed and cleared his throat. "As I already pointed out, this is all highly out of the ordinary."

"Just do it," Big Jim shot back. "If I want ordinary, I'll ask for ordinary."

The flustered minister ran a finger down the page to relocate his place. "All right, fine. But, mark my words, it will probably take me longer to locate the important sections than it would to simply recite the entire—"

"Good grief!" Big Jim interrupted. "Are you tellin' me you don't know the words by heart?" He threw up his hands. "You've been marrying people for the last twenty years, for God's sake! How can you not know the words, William?"

Taking advantage of her father's distraction, Rachel turned to Clint. Leaning close so she might clearly see his face, she whispered, "You can't honestly intend to just stand there and do nothing to stop this."

"Who says?"

"I say!"

He stood with his hands clasped behind him, gaze fixed on the minister, expression deadpan. At the corner of his mouth, she thought she glimpsed a smile and wanted to give him a good kick for not putting a halt to the proceedings. Before she carried through on the idea, she thought better of it. Last night he'd been charming, but he'd been silly with drink and mellow from the valerian. This morning, all boyishness had been wiped from his face. If asked to describe him, she would have said he looked stern and more than a little intimidating, not at all the kind to provoke.

She jerked her gaze away and scanned the church, dismayed to see that the crowd at the back had dispersed to take their usual places in the pews, not for Sunday services as usual, but to witness a wedding. Her wedding.

That thought drove Rachel to desperate measures. Straightening her shoulders and lifting her chin to a stubborn angle, she faced her father. "Daddy, I cannot marry this man," she said, slowly and distinctly. "I absolutely can't. Nothing you can say or do will convince me otherwise."

"Of course you can," her father replied and, without so much as a pause, he drew his Colt revolver from its holster and pressed the barrel to Clint Rafferty's temple. "It's the only thing you can do, honey. Whether he meant to or not, Mr. Rafferty here ruined my little girl. Honor demands that I kill him if he don't marry you. It's the way things are, sort of an unspoken code among men. Ain't that right, Mr. Rafferty?"

"Christ," Rafferty said hoarsely.

Rachel watched her father with mounting horror, an emotion she made every effort to conceal by smiling and folding her arms. "Right. You're just going to shoot him in cold blood. After a lifetime of upholding the law? Come on, Daddy. I realize I'm a little gullible, but that's just plain silly."

With slow deliberateness, her father drew back the hammer of his gun. "You think I'm bluffin'? Think again, Rachel Marie. His fault or not, he has ruined any chance you have of making a decent marriage."

"That isn't so!" Rachel scanned the church and spotted Reverend Wells's son, Lawson, who had been courting her these last three years. "Tell him, Lawson! Tell him it doesn't matter, that you love me and won't hesitate to marry me anyway!"

Looking as though his necktie was choking him, Lawson sprang up from his seat, swallowed spasmodically, and then just stood there looking bug-eyed.

"Well?" Rachel implored him. "Speak now, Lawson, or forever hold your peace!"

To her dismay, Lawson said nothing. She sent

him a scathing glare, barely resisting the urge to call him a bad egg, plug ugly, and a bootlicker, just for starters. She settled for whispering the insults under her breath.

"I guess that proves my case," her father said, gesturing toward Lawson. "Not even your own beau will step forward."

Feeling a little less certain of herself, Rachel let her arms fall to her sides. "That still doesn't mean you'll shoot Mr. Rafferty. You're only trying to frighten me into minding what you say."

"Oh, I'll shoot him," her father assured her. "Before I let him walk off scot-free, I'll blow his brains clear into next week."

She winced at the picture his threat brought to mind. "You don't mean it, Daddy. What about being marshal? You'd have to give up your badge if you shot somebody."

"That's why. Don't you see? An upstandin' man don't let another man ruin his daughter and not do something about it. If you won't marry him, Rachel Marie, I have to shoot the poor fellow. It's just that simple."

Preacher Wells chimed in with, "Do you, Clint Rafferty, take this woman, Rachel Marie Constantine, to be your lawfully wedded wife?"

Beads of sweat had sprung up on Clint's dark face. His Adam's apple bobbed as he tried to swallow. "I do," he said without a second's hesitation. Then, to Rachel, "If it's all the same to you, argue with your father later. He's got a gun held to my head, in case you haven't noticed."

"Don't worry. He won't really shoot you," Rachel assured him.

"Wanna bet?" Big Jim grinned broadly and curled his finger over the trigger.

Clint squeezed his eyes closed. "Jesus Christ! Do what he tells you, Rachel!"

Rachel's stomach plummeted. "Daddy, this has

ceased to be entertaining. What do you think you're doing, threatening an innocent man's life like this?"

"Innocent," Clint inserted, "there's the key word."

The preacher cut in once more. "And, do you, Rachel Marie Constantine, take this man to be your lawfully wedded husband, to love, honor and obey until death do you part?"

Rachel rolled her eyes and smiled sweetly at the minister. "Mr. Rafferty may be quaking in his boots, but I certainly am not. Blizzards will fly in August before any of you hear *me* say 'I do.'"

Big Jim smiled at the preacher. "You heard her. She just said 'I do,' clear as you please."

"I did not!" Rachel said with a scandalized gasp.

"You did so!" Big Jim argued.

Glancing apologetically at Rachel, the preacher said, "I heard her, Big Jim, but I'm not entirely certain she meant—"

"Keep your opinions to yourself and just finish the ceremony," Big Jim instructed.

"By the authority vested in me . . ." the preacher began.

Clint overrode him in a louder voice. "Marshal, would you mind pointing that gun somewhere else besides at my head?"

"Such tactics will never hold up in a court of law," Rachel cried. "These are the nineties, I'll have you know. You men can't marry us women off against our wills anymore. We have legal recourse!"

As though to punctuate that pronouncement, the preacher said, "I now pronounce you man and wife!" and slapped his prayer book closed.

A sudden silence descended over the church. A silence so thick that Rachel felt as if she were drowning in it. She stared at her father, scarcely able to believe he'd betrayed her like this. Her father, who had always loved her so well. Ever since the death of her mother, he had been the only person she could trust.

With a sad smile, he finally drew the gun barrel from Clint's temple. As he slowly let the hammer back down, he said, "Well, honey, for better or worse, you got yourself a husband."

5

Less than an hour later, Rachel found herself a mile outside of town, alone with a complete stranger who also happened to be her lawful husband. To complicate matters further, he'd chosen not to rent a wagon for the return trip to his ranch, which meant that she was ensconced on the saddle in front of him and forced to endure the intimacy of his touch for the duration of the ride. Her valise and satchel, joined together at the handles by a length of rope, were draped over the horse's rump behind him like an ungainly pair of saddlebags.

Convinced he must be furious—she couldn't imagine his being anything else, despite his denials inside the church—Rachel racked her brain for a way to defuse his anger before they reached his ranch and he did something they both might regret.

"Mr. Rafferty?"

At the sound of his name, he stiffened slightly, his hand on her midriff shifting position, the proximity of his fingertips to her breast a subtle reminder that she was now his wife and therefore his possession. "You can call me Clint now, Rachel. It's more or less an accepted thing, the use of first names between husbands and wives."

"Yes, of course, Clint." The lump of anxiety in Rachel's throat felt the size of a goose egg. "I, um . . ." She tried desperately to swallow. Tears of frustration filled her eyes, making the surrounding woods seem even more blurry. In the distance, she could see the craggy peaks of the Cascades, which, without her spectacles, looked like gigantic, indistinct lumps, their snow-swept slopes glistening brilliantly in the July morning sun. "I was just— well, I know you must be angry. Possibly even livid. I certainly can't blame you for that, and I want you to know that I'll do whatever I possibly can to resolve matters."

"Really?" He hunched his broad shoulders around her and tipped his hat back so he might watch her face. "And tell me, Rachel, just how do you plan to resolve matters?" His smoky blue eyes twinkled warmly into hers. "Correct me if I'm wrong, but I thought things were already pretty much settled."

"Settled? We're married, Mr. Rafferty! Don't you realize what that means? I can't believe you've agreed to this."

He smiled slightly, his ebony lashes drifting low over his eyes to partially conceal his expression. "I guess maybe the situation is a little more frightening for you than it is for me."

"Frightening? Why should I feel frightened?" she asked. "I think it would be more accurate to say I feel uneasy."

The creases that bracketed his mouth became deep slashes as his firm lips drew into a smile. "All right, you probably feel more *uneasy* than I do, then. And I can't blame you for that. You barely know me, and now I suddenly have control over your life. That has to be unsettling."

Rachel could have gone all day without hearing him put it into words like that. Control over her life? Oh, God . . . She blinked and averted her face, uncomfortable with the silence that fell over them but uncertain how to break it. With nervous fingers, she plucked at the folds of her skirt, wishing she were anywhere but there.

"If it's any comfort at all," he finally added, "I'm not a mean-natured man. You don't need to feel afrai—" He broke off and fell silent. "Uneasy, you don't need to feel uneasy."

Looking up at him, she felt breathless. To her frightened mind, he seemed taller and broader across the shoulders than he had earlier, a muscular wall of power that might at any moment be targeted at her. *Control over her life?* Oh, it was far more than that, she thought dismally. Far, far more.

Clint heaved a weary sigh and shifted his weight in the saddle. For just a moment his thoughts turned toward home, where his brothers, completely unsuspecting that they had a new sister-in-law, awaited his arrival. Because of them he hadn't protested the marriage to Rachel, and for the life of him, he couldn't regret that decision now. The Raffertys, Clint included, needed a woman in the house, and left to his own devices, Clint wasn't at all sure he could have found one who compared to Rachel Constantine. She wasn't just beautiful, which was a definite plus as far as he was concerned, but she had nice manners and was well-spoken. She'd be a good influence on his brothers, a real good influence. He pictured her in a bib apron with a streak of flour on her cheek. His stomach growled just at the thought. Lord, he couldn't remember when he'd had a good home-cooked meal.

No, he couldn't muster up any regret about marrying Rachel Constantine. The words "manna from heaven" kept popping into his mind. To him, that was what she was, a miracle that had accidentally dropped in his lap. Besides, it wasn't as if this was his fault. He hadn't set out to entrap her or anything. Far from it. And he wasn't the only one benefitting. His own selfish reasons aside, Rachel would have been crucified by the so-called righteous citizens of Shady Corners if he hadn't made an honest woman of her. This marriage was the best thing for her.

Glancing down at her, Clint saw that the bewildered, worried expression was still in her beautiful blue eyes. If they knew each other better, he might be able to guess what she was thinking. How did a young woman feel when she'd just married a man against her will? And a stranger, at that? Clint didn't suppose she felt like whooping for joy.

For just a moment, he toyed with the idea of waiting until he exercised his conjugal rights. Just as swiftly, he discarded the idea. From the instant he'd said "I do," he'd been determined to make the best of this marriage. With that aim in mind, he had no intention of sharing a bed with Rachel and refraining from touching her. Just the thought set his nerves on edge.

He already had enough on his plate without having to deal with sexual frustration. The way he saw it, intimacy between him and Rachel would only make it easier for them to forge a friendship. Some people might say he was going at things ass-backward, but so what. He was new to this marriage business and was making up the rules as he went along.

Though his recollections of last night were a little muddled, some parts were picture clear. He recalled how she had felt in his embrace, how unbelievably sweet she had been, as if God had made her especially for him. Her kiss, as he remembered, had been awkward and shy, definitely not that of an experienced woman, but even so, he knew there was passion within her to kindle. That had been apparent in the way she'd opened her mouth to him and molded her body to his. His main problem would be to get her back into his arms again. Once he had her there, he didn't doubt his ability to arouse her. At the thought, a searing heat formed low in his belly.

Becoming more mindful by the moment that it was still morning and, therefore, a long while till nightfall, Clint forced his thoughts away from love-making. "About your sister Molly," he said softly. "If Matt truly did humiliate her in front of her friends and make her cry, I'm really sorry."

"He didn't just make her cry," she corrected. "He broke her heart." Her large blue eyes flashed to his. "Just because she's only fourteen, that doesn't mean she's too young to fall in love, you know."

"Of course not," he agreed. "If anything, she's probably capable of loving even more intensely because of her age. It's my experience that we tend to guard our feelings a little more closely as we get older."

She looked mildly surprised to hear him say that. "You aren't going to say it's all nonsense then? About Matt breaking her heart, I mean?"

Gazing down at her, Clint had an almost irresistible urge to kiss the little frown wrinkles from her brow. Why, he couldn't say. True, he'd cast an admiring eye in Rachel Constantine's direction more than once since moving to this area. But being a young and healthy bachelor, he'd cast an admiring eye in lots of girls' directions. Maybe that was his trouble. He and his friend Henry hadn't had the pleasure of a lady's company in a good long while, and pent-up need was playing heck with his self-control. "No," he said hoarsely, "I don't think it's nonsense. That isn't to say I believe Matt meant to hurt her, or that he even knows he did."

"How could he not know?"

Clint sighed. "Rachel, my brother has probably broken a dozen hearts, and I doubt he ever realized it. He's a very handsome fellow with a charming way about him. More than one—"

For the first time that day, she smiled. Only slightly and very fleetingly, but it was a smile just the same. The brilliance of it cut him short and left him with absolutely no recollection of what he'd been about to say. "Handsome and charming, is he? Do you realize how much you two look alike?"

For a second, Clint couldn't think how to reply. Then he decided to fall back on plain old honesty, which had never failed him yet. "Matt and I are like two identical chunks of agate, one polished and the other not. I have all the same surface, darlin', but I'm missin' the shine."

Her large blue eyes moved slowly over his face. After looking her fill, she smiled again, still only slightly, but with devastating impact. Looking down at her, Clint decided he could probably become a millionaire if he could figure out a way to bottle that sweetness of hers. "I've never seen your brother, so I can't say for sure, but I find it difficult to believe he outshines you by much."

Uncertain how to accept the compliment graciously, Clint decided to ignore it. "What've you been doin', girl? Walkin' around town with your eyes shut?"

"Pardon?"

"How else could you miss seein' my brother?"

Her cheeks turned an embarrassed pink. "I misspoke. Of course I've seen him, just never from up close."

Clint found it rather incredible that Matt, who was attracted to pretty women like bees to honey, had never homed in on Rachel. She was one pretty little gal, make no mistake. "Well, trust me, honey, he doesn't just outshine me. If women's reactions to him are any indication, we're talkin' a total eclipse. Just you make sure you don't fall for any of his blarney. Mistake or no, you're married to me, not to him.''

He clicked his tongue to the horse and nudged it to a faster pace. At just that moment, a jackrabbit bounded out from a clump of brush onto the road. The unexpected flash of movement spooked Clint's roan, and before he could react, the stallion reared to strike the air with its front hooves. Rachel had no stirrups with which to balance her weight, and the only thing anchoring her to the saddle was Clint's hold on her. Fearful that she might get hurt, he tightened his arm around her waist as he struggled to regain control of the horse.

When the huge animal had finally quieted, Clint realized that in the confusion, he had moved his palm upward on Rachel's ribs to partially cup her breast. She clearly didn't appreciate the familiarity. Either that, or the stupid horse had scared her half to death. As near as he could tell, she had all but stopped breathing.

"Rachel?"

Very carefully, he slid his hand back down to its former resting place, then leaned slightly forward so he might see her face. His heart caught at her expression, her eyes squeezed tightly closed, her sweet mouth acquiver as she waged an obvious battle not to cry out.

"Rachel . . ." he said more softly. "It's all right."

"Did we smash it?"

The question took him totally off guard, and he slowly circled it, not entirely sure what she was talking about. "Did we smash what?"

"The poor bunny," she asked thinly.

The poor bunny? Clint stared down at her pale face, still not convinced he was reading this correctly. True, the girl had been born and raised in town, but surely that hadn't entirely insulated her from the realities of life, rabbit stew ranking high on the list. "No, we didn't smash the rabbit," he replied in a voice that had gone oddly tight. "He made it across without even getting his fur ruffled."

Her breath rushed from her chest and her eyes fluttered open. Splaying a small hand over her throat, she swallowed audibly and gave a weak smile. "Oh, thank goodness. They're such sweet little things, don't you think? I particularly love the way they wiggle their noses."

After studying her for a moment, Clint gave himself a hard mental shake. There was no point in thinking the worst. Just because the girl was worried about one wild bunny, that didn't mean she would be squeamish about cooking up the occasional rabbit stew.

Surely not.

6

The Rafferty ranch was nestled among a stand of tall pines in a grassy valley completely surrounded by forested mountains. As soon as she got close enough to see it clearly, Rachel found it breathtaking.

As Clint steered his stallion down to the house, she couldn't shake the feeling of rightness that came over her. It was as if she'd been waiting all her life for this moment, and possibly for this man. Crazy, so crazy. She was making absolutely no sense. This marriage was a mockery and doomed to be dissolved. To entertain the notion that it might be otherwise was absolute madness.

As Clint drew the horse up at the edge of the porch, she saw a blur of white next to an odd-looking stump. Peering more intently, she realized she was seeing a chopping block, with chicken feathers strewn at the base. Instantly queasy, she jerked her gaze to the house itself. Anything to keep from imagining the blood and gore that must have accompanied the recent slaughter.

The house was simplicity itself, a sprawling structure of rough-hewn logs and a cedar shake roof. It wasn't pretty by any stretch of the imagination, though it could have been charming if any attempt at all had been made to pretty it up.

To say that hadn't happened struck her as a gross understatement. In fact, by the looks of things, just the opposite had occurred. Even without her glasses, she could make out a rusted old washtub on one side of the front porch with a weathered scrub board standing on end inside it and a pair of dirt-encrusted gray socks draped over its rim. Next to the tub lay a discarded flour sack, out of which had spilled some flour gone wet and gooey in the rain, then turned rock hard in the sun. Behind the flour sack, a partially used sack of spuds had been propped against the house within easy reach of the front door. All in all, the place looked as if a band of none-too-tidy squatters had taken up residence.

"Things could use some cleanin' up," Clint said apologetically.

"Oh, it's lovely. Really. I like log houses. Don't you?" In actuality, Rachel preferred clapboard, but she would never risk hurting his feelings by saying so.

Glancing back at him over her shoulder, her gaze caught on his firm mouth. She couldn't help but recall how it had felt to be in his arms last night, how dizzily she had succumbed to his kisses. Thinking back on it, she wondered how it might feel to be kissed by him again. In the light of day, would she find his embrace boring and unexciting, as she had Lawson's? Or as had happened last night, would the first touch of his lips on hers steal her breath away? It would probably be just as well if she never found out, she decided. Her sister Molly wasn't the only young girl who'd ever gotten her heart broken. Rachel had as well, and if she'd learned anything from the experience, it was that handsome men didn't find women like her attractive.

As he shifted forward to drape the horse's reins over the saddle and get a grip on the saddle horn, she felt the powerful play of muscles in his chest and arms. A shiver of awareness went down her spine as he swung from the saddle and reached up to lift her down.

"I can manage by myself," she said.

The protest came too late. Before she could so much as blink, he seized hold of her waist. Placing her hands on his shoulders, she kept her gaze locked with his as he lifted her easily from the saddle.

"I don't want you managing by yourself," he said huskily. "Not with eight of us here to help you. Just you remember that."

She was glad to note that his solemn, almost stern expression was belied by a slight smile flirting at the corners of his mouth. She wondered if he was smiling because he'd somehow sensed she'd been wondering how it might feel if he kissed her again. At the thought, a flush began creeping up her neck.

He was standing with his back to the sun, and his Stetson cast a shadow over his burnished features. Even with the lack of light, however, his smoky eyes had a lustrous glow. As he drew his gaze over her, she felt powerless to move and wasn't certain she wanted to. As she'd noted last night, there was something about Clint that captivated her. What or why was a true puzzle, but the moment he looked at her with those warm, gray-blue eyes of his, she felt sort of, well, boneless. But that was just plain silly.

Grasping her elbow in a large, capable hand, he helped her step up onto the porch. "We would've cleaned up if we'd've known company was comin'." As though to emphasize the point, he gave the flour sack a kick. "With the ranch demandin' so much of our time, things here at the house get sort of neglected." He led her to the door, then leaned around her to boot it open. "Not that I'm sayin' you should think of yourself as company, Rachel. Consider this to be your home."

With that, he swung the door open on a kitchen so cluttered and disorganized it defied description. An unusually long plank table, the surface of which was buried under piles of mercifully blurred clutter, dominated the center of the room. If it hadn't been for the occasional dirty dish mixed in, Rachel wouldn't have believed anyone actually used the table for eating. "Oh, my . . ."

Clint's hand tightened on her arm. "The boys and I will help you get things cleaned up," he assured her. "And on down the road, maybe I can put up some planed wooden walls. I know ladies are fond of hangin' wallpaper and pictures and such."

Rachel squinted to see. The interior of the house seemed unusually dim, probably because the log walls had darkened with age. The kitchen, one half of which was partitioned off from the back of the house by a wall, opened into a parlor area at the unpartitioned end, creating an L-shaped living area over which a large loft loomed.

If Clint's brothers were going to help her clean

up, Rachel hoped they came bearing broad-blade shovels. On second thought, even shovels might not do it. In every corner, as far back into the house as she could see, there were piles of junk. Old newspapers, empty food tins, dirty laundry, school books, slates . . . It looked as if someone had tossed all the contents of the house onto the floor, given them a stir, and then kicked the mixture out of the way to create traffic paths. Never, not in all her born days, had she seen such a horrendous mess.

From out of the rubble, an ebony-haired little boy suddenly appeared. Rubbing one eye with his fist, he surveyed Rachel from his other.

"Who're you?"

As he drew close enough for her to see him clearly, Rachel thought she'd never clapped eyes on a cuter little fellow. She guessed him to be about six, and he looked exactly how she imagined Clint must have at that age, compact and wiry, with burnished skin and an unruly shock of pitch-black hair.

"Well, hello," she said, crouching to greet him at his eye level. "My name's Rachel. What's yours?"

"Cody." When he drew his fist from his eye, he had to blink to get his sooty eyelashes untangled. She noticed that a streak of dirt angled across one of his cheeks. He regarded her for several moments, his expression more serious than a child's his age should have been. With a pronounced lisp that distorted all his S's, he added, "I'm almost seven."

"Not for nine more months," Clint corrected. "And what are you doin', sleepin' in the parlor, tyke? Not to mention it's nigh onto noon."

"Nobody woke me to go upstairs last night." Cody dragged a suspender strap up over his shoulder. "And don't call me 'tyke,' Clint. I'm too old for little kid names."

Rachel couldn't suppress a smile. "I thought you

were at least eight," she fibbed. "You must be very tall for your age."

Cody rewarded her with a pleased grin that revealed large gaps where he was missing front teeth. "Clint says I'm only knee high."

"Yes, well, considering how high his knees are, that's rather tall for someone your age," Rachel observed diplomatically. "I think lofty stature runs in your family." She glanced up at Clint. "You didn't mention having a brother so—" She nearly said "little" but stopped herself.

"Grown up?" he inserted quickly.

Rachel smiled and pushed to her feet. "Exactly."

He flashed her a meaningful look. "Like I said, I have my reasons for wantin' a wife."

Now that Rachel had met Cody, she could understand Clint's willingness to do nearly anything to ensure the little boy's happiness, even playing groom to her bride in a shotgun wedding. The problem was, his feelings were bound to change, if not when he learned she was half blind, then when he saw her in spectacles. Given the severity of her eye problem, her glasses had unusually thick lenses that would have detracted from her looks even if she'd been the most beautiful woman in the world. Rachel had learned the hard way that handsome men wanted to be with equally handsome women, which she definitely was not when she had spectacles perched on the end of her nose.

Before Rachel could stand back up, an older boy came tearing down the loft ladder into the kitchen. In the process of buttoning his blue jeans, he froze when he spotted Rachel. "Well, dammit, Clint!" The youth hurried to get his pants fastened. "You could've hollered out that we had us some company."

"Meet Daniel," Clint said by way of introduction, glancing first at Rachel, then inclining his head at the boy. "Fourteen, goin' on eighty. Excuse his language, but I ran low on soap."

Since soap was clearly a commodity in short supply, Rachel had no difficulty believing that. Daniel's undershirt, which had once been gray, was now more of a brown. Still hunkered in front of Cody, she bestowed a friendly smile on him. "Hello, Daniel. I'm pleased to meet you."

He inclined his head. "Same here."

Good manners, it seemed, were another area Clint had neglected. She stood and surveyed the kitchen, feeling overwhelmed. Clint had gone along with marrying her because he needed a woman around the house; he'd made no secret of that. He was, in short, offering her a life here in exchange for her skills as a housekeeper and cook. It was just that simple.

Most women, Rachel knew, would be insulted. They wanted a man to be attracted to them for their looks, to love them for their personalities, to marry them for reasons of the heart. But Rachel had learned long ago not to expect any of those things. She wasn't insulted by Clint's offer. To the contrary, she was titillated, not to mention sorely tempted to take him up on it.

There was just one problem. A rather big problem. Since the death of Rachel's mother when Rachel was four, Mrs. Radcliff, the housekeeper her father had hired, had seen to the running of the Constantine household. A woman who resented any interference whatsoever, she had not encouraged Rachel or Molly to assist her with any of the chores. Consequently, Rachel's knowledge of homemaking was limited. By closely following a recipe, she could cook simple dishes, and she figured common sense would see her through most of the housecleaning chores. But laundry? She'd rinsed out her ribbed cotton hose a few times, but other than that she'd never washed, starched, or

ironed a single garment. As tempting as she found
Clint's proposition, she wasn't at all sure she was
equal to the challenge.

On the other hand, this was her chance—probably her one and only chance—to have the thing
other girls took for granted, namely a handsome
young husband who made her pulse race and her
skin tingle. For so long now, Rachel had been re-
signed to settling for second or third best. Marrying
Lawson. Playing the role of a minister's wife. Pretending she didn't want or need any excitement in
her life. Now, through a quirk of fate, she had a
chance for more. So much more. Every time she
remembered the kiss she and Clint had shared, she
fairly shivered with anticipation.

Madness! She should know better than to get
her hopes up like this. Hadn't she learned anything the last time she'd gotten her heart broken?
Was she really so foolish that she was willing to
risk that kind of pain again? It wasn't as if she
could keep her poor eyesight a secret from Clint
and all his brothers permanently or even for any
length of time at all. Sooner or later, one of them
would catch her wearing her spectacles, and Clint
would discover the truth—that she was half blind
and, to rectify the problem, had to wear horribly
ugly glasses. Once that happened, there'd be no
more spine-tingling kisses. He would probably
make up any excuse he could think of to get rid
of her.

Unless . . . maybe . . . Oh, God, it was crazy to
even consider it. But she'd heard tell of other marriages that had started shaky and ended up just
fine. Why, even her own father had admitted once
that her mother hadn't been all that crazy about
marrying him at first.

Of course, Mama hadn't been blind as a bat, either. Still—what if she could keep her eyeglasses a
secret? The only time she absolutely had to wear

them was to read, and she could try to avoid doing that in front of anyone. If she was careful, really careful, it might be months before Clint learned the truth, and maybe by then he would like her so much for herself he'd no longer care if she wore spectacles.

As crazy a plan as it was, one glance at Clint cemented it in Rachel's heart. He was, without question, one of the handsomest men she'd ever met. To a girl like her, who'd long since given up on dreaming, his offer was irresistible. She had to take a chance. If she got her heart broken again, so be it. At least she wouldn't go to her grave wanting to kick herself for never trying at all.

Her decision made, Rachel quickly assessed the mess that surrounded her. Everywhere she looked, there seemed to be stacks of dirty dishes. She had an awful feeling that her ability to balance a book on her head while climbing a flight of stairs might not come in very handy around the Rafferty place.

"I, um, don't know quite where to start . . ." She turned to look at Clint. "Did you say you had chores to do?"

"Only a few," he assured her eagerly. "This bein' Sunday, we set aside most of the day for indoor chores. As soon as I finish, I'll come back inside and help."

"Have you any bread baked?" Rachel prayed so, for she'd never turned out a loaf of bread in her life.

"No. We usually make up enough on Sundays to last us the whole week. Like I said, Sunday's our indoor day."

Rachel's stomach tightened. "I hope you have a cookbook. I don't know the ingredients for bread by heart."

"No cookbook, exactly. But we do have a collection of recipes my grandma and ma wrote down over the years. Nothin' fancy, just loose sheets of paper in a wood recipe box my pa made."

"Do you have one for bread?"

"Sure do. Otherwise, I'd be lost. I don't know the ingredients by heart, either."

Rachel relaxed slightly. She'd be successful enough at culinary endeavors so long as she had recipes to follow. The cleaning would be a simple matter of following her nose. The main problem she would have was with the laundry. Then she would definitely need help. Maybe if she did passably well at all the other things, Clint wouldn't mind that too much, though.

So unexpectedly that it startled her, Clint yelled, "Everybody hit the deck up there! It's nigh onto noon! Time to get to work!"

From the loft came the sounds of mattress ropes creaking and feet hitting the planked floor. In less than a minute, one dark head appeared at the top of the loft ladder. Then another. Before she knew it, four indistinct young men were standing above her. Taking turns, they came down to join ranks with Daniel and Cody.

With the arrival of each one, Clint called off his name and age. "Cole, seventeen. Jeremiah, twenty-four. Joshua, nineteen. Zack, twenty-two."

As each young man was introduced to her, Rachel smiled and inclined her head. When Clint wound down, she said, "I'm pleased to meet all of you."

"Not all," Cody corrected her. "Matt ain't here. He's twenty."

"Oh, yes, Matt," Rachel said cautiously. "How could I have forgotten?"

Cody wrinkled his nose and regarded Clint speculatively. "You didn't say how old you are," he reminded his eldest brother.

To Rachel's surprise, Clint stepped up beside her and draped an arm over her shoulders. "I'm twenty-seven, scamp, which makes me plenty old enough to settle down, and that's just what I've decided to do. This morning, Rachel and I got married."

"You what?" "Why didn't you tell us?" "I thought I was gonna be your best man!" "Jumpin' Jehoshaphat! You've gone and done what?" "I thought Lawson Wells was her beau."

"I beat Lawson to the draw and asked her first," Clint said. "Let it be a lesson to you. Don't leave a pretty girl footloose and fancy free for too long a time, or the first thing you know, she may marry some other fellow."

"I didn't even know you knew Rachel that well," Zach said.

"Why didn't you tell us you were thinkin' about marryin' her?" Joshua demanded.

"Oh, wow!" Cody cried excitedly. "You mean she's gonna stay here?"

Clint held up a hand. "Yes, she's gonna stay," he assured Cody. Then to the older boys, "As for all your questions, we just decided to get married, that's all. I'm countin' on all of you to make Rachel feel welcome."

"You're sure enough welcome!" Cody assured her. "Especially if'n you can bake cookies like the kind Clint brought home from the church social last year."

Rachel blinked. Cookies? "Of course I can bake cookies," she assured him. "As long as there's a recipe included in those loose papers Clint mentioned."

Marginally less enthusiastic, but warmly all the same, the older Raffertys expressed welcome, Jeremiah, the next oldest to Clint, finishing with, "We'll be proud to call you sister, Rachel. Welcome to your new home."

Sister. Hearing the word brought a stinging sensation to Rachel's eyes that felt suspiciously like tears. She blinked a little frantically, convinced they would all think her crazy if she got weepy-eyed and sentimental over something so silly. It was just that she'd always wished for a brother, and now she had seven of them, four of them older than she. It was almost as though Clint had known how fiercely she'd wanted an older brother to look out for her.

"And I'll be pleased to call all of you brother," she said in an oddly tight voice.

The courtesies thus observed, Clint drew his arm from around Rachel and systematically began naming off his expectations.

"Rachel's gonna be cleanin' this place up," he started. "I want each of you to help her in any way you can. Understand? Jer, you hightail it out to the porch and bring Rachel's grips into the bedroom. Joshua, you haul her up some buckets of water to heat on the stove. No point in her havin' to wear herself out at the pump. Zach, you gather up all the things she'll need: a broom and mop, clean rags, and whatever else she wants. Cole, while they're doin' that, you and Daniel and Cody get busy pickin' things up and puttin' them away. In their proper places, mind you, not just any old place. And, Cody! Nothin' under the bed, you understand?"

Rachel's head was swimming by the time Clint stopped issuing orders. He drew to a close with, "Now all of you, listen up. From here on out, Rachel's word is law inside this house. I'm sure she'll be makin' up some new rules around here, and I expect each of you to mind what she says, just like it was me. Got that? No sassin' her, or I'll kick your butts."

Zach, who was standing close enough that Rachel could clearly see his face, turned a solemn regard on her. After a long moment, he smiled slightly and winked irreverently. He obviously wasn't intimidated by his older brother.

Clint rubbed his hands together and turned to arch a questioning brow at her. "Did I leave out anything you'd like said?"

"Only thank you." Rachel smiled. "For making me feel so welcome."

Joshua piped up with, "Welcome? Rachel, it's a wonder we ain't on our knees in gratitude. It's been so long since we had a decent meal around here, we've forgotten what good food tastes like."

Rachel could only hope she didn't disappoint them. First things first, though. Before she could try her hand at cooking, she had to muck out the kitchen. Luckily, she had plenty of helpers.

7

Two hours later, Rachel had the kitchen cleaned up enough to start mixing bread dough. After enlisting Cody's help in locating the recipe box Clint had mentioned, she announced to all the older boys that it was time for them to take a much-deserved rest, preferably some place other than in the kitchen.

When they solicitously offered to help her with the cooking, Rachel waved them off, saying, "No, no! I'm funny that way, I guess. I like an empty kitchen when I cook. Too many cooks makes for oversalted porridge, you know."

"I never heard that sayin'," Joshua commented.

Neither had Rachel, but it served her purpose, which was to evacuate the kitchen so she could slip on her spectacles undetected to read the bread recipe.

As the last Rafferty trailed off, Rachel dived her hand into her pocket for her spectacles. Something sharp pricked her fingertip. "Ouch!" She jerked her hand back out, saw a bead of blood, and frowned in bewilderment. "What in heaven's name?"

More gingerly this time, she reached into her pocket. As her fingers curled over the wire frames, her heart felt as though it dropped, not just to the region of her knees, which is how it usually felt when something awful happened, but clear to the floor. Her spectacles! The frames were hopelessly mangled, and as she lifted them from her pocket, she saw that both lenses were absent from their holes. Fishing more deeply in her pocket, she soon learned why. Each lens was shattered. It had been one of the jagged pieces of glass that pricked her finger.

Stunned, Rachel could only stand there for a moment, staring blankly down at her ruined spectacles. How had this happened? She no sooner asked herself that than she remembered falling in the church last night. Evidently her spectacles had been broken then.

As the first wave of shock subsided, she turned her gaze toward the recipe box. Panic rose within her. She quickly tamped it down. Reading without her spectacles was nearly impossible but not absolutely so. If she held the written material right in front of her nose, she could usually make out the letters. It would be tedious, but beggars couldn't be choosers.

"Oh, lands!" she whispered under her breath. "Why my glasses? Why not an arm or leg? I could better do without either."

Returning her ruined spectacles to her pocket, she advanced determinedly on the recipe box, her chin raised high. It took some searching, but she finally located the bread recipe. Peering intently at every ingredient until she could bring the letters and amounts into focus, she managed to mix a triple batch of yeast bread. After letting the three bowls of dough rise once on the cookstove, which still held banked coals from the supper fire the boys had built last night, she punched it down and shaped six loaves. As she recalled, Mrs. Radcliff had always rubbed her loaves with melted lard, covered them with a towel, and left them on the slightly warm stove to double in size. After finding three clean linen towels—no easy feat—Rachel followed the housekeeper's example. When she could finally step back to admire the fruits of her labor, she felt as proud as if she'd given birth to six babies.

Returning to the recipe box, she applied herself to the task of finding something to fix for supper. Since she hated to eat meat, knowing that the practice caused some poor animal to suffer, she settled on venison stew—minus the venison, of course. Oh, yes. This was going to work famously, she assured herself as she began peeling vegetables. Delicious hot bread and stew for supper would make a good first impression on all the Rafferty men, young or old.

"Jesus Christ!"

Clint couldn't quite believe his eyes when he entered the kitchen. His cookstove had been transformed into a huge, misshapen mushroom! At least, that was how it looked at first glance. At second glance, he saw that the mushroomy cap was actually some sort of dough. Mountains of the stuff oozed over the sides of the stove and dripped in gooey rivers toward the floor. Useless, the family's scruffy, mixed-breed excuse for a cattle dog, was pulling off strips of the stuff and eating it.

"Rachel?"

Clint glanced around the kitchen, which had undergone a more favorable transformation than the stove, thank goodness. Even the window over the dry sink now sparkled. Sitting almost regally in the center of the otherwise bare table was a pot of peeled and quartered vegetables covered with water. The makings for a stew or soup, he guessed, and saw that he was right when he spotted the open recipe box. The uppermost recipe was for his ma's venison stew.

Following the sound of voices, Clint went in search of his bride. He found her in the loft with his brothers. The only one of the Raffertys missing, Clint realized, was Matthew, who was still in town, more than likely nursing a hangover. Rachel sat in the center of Zach's bed, her slender back to the log wall, her skirts tucked modestly around her crisscrossed legs. The six boys—no matter how old some of his brothers grew, Clint still thought of them all as boys—were gathered around her, four sitting Indian-style on the bed, two kneeling on the floor with their elbows on the mattress. At the center of their circle was an array of playing cards.

"Here they come, folks, down and dirty," Cole said.

"Down and what?" Rachel asked with a giggle. To Jeremiah she queried, "Are you sure there's such a thing as beginner's luck? I'll never manage to pay all this back to you fellows."

The mess downstairs momentarily forgotten, Clint leaned a shoulder against the partition, one of two half walls that divided the loft into three proportional sleeping areas for his brothers. For a moment, he allowed his gaze to linger warmly on Rachel, then he glanced around at the boys. Apparently they were teaching her how to play poker and were fleecing her in the process. Normally he might have scolded, but it had been so long since he'd seen the six of them interacting this way and having a good time that he didn't have the heart. Even though he didn't hold much with gambling, Clint was a firm believer in having fun, and all of them seemed to be doing that.

"Pair of deuces showin'," Cole said as he dealt a last, face-up card to Zach. "Holy Moly, look at that king. Possible straight!" he cried as he doled out cards to Cody. "And the lady draws a lady! Look at that pair of queens showin'," he yelled as he slapped down Rachel's last card. "Did I hear you askin' if there's such a thing as beginner's luck? Darlin', just look at that. Unless somebody's got somethin' really impressive hidin' in the hole, you're our biggest winner so far."

Rachel touched a hand to her bodice, her big-eyed innocence too genuine to be feigned. "Truly?" She leaned forward to squint at a pile of rocks that lay on the bed. "How much will I win?"

Cody bounced forward to take a quick count. "Fifty dollars!" he said breathlessly. "Wow! If only it was real money, you'd be rich."

Clint relaxed slightly. At least they weren't gambling for actual money. He should be thankful for small blessings, he guessed. At just that moment, Rachel caught sight of him. "Clint? Is that you?"

He chuckled. "Damn, girl, are you stone blind? Of course it's me."

A faint flush touched her hollowed cheeks. "Your hat was shadowing your face," she explained. "I couldn't see you clearly. Besides"—she waved a hand at all his brothers—"just look at all of you. I've never seen so many people look so much alike."

Thus reminded of his manners, Clint swept his hat from his head. "I hate to interrupt the game, but we have a hell of a mess downstairs. What is that stuff that's all over the top of the stove?"

Her eyes went even wider, if that was possible. Tossing down her cards, she scrambled off the bed, elbowing boys out of the way en route. "My bread!"

"Bread? That's bread?" Clint guffawed. "How much yeast did you use?"

Rachel raced by him. Clint caught her arm before she reached the ladder. "Whoa, there. Just slow it down. No point in takin' a tumble."

Setting her back a step, he went down the ladder first so he could ensure her safe descent. "Careful," he cautioned, his gaze fixed anxiously on her small feet. "The rungs are tricky until you get used to them."

After gaining the kitchen, she stood in frozen silence, staring at the stove. "Oh no! My beautiful babies! What on earth happened to them?"

Useless, whose hunger was apparently satisfied for the first time in his misbegotten life, licked his mottled chops, plopped down beside the stove, and whined. It suddenly occurred to Clint that perhaps he shouldn't have allowed the dog to continue eating the dough.

"Christ," he said under his breath, eyeing Useless's belly, "I hope he doesn't get sick."

Rachel huffed indignantly. "Are you saying my bread may make him sick?"

"I was thinking of the yeast, that maybe it isn't good for dogs." Clint dragged his gaze from the canine. "It looks to me like maybe you put too much in."

"Only what the recipe called for, one cup per batch."

"A cup?" Clint whistled. "No wonder you have dough everywhere, honey. You must have misread the ingredients. My ma's recipe calls for one quarter cup yeast per batch."

At that moment, all the boys came spilling down the ladder. When they saw the mess on the stove, their eyes widened in amazement. "Wow!" Cody cried. "Will we cook all of it?"

"No, Cody, I don't think it'll be edible once we get it scraped up," Clint replied. "Useless is the only one who gets bread tonight."

"Oh, darn!" Cody said. "I've had my mouth set for hot bread all day."

Rachel looked so upset that Clint hastened to say, "It's not that bad, Rachel. We can have biscuits tonight, and you can make bread tomorrow."

With that, he rolled back his shirt sleeves and set himself to the task of cleaning up the mess. Ten minutes later he had revised his earlier opinion that it wasn't that bad. He'd never seen so much bread dough. Worse, damn near all of it had stuck to the warm cast iron, creating a mess that was nearly impossible to clean. In the end, he resorted to scraping the goo up with his knife.

"Are you sure you only put in a cup of yeast per batch?" he asked Rachel. "I gotta tell you, I've never seen fifteen cups of flour go so far in my life."

"Nine," she corrected. "The recipe called for three cups of flour per batch, nine if it was tripled."

Clint paused in his scraping to regard her thoughtfully. "No, honey, the recipe calls for five cups of flour per batch, so a tripled amount would be fifteen. You misread more than just the amount of yeast, evidently. Do you have poor eyesight or something?"

At the suggestion, her cheeks flushed a pretty pink and her eyes took on a shimmer of indignation. "Lands, no, I don't have poor eyesight!"

Judging by her expression, Clint could see that he'd made a mistake asking. Females were sensitive about things like that, he guessed. Thinking quickly, he endeavored to mend his fences, making mental note not to call her eyesight into question again. "You're right. It was silly of me to suggest such a thing. No small wonder you misread the writing. Threes and fives look a lot alike, and I've used that recipe so many times, I've probably smeared ingredients all over the numbers, making them hard to see."

Looking relieved to be let off the hook, she nodded decisively. "Yes, I'm sure that's it. The recipe did have lots of smears on it." She wrung out the rag she was using. "I'm so sorry about the mess, Clint. Truly, I am. You really don't have to help me clean up. I can do it by myself."

She looked so adorable standing there that Clint wouldn't have left her to finish by herself for anything in the world. He would have to go out to the barn to do the milking later, but otherwise he was staying inside for the remainder of the day. There was no reason he could think of that he should be separated from his bride. The way he saw it, they had little enough time left before nightfall to get to know one another. If he hoped to make love to the girl before their marriage saw its first sunrise, he had his work cut out for him.

When Clint sat down to supper that night, he nearly broke a tooth on one of Rachel's biscuits, and then he almost went blind looking for the meat in her stew. After taking several bites of the concoction, which was way too salty for his taste, he decided there must not be any meat in it. Regarding his wife the length of the long table, he smiled slightly. She was eating away, clearly oblivious to the fact that there was anything missing.

"Rachel, from now on when you need some meat, just ask the boys and one of them will go fetch you some. We have beef and venison aplenty in the smokehouse."

"Meat?" She fastened startled eyes on him, her spoon suspended partway to her lips. "Whatever would I need meat for?"

Clint deepened his smile. "To cook?"

She returned her spoon to her bowl. "Oh, no, I couldn't."

"Couldn't what?"

"Cook meat."

Her response effectively brought to a halt every spoon at the table. Clint glanced around to see that all his brothers—excluding Matthew, who'd not yet come home—were staring at his bride, their expressions curiously blank. Not that he blamed them. He wasn't sure he'd heard her right himself.

"Did I understand you to say you can't cook meat?" he asked, hoping to clarify matters.

She daintily wiped each corner of her mouth with a fingertip, clearly at a loss without a proper napkin. "That's right. I don't eat meat."

Clint barely managed to suppress a hoot of laughter. "Why ever not?"

Her already wide eyes seemed to grow even larger. "Well, because! It's so cruel!" She looked around at his brothers. "I can't believe a single one of you would be so mean as to actually go out into the woods and shoot an innocent deer just so you could have venison in your stew." She smiled brilliantly. "Not when it tastes perfectly fine without it."

Clint was convinced she was teasing. "Rachel, honey, everyone eats meat."

"Not everyone. I certainly don't. And if I'm to be the cook in this house, none of you shall, either."

Stunned silence. Clint gave each of his brothers a meaningful look. Clearing his throat, he said, "Maybe we should discuss this later."

"There's nothing to discuss," she said sweetly. "Unless, of course, someone else is volunteering to cook." She looked around the table. "You all don't mind, do you? Eating meatless meals, I mean?"

Clint could scarcely believe his eyes and ears when every last one of his brothers shook their heads and said, "No, we don't mind!" almost simultaneously. He scowled his displeasure at each of them. "All of you know very well that you like meat. How can you sit there and say you won't mind doing without it?"

Josh said, "Well, maybe a couple of times a week, one of us can cook, and on those nights, we can have meat."

"Do we get to eat eggs?" Cody asked glumly.

"Yes, of course," Rachel assured him. "And there's no meat in cake or cookies."

Cody brightened at that news. "We don't gotta have meat, Clint. Not if it makes Rachel sad to cook it."

Jeremiah looked as if he were about to bust with laughter. "We wouldn't want to be cruel to animals. I guess eating them qualifies."

Clint didn't see the humor. "Might I remind you that we're operating a cattle ranch here? We raise and sell beef."

Rachel looked appalled. "Oh, my, I never thought about it like that. I suppose the cows are killed once they're sold, aren't they?"

"That's how folks who live in town get their hands on steak, Rachel. They buy cows raised on cattle ranches and butcher them." Clint set his teeth at the distress he read in her expression. Then, before he could stop himself, he added, "A lot of cows aren't butchered, though." He groped for another lie, anything to make her feel better about what he did for a living. "Dairies, for instance. Lots and lots of cows are sold to dairies."

"And a bunch are sold for breeding purposes!" Cole inserted.

"That's right," Daniel agreed. "Without plenty of bulls and cows left to reproduce, we'd have no newborn calves each spring."

Cody beamed a smile. "And they're used to make shoes and boots, too! So, see, Rachel? Not all of 'em get sold for steak."

Rachel touched a hand to her throat. "Oh, my . . . You know, I never stopped to think about it, but my opera pumps and high-button shoes are made out of leather."

Afraid she might try to convince them they should all go barefoot next, Clint broke in with, "This really is good stew, Rachel. What's that spice I taste?"

"Salt," Jeremiah supplied.

Clint reached for his glass of water to wash down the taste. "Mmm-mmm."

8

Shortly after the supper dishes were washed, Clint hustled the boys off to bed and maneuvered Rachel into the downstairs bedroom, which adjoined the parlor. With no lamp lit and only a few feeble moonbeams streaming through the double-hung window, he figured it was dark enough to undress without embarrassing her.

Rachel said nothing when he took off his shirt. But as he removed his gun belt and reached for his belt buckle, she let out a shrill squeak. "What're you doing?"

Clint froze. "Undressing?"

"Why?"

He circled that carefully, not at all sure he knew how to reply. "Well . . ." He sent a loaded look at the bed. "I usually do before I go to sleep." Not that he had any intention of sleeping. "Don't you?"

"But where is your nightshirt?"

"My what?"

"Your nightshirt. Surely you don't—" She broke off and swallowed. Even in the dimness, he saw her throat convulse. "Surely you don't sleep in your altogether."

Clint rubbed a hand over his face. It didn't take a genius to realize she was as nervous as a long-tailed cat in a roomful of rockers. He abandoned his intention to undress and stepped slowly across the room to her, taking care not to make any sudden moves. Judging by her pallor, which made her look sort of luminous in the moonlight, she was already scared half to death.

"I don't have a nightshirt," he informed her cautiously.

She looked scandalized to hear that. "You don't? Well . . . until you can purchase one, I suppose you'll have to sleep in your . . . in your unmentionables."

"My what?"

"Your"—she lowered her voice—"your underwear."

In the summer, Clint wore knee-length cotton underdrawers. Somehow he didn't think that was what she had in mind. "Rachel, honey, I'm not going to hurt you." He smoothed a tendril of dark hair away from her cheek. "In fact, I'm hopin' to make you feel real nice."

Her gaze skittered from his. "That's fine. I mean—well, I know about—well, you know." She airily waved one hand and then leaned slightly toward him, gave a little laugh, and whispered conspiratorially, "It's just that I'd rather not do it naked."

An ache of tenderness swelled in Clint's chest. He traced the hollow of her jaw with his thumb. "How are we going to manage, then?"

"With a minimum of fuss?"

He nearly chuckled. But gazing into her eyes, he

read her fear and realized it wasn't all that funny. With a minimum of fuss? He had a feeling the slower he went and the fussier he was, the better it would be for her. Of course, she didn't know that.

She toyed nervously with the top button of her shirtwaist. "I also absolutely must insist that you buy a nightshirt, posthaste."

Clint imagined how his brothers would tease him if they saw him wearing one.

"We'll see. For now . . ." He caught her chin on the edge of his hand and tipped her face up for his kiss, confident that he could stir her to passion if only she would relax. Instead, she went as stiff as a twice-starched collar.

"Rachel," he scolded huskily, "don't be afraid."

"I'm not." She whispered the denial against his lips.

Settling a hand at her waist, Clint knew the instant he touched her that she was lying. Her body was rigid. Pressed close to her as he was, he could feel the rapidity of her breathing and imagined he could hear her heart pounding. He only hoped he could make her forget her girlish fears by kissing her.

He was about to try when a thump came from somewhere beyond the bedroom door. The next instant, an eerie wail echoed throughout the house. Then someone yelled, "Clint! Hurry! Somethin's wrong with Useless!"

By the time Rachel and Clint arrived in the kitchen, the dog had worked himself up to a full-fledged cacophony, his howls resounding. Instantly aware that the canine's belly was abnormally distended, Clint dropped to his knees.

"Oh, shit! The yeast dough! The poor bugger ate too much, and it wasn't done rising."

Cody gasped. "Is he gonna die?" he asked in a quavery voice.

"No," Clint assured him. "But I bet he's got one heck of a bellyache."

He glanced over his shoulder at Rachel, wishing he could return with her to the bedroom and finish what he'd started. One look into her wary blue eyes told him that it was probably a good thing he couldn't. It was too soon for a consummation of their marriage. She needed time to get to know him first, and it was his responsibility as her husband to see she got it. He might even have to give her as much as a month, perish the thought.

"It looks like I have to stay up and play nurse to Useless. Care to join me?"

She smiled, plainly grateful to be given a reprieve. "Sure."

So it was that the two of them prepared to spend their wedding night fully clothed, playing nursemaid to a sick dog. A little after midnight, Matt finally wandered home. After Clint informed him of his marriage to Rachel, Matt joined them in their vigil, taking a spot beside the dog on the floor. Initially things were tense: Rachel openly hostile, Matt sullen. Clint decided then and there that the two of them had to discuss the bad feelings between them, all of which seemed to revolve around Rachel's little sister Molly.

When encouraged to air her grievances against Matt, Rachel started off by accusing, "You deliberately led my sister on and then heartlessly humiliated her!"

Matt cried, "I did not!"

From there, the fight was on, with Clint playing referee. After the two combatants had vented their spleens, he was able to maneuver them into a more productive exchange, during which it was discovered that Molly had failed to tell Rachel the entire story.

"When she walked up to me on the boardwalk

that afternoon, she had cotton stuffed into her dress," Matt explained.

"Cotton?" Rachel repeated blankly.

"Yeah." Matt gestured vaguely at his chest. "You know . . . to make herself look older."

Rachel's eyes went round with astonishment. "She didn't!"

Matt nodded grimly. "Some of the cotton was poking out, only she didn't know it," he elaborated. "Above her neckline. Everyone saw it. A couple of the younger boys started laughing. When Molly looked down and saw what was amusing them so much, she started to cry." In his earnestness, Matt stopped petting Useless and leaned forward to look her directly in the eye. "I did tell her to go home, Rachel, just like she says I did. But I didn't do it to be mean, and I didn't intend it to hurt her feelings. It was just—well, she was so embarrassed, I don't think she'd have had the presence of mind to move otherwise."

Clearly mortified, Rachel cupped a hand over her eyes. "Oh, dear . . . Cotton? Why would she do something so silly?" She shook her head. "No wonder she came home sobbing. She must have been humiliated to death. Why didn't she just tell me the truth? I would've understood. Instead, I've been blaming you."

"She was probably ashamed to tell you." Matt smiled slightly. "When we're that age, all of us do crazy things in the name of love. I even serenaded a girl under her bedroom window once."

"That isn't crazy, it's sweet."

Matt laughed. "You haven't heard me sing!" He glanced at Clint. "Your turn to share, brother. What crazy stunt did you pull?"

Clint chuckled. "Leave me out of this."

Rachel sighed and nibbled her lower lip. "I guess I owe you an apology, Matthew. I'm sorry my sister made such a pest of herself. It sounds as though she dogged your heels constantly."

"Oh, she wasn't that bad," Matt said. "Not for the most part, anyhow. Except for when she followed me into the bathing house. Three men smoking cigars dived under the water when they saw her, and I had to buy them all new smokes. I could've wrung her neck that time."

"The bathhouse? She followed you into the bathhouse? Oh, just you wait until my father hears. She won't be able to sit down for a week."

Matt began to look worried. "Maybe you shouldn't tell on her," he suggested. "I don't want her getting into trouble. She's just a kid. Kids do dumb things."

Matt's attempt to intervene on Molly's behalf completely won Rachel over. Her eyes took on a suspicious shine. "Maybe you're right. Being embarrassed in front of her friends was probably punishment enough." She glanced at Clint, then averted her face. "I feel really bad. After everything that's happened, and now I learn that Molly brought all her heartache on herself."

"All's well that ends well," Clint assured her.

"Ends well? You've suffered dearly for her antics. Here you are, married to me."

Clint smiled. "Like I said, all's well that ends well."

By morning, Useless was much improved, if not completely recovered. Still a little worried, Clint allowed the dog to remain in the house while he and Jeremiah went out to milk the cows and gather the eggs.

When the two older brothers exited the house, Cole and Daniel were already out in the yard getting that day's stove wood chopped and moved onto the porch. "What's Rachel fixin' for breakfast?'' Cole called out as Clint passed by him en route to the barn.

"Biscuits!" Clint called back, hoping even as he spoke that Rachel's second attempt proved more edible than her first. "Since she was up all night, I said we could make do with hot biscuits and sorghum."

Cole made a face, but he took the disappointment in stride, accustomed as he was to eating whatever he could scrounge.

A few minutes later, as Clint made his way back to the house, Cole yelled, "Shouldn't've left Useless inside! He reared up on Rachel and knocked the gallon of sorghum out of her hands."

"It went all over everywhere," Daniel elaborated. "Rachel, the floor, the table. Talk about a mess. To top it all off, she got sidetracked tryin' to clean up the syrup and burned the biscuits."

Clint groaned. He entered the kitchen to find Rachel still on her hands and knees. By the looks of her face, he guessed she'd been crying. He knelt to help her, and within a few minutes, the majority of the sorghum was mopped up. Unfortunately, the stickiness had seeped into the unvarnished planks, and their shoes stuck to the floor when they walked across that spot.

"Well, this day is off to a wonderful start," Rachel said morosely. Then, out of the blue, she started to giggle.

Clint couldn't see what was so funny. Nothing had gone right since her arrival, after all. Then he realized that was exactly why she was laughing: because they were off to such a bad start. Leave it to Rachel to find some humor in that.

With a weary chuckle, he sank down on a bench. "Well, I guess if we make it through this, we can make it through anything."

Red in the face and holding her sides, she gave a breathless nod and then managed to squeak,

"Oh, Clint! The bench. That's where I spilled more sorghum, and it wasn't wiped up yet!"

He reached back to feel and swore under his breath. "Well, hell." This time it was his turn to dissolve into laughter. He laughed until he ached. Until tears rolled down his cheeks. Until he was weak.

"Things have to get better," he finally managed to say. "They can't get worse."

Rachel could have told Clint that, around her, things could always get worse. Bad luck was to her what miracles had been to Jesus, and over the next few days, it seemed that fate was out to prove it. One morning as she walked from the chicken coop back to the house, she didn't see a piece of firewood one of the boys had dropped on the steps. When she tripped over the wood, she smashed every one of the eggs she'd just collected for breakfast. Since eggs were one of the few things she seemed able to cook without disastrous consequence, it was no small matter.

Her cooking . . . It wasn't just bad, it was awful. Since she still hadn't worked up the courage to tell anyone how blind she was, Rachel had no idea what Clint must think. That she was the stupidest creature ever born, she supposed. And she couldn't much blame him. One time she misread the labels on the storage barrels and accidentally used salt instead of sugar in an apple pie. Another time, she used three times the soda called for in a cookie recipe. It got so bad that Rachel wanted to duck every time anyone took a normal-sized bite of anything she cooked. Unless she remembered to taste things herself as she went along, she could never be sure she hadn't misread a recipe or mistaken one ingredient for another.

Unfortunately, her failures didn't occur only in the kitchen. In addition to being unable to follow a simple recipe accurately without her spectacles, Rachel soon discovered another flaw in her character: extreme absentmindedness. No matter how important the chore, if she allowed herself to be distracted midway, it was a sure bet she would forget whatever she had been doing, oftentimes with catastrophic results. On one such occasion, she had put a laundry tub full of white clothes on to boil over a fire out in the yard. As she stood there, stirring away and gazing off into a blur of nothingness, she heard Cody crying and abandoned her post to go find him. He was horribly upset, and she soon discovered why. Clint's birthday was coming on July sixteenth, and Cody had nothing to give him as a present.

Unable to bear seeing the six-year-old cry, Rachel applied herself to the task of cheering him up. Since they had an oversupply of old newspapers and plenty of flour, she suggested they make Clint a gift from papier-mâché. They had decided that a bowl to hold his pocket change would be an ideal gift, and Rachel was just mopping up Cody's last tears when a shout came from out in the yard. In a twinkling, she remembered her laundry. But by then it was too late. To say that it had gotten scorched was an understatement. Incinerated, more like.

Failure . . . It might not have been so hard to take if only she hadn't come to care so deeply, not just about Clint, with whom she strongly suspected she was falling in love, but about Cody and Matt and all the others. Each of Clint's brothers had become special to her in some way: Cody because he so desperately needed a mother, Matt because of his tendency to drink, and Cole because he needed help with his spelling, something Rachel was able to assist him with by having him spell out loud. The list went on and on. For the first time in her life, Rachel felt needed, truly needed. She wanted so badly to stay with the Raffertys, to feel as though she belonged with them, to know she wasn't just a temporary fixture. Instead, because of her continual bungling, she half expected Clint to send her packing. She certainly wouldn't have blamed him if he had.

To ensure that he didn't, Rachel made plans to bake him a special cake for his birthday—chocolate with fudge frosting—according to Cody, his absolute favorite. On the big day, everything went perfectly. The cake came out of the oven looking divine. Her frosting was flawless, exactly the right consistency. When everyone gathered around the table to eat, Rachel was so proud of herself she had tears in her eyes.

Then Clint took his first bite of cake. Though he was far too polite to let on, Rachel knew something was wrong by the way his eyes darkened.

"What?" she cried.

He waved a hand and tried to smile. "It's nothing," he managed. "Really, Rachel."

She didn't believe that for a second. She took a bite to see for herself. Salt. The frosting was delicious, but the cake itself tasted awful. Rachel nearly gagged. She couldn't imagine how Clint managed to sit there, pretending it wasn't so bad.

Suddenly, it was all just too much. In a twinkling, she remembered every disastrous mistake she'd made since coming there. Now, to add insult to injury, she had ruined Clint's birthday. Even Cody looked at her with accusing eyes.

"I'm sorry," she whispered to no one in particular. "I'm so—sorry."

The final blow occurred when Rachel turned to flee the house. Useless was lying on the floor behind her, and with tears blurring her already poor vision, she mistook him for a rug, tripped over him, and sprawled face first on the floor. Matt reached her first. He was the one to help her stand, the one to check her hands for scrapes and brush her off. The others hovered around, all of them making sympathetic noises, none of them saying what she needed to hear. What that might have been, Rachel didn't know. She just knew she was humiliated to the marrow of her bones.

Looking up at Matt through her tears, she remembered his saying that he'd once advised Molly to run along home, not because he wished to hurt her, but because she needed the prompting. For different reasons, Rachel wished he'd given her the same advice. Anything to have avoided this.

With agonized movements, she retreated toward the door. With each step she took, all their faces became less distinct. Except for Clint's, of course. His, she decided, had been carved in her heart, never to be forgotten, never to blur, no matter how far away she was from him.

With a low sob she couldn't stifle, she jerked open the door and fled. She couldn't go on like this. It wasn't just she who was suffering; all of them were.

9

For at least a full minute after Rachel fled from the house, no one spoke. Then everyone tried to say something at once. Clint held up his hands.

"I'll go get her."

Cody ran up to hug his leg. "Tell her it don't matter. We can make another cake."

"Sure we can!" Daniel agreed.

"She just needs more practice cooking," Jeremiah insisted.

Glancing around at all their faces, Clint realized that his brothers were as hopelessly in love with Rachel as he was, albeit in a different way. He ruffled Cody's hair. "I'll bring her back, tyke. Don't you worry." Glancing at Jeremiah, he added, "This could take a spell. While you guys are waiting, why don't you whip up another cake real fast?" He glanced meaningfully at Cody. "A birthday party just isn't a birthday party without cake."

Jeremiah nodded. "Sure, Clint. Just don't expect much. My cake may not taste much better than Rachel's."

Clint nearly said that *anybody's* cake would taste better than Rachel's, but he bit back the words. The less said, the better, he decided.

He found Rachel hiding in the barn loft. She was weeping copiously, her sobs deep and tearing. Just listening to her was enough to break Clint's heart. Swinging a leg over the top ladder rung, he stepped off into the loose hay and made his way toward her. Where bales were missing, there was no bottom to the softness, and he lurched. Dust particles seared his nostrils.

The instant Rachel sensed his presence, she held her breath to stop crying. Crossing his ankles, he dropped to a sitting position beside her, propping his elbows on his knees. After a long moment, he said, "You know, Rachel, none of us care if you can cook."

With a catch in her voice, she cried, "What do you mean, you don't care? That's why you brought me here! To cook and clean and make the house nice."

"And you've done that." He recited a list of things she'd done. "Seeing Cody all cleaned up for supper every night, havin' flowers on the table and the place all shiny clean, those are the things that matter. You bein' a great cook doesn't."

"You're just saying that!" she said shakily.

Clint turned his hands to gaze at his palms. As he listened to her stifled sobs, he curled his fingers into tight fists. "Rachel, I'm not just saying it. You've no idea what it was like around here for the boys before you came. Daniel and Cody used to have terrible dreams almost every night about our folks dyin' and the hard times we went through after. Now they hardly ever wake up crying." He waited for a moment to let that sink in. "Your bein' here has given them a sense of security, that everything is okay in their world. And—" His throat went tight. "And, all that aside, I think I'm falling in love with you."

She went instantly silent and turned to look at him. Clint met her gaze steadily.

"You'll stop thinking so the minute you hear the truth," she informed him in a tremulous voice. "I'm not just a bungler, like you think. I can't see."

"Can't see what?"

"Anything! I'm nearly blind. To see, I have to wear spectacles over a half inch thick."

"I thought you said you didn't have poor eyesight."

She cast him a look that spoke volumes. "That wasn't a lie. My eyesight isn't poor, it's downright awful."

Clint regarded her for several long seconds, remembering all the times she'd looked up at him just as she was doing now. Before, he'd always believed she was enthralled and hanging on his every word. Now he realized she looked at him with that wide-eyed intentness because she was trying to *see* him.

"My God . . ." he whispered. There had been so many signs. Now that she'd told him the truth, he couldn't believe he'd been so blind. "Why haven't you been wearing your glasses then, sweetheart?"

"They got broken. I always carry them hidden in my skirt pocket and only sneak them out when I have to. When I fell in the church, they got shattered. At home I have extra pairs, but here I don't."

"You should've told me! I would have gone to town and gotten your spare spectacles, honey. I can't believe you've gone around all this time unable to see." He sighed. "As soon as I can get away—let me see—Saturday, I reckon. That's only four days. I'll take you into town and we'll get your spare spectacles. Can you wait that long?"

Her chin started to quiver, and her beautiful eyes filled with sparkling tears. "You wouldn't mind?"

"Mind what?"

"My wear—" Her voice broke. "The spectacles? How ugly they make me look? You wouldn't care?"

It hit Clint then, like a fist in his guts. This girl that he was coming to love so much had been badly hurt, and he had a nasty feeling it had been by a man. He caught her small chin in his hand. "Rachel, you couldn't look ugly if you tried."

"Yes," she squeaked.

That single word imparted a wealth of pain. Clint bent to kiss the tears from her cheeks. "Not in spectacles a half inch thick or even an inch thick. You're the most beautiful girl I've ever seen, Rachel, and I'd like to kill the bastard who told you otherwise. Who was he?"

"Nobody. Nobody important, anyhow. He left town after I told him about my eyes. He sort of eloped without me."

Word by word, Clint dragged the story out of her and then pieced it all together. It sounded to him as though Rachel had come perilously close to being seduced by an opportunistic scoundrel. She'd been fifteen, only a year older than her sister Molly. The man, a Bible salesman who peddled tonics on the side, had reneged on his promise to marry her when he realized she had poor eyesight. The way Clint saw it, that had probably been Rachel's lucky night. A man like that would have used her, then abandoned her along the wayside somewhere.

"No wonder you went after Matt with such vengeance when you thought he'd deliberately hurt Molly." Clint drew her into his arms. "You were getting revenge for yourself as well." He ran a hand up her back. "Ah, Rachel. So many wasted tears. Don't cry any more, sweetheart. I'll think you gorgeous in spectacles, I promise."

"You will?"

"Absolutely."

She sniffed. "I won't wear them except for when I have to. Like when I'm cooking and stuff." She drew back slightly. "I'm really not a bungler that often when I can see what I'm doing."

Clint smiled slightly. "You can wear your eyeglasses all you want. I'll be so busy thinking about other things when I look at you, I probably won't notice."

"What other things?"

"Let me show you." It was all the opening Clint needed. Bending his head, he settled his mouth over hers. "Oh, yes, Rachel, girl," he whispered against her lips. "Let me show you."

Rachel . . . As their kiss deepened, her name was like a song in Clint's mind. He peeled off his shirt and spread it over the hay to protect her from the scratchiness. Then, so sweetly he could scarcely credit it, she surrendered to him. Over the years, Clint had heard lovemaking described in every possible way, but this was the first time he had ever thought of it as sacred.

That was how it seemed with Rachel, sacred. She was like an angel in his arms. A silken, wonderfully warm little angel who made all his dreams come true. Never had he seen anyone so beautiful. Ivory skin. Full, perfectly shaped breasts with rosy tips that tasted like nectar. A slender waist, just perfect for his hands. Gently flared hips. Long, shapely legs. Clint went over every inch of her and decided there wasn't a single thing about her he would change. Including her eyes . . .

He made love to her carefully, taking his time, lingering over her body to make certain she was as aroused as he was before he took her. It was the most incredible joining he had ever experienced, and judging by Rachel's cries of elation, she felt the same way.

Contentment . . . Utter fulfillment. Afterward, Clint held her in his arms, wishing they could stay right where they were and make love again and again. Instead he would have to pluck the hay from her hair and take her back to the house for his birthday party. Wasn't that a fine kettle of fish? The only present he really wanted was to make love to his wife again, which he probably wouldn't be able to do until everyone in the family went to bed that night.

Ah, but then, what a birthday celebration he would have. Clint sighed and pressed his lips against Rachel's temple, promising himself he would make love to her all night, that dawn would find her still whimpering with pleasure in his arms.

The sun was just peeking over the horizon when Rachel opened her eyes the next morning. As usual, Clint's side of the bed was empty. Running her hand caressingly over the sheet, she found it still warm from the heat of his long, lean body. Even as the memory of last night's coupling ran through her, the familiar sound of the rustling husks under her fingers made her smile. While making love to her, Clint had cursed the husks for the noise they made and suggested they get a feather-tick mattress as soon as possible. When she had pointed out how many chickens would have to die to fill a mattress with feathers, he'd nearly laughed until he cried. Then he'd settled back down to making love to her again. Sweet, wonderful love.

Finally, after a month of tension and nervous, sidelong glances, he'd decided to make love to her. And make love he had, taking her higher and higher until she was drenched in the purest bliss.

Even though her experience was admittedly limited, she was sure now that no wanton could have responded more totally. And, oh, how glorious it had felt to surrender to the man she loved.

She was well and truly a woman now. A woman desperately, totally, and forever in love with her husband. Her smile took on soft edges, and she let her eyes drift closed. Deep inside, where the sweetest of sensations still throbbed ever so gently, she felt different. Changed. And yes, beautiful.

All because Clint had touched her where she'd never been touched before. And kissed her. And fused his hard, strong body with hers until she'd nearly exploded with the pleasure and joy of it.

She'd expected pain, and he'd given her ecstasy. She'd be prepared for disappointment and found herself soaring. She'd feared a maidenly embarrassment, and instead had found herself entranced. Desire rose in her again like a river of warm honey, and, suddenly restless, she stretched out her legs. Beneath the faded quilt, her skin tingled, eager to feel again the slow stroking touch of Clint's big hand.

Lifting drowsy lids, she looked toward the window where a blur of pink and gold promised a glorious sunrise and an even more glorious day. A good day for outside chores, she thought, pleased that she was beginning to think like a rancher's wife.

After all, a rancher's wife was just as involved with the successful functioning of the place as any hired hand. More so, she thought, thinking of the mountains of clean clothing required by eight men, not to mention the victuals they needed to fuel those active Rafferty bodies. Clint and Jeremiah had more fence wire to string today, and Zach needed to finish patching the roof on the chicken house. She herself had a mound of ironing to tackle right after breakfast, and she really should get to the mending today. And then there was bread to make, and while Cody was busy helping Daniel muck out the stable, she would try once more to bake him that mess of cookies he wanted so desperately.

An annulment? Not on her life. She threw off the quilt with a newfound confidence. So what if she wasn't the greatest cook in the county and the kitchen floor always seemed to need sweeping? Clint smiled a lot more often than he frowned these days, and Cody was thriving. She'd even heard Josh whistling in the bathtub Saturday night, and Matt hadn't spent a Sunday nursing a hangover for more than three weeks running. As for Daniel, that boy was going to break hearts someday.

All because there was a woman in the house. A married woman, she thought, reaching for her bloomers. A wife and mother.

A mother? Dear God, it was possible now. More than possible. Holding her breath, she reverently placed a hand over the slight swell of her belly. Oh, it would be so wonderful to know that a baby was already growing inside her. Clint's baby.

Tears came to her eyes at the thought of giving him a child of his own, perhaps a dark-haired little girl with the lopsided Rafferty grin she adored. A sweet-smelling, pink-cheeked daughter, maybe even a whole passel of pigtailed little girls to spoil him rotten. After all he'd sacrificed for his brothers, all the backbreaking hours of labor he'd put in to

keep them fed and clothed and safe, he deserved
to be pampered a little.

As she dressed hurriedly, she envisioned this
same house with cheery wallpaper covering the
rough-hewn logs and the happy laughter of children mingling with the deeper chuckles of adoring
uncles. At Christmastime, Clint would play Santa
Claus. And on Easter Sunday, after they'd all
trooped home from church, Cody and Daniel
would hide the colored eggs while she prepared
perfectly brewed coffee and featherlight biscuits.
And then, they would watch as the little ones
searched for the eggs, one huge, happy family of
Raffertys. Later, when everyone was bedded down,
she and Clint would come together in this same
bed. Their marriage bed.

Still smiling, she tied her hair away from her face
with a plaid taffeta ribbon as bright as her mood
and headed for the kitchen. Her family needed her.

10

"**O**h, no!"
Rachel raced across the kitchen, waving away smoke as she went. Using her apron as a
pot holder, she jerked open the oven door and
snatched the cookie sheet from the rack. She'd
failed again. In place of the deliciously browned
gingerbread men she'd envisioned as she'd mixed
and rolled and formed the batter, she had con-
torted lumps of burned, foul-smelling dough.

After starting the day so positively, Rachel could

scarcely believe things had gone sour so quickly. A ranch wife, was she? Sick with disappointment, she carried the ruined cookies to the open window and tossed them onto the dirt. At the same time, she saw Clint heading with long, impatient strides toward the porch. "Dammit, Rachel, are you trying to burn the house down?" he called teasingly when he caught sight of her at the window.

"It isn't funny, Clint Rafferty!" she shouted back. "I swear I did everything right this time, and they just up and burned. I even had Cody read the recipe to me three times so I'd be sure not to make a mistake. I think it's the dad-blamed stove, that's what I think. I hate the darned old thing!"

"Now, darlin'," Clint began as he entered the kitchen, only to stop dead when she whirled toward him, her eyes huge and wisps of soft brown hair curling against her neck where it had escaped the ribbon.

"It *is* the stove," she declared, waving her hand toward the smoke that billowed from the oven. "Not even God himself could produce a decent meal on that . . . monster."

Clint only just managed to keep from grinning. "Guess it is a mite old at that, but Sam Butts at the mercantile swore it was in good working order when he sold it to me."

"Old," she insisted, her slightly narrowed eyes darting blue daggers, first toward the stove and then toward him. "That contraption was *old* when Methuselah was still a boy."

"Did you test the temperature by sprinkling flour on the bottom of the oven?"

"Of course I did! It's the stove, I tell you."

"And when you checked the flour to see how brown it was, could you see it clearly?"

She gestured vaguely with a hand. "Sort of."

The smoke had cleared enough now that Clint could see her cheeks, and he couldn't help but admire the lovely pink they were suddenly turning. And with each agitated breath she took, her breasts pushed against the thin material of her pretty blue shirtwaist.

He advanced slowly, careful to keep his expression sober. But Lord save his sorry hide, she was pretty when she got upset. And almost as pretty when she wasn't, come to think of it. He could have done a lot worse for himself. Hell, he still couldn't believe his luck.

"Well, if you're right, I guess we'll just have to add a new stove to our list," he offered in as sincere a tone as he could manage. "Right after I buy a new pair of spectacles for my nearsighted little wife." When she shot him another glare, he held up a staying hand. "Just on the off chance it's your eyes that's the problem and not the stove. If you can't see to do a proper sprinkle test, honey, it's a little hard to get the oven temperature just right. Not saying that's the case."

Her soft mouth firmed, and her chin hiked a little higher. "But I was so careful!"

Clint's heart caught at the pain in her eyes. To him it was just a sheet of burned gingerbread, but to Rachel it obviously meant a lot more. "It isn't your fault. Once we go to town and get your spare spectacles, stuff like this won't happen anymore."

"I promised Cody gingerbread and milk when he finished his chores."

Her lips quivered ever so slightly before she turned away. In the past, Clint had had a busy man's impatience with displays of emotion. Not only were they nonproductive and time-consuming, but he'd always considered them to be a surefire sign of weakness. With Rachel, however, he couldn't quite manage to feel impatient. He guessed he should thank the good Lord he'd never had sisters. They would have all been spoiled rotten.

"Cody'll understand," he said, turning her toward him again. His breath caught when he saw tears dulling the vibrance of those out-of-focus blue eyes.

"No, he won't, and I don't blame him," she murmured, lowering her gaze to the level of his chest. "A promise is a promise."

Unable to resist, Clint slid his arms around her waist and pulled her closer, remembering as he did how soft and warm her skin felt against his palms. And how eagerly she'd welcomed him into the moist cradle of her thighs.

"Then we'll make more," he found himself promising, and in a voice so husky it sounded alien. "I'll help you."

She smiled a little at that before shaking her head. "There's no more flour," she murmured, bringing one hand up to rest against his midriff. "At least none I'd want to use."

Cupping her face, he nudged her chin higher, waiting until her gaze found his before he gently asked, "What happened?"

She shook her head, and he found himself wanting to kiss her so badly he was all knotted up inside. All morning long he'd been looking for an excuse to ride back to the house. And her. Not so much to kiss her again, though that was on his mind, but more to make sure he hadn't imagined the look of pure happiness he'd seen in her eyes over breakfast. It wasn't every day a man found himself in danger of busting his buttons out of sheer male pride, but damn, he felt good. Just knowing he'd been the first to see that creamy skin in lamplight put a lump the size of an egg in his throat.

Damn, he loved her. Not that he was anywheres near ready to say that out loud. Last night he'd gone so far as to tell her he *thought* he was falling in love with her, but that was a far cry from admitting he was already a goner. A man had to consider the consequences before he gave up that much of himself, especially to a woman who'd been so reluctant to share his name—and so nervous about sharing his bed.

"Tell me what happened to the flour," he urged, more to hear the music of her voice than from any burning curiosity.

"You'll think I'm hopeless."

Using his thumb, he brushed away a smudge of flour from her chin and felt her tremble. Her skin was supple and warm, her milk-white flesh rose-petal soft. Beneath the plain blue skirt that hid all but the toes of her shoes, her thighs were sleek and delectably plump, her calves perfectly formed, her ankles trim. Tonight, when the lamp was turned low and the door locked, he would lap every inch of her with his tongue, and she would make that little growling sound in her throat again.

His body swelled against the fly of his jeans. "I think you're adorable."

"No, I'm not. I'm clumsy and nearsighted and I can't sew a straight seam."

"You just need your glasses and a little practice, that's all."

Rachel felt a little flutter in the vicinity of her heart. Though it hurt to admit it, even to herself, she craved Clint's approval. Almost as much as she craved his love.

Even so, she forced herself to be honest. Despite the fact that their marriage had been precipitated by trickery, or perhaps because it had, she desperately wanted their life together to be based on mutual trust. Still, it took her three gulping deep breaths before she was able to blurt out, "I tripped over the train you carved for Cody and, uh . . . dropped the flour crock."

"It broke?"

She nodded and said, "It took me an hour to get

the flour swept out of the floor cracks. And while I was busy doing that, Useless stole the chicken Daniel plucked for tonight's dinner."

"You let Daniel kill a chicken?"

"Oh, no. The poor thing died of old age. That's why it's so awful that Useless stole it. I mean, it's probably not very often that a chicken just up and dies like that."

"Probably more often than you think. Every spring we buy batches of chicks, all at the same time, so when they get old and start keelin' over, they tend to go one right after another. I wouldn't be surprised if another one isn't breathin' its last right this minute. We might have chicken for supper yet."

"Only if I don't let Useless steal the meat!"

"Heaven help us," Clint drawled, his eyes taking on a sudden twinkle within the frame of his sin-black lashes.

"That's just it, Clint. I'm beginning to think that not even Gabriel and all his archangels can make me into the kind of wife you deserve."

His firm mouth twitched at the corners. Then it curved slowly into a lopsided, boyish grin. The look in his eyes, however, was hot enough to heat her blood.

"Far as I'm concerned you can burn gingerbread from now till doomsday, Rachel, and I'll not offer one word of complaint," he said in that gravelly voice she had come to love. "Not so long as you keep snugglin' that nice little fanny of yours up against me of a night."

He skimmed a hand up her side to her breast. His fingers were hard, his touch gentle as he cupped her flesh. "As for the damned flour, it isn't your fault Cody left his train layin' out."

Though two layers of clothing prevented skin

from caressing skin, she began to burn where his hand pressed. "Mmm," was all she could manage as a response.

"As for the stolen chicken, I guess I could shoot Useless," he offered.

Unable to restrain herself, Rachel arched toward him and at the same time encircled his strong brown neck with her arms. "Just kiss me," she whispered, drawing him down to her.

His groan shuddered against her parted lips a split second before his mouth closed over hers. His lips were hot, his breath moist, his tongue arrogantly demanding.

Rachel felt her heart begin to race and a dull roaring filled her ears, as eagerly, desperately, she arched against him, her body responding as though driven by a will of its own. She exulted in the harsh rasp of his breathing.

When his hands tugged her shirtwaist free, she gasped. When his fingertips sought her breast again, she moaned. Between hard, eager kisses, she tore at the buttons of the chambray shirt he'd plucked straight from the ironing basket that morning.

Just as her shirtwaist fell open, she heard a sound. A voice, calling Clint's name. A woman's voice. He jerked free, his hands instinctively drawing her against the protection of his big chest, even as he turned toward the sound.

Heart thundering, and lungs starved for air, Clint fought to clear his head. He knew that voice. . . .

"Clinton? Is that you?"

"Aunt Hester?" he said in stunned disbelief, a split second before his aunt's rotund form filled the doorway.

Like a plump blackbird spreading its wings, his

aunt, dressed head to toe in mourning, held her
arms out at her sides. "I got your letter, and here
I am, come to keep your house and help raise those
dear great-nephews of mine!"

11

Rachel poked her fork forlornly at the stewed
turnips remaining on her plate, unable to
force another bite past the bitter lump lodged in
her throat. To her right, Cody was busily gnawing
the last few shreds of meat from his second chicken
leg. To her left, Matt was shoveling down his third
piece of sour lemon pie. Rachel had to admit that
prior to Aunt Hester's arrival two days ago, the
boys had never eaten so heartily nor praised the
food more fulsomely. Even Clint had taken to coming to the table with an eager glint in his eyes.

Oh, he never came right out and said he preferred Aunt Hester's cooking to the pathetic offer-
ings *she'd* put on the table, but the signs of his
newfound contentment were so obvious that even
she, blind as she was without her spectacles, could
see them.

Take this morning, for example, she thought,
stabbing her fork at another perfectly cooked tur-
nip slice. Why, the man had actually waxed poetic
over his portly aunt's buttermilk biscuits. His
brothers had been too busy to comment in kind,
engaged as they had been, slathering on strawberry
jam that Hester had brought with her from Ohio.
The mound of biscuits had disappeared from the

basket in a trice—unlike *her* biscuits, which generally lasted a good three days.

"There's more pie, boys," Aunt Hester sung out from her place to Clint's right.

"I'll have another piece," Cole said eagerly, shoving his plate forward.

"Me, too, Aunt Hester," Cody shouted. "I ain't never tasted anything so good."

Aunt Hester beamed as she slid huge slabs of pie onto each of their plates. "Clint? There's one last piece of pie here with your name on it."

"No, thanks, Aunt Hester." Clint put down his fork and leaned back. "But like Cody said, that's about as good as pie gets."

"Why thank you, Nephew. That's just about the nicest compliment a lady can get from a gentleman."

At that, Matt leaned close to Rachel's ear to whisper, "Remind me to use that line on Dora Faye next time I'm in the Golden Goose."

Rachel gave his booted foot a good kick, which only served to widen his wicked grin. "Careful, Sis," he whispered, offering her a broad wink. "That there's the foot I use to prop up the bar of a Saturday night."

Seeing his brother cozying up to Rachel like a stallion sniffing heat would normally put Clint into a foul mood, but with his belly full of his aunt's good cooking he was too mellow to do more than scowl a warning in Matt's direction.

For some reason he couldn't fathom, Rachel seemed different since Aunt Hester's sudden arrival. Though he wasn't partial to analyzing emotions—his or anyone else's—he couldn't help noticing how quiet she'd turned, like an unshielded lamp suddenly extinguished by an unexpected gust of wind.

Rubbing a hand across his belly, he thought back to the scolding Aunt Hester had given him her first night on the place. "Why, the poor girl is plumb

worn to a nub," she'd chastized. "Trying to handle
a house full of rowdy men and deal with all their
trappings is more than a new bride should have to
do."

Maybe Aunt Hester was right, Clint thought,
staring the length of the table at his wife's bowed
head. Unlike other nights when she'd been slaving
over steaming pots, her shiny brown hair was
neatly tied back by a plain black ribbon, and her
white shirtwaist was crisp with fresh starch and
neatly tucked. Damned if she didn't look as young
and innocent as a school girl, he thought, covertly
eyeing the swell of her breasts under the modest
attire.

Guilt stabbed him hard, reminding him of all
that he and his brothers had demanded of her these
past weeks. Hell, he'd brought her home to a pigsty
and all but insisted she turn it into a home. And
without much help, if truth were told. At least, not
much from him.

But that was about to change. Now that Aunt
Hester had a good hold on the running of the
house, Rachel would have more time for fun. In a
day or two, the branding would be done and he'd
be able to take some time off. If he got a decent
price for the beef this year, he might be able to treat
Rachel to a few days in San Francisco. He'd heard
tell of some right fancy hotels, with beds soft
enough even for her delicate skin.

Just thinking about the two of them stealing off
alone had his blood heating. Aunt Hester's arrival
had put a crimp in his lovemaking, no doubt about
it. This winter, he would build on another bedroom
for himself and Rachel that would afford them a
little more privacy, but for now he couldn't help
worrying about making noise. The boys had all
moved into two of the sleeping areas upstairs, leaving the third empty for Aunt Hester. But that didn't
put the woman far enough away to suit Clint.

Those damned corn husks! They crinkled every time a man so much as wiggled a toe.

Which was why Clint looked forward to a stay in San Francisco like a parched man did drink. Lord, but Rachel'd be a pretty sight with her hair spread out on one of those lacy hotel pillows.

"Aunt Hester's promised to make me cookies after the dishes are done," Cody piped up between bites. His announcement jerked Clint from his mental meanderings back to the present. "Didn't you, Aunt Hester?"

"I recollect I did," Hester acknowledged with a nod of her graying head.

"I'll help," Rachel volunteered, rising quickly to take up her still half-filled plate.

"No!" chorused Cody and Daniel before exchanging sheepish looks.

"Uh, that is, you're lookin' kind of tired tonight," Daniel amended quickly. "Ain't that right, Clint?"

Still clutching her plate, Rachel squinted the length of the table at the blur she knew to be her husband.

"Actually, I was just thinkin' she looked particularly tidy tonight," Clint drawled.

Tidy? Rachel glanced down at the plain black skirt more suited for a matron of advanced years than a bride. She'd worn it because the wide sash reduced her waist to a mere wisp, something she'd heard men found irresistible. Instead, Clint thought she looked *tidy*. Lord, he might as well stand up in church and declare her a miserable failure as a wife *and* lover.

The lump in her throat took on sharp edges. Just when she had finally begun to feel at home, the family she'd grown to love was letting her know how little they valued her. "I suppose I should really attend to the mending—"

"Bless your heart for offering, but there's no need," Aunt Hester interrupted in her hearty midwestern twang. "Since I had a few spare minutes, I managed to finish the last of it before supper."

Rachel blinked, seeing the overloaded mending basket in her mind's eye. It had always seemed like an unscalable mountain. "All of it? The socks, too?"

Though she couldn't see Aunt Hester's face, she could hear her answering chuckle. "Why, child, it wasn't such a chore, not when a body knows what she's doing."

Which I don't, Rachel thought, turning away from the table.

Just a few minutes before noon the following day, Clint came in from the fields in hopes of stealing Rachel away on a nice long ride for a picnic. For dessert, he planned to make wild and noisy love to her. As he entered the kitchen, he slapped the dust from his hat and tossed it onto the table. Aunt Hester was outside boiling linen, and the house seemed strangely quiet. Too quiet, come to think of it.

"Rachel? Where are you, girl?" Hearing no answer, he strode impatiently toward the master bedroom, his boot heels thudding noisily on the freshly waxed planks. "Rachel?"

The door stood open. Inside, where the knotty pine bedstead gleamed under a fresh coat of polish, the rag rugs were almost bright as new and the windows actually sparkled. Aunt Hester had worked her magic once more, and Clint allowed himself a rare moment of self-congratulation. Despite temporary inconveniences because of inadequate sleeping arrangements, writing to Aunt Hester had been a stroke of genius, sure enough. Finally, he had the smoothly running home he'd craved. Once he got a master bedroom built onto the existing house, everything would be perfect.

As Clint moved into the immaculate bedroom,

he thought it seemed too empty. Even the dresser
that had held Rachel's female doodads looked a
little too naked for his peace of mind. Alarm
snaked through him, settling its coils around his
gut and squeezing hard. Heart tripping, he strode
to the armoire and tore open the door. Rachel's side
was empty. There wasn't a fussy shirtwaist or leg-
of-mutton sleeve or long skirt in sight. Even the
jumble of small shoes in the bottom had disappeared.

"Shit!"

Leaving the armoire door open, he turned to the
chiffonier and jerked open the drawers one by one.
All empty, save for the last which held his long
johns and socks. Damn the woman's hide; she had
a wagon load of explaining to do.

Seconds later Clint strode furiously across the
yard toward his aunt. "Have you seen my wife?"
he demanded, planting his feet wide and jamming
hard fists on his hips.

Aunt Hester finished pinning one of Cody's
shirts to the line before turning her gaze in his direction. "Last I seen, she was riding out of here on
a bay mare with all her belongings strapped on the
rump," she declared, her mouth tugged down by
the weight of her glum mood. "Riding astride, I
might add, with her petticoats hiked clear to her
knees and her bloomers displayed for the whole
county to see."

Clint snapped a fast look at the rutted trail heading toward town. Whatever dust Rachel had raised
had long since settled, and the only thing moving
between him and the distant horizon were swaying
pine trees.

"Why?" he muttered, forgetting for a moment he
wasn't alone.

"Don't know the why of it myself. I asked, mind.
But all she gave me was a damned fool answer."

"Which was?"

"That she kept up her end of the bargain, but now that I'm here, she don't have to anymore." Hester fastened worried eyes on him. "Nephew, never mistake it. I'd rather leave than cause trouble between you and your missus. I guess, in my eagerness to make myself needed, I might've started off a little strong. Maybe she felt like I was pushing her out."

"That's ridiculous," Clint bit out. And he truly believed it was. "You've been nothin' but sweet and kind since you've been here, Aunt Hester. If Rachel felt shoved out, it was because she wanted to feel that way."

His aunt didn't look reassured. "Sometimes we women see things a little different than you men." She sighed, snapping the wrinkles from a shirt. "She said to tell you to pick up the mare at the livery, by the way, rather than at her house."

That news only added more fuel to Clint's mounting rage. So, she didn't wish to see him, did she? Not even for the few short minutes it would take for him to pick up the horse? Well, fine. That was just fine.

He raked a hand through his hair, his temper aboil and his gut tight. Damn it to hell, no woman was worth this kind of aggravation, especially when he'd been as patient as a man could be.

"I expect you're aiming to go after her," Aunt Hester said.

Damn straight he was going after her, Clint thought, clenching his teeth so hard something popped alongside his jaw. She was his wife, wasn't she? She belonged here with him. In his bed—

Shit! Maybe his lovemakin' wasn't as great as he liked to think. Could be he hadn't been patient enough with her that first time. Or skilled enough, for that matter. Given his limited experience with women, he'd tried his best to do right by her. But maybe his best hadn't been good enough. Especially not after those first nights, what with Aunt Hester listening in, and all.

Clint stared off into the distance, his throat stinging so sharply with unshed tears, he felt about as old as Cody. Was that the reason Rachel'd hightailed it back to her da at the first opportunity? Because he had disappointed her? Shame scalded his insides, burning deeper and deeper until he damn near doubled over. If a man couldn't satisfy his woman in bed, he didn't *deserve* to keep her.

"No, I'm not aimin' to go after her," he said in belated answer to his aunt's question.

"But, Nephew, that's just plain—"

"No buts, Aunt Hester. I'm not goin' after her. I have better things to do."

Squaring his shoulders, he turned away and headed for the barn. He was a Rafferty, damn it. Rafferty men had pride. Rafferty men didn't beg any woman to stay if she really wanted to leave. But, damn, it hurt.

Clint shoved open the bat-wing doors and headed into the Golden Goose. The monthly cattlemen's meeting had lasted longer than usual, and remembering how he'd met Rachel after the last meeting a little over two months ago, he'd been so tense all evening, his throat was raw with thirst. Squinting in the smoke and lamp oil haze, he cast a look-see toward the bar, half expecting to spot Matt or one of his other brothers bending an elbow. This time he saw only Dora Faye. Judging by her scowl, she wasn't planning to lay out any welcome.

"You got your nerve comin' here tonight, Clint Rafferty," she said when he drew up next to her.

"How so?" he asked before signaling the barkeep to bring him a bottle. "Rye," he amplified. "The kind you keep on hand for bankers and politicians." He flicked Dora Faye a glance. "And two glasses."

"One," she corrected in a trice. "I'm particular about who I drink with."

Clint shoved back his hat. "Meaning you ain't interested in drinkin' with me?"

She turned her back to the bar and rested her elbows on the polished surface. Another time Clint might have enjoyed the snowy expanse of female bosom above the gaudy lace of her cheap green dress. Tonight, however, he had one thing on his mind, and one thing only—pouring enough whiskey down his throat to take away the empty feeling in his belly. Now he knew how his da must have felt after losing his ma. Hollow clear to his marrow. Not really caring if he lived or died. Rachel had been gone a month now, and every second had been an agony for him.

"Suit yourself," he said to Dora Faye as he tipped the bottle over the glass. A second later, he slugged down the liquor. Five drinks later, some of the knots in his mood had come untangled, but not all.

"For someone claimin' she's not eager for my company, you sure are hangin' fast to my shirt-tails," he told the soiled dove sourly.

"Only so's I can tell you what an ass I think you are. You broke Rachel's heart, you bastard."

Clint bit down hard. "The hell I did," he retorted. This time when he poured, his hand wasn't as steady as it should have been. And when he downed the triple shot, the whiskey had suddenly acquired a foul bite. Or was it loneliness he was tasting?

"She's lost weight since she come home. Big Jim's at his wit's end."

Clint tapped the bottle with a forefinger. "Sure you won't have a drink?" he offered, trying to ignore what she said. "There's plenty left." A good half jug, by his reckoning. Too much to waste.

"Last time I saw her at the mercantile, her eyes were all red from crying."

Clint poured faster this time, slopping the equivalent of a shot on the bar. Shrugging, he swiped his forearm across the spill, then downed the whiskey that *had* ended up in the jigger. No good. He could still see Rachel's face on the pillow, her thick brown hair spread like a dark angel cap on the slightly singed linen.

"Nobody told her to go," he muttered, his voice whiskey thick.

"Maybe not in so many words," Dora Faye exclaimed in a low hissing whisper. "But a woman as sensitive as Rachel can read between the lines."

"What the devil are you talkin' about?" Clint demanded, his head beginning to swim ever so slightly.

"You jackass! I'm talkin' about that bully of an aunt you imported."

Clint drew his head back and squinted down his nose at his red-headed accuser. It took a full second to get her face in good focus, and then he realized he liked it better when he couldn't see the green sparks shooting out of her eyes. Was this the way Rachel felt without her glasses? he wondered. Like the whole world was on the opposite side of fogged glass?

"Bully? Aunt H—Hester?" Damned if the whiskey hadn't numbed his tongue instead of his head. "Is that what Ra—Rachel told you?"

"Not in so many words, but I could tell she was hurting." She poked a finger at his chest. "Rachel gave everything she had to that ungrateful family of yours, and what did she get back? Not so much as a 'thank you, ma'am' or a 'don't let the door hit you where the good Lord split you.' "

"Where the good Lord what? Now wait just a minute—"

She jabbed a finger at his nose this time. "So she

can't cook as good as a woman who's been doing it for thirty years or more? She tried her best, didn't she? And maybe she did singe a few underdrawers, but that don't mean you boys didn't have clean clothes when you needed 'em, along with a smile and a cheery word when you come home tired and hungry."

"I never said—"

"That's just it, you fool cowboy. You never *said* nothing she needed to hear, like how much you appreciated her tryin' so hard. Or how nice it was that she was there when you come home, or how pretty she looked, or how sweet it was at night to pull her close." She paused to haul in a breath. "Instead, you washed your hands of her the minute you didn't need her any more. Even in the bedroom, behind closed doors, you worthless toad."

Recalling the nights after his aunt's arrival when he'd felt too self-conscious to make proper love to his wife, Clint felt heat sear his cheeks. "What occurs between a man and his wife behind closed doors is no concern of yours," he muttered, staring at the amber liquid in the bottom of his glass.

"Pathetically little happened for you to keep secret, from what I heard! Crinkling corn husks, my hiney."

Clint stared at her in amazement. "Is *that* why she left? Because I was worried about makin' noise and wasn't very—well, you know?"

"That and other things. Like maybe because you never told her you loved her. Don't deny it. If you had, she never would of left, not in a million years."

Clint bristled at that. "I did so! Plain as can be! I told her several times."

"Not according to Rachel. She says you told her you *thought* maybe you did."

Clint had no answer for that. Thinking back on it, he recalled now that he had skirted the issue, telling Rachel he thought he loved her, but never saying he knew it for certain. "That still didn't give her any call to leave," he said under his breath.

Dora Faye, who glared at him nearly nose to nose, caught the words. "Oh, really? And what would have convinced her to stay, you stubborn mule? You married her for her talents as a housekeeper. As I understand it, you never made any bones about it, not from the very first, and Rachel feels like she failed you at every turn." When Clint tried to protest, she waved him to silence. "Her words, not mine. After good old Aunt Hester showed up, she didn't feel needed anymore. In fact, she felt like she'd done such a miserable job that you were all hoping she'd leave."

"That is *not* so."

A pulse throbbed in Dora Faye's temple. "She thinks you wish you'd never married her in the first place."

"That's silly."

"Is it? I don't think so. And after you think about it, I don't think you will, either." She fixed him with those fiery green eyes of hers for a long moment. "She's leavin' on Monday, you know. Goin' back east to stay with some relatives and go to some kind of school. And why wouldn't she? Now that you've tossed her back, she has no hope for making a life here in Shady Corners."

12

The church seemed to be unusually crowded for early services. Rachel stood just outside the doors with her father and sister, held back by the press of people trying to move en masse into the church. Molly kept standing on tiptoe, craning her neck to see. "I wonder what's happening?" she asked for at least the dozenth time.

"I have no idea," Rachel replied.

"Well, I'm going to find out!" her father vowed.

He began shoving his way through the crowd, cutting a path for Rachel and Molly in his wake. They fell in after him like farmers behind a plow. Just inside the church doors, Rachel realized the interior of the building seemed oddly quiet. Once people got inside, they usually visited right up until the preacher stepped to his pulpit. She strained to see over the shoulders of men, wondering why the crowd seemed to have gathered at the back of the church.

When at last her father had worked his way through the throng, Rachel felt sure she would discover what was holding everyone back from finding their seats. But at first glance around the church, she saw nothing unusual.

"Hells bells, there she is. Took you long enough, darlin'. We were about to give up on you."

Rachel's heart leaped. She would have recognized Clint's voice anywhere. She homed in on the sound and finally made out his blurry outline. He was sitting on the floor, almost precisely where the two of them had been discovered together that other ill-fated morning over two months ago. His back was supported by the rear church pew, one knee raised so he might rest his arm. Beside him sat a jug of liquor.

"Folks, may I present to you my wife?"

Her only thought to get out of there, Rachel pivoted to leave. But the crowd had closed ranks behind her, and there was no way out.

"You can't run from me, Rachel. Hightail it, and I swear I'll come after you."

She turned back to find that he had pushed to his feet. "Why are you doing this?" she asked thinly.

"The way I hear it, you're planning to leave town. I thought maybe I should clear up a few things before you take off."

"What things?" she asked expressionlessly.

"Like the fact that I love you." He took a step toward her. "And that I think you're beautiful and sweet and absolutely wonderful. And that's not to mention that I can't live without you."

Rachel felt her skin pinken, and she lowered her gaze to the floor. "Oh, Clint, don't."

"Oh, Clint, don't? Why not? Do you think I want to lose you? Dammit, Rachel, you had no business runnin' off without talkin' to me. Do you think I care that much if Aunt Hester makes good pies? Hell, no. I like pie as much as the next man, but I can live without it, and so can my brothers. What we can't do without is the heart of our family. The love and the laughter. Havin' someone around who'll leave the laundry tub to boil dry if we need her. Someone to tell stories. Hell, even Useless misses you."

She squeezed her eyes closed. "You don't need me. None of you do!"

"Matt's drinkin' again!" he bit out. "And last

night I joined him. Cody's got the nightmares again, too. To top that all off, there's beef and venison hangin' in the smokehouse again, and I gotta tell you that neither the buck or the steer died of old age. And there's chickens gettin' their heads chopped off right and left. You gotta come back, Rachel. That's all there is to it. To save the poor animals, if for no other reason."

"You'll just have to save them yourself."

"The place is goin' to rack and ruin without you."

"Not with Aunt Hester there! I'm sure she has everything under control. She's a paragon."

"She's someone to help you with the work, and nothin' more. Someone to make life a little easier so you can have more fun with your family. When the babies start comin', she'll be an even bigger help. But the bottom line is, she's just a side dish, Rachel, not our main meal. We need you, honey." He broke off and swallowed hard. "*I* need you."

Rachel gave a start when his scuffed boots suddenly came into view. The next instant, his large warm hand curled under her chin, and he forced her to look up at him. Rachel discovered that she was standing so close to him that she could see the sooty lashes that lined his eyes, the stormy gray-blue of his irises, the burnished tone of his skin. Her heart kicked hard against her ribs. He looked good enough to eat. He surely did.

"You have to come home," he said huskily. "There aren't any flowers on the table, and I love you so much, I can't live without you."

With no warning, he bent and began fishing in her skirt pocket. When he came up with nothing, he dived his hand into her other pocket as well. A satisfied gleam entered his eyes. The next thing Rachel knew, he was settling her spectacles on her nose. Bending slightly at the knees, he made a great show of looking her over. Then he flashed her a devastating grin.

"I knew it. You look adorable in spectacles." He glanced around, as if to draw comment from others present.

Someone nearby said, "I didn't know you wore spectacles, Rachel."

Clint replied, "She darn sure does. She just doesn't wear them in public because she has the fool notion they don't look good on her. I disagree. I think she looks beautiful in them."

Rachel cried, "Clint, stop it. You're embarrassing me!"

"Then come home with me," he demanded in an oddly gruff voice, "so I can tell you in private how beautiful I think you are."

Tears filled Rachel's eyes, and her spectacles began to fog over. Clint took hold of her hand.

"Please, Rachel. Come back home where you belong. Every hour I spend apart from you, I die a little more inside. Please . . ." When she didn't immediately speak, he hastened to add, "I'm sorry you felt cast aside after Aunt Hester came. Lookin' back, I can see how it must have seemed to you, me all of a sudden backin' off and usin' the corn husks as an excuse. But I swear it wasn't that way. I truly was worried about her hearin' us."

Rachel shot a horrified look around. "Be quiet! Do you want everyone to hear!"

"See?" he said with a devilish grin. "It's a private affair, isn't it?"

She narrowed her eyes, but it was all she could do not to smile. "You've made your point."

"Then come home," he said huskily. "Where we can talk in private."

"Oh, Clint. Are you certain you really want—"

He cut her off with a kiss that answered her question far more eloquently than words. A sweet, wonderful kiss that sent tingles down her spine and made her toes curl. Exactly the kind of kiss Rachel had always dreamed of and had never received. Until she met Clint Rafferty, of course.

"I love you," he whispered against her cheek. "Please believe that, Rachel. I'll love you forever."

The throbbing timber of his voice, so packed with emotion, would have convinced Rachel. The way his hands shook when he touched her was added proof that he was sincere. Joy welled in her chest, nearly cutting off her breath, and she threw herself into his arms.

His arms . . . His wonderful strong arms. The instant they closed around her, Rachel knew she was where she belonged and where she would remain.

For the rest of her life.

Catherine Anderson

CATHERINE ANDERSON lives with her "wonderful" husband, Sid, and her beloved Rottweilers, Goliath and Sampson, in a secluded mountaintop chalet that is surrounded by towering fir trees and overlooks the beautiful Umpqua Valley of central Oregon. The entire west side of their house is glass, and of an evening, their loft bedroom is softly illuminated by the gorgeous sunsets and the city lights of Sutherlin, a quaint little town that was founded well over a century ago. It is, according to her, the perfect setting for a historical romance writer, for everywhere she looks there is something to inspire her.

An award-winning author of eleven published books, Catherine is presently working on her second full-length historical romance for Avon Books. Her first, *Annie's Song*, will be released in January 1996.

The Mad Earl's Bride

Loretta Chase

Prologue

Devon, England
June, 1820

The Devil was partial to Dartmoor.

In 1638, he rode a storm into Widdecombe, tore off the church roof with a lightning bolt, and carried off a boy who'd been dozing during the service.

This was merely one of several personal appearances. More often, though, Satan appeared in disguise as an enormous black hound or a ghostly stallion galloping across the moors.

His attachment to the area surprised no one, for Dartmoor could not have been better fashioned to suit satanic natures.

Storms lashed the rocky uplands, which loomed stubbornly in the path of Atlantic gales. Heavy damps swirled into the valleys, blanketing villages in impenetrable mists, shutting off communication and travel for days.

Then there were the bogs, filling the hollows and crevices of the highlands, shrinking and swelling with changing weather and season.

Narrow tracks of firm ground coiled through this

unwelcoming terrain, yet even the paths could be perilous. At night, or in a mist or storm, it was easy enough for the unwary traveler to lose his way and—if he were especially unlucky—slip into a pulsing morass from which he would never emerge.

Some believed Dartmoor's mires were the Devil's own traps, devised to suck their victims straight down to Hell, Aminta Camoys told her son.

It was twenty-year-old Dorian Camoys's first visit to Dartmoor and the first time he'd seen his mother since Christmas.

"Most considerate of the Archfiend," he replied as he walked with her to the edge of the narrow track. "After slow suffocation by quicksand, the unfortunate sinner will find Hell's torments less shocking to his sensibilities."

She pointed to a suspiciously verdant patch in the bleak wastes below. "Some are bright green like that. There's a larger one half a mile ahead, but it's gray—much better camouflage."

The afternoon had been bright and warm when they'd first ridden out, but a chill wind whirled about them now, and gray clouds swept in, driving out their wispy white predecessors and blanketing the moorland in shadows.

"Thank you for the directions, Mother," Dorian said. "But I do believe I can find my own route to Hell."

"I collect you've found it." She glanced at him and laughed. "Like mother, like son."

He was like her, in more ways than many would suspect.

Although at six feet tall he was by far the larger, the physical resemblance was inescapable. While fully masculine—and puffy and pale at present, thanks to months of dissipation pursued as diligently as his studies—his was the same exotically sculpted countenance.

At the moment, one would never suspect that she, too, was addicted to sins of the flesh. He was the only one, apart from her lovers, who did know. Dorian was her sole confidante.

My mother, the adultress, he thought, as he gazed at her.

Like him, she detested hats, resenting even that small concession to propriety. She'd taken off her bonnet as soon as they'd ridden out of sight of the house. Thick raven hair like his, though much longer, whipped about her face and neck in the sharpening wind. And when she turned to him, the same unblinking yellow stare met his.

Because of those odd-colored eyes and their disconcerting stare—and because he kept to himself and hissed at anyone who came too close—the boys at Eton had nicknamed him Cat. The nickname had followed him to Oxford.

"You'd better take care," she said. "If your grandfather finds out something besides studying is to blame for your pallor, you'll see all your carefully laid plans swept into the maelstrom of his righteous wrath."

"I've exercised considerable ingenuity to make certain he doesn't find out," Dorian said. "You may be sure I shall make a deceptively healthy appearance at Christmas for the annual lecture intended to guide me through the new year. After which I shall watch him scrutinize—for doubtless the hundredth time—every penstroke of the academic reports, looking for an excuse to yank me out of university. But he won't find his excuse, no matter how hard he looks. I'll have my degree—with honors—at the end of next Easter term, and he'll be obliged to reward me with a year's trip abroad, as he's done for the others."

"And you won't return," she said. She moved

away, her gaze turning to the surrounding moors.

"I'll never be free of him if I do. If I don't find
work abroad, I'll be tied to his purse strings until
the day he dies."

That prospect was intolerable.

His grandfather, the Earl of Rawnsley, was a des-
pot.

Dorian's father, Edward, was the youngest of the
earl's four sons, all of whom, with their spouses
and offspring, lived at Rawnsley Hall in Gloucestershire, where His Lordship could control their
every waking moment. The adults might go away
on short visits and spend time in London during
the Season, and the boys eventually went away to
school; but Rawnsley Hall was their home—or
prison—and its master ruled them absolutely. Always, wherever they were, they must behave and
think as he told them to.

They did it because they had no choice. Not only
did he control all the Camoys money, but he was
utterly ruthless. The smallest hint of rebellion was
promptly crushed—and the earl had no scruples
about how he did it.

When, for instance, whippings, lectures, and
threats of eternal damnation proved ineffective
with Dorian, Lord Rawnsley turned his vexation
upon the incorrigible boy's parents. That had
worked. Dorian could not stand by and watch his
parents punished and humiliated for his faults.

Consequently, though he'd been born quick-
tempered and rebellious, Dorian had learned very
young to keep his feelings and opinions to himself.

His outward behavior strictly regulated, all he
had to call his own was his mind—and it was an
exceptionally good one. That, too, he'd inherited
from his mother, the Camoys not being renowned
for intellectual acuity.

Since Dorian had performed brilliantly at Eton,
his grandfather had been obliged to send him on

to Oxford. In another year, Lord Rawnsley would be obliged, likewise, to finance the year abroad.

Dorian would have one year on the Continent to look for work. He was sure he'd survive, and he wasn't concerned about living in poverty at first. He would move up in the world eventually. All he had to do was concentrate as he did with his studies . . . and keep his sensual weaknesses under stricter control.

The thought of his weaknesses drew his mind and his gaze back to his mother. She had taken off her gloves and was playing with her rings.

Gad, but she loved trinkets—and fashionable gowns, and Society . . . and her romantic intrigues.

He wondered why she'd come to Dartmoor. She'd been born and reared here, yet it hardly suited her nature. She was meant for the gaiety of Society, for parties and gossip and admiring men swarming about her.

He'd expected to find her bored frantic. Instead, she seemed quieter than he could remember her ever being. He supposed her recent illness accounted for the apparent tranquillity. All the same, he couldn't help wondering why, when the doctor proposed a change of air, she'd asked to come here, of all places. She'd been quite adamant about it, Father said.

He approached her. "I wish you would think about coming to stay with me on the Continent," he said.

"Don't be absurd," she said. "I cannot live in a garret. And don't pretend you'll miss me," she added irritably. "I never was the least use to you. I had all I could do to look out for myself. It isn't easy, as you well know. Lud, I'm so tired of it. You've no idea the relief it is to be here, away from temptation and the everlasting thinking and planning and lying. And pretending, always pretending. No wonder my head still aches. It's so in the habit of laboring, it doesn't know how to stop. When there's nothing to think about, it makes something."

She thrust her hair back from her face—a habit of his, too, and one that had always irritated his grandfather. "That's the trouble with secrets," she said. "You can never be rid of them. They haunt you . . . like ghosts."

He smiled. "Your sins are not so grave, Mother. Bertie Trent's grandmother* goes through lovers as she goes through bonnets, they say."

Her brooding gaze upon the bleak wastes beyond, she did not seem to hear him. "I dreamt my sins took the shape of phantasms," she said in an odd, low voice. "They pursued me, like the Furies in Greek myths. It was frightful—and so unjust. I can't help my nature. You understand."

Dorian understood all too well. He loathed the weakness in himself, but no matter what he did, he could not master it. He could not resist the scent of a woman; he could scarcely resist the mere thought of one. Time and again the need drove him—and Lord, the distances he traveled, the subterfuges he resorted to . . . for what always, afterward, left him sick with disgust.

It was not nearly so bad with her, he was aware, but then she was constantly under scrutiny, which he wasn't, and she was a female, smaller in her sensual appetites as she was in size. Still, even her little escapades had taken their toll on her health.

He ought to heed the warning, Dorian knew. She'd only recently recovered. That made it more than six months since Mr. Budge, the Camoys family physician, had diagnosed a "decline." She'd spent half that time between a chaise longue and her bed.

---

*See *Lord of Scoundrels* by Loretta Chase, published by Avon Books.

Dorian could not afford so long a period of debility. He would fall behind in his studies . . . and the trip abroad would be delayed . . . and his bondage to his grandfather would stretch on . . .

He shook off the grim prospect. "It's Dartmoor," he said lightly. "Every foot of ground seems to have a spook attached to it. Small wonder you dream of ghosts and demons. I should be amazed if you didn't."

She laughed and turned back to him, her melancholy mood lifting as swiftly as it had descended.

From then until the end of Dorian's two-day visit, his mother seemed to be her lively self again. She related, along with more Dartmoor legends, all the London gossip gleaned from her friends' letters, and told slightly improper anecdotes that made Father blush, yet laugh all the same. Away from Rawnsley Hall, Edward Camoys was more human and less his father's puppet, and though he still treated his wife like a wayward child, that had suited them both for years.

All seemed well when Dorian departed.

He had no idea that his father had secrets, too, and as the months passed, Edward Camoys would find them increasingly difficult to conceal.

Aminta Camoys's letter writing, like Dorian's, was erratic at best. That was why he suspected nothing, though he didn't hear from her after early September.

It wasn't until shortly before Christmas, when Uncle Hugo, the earl's eldest and heir, turned up at Oxford unexpectedly—and, as it turned out, against the earl's orders—that Dorian learned the truth.

Then, deaf to his uncle's warnings, Dorian boarded a mail coach headed north.

He discovered his mother where Hugo had said she was.

It was a private, exclusive, and very expensive lunatic asylum.

Dorian found her in a small, rank room, strapped to a chair. She wore a stained cotton gown and thick, rough stockings on her delicate feet. Her long black hair had been sheared to a dark skullcap. She didn't know who he was at first. When, finally, she recognized him, she wept.

Dorian did not weep, only cursed inwardly while he unfastened the cruel straps. That sent the attendant running out of the room, but Dorian was too distraught to care. He carried his mother to the narrow bed and laid her down and sat beside her and chafed her icy hands and listened, his gut churning, while she told him what they'd done to her.

She'd fallen ill again, she said, and in her weakness, she'd let her secrets out. The earl knew everything now, and so he'd locked her up to punish her because she was a scarlet woman. Her keepers mortified her flesh to make her repent: they starved her and dressed her in stinking rags and made her sleep on filthy linens. They thrust her into ice baths. They shaved her head. They would not let her sleep: they beat on the door and called her a whore and a Jezebel and told her the Devil was coming for her soul.

Dorian didn't know what to believe.

Though she sobbed uncontrollably, her speech was coherent. Yet Uncle Hugo had said she'd gone after Father with a knife and tried to burn down the Dartmoor manor house. She heard voices, he said, and saw things that weren't there, and screamed of ghosts and cruel talons ripping into her skull. Edward Camoys had told nobody about her condition and tried to look after her himself, with the help of the local doctor, Mr. Kneebones.

But the earl had visited them in Dartmoor a month ago and, horrified at what he found, summoned physicians from London. Deciding she needed "expert care," they'd recommended Mr. Borson's private madhouse.

"Don't look at me so," she cried now. "I was ill, that was all, and the pain was dreadful, tearing at my skull so that I couldn't see straight. I couldn't think. I couldn't watch my tongue. Too many secrets, Dorian, and I was too weak to keep them in. Oh, please, darling, take me away from this wicked place."

Dorian didn't care what the truth was. He knew only that he couldn't leave her here. He looked about for something to wrap her in, to keep her warm, so that he could carry her away, but there were only the rank bedclothes.

He was tearing them from the bed when the attendant returned, with reinforcements—and Dorian's grandfather.

The instant the earl entered, Aminta turned into a she-demon. Uttering obscenities and threats in a guttural voice Dorian couldn't believe came out of her, she lunged at Lord Rawnsley. When Dorian tried to pull her away, she clawed his face. The attendants grabbed her and swiftly shackled her to the bed, where she alternated between bloodchilling curses and heartwrenching sobs.

When Dorian objected to the painful restraints, the attendants—on the earl's orders—removed him from the room, then from the building altogether. Shut out, Dorian paced by his grandfather's carriage while his mind replayed the scene over and over.

He could not stop shuddering because he could not shake off the sickening comprehension of what his mother must feel. In the unpredictable moments of clarity—like the one he'd encountered first—she could look about her and recognize what she'd become and where she was. He could imagine her rage and grief at being treated like a mindless animal. He could imagine, all too vividly, her terror as well—when she felt her control slip and the darkness begin swamping her reason. He had no doubt she knew what was happening to her: she'd said as much, that she was weak and couldn't keep things in.

She knew her once-formidable mind was betraying her, and that was worst of all.

And that was why, when his grandfather came out, Dorian gathered his shattered composure and swallowed his pride—and begged.

"Please let me take her elsewhere," he said. "I'll help look after her. I needn't return to Oxford. I can finish later. I know Father and I can manage with the help of a servant or two. I beg you, Grandfather, let—"

"You know nothing about it," Lord Rawnsley coldly cut in. "You know nothing of her tricks and subterfuges, her madwoman's cunning. She played your father for a fool and did the same with you this day. And now Borson says there is no telling what damage you've done—taking her part against those who know better, and making promises you cannot keep. She will be agitated for days, weeks, perhaps." He pulled on his gloves. "But it was ever this way. You were always her creature, in character as well as looks. Now you mean to throw away your future—to care for one who never cared for anybody but herself."

"She's my mother," Dorian said tightly.

"And my daughter-in-law," was the grim retort. "I know my duty to my family. She will be looked after—properly—and you will return to Oxford and do your duty."

Two weeks later, in the midst of a violent fit, Aminta Camoys collapsed and died.

She died in the madhouse Dorian had been unable to rescue her from, while he was at Oxford, burying his rage and grief in his studies because he had no choice. He had no money and no power to rescue her, and his grandfather would punish anyone who dared to help him.

He told nobody what had happened, not even Bertie Trent, the only friend Dorian had.

And so no one but the Camoys family—and then it was only the immediate family—was aware that Aminta Camoys had died, a raving lunatic, in Mr. Borson's expensive hellhole of a madhouse.

Even then, she wasn't left in peace. His grandfather let the curst doctors hack into her poor, dead brain to satisfy their grisly curiosity. The brain tissue was weak, and they'd found evidence of blood seepage. A vessel had burst during the last fit— one of many that might have burst at any time, so fragile they were. Her earlier decline, the doctors decided, must have been the first outward sign of an inner deterioration that had begun long before. The headaches were further symptoms, caused by the slow leakage.

There was nothing anyone could have done for her, they claimed. Just as medical science had no way of detecting such defects early on, it had no way of curing them.

And so Borson and his associates absolved themselves of all blame—as though they had not made her last months a living hell.

And the Camoys saw to it that no blame or shame would be attached to the family, either.

She had "sunk into a fatal decline"—that was the story they gave out, because no Camoys, even one by marriage, could possibly be mad. No hint of insanity had ever appeared in the family in all the centuries since Henri de Camois had come over from Normandy with the Conqueror.

Even among themselves, they never openly re-

ferred to her insanity, as though giving the truth
the cut direct could make it go away, like an un-
suitable acquaintance.

That was just as well, as far as Dorian was concerned. If he had to listen to the heartless hypo-
crites pontificating about his mother's madness, he
was bound to commit some outrage—and be destroyed, as she had been.

After the funeral, he returned to Oxford and buried his feelings, as usual, in study. It was the one
thing he could do, the one thing his grandfather
could not crush or twist to suit his tyrannical purposes.

Consequently, at the end of the term, Dorian not
only earned his degree but did what no Camoys
had ever done before: he won a first, *In Literis Hu-
manioribus*.

The traditional celebration followed at Rawnsley
Hall. It was the usual hypocrisy. Dorian had never
truly been one of the Camoys and he knew his academic triumph stuck in the collective family craw.
Still, they must give the appearance of family unity,
and for Dorian, pretending was easier this time,
with freedom so near. In a few weeks, he would
be upon the Continent—and he would not return
to England until his grandfather was sealed in the
tomb with his saintly ancestors.

In the meantime, Dorian could play his role, as
he'd done for years, and bear their pretense and
hypocrisy.

Pretending, always pretending, his mother had
said.

Her mind had broken down under the strain,
she'd believed.

Too many secrets . . . too weak to keep them in.

He didn't know that hers were not the only secrets she'd let out.

He did not find out until twenty-four hours after

the so-called celebration. And then Dorian could
only stand and listen helplessly for an endless,
numbing hour to the chilling speech that shattered
and scattered his plans like so much dust and left
him with nothing but his pride to sustain him.

Dorian was turned out of Rawnsley Hall with six
pounds and some odd pence in his pocket. This
was because Lord Rawnsley had expected him to
hang his head and make penitent speeches and beg
for forgiveness—and Dorian had decided that the
earl could wait until Judgment Day.

His grandfather had called him a whoremonger,
a slave to the basest of appetites, who shamelessly
and recklessly pursued a path that could only lead
to madness and a hideous death from the foul diseases contracted from the filth with which he con-
sorted.

Though Dorian knew this was true, he found he
must be sunk beyond shame as well because he
could not find a shred of remorse in his heart, only
rage. He would not, could not submit to his grandfather, ever again. He would starve and die in a
filthy gutter, rather than go crawling back.

He left fully aware that he'd have to survive entirely on his own. The earl would make trouble for
anyone who aided his errant grandson.

And so Dorian went to London. There he assumed a new identity and made himself one of the
insignificant masses. He found lodgings—a dank
room among the teeming tenements of the East
End—and employment as a dockworker by day
and a legal copyist at night. There was no future
in either occupation, but then, he had no future,
with all respectable doors shut to him. Still, even
when the dock work dwindled from time to time,
the lawyers kept him busy. There was little danger
of their running out of documents. And when the

drudgery threatened to crush his spirit, a few coins could buy him the temporary surcease of a relatively clean whore and a bottle.

The months stretched into years while his grandfather waited for the prodigal to crawl back on his hands and knees and the prodigal waited for his grandfather to die.

But the influenza epidemic that bore off Dorian's father, his Uncle Hugo, two aunts, and several cousins in 1826 left their lord and master untouched.

Then, in the summer of 1827, Dorian suddenly fell ill—and sank into a decline.

1

Dartmoor, Devon
Early May, 1828

Dorian stood in the library of Radmore Manor, looking out the window. In the distance, the moors stretched out in all their bleak beauty. They beckoned to him as strongly now as they'd called to his sickly fancy months before in London, when he'd fallen so dangerously ill, too weak even to hold his pen.

In August, Hoskins, a solicitor's clerk, had found him barely conscious, slumped over an ink-splotched document.

I'll fetch a doctor.

No. No doctors, for God's sake. Dartmoor. Take me to Dartmoor. There's money . . . saved . . . under the floor-board.

Hoskins might have absconded with the little hoard, and heaven knew he needed money, living on a clerk's pittance. Instead, he'd not only done as Dorian asked but stayed on to look after him. He'd remained even after Dorian recovered—or seemed to.

That apparent recovery had not deluded Dorian.

He'd suspected, early on, that the illness, like his
mother's years earlier, had simply been the beginning of the end.

In January, when the headaches began, his suspicions were confirmed. As the weeks passed, the
attacks grew increasingly vicious, as hers had done.

The night before last, he'd wanted to bash his
head against the wall.

. . . *pain . . . tearing at my skull . . . couldn't see
straight . . . couldn't think.*

He understood now, fully, what his mother had
meant. Even so, he would have borne the pain,
would not have sent for Kneebones yesterday
morning, if not for the shimmering wraith he'd
seen. Then Dorian had realized something must be
done—before the faint visual illusions blossomed
into full-blown phantasms, as they had for his
mother, and drove him to violence, as they had
done her.

"I know what it is," Dorian had told the doctor
when he came yesterday. "I know it's the same
brain disease and incurable. But I had rather finish
my time here, if it can be managed. I had rather
not . . . end . . . precisely as my mother did, if it can
possibly be helped."

Naturally, Kneebones must satisfy himself and
arrive at his own conclusions. But there was only
one possible conclusion, as Dorian well knew. His
mother had died within eight months of the onset
of the "visual chimera"—the "ghosts" she'd begun
seeing while awake, not simply in dreams, as she'd
said.

Six months was the most Kneebones could promise. He said the degeneration was progressing more
rapidly in Dorian's case, thanks to "a punishingly
insalubrious mode of living."

Still, Kneebones had assured him that the violent
fits could be moderated with laudanum, in large
doses.

"Your father was too sparing of the laudanum, fearing overdose," the doctor explained. "Then, when your grandfather came, he raged about my turning that unhappy woman into an opium addict. And then the fancy experts came, calling it 'poison' and saying it *caused* the hallucinations—when it was the only means of subduing them and quieting her."

Dorian smiled now, recalling that conversation. Opiate addiction was the least of his anxieties, and an overdose, in time, might offer a welcome release.

In time, but not yet.

Outwardly, he was healthy and strong, and in Dartmoor, he'd been free of the self-loathing that had haunted him since his last year at Eton, when temptation, in the shape of a woman, had first beckoned, and he'd found he was no match for it. Here, as his mother had said, there was no temptation. When he felt the old itch and grew restless, he rode through the moors, riding long and hard, until he was exhausted.

Here he'd found a refuge. He meant to enjoy it for as long as he could.

Hearing footsteps in the hall, Dorian turned away from the window and thrust his hair back from his face. It was unfashionably long, but fashion had ceased signifying to Dorian years ago, and it certainly wouldn't matter when he lay in his coffin.

The coffin didn't trouble him much, either, and hadn't for some time. He'd had months to get used to the idea of dying. Now, thanks to the promise of laudanum, his remaining anxiety was eased. The drug would stupefy him, sparing him full awareness of the wretched thing he would become, while those who looked after him needn't fear for their lives.

He would die in something like peace with

something like dignity. That was better than the lot
of scores of wretches in the cesspits of London, he
told himself. It was better than what his mother
had endured, certainly.

The library door opened, and Hoskins entered,
bearing a letter. He set it face down on the library
table so that the seal was plainly evident.

It was the Earl of Rawnsley's seal.

"Damn," Dorian said. He tore the letter open,
scanned it, then handed it to Hoskins.

"Now you see why I chose to be a nobody," Dorian said.

Hoskins had learned Dorian's true identity only
yesterday, at the same time he'd been informed of
Dorian's medical condition—and offered the opportunity to depart, if he wished. But Hoskins had
fought and been wounded at Waterloo. After the
horrors he'd experienced there, looking after a
mere lunatic was child's play.

Moreover, to Dorian's vast relief, Hoskins's manner remained matter-of-fact, with occasional ven-
tures into a gallows humor that lifted Dorian's
spirits.

"Is it the irascibility of age?" Hoskins asked
mildly as he handed the letter back. "Or was the
old gentleman always like this?"

"He's impossible," Dorian said. "Born that way,
I suppose. And quite convincing. For most of my
youth, I actually believed I was always the one at
fault. There is no dealing with him, Hoskins. All
one can do is try to ignore him. That won't be
easy." He frowned at the letter.

His remaining aunt, Hugo's widow, had visited
Dartmoor a short while ago and spotted Dorian on
one of his gallops through the moors. She'd written
the earl a highly exaggerated description of Dorian's riding garb—or lack thereof—and passed on
a lot of local gossip, mostly ignorant speculation

about the reclusive eccentric living at Radmore Manor.

The earl's letter ordered Dorian to appear—his hair properly shorn and his person decently attired—at a family council on the twelfth of May, and explain himself.

If they wanted him, they'd have to come and get him, Dorian silently vowed, and they would never take him away alive.

"Did you wish to dictate a reply, sir?" Hoskins asked. "Or shall we chuck it into the fire?"

"I'll write my own reply. Otherwise you'll be targeted as an accomplice, and made to feel the weight of his righteous wrath." Dorian smiled faintly. "*Then* we'll chuck it into the fire."

On the twelfth of May 1828, the Earl of Rawnsley and most of his immediate family were gathered in Rawnsley Hall's drawing room at the moment that a section of the ancestral roof above them chose to collapse. In a matter of seconds, several tons of timber, stone, and miscellaneous decorative debris buried them and made Dorian Camoys— one of the very few family members not in attendance—the new Earl of Rawnsley.

In a small sitting room in a house in Wiltshire, Gwendolyn Adams read the weeks-old newspaper account several times before she was satisfied she had not overlooked any details.

Then she turned her attention to the other three documents on her writing desk. One was a letter written by the present earl's recently deceased aunt. According to it, her nephew had turned into a savage. His hair hung down to his knees, and he galloped half-naked through the moors on a murderous white horse named after a bloodthirsty pagan god.

The second document was a draft of a letter from the earl to his "savage" grandson. It gave Gwen-

dolyn a very good idea why the heir had failed to
attend the funeral.

The third document was the present Lord Rawnsley's reply to his grandfather's obnoxious letter,
and it made Gwendolyn smile for the first time
since the duc d'Abonville had arrived and made
his outrageous proposal.

Abonville's mother had been a de Camois, the
French tree from which the English Camoys branch
had sprouted centuries earlier—and thus Rawnsley's very distant cousin. Abonville was also the
fiancé of Gwendolyn's grandmother, Genevieve,
the dowager Viscountess Pembury.

The pair had attended the Camoys's funeral,
after which a harassed solicitor had sought the
duc's assistance as nearest male kin: papers needed
signing, and any number of legal matters must be
attended to, and the present Lord Rawnsley had
refused to assume his responsibilities.

Accordingly, the duc and Genevieve had jour-
neyed to Dartmoor. There, they discovered that the
new earl had fallen victim to a terminal brain disease.

Gwendolyn's smile faded. Bertie Trent, her first
cousin, had taken the news very hard. At present,
he was hiding in the stables, sobbing over an old
letter, creased and faded past legibility, from his
boyhood friend Cat Camoys.

She moved the papers aside and took up the
miniature Bertie had given her.

The tiny likeness allegedly represented Bertie's
friend. It had been painted years earlier by a singularly inept artist, and it did not tell her much.

Still, twenty-one-year-old Gwendolyn was too
levelheaded a girl to base the most momentous decision of her life upon a picture two inches in di-
ameter.

In the first place, she knew she was no great
beauty herself, with her pointy nose and chin and

impossible red hair. She doubted that her green eyes, to which several suitors had composed lavish—and very silly—odes, compensated for everything.

In the second place, physical attractiveness was irrelevant. Rawnsley had not been asked to fall in love with her, nor she with him. Abonville had simply asked her to marry the earl and bear him a son to save the Camoys line from extinction.

She'd been asked to do this because she came of a phenomenally fertile family, famous for producing males. Both characteristics were critical, for the Earl of Rawnsley hadn't much time to sire an heir. His physician had given him six months to live.

Unfortunately, there were no documents offering any insights into the brain disease itself. The little Genevieve and Abonville knew they'd learned mainly from the earl's manservant, Hoskins. His Lordship had volunteered no details, and pressing him for information would have been unkind, Genevieve had said.

Gwendolyn frowned.

Her mother entered the room at that moment and softly closed the door behind her. "Are you truly thinking it over?" she asked as she took the seat next to Gwendolyn's desk. "Or are you only making a show of hesitation for Papa's benefit?"

Though she had taken time to reflect, Gwendolyn did not feel hesitant. She knew the task she'd been asked to undertake would not be pleasant. But that did not daunt her in the least.

Unpleasantness was only to be expected. Illness, whether of the mind or the body, was disagreeable; otherwise so much labor wouldn't be dedicated to making it go away. But illness was also exceedingly interesting, and lunatics, Gwendolyn felt, were the most interesting patients of all.

Lord Rawnsley's case, combining both a mysterious neurological disease and aberrant behavior, could not have excited her more.

If the Almighty had sent her a letter, signed, witnessed, and notarized, she could not have felt more certain that He, in His infinite wisdom—about which she had entertained doubts on more than one occasion—had made her expressly for this purpose.

"I was making absolutely certain there wasn't anything to think about," Gwendolyn told her mother. "There isn't."

Mama gazed at her for a long moment. "Yes, I heard the celestial summons—as clearly as you did, I don't doubt. Papa is another matter, however."

Gwendolyn was well aware of this. Mama understood her. Papa did not. None of the males of the family did. That included Abonville. Gwendolyn was sure the marriage idea was one her grandmother had planted in his head while convincing him it was his own. Fortunately, Genevieve had an enviable talent for making men believe just about anything she wanted them to.

"We'd better let Genevieve talk him round," Gwendolyn said. "Otherwise he will create delays by raising a lot of needless obstacles, and we have no time to lose. There's no telling how long Rawnsley will retain his reason, and he must be of sound mind for the legalities."

That wasn't Gwendolyn's only anxiety. At this very moment, the Earl of Rawnsley might be taking one of his reckless rides and risking a fatal tumble into a mire.

Then she would never have a chance to do something truly worthwhile with her life.

Before she could voice this concern, her mother spoke.

"Genevieve has already begun working on your father," she said. "She knew what your answer would be, as I did. "I shall go downstairs and signal her to administer the coup de grâce." She rose.

"Thank you, Mama," Gwendolyn said.

"Never mind that," Mama said sharply. "It is not what I would have wished for you, even if you will be Countess of Rawnsley. If that young man had not been Bertie's friend, and if he had not looked after your idiot cousin all through Eton—and doubtless saved his worthless neck a hundred times—" Her eyes filled and her voice was unsteady as she went on, "Oh, Gwendolyn, I should never let you go. But we cannot leave the poor boy to die alone." She squeezed Gwendolyn's shoulder. "He needs you, and that is all that ought to matter, I know."

Dorian Camoys stood, trapped, in his own library.

Less than a fortnight had passed since the duc d'Abonville had turned up at the door.

Now the Frenchman was back—with a special license and a female he insisted Dorian marry forthwith.

Dorian could have dealt with the Frenchman and his ludicrous command easily enough. Unfortunately, along with Lady Pembury and the girl Dorian had not yet met and knew better than to consider meeting, Abonville had also brought his future grandson, Bertie Trent.

And Bertie had got it into his head that he would stand as his friend's groomsman.

When Bertie got something into his head, it was next to impossible to get it out. This was because Bertie Trent was one of the stupidest men who'd ever lived. This, Dorian had long ago recognized, was the reason Bertie was the only friend he'd ever had—and one whose childlike feelings Dorian couldn't bear to hurt.

It was impossible to rage at Abonville properly

while trying not to distress Bertie, who was so thrilled about his best friend marrying his favorite female cousin.

"It's only Gwen," Bertie was saying, misconstruing the issues, as usual. "She ain't half bad, for a girl. Not like Jess—but I shouldn't wish m'sister on anybody, especially you, even though you'd be m'brother then, because I can't think of anything worse than a fellow having to listen to her the live-long day. Not but what Dain can manage her—but he's bigger than you, and even so, I daresay he's got his hands full. Still, they're already shackled, so you're safe from her, and Gwen ain't like her at all. When Abonville told us you was wanting to get married, and he was thinking Gwen would suit, I said—"

"Bertie, I wasn't wanting to get married," Dorian broke in. "It is a ridiculous mistake."

"I have made no mistake," said Abonville. He stood before the door, his distinguished countenance stern, his arms folded over his chest. "You gave your word, cousin. You said you recognized your duty, and you would marry if I could find a girl willing to have you."

"It doesn't matter what I said—if I did say it," Dorian said tightly. "I had a headache when you came, and had taken laudanum. I was not in my senses at the time."

"You were fully rational."

"I could not have been!" Dorian snapped. "I should never have agreed to such a thing if I had. I'm not a damned ox. I shan't spend my last months breeding!"

That was a mistake. Bertie's round blue eyes began to fill. "It's all right, Cat," he said. "I'll stick by you, like you always stuck by me. But you must have promised, or Abonville wouldn't have said you did, and talked to Gwen. And she'll be awful disappointed—not but what she'll get over it, not being the moping sort. But only think how we could be cousins, and if you was to make a brat, I could be godfather, you know."

Dorian bent a malignant glare upon the accursed duc. This was his doing. He'd filled Bertie's head with the kinds of ideas he was sure to set his childish heart on: standing as groomsman for his dying friend, becoming Dorian's cousin, then godfather to imaginary children.

And poor Bertie, his heart bursting with good intentions, would never understand why it was impossible. He would never comprehend why Dorian needed to die alone.

"I'll stick by you," he'd said—and Bertie would. If Dorian wouldn't wed his cousin, Bertie would stay. Either way, Dorian wouldn't stand a chance. They would never let him die in peace.

Once Dorian was no longer capable of thinking for himself, Bertie—or Abonville or the wife—would call in experts to deal with the madman.

And Dorian knew where that would lead: he would die as his mother had, caged like an animal . . . unless he killed himself first.

But he would not be hurried to his grave. He still had time, and he meant to enjoy it, to relish his sanity and strength for every precious moment they remained.

He told himself to calm down. He was not trapped. It only seemed that way, with loyal, dim-witted Bertie on one side, prating of godchildren, and Abonville on the other, blocking the door.

Dorian was not yet weak and helpless, as his mother had been. He'd find a way out of this so long as he kept a cool head.

Half an hour later, Dorian was galloping along the narrow track that led to Hagsmire. He was laughing, because the ruse had worked.

It had been easy enough to feign a sudden attack

of remorse. Given years of practice with his grandfather, Dorian had no touble appearing penitent, and grateful for Abonville's efforts. And so, when Dorian requested a few minutes to compose himself before meeting his bride, the two guests had exited the library.

So had he—out the window, through the garden, then down to the stables at a run.

He knew they wouldn't pursue him to Hagsmire. Even his own groom wouldn't venture onto the tortuous path this day, with storm clouds roiling overhead.

But he and Isis had waited out Dartmoor storms before. There was plenty of time to find the cracked heap of granite where they'd sheltered so many times previously, while Dorian beat back the inner demons urging him toward the old habits, the illusory surcease of wine and women.

Even if they searched, his unwanted guests would never find him, and they would give up awaiting his return long before he gave in. He had not yielded to his private demons or to his grandfather, and he would not yield to an overbearing French nobleman obsessed with genealogy.

There would be no more submitting to Duty. The new Earl of Rawnsley would be dead in a few months, and that would be the end of the curst Camoys line. And if Abonville didn't like it, let him uproot one of the French sprigs and plant him here, and make the poor sod marry Bertie's cousin.

Because the only way she would marry Dorian Camoys, he assured himself, would be by coming into Hagsmire with the entire bridal party and the preacher, and even then someone would have to pin the groom down with a boulder. Because he would dive into a bottomless pit of quicksand before he would take any woman into his life now and let her watch him disintegrate into a mindless animal.

Thunder rumbled faintly in the distance.

Or so Dorian thought at first, until he noticed that the rumble didn't pause, as thunder would, but went on steadily, and steadily grew louder. And the louder and nearer it came, the less it sounded like thunder and the more it sounded like ... hoofbeats.

He glanced back, then quickly ahead again.

He told himself the recent confrontation had agitated him more than he'd suspected, and what he believed he'd just seen was a trick of his degenerating brain.

The ignorant rustics, who believed pixies dwelt all over Dartmoor, had named Hagsmire for the witches they also believed haunted the area. During mists and storms, they mounted ghostly steeds and chased their victims into the mire.

The hoofbeats grew louder.

The thing was gaining on him.

He glanced back, his heart pounding, his nerves tingling.

Though he assured himself it couldn't be there, his eyes told him it was: a demonic-looking female riding an enormous bay. A tangled mane of fiery red hair flew wildly about her face. She rode boldly astride, a pale cloak streaming out behind her, her skirts hiked up to her knees, shamelessly displaying her ghostly white limbs.

Though it was only a moment's glance, the brief distraction proved fatal, for in the next instant, Isis swerved too sharply into a turning.

Dorian reacted a heartbeat too late, and the mare skidded over the crumbling track edge and down the slippery incline—toward the quagmire waiting below.

The pale mare managed to scramble back from the edge of the murky pit, but she threw off her master in the process.

Gwendolyn leapt down from her mount, collected the rope she'd brought, and climbed down the incline to the edge of the bog.

Several feet from where she stood, the Earl of Rawnsley was thrashing in a pit of grey muck. In the few minutes it had taken her to reach the bog, he'd slid toward its heart, and his efforts to struggle for footing where there wasn't any only sucked him in deeper.

Still, the muck had climbed only as far as his hips, and an assessing glance told Gwendolyn that this patch of mire was relatively narrow in circumference.

Even while she was studying her surroundings, she was moving toward the mare, making reassuring sounds. She was aware of Rawnsley cursing furiously, in between shouting at her to go away, but she disregarded that.

"Try to keep as still as possible," she told him calmly. "We'll have you out in a minute."

"Get away from here!" he shouted. "Leave my horse alone, you bedamned witch! Run, Isis! Home!"

But Gwendolyn was stroking under the mare's mane, and the creature was quieting, despite her master's shouts and curses. She stood docilely while Gwendolyn unbuckled the stirrup strap, removed the stirrup iron, and rebuckled the strap. She looped one end of the rope through the strap and knotted it. Then she led the mare closer to the bog.

Rawnsley had stopped cursing, and he was not thrashing about so much as before. She did not know whether he'd come to his senses or was simply exhausted. She could see, though, that he'd sunk past his waist. Swiftly she tied a loop at the free end of the rope.

"Look sharp now," she called to him. "I'm going to throw it."

"You'll fall in, you stupid—"

She flung the rope. He grabbed . . . and missed. And swore profusely.

Gwendolyn quickly drew it back and tried again. On the fifth try, he caught it.

"Try to hold on with both hands," she said. "And don't try to help us. Pretend you're a log. Keep as still as you can."

She knew that was very difficult. It was instinctive to struggle when one was sinking. But he would sink faster if he fought the mire, and the deeper he was, the harder it would be to pull him out. Even here, where it was safe, the soggy ground was barely walkable. Her boots sank into mud up to the ankles. Isis, too, must contend with the mud, as well as her master's weight, and the powerful mire dragging him down.

Still, they would do it, Gwendolyn assured herself. She looped the reins through one hand and grasped the stirrup strap and rope with the other.

Then she turned the mare so that she'd be moving sideways from the bog, and started her on the first cautious steps of rescue. "Slowly, Isis," she murmured. "I know you want to hurry—so do I— but we cannot risk wrenching his arms from their sockets."

He collapsed as soon as he escaped the mire, but Gwendolyn had to leave him while she returned to the bridle path with Isis. Though the horse had been good and patient through the ordeal, she was restless and edgy now, and Gwendolyn was worried she might stumble into the mire if left unattended. One could not look after horse and master simultaneously.

By the time she'd settled Isis with Bertie's gelding, retrieved a brandy flask from the saddlebag, and hurried back to Rawnsley, he had returned to full consciousness. To extremely bad-tempered consciousness, by the looks and sounds of it.

His black mane dripped ooze from the mire, and he was cursing under his breath as he shoved it out of his face and dragged himself up to a sitting position.

"Devil take you and roast you in Hell!" he snarled. "You could have killed yourself—and my horse. I told you to go away, curse you!"

A mask of grey-green slime clung to his face. Even under the mucky coating, however, his features appeared stronger and starker than in the miniature. This was a hard, sharply etched face, while the painted one had been sickly looking and puffy.

The rest of him was not sickly looking either. The earl's bog-soaked garments clung to broad shoulders and back, a taut, narrow waist, and long legs—and every inch of that was solid muscle.

The reality was so unlike the picture that Gwendolyn wondered for a moment whether someone had played a joke on her, and this wasn't Rawnsley at all.

Then he pulled off his mud-encrusted gloves and wiped the filth from his eyes with his fingers and looked at her ... and she froze, the breath stuck in her throat as her heart missed the next scheduled beat.

Bertie called him Cat because, he said, that's what all the fellows at school had called him. Now Gwendolyn understood why.

The Earl of Rawnsley's eyes were yellow.

Not a human brown or hazel but a feline amber gold. They were the eyes of a jungle predator, burning bright—and dangerous.

Fortunately, Gwendolyn was not easily intimidated. The shock passed as quickly as it had come, and she knelt down beside him and offered the flask with a steady hand.

Her voice was steady, too, as she answered. "No

self-respecting witch would go away on a mere mortal's orders. She'd be drummed out of the coven in disgrace."

He took the flask from her and drank, his intent yellow gaze never leaving her face.

"You may not know that all the best witches come to Dartmoor for their familiars," she said. "A black cat is de rigueur. Since you're the only one available—"

"I'm not available, and I'm not a damned tabby, you demented little hellhound! And I know who you are. You're the curst cousin, aren't you? Only one of Bertie's kin would come galloping into a mire in that lunatic way and blunder about, risking a horse, as well as her own scrawny neck, saving a man from what she got him into. And I didn't ask to be saved, Devil confound you! It's all the same to me—I've already got one foot in the grave—or didn't they tell you?"

"Yes, they did tell me," she answered calmly. "But I did not come all this way only to turn back at the first obstacle. I am aware it is all the same to you. I realize the mire would have saved you the trouble of putting a pistol to your head or hanging yourself or whatever you had in mind. But you may just as easily do that later, after we're wed. I regret the inconvenience, my lord, but I cannot let you die before the ceremony, or I shall never get my hospital."

In the past, Gwendolyn often obtained satisfactory results from startling statements.

It worked this time, too.

He drew back slightly, and his furious expression softened into bewilderment.

"It is simple enough," she said. "I need you, and you need me—although I cannot expect you to believe that at present since you know next to nothing about me."

She glanced upward. "We are about to be in-

undated. We will need to find shelter—for the
horses' sake, I mean, since you won't mind dying
of lung fever, either. That is not altogether inconvenient. Waiting out the storm will give us a
chance for private conversation."

2

"Oh, no, you don't," Dorian said. The words
came out in croaks. His throat was raw
from shouting the objections she'd been so stubbornly deaf to.

Ignoring her outstretched hand, he staggered to
his feet. Staying upright proved even harder than
getting up.

Mires, it turned out, didn't simply swallow you.
His mother had failed to explain that they chewed
first. They tried to suck the skin off your bones and
crush your organs and muscles into jelly. Every
inch of his body, inside and out, was throbbing
painfully. He ignored it.

"There will be no private tête-à-têtes," he said,
grasping her arm and marching her to the incline.
"We have nothing to say to each other. I am taking
you back to the house, and then you will go back
where you came from."

"I don't think that's a good idea," she said. Her
voice remained level, and she made no effort to
free herself from his grasp.

He let go abruptly, wishing he hadn't grabbed
her slim arm in that oafish way. She had no choice

but to follow him, unless she meant to take up residence in Hagsmire.

He started up the slope alone.

After a moment, she followed. "Why did you bolt?" she asked.

"I took a lunatic fit." He trudged on.

"That often happens when one converses with Bertie for any length of time," she said. "Sometimes I have to shake him. Otherwise, he will go on and on and lose track entirely of what he's saying, and one can grow quite giddy trying to follow."

"I'm very fond of Bertie," he said coldly.

"So am I," she said. "But he is miraculously stupid, isn't he? Cousin Jessica says he was born with his foot in his mouth and has been unable to get it out since. I suppose he must have made the most harrowing vows of eternal devotion to you. He was blubbering into his handkerchief when he came out to tell me you'd bolted. So there was no getting an intelligible explanation out of him. And Abonville said only that he'd made a terrible mistake, and Genevieve must take me back to the inn."

"Obviously you heeded Abonville no more than you did me," Dorian said irritably. "The words 'go away' appear to have no meaning for you."

"If I always did what I was told, I should never accomplish anything," she said. "Fortunately, Abonville is aware that I do not blindly obey orders. And so, when I said I must go after you, and my grandmother agreed, he took Bertie back into the library, and they made direct for the brandy."

They had reached the bridle path. Dorian wanted to get on his horse and ride so he wouldn't have to listen to her, but his leg muscles were giving way.

His hair was thick with mire ooze, and the cold slime dribbled down his neck. Thanks to the slime, he stank to high heaven. He was too tired and shaken to care.

He staggered to a boulder and sat down and stared at his sodden trousers while he waited for his respiration to slow and his brain to quiet.

"It would appear there has been a misunderstanding," she said.

He couldn't understand why she wouldn't keep her distance from him when it must be obvious to her by now that he was deranged. It was certainly obvious to him.

He pushed a hank of soggy hair from his eyes and looked up at her. Though she didn't appear as demonlike as she had before, galloping after him, she still looked like a witch. A young witch, with her sharp little nose and chin and narrow, uptilted green eyes—and the hair, the wild mass of red hair. It wasn't even a normal red but a strange maroon, glinting fire even in the gloom of the approaching storm.

All the same, strange as she was, Dorian couldn't believe he'd actually mistaken this young Englishwoman for one of Satan's handmaidens.

He should not have let himself become so overwrought, he reproached himself. If he had stayed with the two men and argued patiently and rationally . . . but he hadn't. Instead, he had run away—from temptation, yes, but they would think he'd fled a mere girl—and now they would have no doubt he was a lunatic. Abonville would probably have him examined and certified non compos mentis.

"Damn me to hell," he muttered.

"I don't mean to plague you," she said, "but I cannot work out what happened, exactly. What did they say about me that made you bolt? I have been wracking my brains, but all I could think was that Bertie—"

"I didn't know what to do with him!" he

snapped. "The silly sod wants to stay with me—to the tragic bloody end—and I'll never get rid of him without resorting to violence." *Then they'll lock me away,* he added silently.

"I can make him go away," she said. "I'm one of the few people who can actually communicate with him. Is that all?"

"All?" he echoed. "No, that isn't all. I want the lot of you gone. I don't need Bertie about, sobbing the instant my tragic condition is hinted at. I don't need Abonville telling me what's good for me and what I ought to do. I've had a lifetime of that. And most of all, I don't need a wife, damn and blast him!"

The demons in his breast cried that a wife was what he most needed, and conjured erotic images he hastily thrust away.

A pucker appeared in her brow. "That is odd. I should not have thought Abonville would misunderstand. His English is excellent. Or have you changed your mind about getting married? I do wish you would explain, my lord. It is very difficult to respond sensibly to a situation when one is so utterly in the dark."

"I did not change my mind," he said, beating back an insane urge to smooth the furrow from her young—too young—brow. "I vaguely remember Abonville's and your grandmother's visit—whenever it was—and his explaining how he and I were cousins about a thousand times removed. That's all I remember, and it's amazing I recall so much, considering I had swilled about a gallon of laudanum shortly before he arrived."

Her expression cleared. "Oh, I do see now. Some individuals become extremely docile under the influence of opiates. You must have amiably agreed with every word they said—and all the while you had no idea what they were talking about."

Thunder grumbled in the distance, and black

clouds were massing above their heads. She appeared to heed the threatening weather not at all. She only watched him with quiet concentration. The steady green perusal was stirring a dangerous yearning in his breast. He beat that back, too.

"I tried to explain," he said stiffly, "but he refused to listen to me."

"I am not surprised," she said. "He was sure to think the Rawnsley he encountered the first time was relatively sane—because that Rawnsley sensibly agreed with everything Abonville said. Today, when you disagreed, he was bound to ascribe it to a temporary fit of insanity."

"The thought has crossed my mind," he muttered.

"Many people respond to seemingly irrational behavior in the same way," she said. "Instead of listening to what you said, he probably tried to drum rationality into you by repeating his point over and over, as one drums the multiplication tables into children. Even medical experts, who ought to know better, believe this is an 'enlightened' way of dealing with individuals in an agitated state."

She wrinkled her pointy nose. "It is most annoying. No wonder you lost your patience and dashed off."

"That was a mistake, all the same," he said. "I should have stayed and reasoned with him."

"Waste of breath," she said briskly. "Your mental balance is in doubt. The explanation must come from one whose sanity is not doubted. I will explain to him, and he will listen to me."

She paused, looking about her. "The storm is not rushing upon us as quickly as I expected. For once, Providence shows some consideration. I should have hated going back without having the least idea what was wrong. Not that I am altogether happy with the answer. Still, one cannot hold a man to a promise made when he was not properly in his senses.''

Bertie had said she wasn't the moping sort. Even so, the faint note of resignation in her voice made Dorian feel guilty. She had saved his life. Though he wasn't at all sure he'd wanted to be saved, he could appreciate the courage and efficiency with which she'd acted. She'd also calmed him. She'd listened. She'd understood.

He looked away, wondering how much of an explanation he owed her and how much he could trust himself to utter.

A jagged branch of fire darted over a distant ridge. The heavens rumbled.

He brought his gaze back to her. "Does it not strike you as . . . morbid?" he asked. "That I should take a wife, now of all times?"

She shrugged. "I can understand how it might seem so to you. Yet it is not much different than a decrepit old man marrying a young woman, which happens often enough."

It did happen, Dorian knew. Such a marriage meant a few months, perhaps a few years, of catering to a drooling invalid. The reward of a wealthy widowhood and independence more than compensated, evidently.

He was hardly the one to revile a woman for acting out of greed. It wasn't as though he'd ever been a saint.

Moreover, he was aware that some women had remarkable powers of endurance. Was there so much difference, he wondered, between lying with a man who was as good as a corpse and lying with a drunken, lusting oaf, insatiable while the need was upon him and soddenly morose afterward?

That was the man he'd been, not so very long ago.

He shuddered—at the past and at what his fu-

ture held if he yielded to his baser self and took
what she offered.

"We had better start back," she said. "You are
tired and wet and chilled."

She turned and moved toward her horse.

Dorian rose and followed, relieved that she
sought no further explanation. Though he'd already said more than he wanted, he still wanted to
tell her more, to explain. But that would mean de-
scribing the sordid life that lay behind him and the
helpless imbecility that lay ahead. Better to leave it
as it was, he told himself. She seemed to accept the
situation.

They reached the bay gelding, and Dorian was
so busy telling himself to hold his tongue before it
got him into trouble that he didn't pause to think
but picked her up and set her upon the saddle.

Too late, he remembered it was a man's saddle.

She swung her leg over and settled comfortably
astride, naively exposing to his view several inches
of feminine underthings.

Between the dirty draggle of her petticoats and
the slime-encrusted boots, her muddy stocking
hugged a slender, curvaceous calf.

Dorian backed away, silently cursing himself.

She didn't need his assistance. He could have
mounted his own horse and started for home and
let her take care of herself. He had just escaped a
mire. No one would expect him to play the gallant
at such a time, and she was obviously not a helpless female.

He should not have allowed his mind to wander
into the past. He should not have touched her or
come close enough to notice what her legs were
like. Already he could feel his resistance weaken-
ing, was aware of the excuses forming in his treacherous mind—the false promises he knew better
than to trust. There would be no relief for him, or
release, if he yielded to this temptation. There

never had been before: only a temporary oblivion
and self-loathing afterward.

He hurried to Isis and hastily mounted.

Gwendolyn Adams was not the granddaughter
of a famous femme fatale for nothing. Though she
had not inherited Genevieve's raven hair or heart-
stopping countenance or subtly seductive ways,
Gwendolyn had inherited certain instincts.

She did not have much trouble interpreting the
Earl of Rawnsley's expression when his exotic yellow gaze wandered to her leg.

She did not have much trouble, either, interpreting her own reaction when his gaze lingered at
least two pulse beats longer than delicacy allotted.
The hot spark in his eyes had seemed to leap to
her limb and set a little fire to it that darted up
under her petticoats and past her knee, teasing her
thighs with its naughty warmth before it swirled
into the pit of her belly. There it set off sensations
she had heard of but never before experienced in
her life.

She had never dreamed the mad Earl of Rawnsley would arouse such sensations, but then, he
was nothing like what she'd expected.

She had read about quicksand and the agonizing
pressure it exerted. She was sure he must feel as
though he'd been run over by a herd of stampeding
bulls. Yet he had picked her up as easily as he
might pluck a daisy from the thin Dartmoor soil.
Now she watched him swing his long, powerful
body up into the saddle in one easy motion, as
though he'd done nothing more tiring than pick
wildflowers.

Puzzled, she followed the earl in silence down
the narrow, winding track.

Rain was falling, but halfheartedly. The worst of
the storm seemed to be rampaging in the southeast.

Rawnsley trotted on steadily, never once glancing back at her. If his horse had been fresh, Gwendolyn had no doubt he would have galloped out of Hagsmire in the same desperate manner he'd galloped in.

Abonville had—with the best of intentions, assuredly—thrown him into a dangerously agitated state. It was bound to happen again, and the duc was sure to make the worst possible decisions out of the best possible motives. She had seen it happen too many times: greedy physicians, eager to make heaps of money trying their ludicrous theories out on hopeless cases, and loving families blindly agreeing out of desperation.

But the medical experts were men, and with men, everything was a war of sorts. Doctors were bound to battle disease, at times, as though the victims as well as the illness were mortal foes. Then the physicians wondered why their patients turned hostile.

What Rawnsley needed was a friend. At present, though, thanks to Abonville—and poor, stupid Bertie—he viewed Gwendolyn as the enemy.

"Drat them," she muttered. "Leave it to men to make a muck of things."

She was silently reviewing her long litany of grievances against the male of the species when Rawnsley drew his mare to a halt.

Gwendolyn noticed that the track had widened. There seemed to be enough room to ride abreast.

Rawnsley was waiting for her to catch up, she realized with amazement. Her spirits rose, but only a very little bit. Experience had taught her not to leap to conclusions, especially optimistic ones.

When she came up beside him, he spoke.

"You mentioned a hospital," he said, moving on again. His voice was hoarse and unsteady. Exhaustion and inner distress were easy enough to diagnose. The distress itself was more difficult to analyze. He was not looking at her but watching the path ahead, and his long, wet hair hung in his face, concealing his expression.

"I have been trying to guess why you would come to marry a dying madman," he continued. "You said you needed me. I assume it's the money you need." He gave a short laugh. "Obviously. What other reason could there be?"

That was rather a crass way of putting it. Nevertheless, it was true enough, and Gwendolyn had determined at the outset to be honest with him.

"I do need the money, to build a hospital," she said. "I have definite ideas about how it should be constructed as well as the principles according to which it must be run. In order to achieve my goals—without negotiation or compromise—I require not only substantial funds, but influence. As Countess of Rawnsley, I should have both. As your widow, I should be able to act independently. Since you are the last of the males of your family, I should have to answer to no one."

She glanced at him. "You see, I did take all the details of your present situation into account, my lord."

He was looking straight ahead. He had pushed his sopping mane back from his face. She still couldn't read his expression, but she saw no signs of shock or anger.

"My grandfather would turn over in his grave," he said after a moment. "A woman—the Countess of Rawnsley, no less—building a hospital with the family fortune. All that money thrown away upon peasants."

"Wealthy people don't need hospitals," she said. "They can afford to keep physicians about to attend every trivial discomfort."

"And you mean to run it according to your principles," he said. "My grandfather had a very low opinion of feminine intelligence. A woman with ideas of her own, in his view, was a dangerous

aberrant of Nature." He glanced at her, then
quickly away. "You present me with an almost irresistible temptation."

"I hope so," she said. "There is not another man
in England whose circumstances are more neatly
suited to my aspirations. I grasped this almost immediately and was quite frantic to get here before
you killed yourself. You see, I am much more desperate to marry you than you could possibly be to
marry anybody."

"Desperate," he said with another short laugh.
"I am the answer to your prayers, am I?"

The halfhearted rain was building to a steady
drizzle, and lightning skittered at the edges of the
moorland. Still, they were not far from the house
now, and traveling on lower ground than before.

He seemed to be mulling the matter over.

Gwendolyn waited silently, resisting the urge to
pray. She did not wish to tempt Fate into more
practical jokes. It had already landed him in a mire.

She contented herself with a few cautious sidelong glances at the man she'd come to marry. The
rain was washing some of the muck away, and
even though his face was still dirty, there was no
mistaking the nobly chiseled profile.

He was terribly handsome.

She had not expected that. But then, she was
used to expecting the worst. The possibility of finding him attractive had not entered her calculations.
She was adjusting those calculations when he
spoke again.

"I came here to finish my time in peace," he said.
"I hoped that if I kept to myself in this isolated
place and didn't bother anybody, no one would
bother me."

"But we have come and turned everything up-
side down," she said. "I can understand how frustrating that is."

He turned to her. "Abonville won't leave me alone, will he?"

"I shall do my utmost to persuade him to respect your wishes," she said cautiously. She couldn't promise Abonville would keep away forever, yet she did not want to use the duc as a threat. She did not want Rawnsley to feel he must hide behind a woman's skirts. One of the most disagreeable aspects of being ill was feeling helpless and utterly dependent upon others.

"If I do as he asks and marry you, he'll probably leave me in peace, at least for a time," Rawnsley said. "The trouble is, I should have you about instead, and yet . . ." His gaze drifted to her leg, then upward. After studying her face for a brooding moment, he returned his attention to the track ahead.

"I have not had a woman in nearly a twelve-month," he said tightly. "I had determined to put such matters behind me. Apparently, that species of saintliness is not in my nature, and a year is not nearly long enough to cultivate it. I should need decades, I suppose," he said bitterly.

Gwendolyn had not come expecting the kind of "saintliness" he referred to. She had been prepared to go to bed with him and try to make a baby regardless of what he looked like or how he behaved. If it had not seemed like cruel and unusual punishment then, it could hardly alarm or disgust her now. If a long period of celibacy—and for a man, a year must seem like eternity—and a glimpse of her leg was swaying his judgment in her favor, that was fine with her.

"If you are saying you do not find me abhorrent," she said, "I am glad."

"You have no idea what might be demanded of you," he growled. "You have no idea what kind of man I am."

"Considering what I shall eventually gain by this

marriage, it would be absurd, not to mention ungrateful, of me to fret about your personal flaws,"
she said. "It is not as though I am perfect, either. I
have made it clear that my motives are mercenary.
You have seen for yourself that I am disobedient
and sharp-tongued. And I know I am no great
beauty. I am also obstinate. That runs in the family,
especially among the females of my generation.
The time may come, in fact, when you will view
your loss of reason as a blessed relief."

"Miss—miss . . . Hell, I can't remember," he said.
"I know it isn't Trent, but—"

"The name is Adams," she said. "Gwendolyn
Adams."

He scowled. "Miss Adams, I should like to know
whether you are trying to convince me to marry
you or to kill myself."

"I merely wished to point out how pointless it
is, in the circumstances, to quibble about our re-
spective character flaws," she said. "And I wished
to be honest with you."

A wicked part of her did not wish to be honest.
She realized he was worried about his male urges
clouding his judgment. The wicked part of her was
not simply hoping the urges would win; it was also
tempting her to encourage them with the feminine
tactics other girls employed.

But that was not fair.

They had turned into the narrow drive leading
to the stables. Though the rain beat harder now,
Gwendolyn was aware mainly of the beating of her
own heart.

She did not want to go away defeated, yet she
did not want to win by unfair means.

She supposed the display of her limbs—however
much her immodest mode of riding had been dic-
tated by the need for haste and the unavailability
of a sidesaddle—constituted unfair means.

Consequently, as they rode into the stable yard, she headed for the mounting block.

But Rawnsley was off his horse before she reached it, and at the gelding's side in almost the same moment.

In the next, he was reaching up and grasping her waist.

His hands were warm, his grasp firm and sure. She could feel the warmth spreading outward, suffusing her body, while she watched the muscles of his arms bunch under the wet, clinging shirtsleeves.

He lifted her up as easily as if she'd been a fairy sprite. Though she wasn't in the least anxious that he'd drop her, she grasped his powerful shoulders. It was reflex. Instinctive.

He brought her down slowly, and he did not let go even after her feet touched the ground.

He looked down at her, and his intent yellow gaze trapped her own, making her heart pound harder yet.

"The time will come when I will have no power over you," he said, his low tones making her nerve ends tingle. "When my mind crumbles, little witch, I shall be at your mercy. Believe me, I've considered that. I've asked myself what you will do with me then, what will become of me."

At that moment, one troubling question was answered.

He was aware of the danger he was in. His fears were the same as those she felt for him. His reason was still in working order.

But he continued before she could reassure him.

"I can guess what will happen, but it doesn't seem to matter, because I'm the man I always was. A death sentence has changed nothing." His hands tightened on her waist. "You should have left me in the mire," he told her, his eyes burning into her. "It was not pleasant—yet Providence does not

grant all its creatures a pretty and painless demise.
And I'm ready enough for mine. But you came and
fished me out, and now . . ."

He let go abruptly and stepped back. "It's too
late."

He was in no state to listen to reassurances,
Gwendolyn saw. If he was angry with himself and
didn't trust that self, he was not likely to trust anything she said. He would believe she was humor-
ing him, as though he were a child.

And so she gave a brisk, businesslike nod. "That
sounds like a yes to me," she said. "Against your
better judgment, evidently, but a yes all the same."

"Yes, drat you—drat the lot of you—I'll do it,"
he growled.

"I am glad to hear it," she said.

"Glad, indeed. You're desperate for your hospital, and I'm the answer to your maidenly prayers."
He turned away. "I'm desperate, too, it seems.
After a year's celibacy, I should probably agree to
marry your *grandmother*, Devil confound me."

He strode down the pathway to the house.

3

Dorian made straight for the library, the red-
haired witch close on his heels.

He flung the door open.

Abonville was pacing in front of the fireplace.

Genevieve was reading a book.

Bertie was building a house of cards.

Dorian strode in and paused a few feet from the threshold.

Abonville stopped short and stared. Genevieve laid aside her book and looked up. Bertie leapt from his chair, the cards flying about him and fluttering to the carpet.

"By Jupiter's thunderbolts!" he cried. "What's happened to you, Cat?"

"Your cousin drove me into a mire," Dorian said levelly. "Then she fished me out. Then we agreed to wed. Today. You may stand as my groomsman, Bertie."

The two elders did not so much as raise an eyebrow.

Bertie opened his mouth, then shut it. He retreated a pace, his brow furrowing.

Dorian bent his gaze upon Miss Adams, who had advanced from the doorway to stand beside him. "Any objections, Miss Adams?" he asked. "Or second thoughts?"

"Certainly not," she said. "The ceremony may take place whenever you wish."

"I understand that everything has been prepared for speedy nuptials," he said. "If you've the preacher somewhere about, we can do it now."

He turned his stare upon the trio of relatives, bracing himself for an outburst of hysteria.

They believed he was a madman. He knew he looked like one. The rain had merely diluted his coating of mire ooze, which streamed from his sopping garments onto the carpet.

No one uttered a word.

No one moved.

Except the witch, who paid no more attention to her relatives than if they'd been the statues they were doing a splendid imitation of.

"You'll be more comfortable after you have a bath," she said. "And something to eat. And a nap. I know you are exhausted."

Every muscle in his body ached. He could scarcely stand upright. "I can be comfortable later," he said, darting another defiant glance over the mute trio. "I want to get married. Now."

"I should like to wash and change, too," she said. She stepped nearer and tugged at his soggy shirt cuff. "It will take time to send for my maid and my clothes, as well as the minister. They are all waiting at the inn, along with our solicitors. The lawyers must come, too, so that you can sign the settlements. You don't want to be waiting about for everybody in wet clothes, I'm sure."

Lawyers.

Chill panic washed through him.

They would examine him to make sure he knew what he was doing. Very recently, the Earl of Portsmouth's fourteen-year marriage had been annulled on grounds he'd been of unsound mind when it was contracted. Miss Adams would not want to risk an annulment and lose all claim to his fortune and the title whose influence she needed.

But if they found him unsound . . . He shuddered.

"Look at you," she said sharply. "You're shivering, my lord. Bertie, do stop gaping in that fishlike way and come and make yourself useful. Take your stubborn friend upstairs before he collapses, and tell the servants to ready his bath and find him something to eat. Genevieve, you will send to the inn for what we need, won't you? Abonville, I wish to speak with you."

No one uttered a protest, not so much as a syllable.

Bertie hurried toward him, took the bemused Dorian by the arm, and steered him back through the library door.

Moments later, when they reached the stairs, Dorian saw Hoskins dart through the servants' door and hasten to the library.

He wondered whether the witch had cast a spell over the lot of them.

"Shouldn't dawdle if I was you," Bertie warned. "If Gwen catches us hanging about, she'll take a fit, which I'd rather she didn't, seeing as how she took one already and my ears are still ringing. Not but what she was right. We wasn't listening proper, was we?"

He grasped Dorian's arm and tugged. "Come along, Cat. Hot bath, Gwen said, and she got that right, too, by gad. You look like what the cat dragged in, and meaning no offense, but you smell like I don't know what."

"I told you she drove me into a mire," Dorian said. "What do you expect a man to smell like after a soak in a reeking bog?"

Unwilling to be dragged up the stairs by his overanxious friend, Dorian shook off the helping hand and started up on his own.

Bertie followed. "Well, she wouldn't've had to chase you, would she, if you hadn't gone and bolted," he said. "Couldn't think why you'd do it. I told you she wasn't like Jess, didn't I? I told you Gwen was a good sort of girl. Did you think I'd let them shackle you to any beastly female? Ain't we friends? Don't we look out for each other? Well, I should think so, or at least I did, but then you was away a long time and never told me where you was. But you never was much for letters, and I never was much good at answering 'em anyhow, and I figured you didn't hear yet I was back from Paris."

They had reached the landing. He gave Dorian a worried look. "But it's all right now, ain't it? Mean to say, if you was looking at her over the breakfast table, you wouldn't cast up your accounts, would you?"

If he were looking at her over the breakfast table, he would probably leap on her and devour her,

Dorian thought. Even now, he wondered how he'd managed to keep his hands restricted to her waist after seeing the soft, dazed expression in her eyes when he'd helped her dismount. No woman had ever gazed at him in that way. Under that look, reason, conscience, and will had simply melted away, leaving him defenseless and nigh trembling with longing. Even now, merely recalling, he could not summon up a fragment of common sense.

"I like her . . . eyes," he told Bertie. "And her voice is not disagreeable. She does not seem silly or missish. She seems a capable, sensible girl," he added, recollecting the terrifying efficiency with which she'd extricated him from the mire.

Bertie's worried expression vanished, and he broke into the amiably stupid grin that had softened Dorian's heart toward him years ago.

"There, I knew you'd see it, Cat," he said. "Sensible's the word. Tells you what's to be done and says it plain so you always know how to go about it. And when she says she'll do it, Gwen goes and does it. Said she was going after you, and we was to stay put and keep our mouths shut tight and stay out of her way. And she did it and you come back and said you'd have her, and now we're all in order, ain't we?"

He'd had his life in order before, Dorian thought: everything in hand, his short future so carefully planned. Kneebones had promised, and he could be trusted to keep his part of the bargain: laudanum, as much as Dorian needed to keep him quiet, to let him die in peace.

Now there was no telling what would happen. He could tell his bride what he wanted, but he could not make her do it. He could exact promises, but he couldn't make her keep them. Before long, he would have no power over her.

But he could not keep his mind on the future because he could not drive out the recollection of

the melting look in her green eyes. All he could
think of was the night to come and the little witch
in his arms ...

Oh, Lord, and if his mind failed and he hurt
her—what then?

For Bertie's sake, he manufactured a smile.

"As you say, Bertie," he answered lightly. "All
in order and everyone happy."

Some hours later, Gwendolyn was sitting on a
stone bench in the Earl of Rawnsley's garden,
watching the blood-red sun's slow descent over a
distant hill. The storm had long since swept off to
ravage another part of Dartmoor, leaving the air
cool and clean.

She was clean and neatly dressed in the green
silk gown Genevieve had brought her from Paris,
and her unruly hair had been temporarily tamed
into a relatively tidy heap of curls atop her head.
She hoped it would still be tidy by the time Rawnsley emerged from his meeting with the lawyers.

Gwendolyn's hair was the bane of her existence.
The Powers that Be, with their usual perverse idea
of a joke, had given her Papa's hair instead of
Mama's.

She did not mind the color so much—at least it
was interesting—but there was so much of it, a
hodgepodge of twists and bends and corkscrews,
each of which had a mind of its own, and all of
them demented.

Her hair, which was the complete antithesis of
her level, steady, and orderly personality, made it
very difficult for people to take her seriously—as
though being a female didn't make that hard
enough already. Thanks to the crazed mass of red
curls and corkscrews, every new person she met
represented yet another uphill battle to prove herself.

She wished wimples would come back into fashion.

She wondered what Rawnsley's raven mane was like when it was clean and combed. She had not seen him since Bertie had taken charge of him.

She wondered why the earl kept his hair long, whether it was merely some odd masculine vanity or an act of defiance—against convention in general or, more likely, his straitlaced grandfather in particular. She could certainly understand that.

Rebellion did not explain, however, why the earl so little resembled his tiny portrait. The puffy face in the miniature had seemed to belong to a rather corpulent man. The one Gwendolyn had met hadn't an ounce of excess flesh upon his six-foot frame. His drenched shirt and trousers had clung like a second skin, not to rippling rolls of fat, but to lean, taut muscle.

Whatever was wrong with him was obviously confined to the contents of his skull.

Gwendolyn watched the light of the lowering sun spread a red stain through the deepening shadows of the moors while she searched her mental index of brain diseases. She wondered what malady corresponded to the "crumbling" he'd mentioned.

She was considering aneurisms when she heard footsteps crunch upon the gravel path.

Turning toward the sound, she beheld her betrothed advancing toward her, his face set, his right hand clutching a piece of paper.

At that moment, medical hypotheses, along with all other intellectual matters, sank into the deepest recesses of Gwendolyn's mind. When he paused before her, all she could do was stare while her heart beat an erratic rhythm that made the blood hum in her veins.

He wore a coat of fine black wool, whose snugly elegant cut hugged his powerful, athletic physique.

Her glance skidded down over the equally snug trousers to the gleaming toes of his shoes, then darted up again to his face.

Cleaned of the mire's vestiges, his countenance was pale, chiseled marble. The long black hair, gleaming like silk, rippled over his broad shoulders. A burning golden gaze trapped hers.

If she had been a normal female, she would have swooned. But she was not normal, never had been.

"Good grief, you are impossibly handsome," she said breathlessly. "I vow, I have never experienced the like. For an instant, my brain stopped altogether. I must say, my lord, you do clean up well. But next time, I wish you would call out a warning before you come into view, and give me a chance to brace myself for the onslaught."

Something dark flickered in his eyes. Then a corner of his hard mouth quirked up. "Miss Adams, you have an interesting—a unique—way with a compliment."

The trace of a smile disoriented her further. "It is a unique experience," she said. "I never knew my brain to shut off before, not while I was full awake. I wonder if the phenomenon has been scientifically documented and what physiological explanation has been proposed."

Her eyes would not focus properly but wandered fuzzily downward again . . . and stopped at the piece of paper. The document snapped her back to reality. "That looks official," she said. "Legal drivel, I collect. Is it something I must sign?"

He glanced back toward the house.

When his attention returned to her, the half-smile was gone, and his expression had hardened again. "Will you walk with me?" he asked.

The backward glance gave Gwendolyn a good idea of what the trouble was. She kept her thoughts to herself, though, and stood obediently and walked with him in silence down a path bordered by roses. When they reached a planting of shrubs that shielded them from view of the house, he spoke.

"I am told that, in view of my prognosis, a guardian ought to be appointed to oversee my affairs," he said. His voice was not altogether steady. "Abonville proposes to act as guardian since he's my nearest male kin. It is a reasonable proposal, my own solicitor agrees. I've inherited a good deal of property, which must be protected when I become incapable of acting responsibly."

A stinging stream of indignation shot through her. She did not see why he must be plagued with such matters this day. All he needed to sign were the marriage settlements. He should not be asked to sign his whole life away in the bargain.

"Protected from whom?" she asked. "Grasping relatives? According to Abonville, there's no one left of the Camoys but a few dithering old ladies."

"It isn't merely the property," he said. His voice was taut, his face a rigid white mask.

She wanted to reach up and smooth the turmoil and tension away, but that would look like pity. She plucked a leaf from a rhododendron and traced its shape instead.

"The guardianship includes legal custody . . . of me," he said. "Because I cannot be responsible for myself, I must be considered a child."

He was not irresponsible yet or remotely childlike. Gwendolyn had told Abonville so. She knew her lecture had calmed the duc down, yet it was too much to hope that her speeches could fully quell his overprotectiveness. He meant well, she reminded herself. He assumed the marriage would be too great an ordeal for her and wished to share the burden.

She could hardly expect her future grandfather to fully understand her capabilities when none of the other men in her family did. None of them took her medical studies and work seriously. Her dedicated efforts remained, as far as the males were concerned, "Gwendolyn's little hobby."

"It is very difficult to think clearly," Rawnsley went on in the same ferociously controlled tones, "with a pair of lawyers and an overanxious would-be grandpapa hovering over me. And Bertie's holding his tongue was no help, when he had to stuff his handkerchief into his mouth to do it, and he still couldn't stop sniffling. I came out to clear my head, because . . . *damnation.*" He dragged his hair back from his face. "The fact is, I do not feel reasonable about this. I wanted to tell them to go to the Devil. But my own solicitor agreed with them. If I object, they'll all believe I'm irrational."

And he was worried he'd end up in a madhouse, Gwendolyn understood.

That he'd come to her with his problem seemed to be a good sign. But Gwendolyn knew better than to pin her hopes on what seemed to be.

She moved to stand in front of him. He did not look down at her.

"My lord, you are aware, I hope, that the 1774 Act for Regulating Madhouses included provisions to protect sane persons from improper detention," she said. "At present, only an examining body composed of imbeciles and criminal lunatics could possibly find you non compos mentis. You need not sign every stupid paper those annoying men wave in your face in order to prove you are sane."

"I must prove it to Abonville," he said stiffly. "If he decides I'm mad, he'll take you away."

She doubted the prospect was intolerable to him. She knew he'd agreed to marry her for what he believed were the wrong reasons. She doubted he'd developed a case of desperate infatuation during the last few hours.

It was far more likely that he'd come to test her.

If she failed, he would believe it was wise to let her go.

Gwendolyn had been tested before, by certified lunatics, among others, and this man was no more deranged at present than she. Nevertheless she did not make the mistake of imagining this trial would be easier—or less dangerous. She had marked him as dangerous from the first moment he had turned his smoldering yellow gaze upon her. She was sure he fully understood its compelling effect and knew how to use it.

Her suspicions were confirmed when the brooding yellow gaze lowered to hers. "What's left of my reason tells me you represent an infernal complication, Miss Adams, and I should be better off rid of you. The voice of reason, however, is not the only one I hear—and rarely the one I heed," he added darkly.

His gaze drifted down . . . lingered at her mouth . . . then slid downward to her bodice.

Beneath layers of silk and undergarments, her flesh prickled under the slow perusal, and the sensations spread outward until her fingers and toes tingled.

He was trying to make her uneasy.

He was doing a splendid job.

But he faced madness and death, she reminded herself, next to which her own anxieties could not possibly signify.

By the time the potent golden stare returned to her face, Gwendolyn had collected at least a portion of her composure.

"I am not sure you have identified the correct voice as reason's," she said. "I am absolutely certain, though, that if Abonville tries to take me away, I shall take a fit. I went to a good deal of trouble to get ready for the wedding. My head is stuck full of pins and my maid laced my stays so tight it is a wonder my lips haven't turned blue. It took her a full hour to tie and hook me into this gown, and I shall likely be three hours trying to get out of it."

"I can get you out of that gown in a minute," he said too quietly. "And I shall be happy to relieve you of your painful stays. It would be better for you not to put such ideas into my head."

As though they weren't already there, she thought. As though he hadn't warned her: he hadn't had a woman in a year.

Though she knew he was testing her maidenly fortitude, his low voice set her nerves aquiver.

He was taller than she. And heavier. And stronger.

A part of her wanted to bolt.

But he was not on the brink of a violent lunatic fit, she scolded herself. He was feigning, to test her, and allowing him to intimidate her was no way to win his trust.

"I do not see why it would be better," she said. "I do not want you to be indifferent to me."

"It would be better for you if I were."

He had not moved an inch nearer, yet his low voice and glowing eyes exerted a suffocating pressure.

Gwendolyn reminded herself that the Almighty had been throwing obstacles in her path practically since the day she was born and had confronted her repeatedly with men determined to browbeat or frighten her.

That was sufficient practice for dealing with him.

"I know I am an infernal complication," she said. "I realize you feel put upon, and I do understand your resentment of your—your masculine urges, which incline you to act against your better judgment. But you are not looking on the bright side. A lack of such urges would indicate a failure of health and strength."

She caught the flicker of surprise in his eyes in the instant before he masked it.

"You ought to look upon your animal urges as a positive sign," she persisted. "You are not as far gone as you thought you were."

"On the contrary," he said. "I find myself in far worse case than I had imagined."

He directed his yellow stare to a point on her left shoulder where the neckline of her gown left off and her skin began . . . and instantly she became hotly conscious of every square inch of her skin.

She heard a crackling sound. Looking down, she saw the paper crumpling in his tightly clenched hand.

He looked there, too. "It hardly matters what I sign," he said. "Nothing matters that should." He crushed the document into a ball and threw it down.

Her heart was pumping double-time, speeding the blood through her veins in preparation for flight.

"Damn me," he said. He advanced.

She sucked in her breath.

He grasped her shoulders. "A pretty fellow, am I? Take a fit, will you? I'll show you a fit."

Before she could exhale, he clamped one hand on the back of her neck, pulled her head back, and brought his mouth down upon hers.

It was her fault, Dorian told himself. She should not have looked at him in that bone-melting way. She should not have stood so near and caught him in her scent, rich and heady as opium to his starved senses. She should have run, instead of staying so close and snaring him in awareness of the fine, porcelain purity of her skin.

He could not help yearning for that purity and softness, and then he could not keep from reaching for her.

He clamped his needy mouth upon her soft, trembling one, and the clean, sweet taste of her made him shiver—in pleasure or despair, he couldn't tell. For all he knew the chill was the emptiness inside him, ever-present, impossible to fill.

He should have stopped then, for his sanity's sake, if nothing else. He knew it was hopeless. This innocent could never sate him. No woman, no matter how experienced and skilled, had ever done it.

But her lips were so soft, warming and yielding to the pressure of his. He had to draw her nearer, seeking the warmth of her young body while he savored the untutored surrender of her innocent mouth.

He pressed her close, greedy for her warmth and softness. He pressed her to his famished body while he deepened the kiss, seeking desperately, as always, for more.

He felt her shudder, but he couldn't stop—not yet. He couldn't keep his tongue from searching the mysteries of her mouth ... feminine secrets, promising everything.

Lured by scent and taste and touch, he slipped into the darkness. He stroked over her back, heard silk whisper under his fingers, and felt her shift under his touch. Then he was truly lost because she moved into his caress as though she'd done it many times before, as though she belonged in his arms, had always belonged.

Warmth ... softness ... sinuous curves under whispering silk, melting against him ... woman-scent, enveloping him ... and her skin ...

He trailed his lips over her satiny cheek, and she sighed. The soft sound ignited the too-quick inner fuse of desire. His fingers found a fastening ...

"If you're trying to scare me off," came her foggy voice, her breath tickling his ear, "you're going about it all wrong."

His hands stilled.

He raised his head and looked at her. Her eyes opened, and slowly her hazy green gaze sharpened into focus. His own haze instantly dissipated under that penetrating study.

"I was taking a lunatic fit," he said, aware that his thick tones told another story. He wrenched his gaze from the mesmerizing trap of hers and drew back.

Curling red tendrils had escaped their pins to tumble wildly about her flushed face and neck. Her gown was twisted askew.

He stepped back and looked at his hands, afraid to think where they'd been and what he might have done to an innocent, lusting oaf that he was.

"What is wrong with you?" he demanded. "Why didn't you make me stop? Do you have any idea what I might have done?"

She tugged her gown back into place. "I have a very good idea," she said. "I am familiar with the mechanics of human reproduction, as I told Mama. But she felt it was her maternal duty to explain it herself."

She smoothed her bodice. "I must say, she did point out a few subtleties I was unaware of. And Genevieve, as you would expect, enlightened me further. It turned out to be not quite as simple as I thought." She pushed a few pins back into her hair. "Which is not to say I haven't experienced considerable enlightenment under your tutelage, my lord," she added quickly. "It is one thing to be told about intimate kisses. Experiencing them is another matter altogether. What are you staring at?" She looked down at herself. "Have I missed something? Is anything undone?" She turned, presenting her slim back. "Do I need fastening?"

"No." *Thank God*, he added silently.

She turned back and smiled.

Her mouth was overwide. He had noticed that

before . . . and felt and tasted every luscious atom
of it.

He could not remember seeing her smile before.
If he had, he would not have forgotten, for it was
a long, sweet curve that coiled about him like an
enchantment.

He did not know how to resist its warm promise.
He did not know how to fight her and himself simultaneously. He did not know how to drive her
away, as he must, when she made him want so
desperately to hold her.

It seemed he did not know how to do anything.

The document he'd been asked to sign, the reasons they'd given him for signing, had made him
face what he'd tried to ignore. He'd come, intending to scare her off for her own safety—and his
peace of mind. Yet he, once capable of making
hardened whores tremble, could not stir the smallest anxiety in her, any more than he could rouse
his feeble conscience.

Once capable.

Past tense.

Before the headaches. Before the disease had begun its insidious work.

The answer came then, chilling him: the tenuous
link between will and action, mind and body, was
breaking down already. He was healthy and
strong, she'd claimed, but that was only outwardly.
His degenerating mind was already sapping his
will.

He turned away, lest she read his despair in his
countenance. He would master it. He needed but a
moment. It had caught him unawares, that was all.

"Rawnsley."

He felt her hand upon his sleeve.

He wanted to shake it off, but he couldn't, any
more than he could shake off his awareness of her.
The taste of her lingered in his mouth, and her
drugging scent wafted about him. He recalled the

soft look in her beautiful eyes and the smile . . . warm promises. And he was cold, chilled to his soul.

And too selfish, too weak, he thought with bitter resignation, to let her go.

He brought his hand up and covered hers. "I do not want to go back into that curst library and listen to their solemn speeches and read their bloody documents," he said levelly. "I signed the settlements. You'll get your hospital. That is enough. I want to be wed. Now."

She squeezed his arm. "I'm ready," she said. "I've been ready for hours."

He looked down at her. She smiled up at him.

Warm promises.

He drew her arm through his and led her back to the house. It wanted all his will not to run. The sun was setting, evening closing in with its blessed darkness. Soon, this night, they'd be wed. Soon, they would go up to his room, to the bed. And then . . . God help them both.

He took her through the door and hurried her down the hall. He saw the library door standing open, the light streaming into the gloomy corridor.

He turned to speak to her—then he caught it, faint but unmistakable, at the periphery of his vision.

Tiny zigzags of light.

He blinked, but they would not wash away. They hovered, sparkling evilly, at the edges of his vision.

He shut his eyes, but he saw them still, winking their deadly warning.

He opened his eyes and they were there, inescapable, inexorable.

No, not yet. Not so soon. He tried to brush them away, though he knew it was futile.

They only signaled back, glittering, remorseless: *soon, very soon.*

4

"This is your doing," Mr. Kneebones raged at Hoskins. "I told you my patient's fragile health could not withstand *any* strain. I told you he must be insulated from all sources of nervous agitation. No newspapers. No visitors. You saw what the news about his family did to him: three attacks in one week. Yet you let strangers descend upon him at a time when he was most vulnerable. And now—"

"A man becomes a peer of the realm, he ought to know about it," Hoskins said. "And attacks or no attacks, it was a relief to him to learn the old gentleman couldn't trouble him anymore. And as to letting in strangers, I reckon I can tell the difference between a friend and an enemy. Even if I couldn't, I'd like to see you shut the door in Lady Pembury's face—and her the grandmother of the only friend my master ever had. Maybe it wasn't my place to tell her what was wrong with him, but I judged it best to warn her beforehand that he wasn't as strong as he looked, and his nerves weren't what they used to be."

"Which means they should not have been subjected to *any* source of agitation," Kneebones snapped.

"With all due respect, sir, you never clapped eyes on him until a few weeks ago," Hoskins said.

"You may be qualified to judge his medical condition, but you don't know his character or his wishes. I've had more than nine months to learn, and I promise you, the last thing he wishes is to be treated like a vaporish female." He glanced at Gwendolyn. "Meaning no offense, my lady."

"None taken," she said. "I've never succumbed to vapors in my life."

The middle-aged veteran smiled.

Kneebones glared at her.

He'd been glowering at her ever since she'd summoned him into the drawing room, after he'd visited his patient. They had not spoken together ten minutes before hostilities broke out. Hoskins, waiting outside in the hall, had hurried in and leapt to her defense, unaware she didn't need defending.

Still, that had not been unproductive. The manservant's skirmish with the doctor had clarified several matters, and heaven knew Gwendolyn needed as much enlightenment as she could get.

Rawnsley seemed determined to keep her completely in the dark about his illness.

She had noticed something was wrong within minutes of their returning to the house, after the episode in the garden. During the following hours, while Gwendolyn was marshalling everyone into order, she had watched the earl change. By the time of the ceremony, his voice had settled into a monotone . . . while his movements became painfully slow and careful, as though he were made of glass and might shatter at any moment.

The fingers slipping the wedding ring onto hers had been deathly cold, the nails chalk white.

Only after it was done, though, and they had signed their names as husband and wife, had Rawnsley told her he had a headache and was going to bed.

She'd sent her relatives away, as he'd asked, saying the earl needed absolute quiet.

He had spent his wedding night in bed with his laudanum bottle. He had locked his bedroom door, refusing to let even Hoskins in.

This morning, Gwendolyn had taken up the earl's breakfast herself. When she tapped at the door and called softly to him, he told her to stop the infernal row and leave him alone.

Since the servants hadn't seemed unduly alarmed by his behavior, she'd waited patiently until late afternoon before sending for Kneebones.

After the doctor left the room, the patient's door had been locked again—and Kneebones refused to discuss his condition with her.

Gwendolyn regarded the physician composedly, ignoring his threatening expression. Medical men had been glowering and glaring and fuming at her for years. "I should like to know what dosage of laudanum you have prescribed," she said. "I cannot get into my husband's room to determine for myself, and I am most uneasy. It is all too easy for a patient in extreme pain to lose track of how much he's taken and when he last took it. Laudanum intoxication rarely improves either calculating abilities or memory."

"I'll thank you not to tell me my business, madam," Kneebones said stiffly. "I have discussed the benefits and risks with my patient—for all the good that does him now, after what he's been subjected to. One shock after another—capped by a hurry-up wedding to a female he doesn't know from Adam. It was as good as killing him outright. You might as well have taken a hammer to his skull."

"I have discerned no symptoms of shock," Gwendolyn said. "What I have observed—"

"Ah, yes, during *your* lengthy acquaintance with His Lordship," Kneebones said with a cold glance at Hoskins. "My lady has known him all of what—thirty-six hours, if that?"

Gwendolyn suppressed a sigh. She would get nowhere with him. He was like virtually every

other physician—with the blessed exception of Mr.
Eversham—she'd ever encountered. How they resented being questioned! And how they loved to
be mysterious and all-knowing. Very well. She
could play that game, too.

"I noticed that the hallucinations were of very
brief duration," she said.

Kneebones started. He recovered in an instant,
his expression wary.

She could have told him she'd been trained to
observe, but she said nothing of her background or
of the conclusions she'd drawn after noticing the
way Rawnsley had angrily blinked, and brushed at
the air near his face, as though trying to clear cobwebs. If Kneebones chose to keep her in the dark,
he must expect the same treatment.

She gave him the faintest of smiles. "Did His
Lordship not tell you, sir? I am a witch. But I must
not waste your valuable time. You have other sick-
beds to attend, I know—and I must set my cauldron aboil . . . and look about for a fresh batch of
eye of newt."

Kneebones's mouth set in a grim line, and without another word, he stalked out.

Gwendolyn met Hoskins's quiet gaze.

"I don't know the dosage," he said. "All I know
is what the bottle looks like—and there's more than
one."

Dorian awoke from a restless, nightmare-
plagued sleep to nightmarish pain.

His head pounded relentlessly. His insides
churned, raw with bile.

Slowly, carefully, he inched up to a sitting position and reached for the bottle on the nightstand.
He put it to his lips.

Empty.

Already? he wondered dully. Had he finished it
off in a single night? Or had several nights passed

in the oppressive haze of pain and opiates?

It didn't matter.

He had seen the silvery wraiths again. Today, they'd slowly closed in from the peripheries and shimmered everywhere he looked. He had watched the wedding preparations through sparkling ripples undulating in the air like waves in a ghostly sea.

Then, finally, the silver shards had vanished from his vision and sliced into his skull like white-hot blades.

Now he understood why his mother had claimed the "ghosts" had vicious talons, and why she'd screamed and torn at her hair. She had been trying to rip the wicked claws away.

Even he had trouble reminding himself there were neither ghosts nor claws, that it was all a sick fancy.

He wondered how much longer he would be able to distinguish between sick fancy and reality, how long before he began confusing those about him with ghosts and demons—and attacked them in mindless rage.

But he would not, he told himself. Kneebones had promised that the laudanum would quiet him, quelling the delusions along with the pain.

Dorian edged closer to the nightstand and opened the door. He reached in and found the porcelain cylinder.

He took it onto his lap and pried off the lid.

The narrow bottle, nestled in a woolen cloth, lay within.

The elixir of peace . . . perhaps eternal.

He took it out and with trembling hands set the cylinder upon the nightstand.

Then he hesitated, but it was not the prospect of eternity that gave him pause. No, he was too shallow and base for that. It was the witch he thought of, and her soft mouth and slimly curved body.

And that image was enough to set his mind to fabricating noble reasons for avoiding laudanum's risks: if he died before the marriage was consummated, it might be annulled, and she would not get her hospital . . . and it was his duty, besides, to get an heir.

But her hospital and the end of the Camoys would not matter to him when he was dead, Dorian reminded himself. Nor would she. He would be gone, and good riddance, and God forbid he should leave a child behind. With his luck, his offspring would inherit the same defective brain and live—briefly—and die in the same mortifying way.

He unstopped the bottle.

"I should be careful, if I were you," came a quiet, familiar voice out of the darkness. "You are married to a witch. What if I've turned it into a love potion?"

The room was black as Hades. He couldn't see her—couldn't focus past the throbbing anyhow—but he could smell her. The oddly exotic scent stole through the thundering sea of pain like ghostly fingers and lifted him up to consciousness.

"It might even be a potion to turn you into a cat," she said.

He could not hear her approach past the relentless hammering in his head, but he could smell it, the faint scent growing richer, more potent. Jasmine?

Slim, warm fingers closed over his icy ones.

He tried to speak. He moved his lips, but no sound came out. Pain slammed his skull. His stomach lurched. The bottle slipped from his hands.

"Sick," he gasped. "Christ, I—"

He broke off as something else, cold and round and smooth, pressed into his hands. A basin.

His body shuddered violently. Then all he could do was hold on to the basin, his head bowed, and give himself up to spasm after spasm after spasm, uncontrollable.

Retching. Endlessly. Helplessly.

All the while, he felt her warm hands upon him, holding him. He heard her soft murmurs above him.

"Yes, that's right. It can't be helped. It's a sick headache, I know. Beastly thing, isn't it? Hours and hours. Then it won't go quietly, will it? Instead, it must rip out of you and take your insides with it. I don't doubt it seems that way, but you shall feel better in a moment. There. You're done."

It was not a moment, but an eternity, and Dorian didn't know whether he was done or dead. His body had stopped the spasmodic heaving, but he couldn't lift his head.

She caught him before he could sink into the revolting mess in the basin. She raised his head and put a cup to his lips. He smelled mint—and something else. He didn't know what it was.

"Rinse your mouth," she commanded quietly.

Too weak to fight, he obeyed. The tangy draught cleansed the foul taste from his mouth.

When he was done, she gently guided him back onto the pillows.

He lay there, exhausted, aware of movement. The basin disappeared, and its stench with it.

In a little while, a cool, wet cloth touched his face. Gentle, quick, efficient—cleansing and cooling him. He knew he should protest—he wasn't a babe. He couldn't summon the strength.

Then she was gone again, an everlasting time, and the pain rolled in during her absence. Though it was not so ferocious as before, it was there still, pounding at him.

This time, when the scent returned, light came with it, a single candle. He watched her shadowy form approach. He winced at the light. She moved away toward the fireplace and set the candle on the mantel.

She returned to the bed. "You are still in discomfort, it seems," she said very softly. "I don't know whether that's the original headache or the aftereffects of laudanum."

He remembered, then, the bottle she'd stolen from him. "Laudanum," he choked out. "Give me the bottle, witch."

"Maybe later," she said. "At present, I have to work a spell. Do you think you can climb into the cauldron unaided, or shall I summon Hoskins to help?"

The witch's "cauldron" was alleged to be a steaming bath, and the spell appeared to involve her holding an ice bag on his head while she boiled the rest of him.

That, at least, was the sense Dorian made of her explanation.

He had no trouble deciding that the last thing on earth he wanted to do was climb out of his bed and stagger down to the ground-floor bath chamber.

He changed his mind when he learned his servants were prepared to carry him. He couldn't bear to be carried by anyone, anywhere.

"Your extremities are icy cold," she said as she handed him a dressing gown. She looked away while he angrily struggled into it. "Above the neck, you are much too hot. Your system is unbalanced, you see. We must correct it."

Dorian didn't care if he was unbalanced. On the other hand, he could not bear her seeing him lying helpless and trembling like an infant.

And so he dragged himself from the bed and stumbled across the room and through the door. Rejecting her helping hand, he made his way out of the room and down the stairs.

He found the small, tiled room filled with lavender-scented steam. Candles flickered in the narrow wall niches.

The scented mist, the warmth, the gentle light enveloped him and drew him in. Entranced, he walked to the edge of the sunken bath. Towels had been laid on the bottom and draped over the sides.

His impotent rage dissipated in the sweet warmth and quiet.

He flung off his dressing gown and climbed in, groaning as he slid into the steaming water and the heat stole into his aching muscles.

A moment later, a small pillow slid behind his neck. His eyes flew open.

Mesmerized by the delicious warmth, the inviting water, he had forgotten about the witch . . . and he was stark, screaming naked.

"All you need to do is soak," she said. "Lean back on the cushion. I'll do the rest."

He couldn't remember what the rest was and winced when the soft, icy bag settled onto his head.

"I'll hold it in place," she said. "You needn't worry about it slipping off."

The ice bag was the least of his concerns.

He looked down into the water. The sunken tub was not the deepest one in the world. He could see his masculine possessions all too distinctly.

Though it was too late for modesty, he drew a bit of towel over the place and set his hand over it to keep it from floating up.

He heard a faint sound, suspiciously like a giggle. He refused to look up.

"It's nothing I haven't seen before," the witch said. "Admittedly, the others were live babies or adult corpses, but the equipment is essentially the same in all males."

Something stirred in his sluggish mind. He laid his head back and closed his eyes, trying to collect the elusive bits and pieces. The hospital . . . definite ideas and . . . principles. Her relatives' puzzling obedience. Her lack of fear. The basin in his hands the instant he needed it . . . the quiet efficiency.

He began to understand, but not altogether. Many women had nursing experience, and yet . . .

He returned to the last piece of news. He could understand about the babies. Plenty of women saw infants naked—but adult male . . . corpses?

"How many deathbeds have you attended, Miss Adams?" He kept his eyes closed. It was easier to think without trying to see at the same time. His eyes still hurt. Though the pain was easing, it was still there.

"I am not Miss Adams any longer," she said. "We are wed now. Don't tell me you've forgotten."

"Ah, yes. It slipped my mind for a moment. Because of the . . . dead bodies. I am vastly interested in your corpses, Lady Rawnsley."

"So was I," she said. "But you will not believe the difficulties I encountered. Admittedly, fresh corpses are not so easy to come by. Still, that is no excuse for medical men to be so selfish about them. How is one to learn, I ask you, if one is not permitted even to witness a dissection?"

"I haven't the least idea."

"It is ridiculous," she said. "I finally had to resort to challenging one of Mr. Knightly's students. The condescending coxcomb claimed I would lose my breakfast and swoon and fall on the stone floor and get a severe concussion. I bet him ten pounds I wouldn't." She paused. "As it turned out, he was the one who went to pieces." Her voice held a quiet note of triumph. "After I'd dragged his unconscious body out of the way—I did not wish to step on him by accident—I continued the dissection myself. It was most enlightening. You cannot learn a fraction as much from a living person. You can't see anything."

"How frustrating," he murmured.

"It is. You'd think that proving myself once would be sufficient, but no. It was the one and only time I had the instruments in my hand and a corpse all to myself. All I won was permission to observe, and that must remain a dark secret, lest my family get wind of it. Even with the patients— the living ones—it was no good proving my competence to anybody. As long as Mr. Knightly was in charge, I might only assist, discreetly. He must rule absolutely, and mere females must obey orders, even when they are based upon the most antiquated theories."

Behind his closed eyes, Dorian saw the answer now, with stunning clarity.

A day earlier, the insight would have had him leaping from the bath and running hell for leather for the nearest available mire.

At present, a part of his mind suggested that fleeing was not an altogether bad idea.

But he was so comfortable, his muscles relaxing in the steaming water, his tormented head pleasantly cool.

And so he said, very mildly, "Small wonder, then, that you should leap at the chance to have a patient of your very own."

And before very long, a corpse of her very own, he added inwardly. Not that it mattered. If she wished to dissect his remains, he would hardly be in a position to object.

She did not respond immediately. Dorian kept his eyes closed, savoring the scented mist drifting about him. Her scent was there as well, rich and deep, coiling with the lavender. He did not know whether it was the scent or his ailment that made him feel so lightheaded.

"I was not implying that all members of the medical profession are imbeciles," she said at last. "But I could not trust Abonville to distinguish among them. Bertie would be worse. He'd be sure

to send for experts from London and Edinburgh,
and he has such a knack for blundering."

"I understand," he said. "You came to . . . save
me."

"From medical bedlam," she said hastily. "I am
not a miracle worker, and I know precious few
brain diseases are curable. Not that I know much
about yours," she added with a trace of irritation.
"Mr. Kneebones is as obstinately closemouthed as
Mr. Knightly was. I knew it was a waste of breath
to argue with him. Words are rarely of any use. I
shall have to prove myself, as usual."

Dorian recalled her brisk, unruffled mode of
freeing him from the mire. He recalled the cool
steadiness with which she'd met his attempt to
frighten her away. He recalled her calm, efficient
ministrations of a little while ago, when he'd been
so disgustingly sick.

He considered his present comfortable state. He
had not felt so tranquil in months. He couldn't remember, in fact, when he'd last felt so much at
peace. Had he ever?

He couldn't recall a time when he hadn't been
angry with himself for his weaknesses and seething
with resentment of his grandfather, who, like the
doctors she spoke of, insisted on ruling absolutely.

He opened his eyes and slowly turned his head
to look up at her. She kept the ice bag in place
while her cool green gaze shifted to meet his.

He wondered whether the cool detachment came
naturally, or if she'd had to train herself to suppress emotion, in order to survive in a world that
didn't trust or want her. He knew what that was
like, and what the training cost.

"The damp does strange things to your hair," he
said gruffly. "All the little curls and corkscrews
sprout up every which way, making a fuzzy red
cloud. Even in dry air, it seems alive, trying to do
whatever it is bent on doing. 'What on earth is her

hair doing?' the medical men must ask themselves. One can't be surprised at their failing to attend closely to what you say."

"They should not allow themselves to be distracted," she said. "It is unprofessional."

"As a group, men are not very intelligent," he said. "Not in a steady way, at least. We have our moments of lucidity, but we are easily distracted."

He was—oh, so easily.

The room's steamy fog had settled upon her. A fine dew glistened on her porcelain skin. Damp curls clustered about her ears. He thought of pushing the curls away and tracing the delicate shape with his tongue. He thought of where his mouth and tongue would go if he let them... along the moist flesh of her neck to the hollow of her throat.

His gaze skimmed down to her neckline, then lower, to where the damp fabric clung to the curve of her breasts.

Mine, he thought. And then he could not think about the future. He could scarcely think at all.

"Some men can be distracting," she said. "At times. You, especially."

If he had not been so keenly, yearningly aware of her, he would not have caught the faint, unsteady thread in her voice.

"Ah, well, I'm mad." What he felt might as well be madness. Beneath the concealing corner of the towel, the part of him that never heeded reason stirred from its slumbers.

"This treatment is supposed to have a soporific effect," she said, frowning as she studied his face.

She did not appear anxious but puzzled, which would have amused him if he had been capable of detached observation. That was impossible.

She sat near his shoulder, at the edge of the sunken tub, her legs curled up under her gown, and his base mind was fixed upon what lay beneath. He brought his hand up out of the water and rested it on the tub's curved rim, inches from the hem of her gown.

"Treatment?" he said. "I thought this was supposed to be a spell."

"Yes, well, I must not have added enough eye of newt. It is supposed to induce a pleasant drowsiness."

"My brain is becoming somnolent." His fingers touched the ruffled muslin . . . and closed upon it.

Her frowning attention shifted to his hand. "You have a headache," she said.

He toyed with the ruffle. "That does not seem terribly important at the moment."

Though the pain lingered, it no longer mattered. What mattered was his treacherous recollection of what lay under the muslin. He drew it back.

Soft kid slippers . . . a few inches of prettily turned ankle . . . and no stockings. "No stockings," he said, his voice as foggy as his mind. "Where are your stockings, Lady Rawnsley?"

"I took them off before," she said. "They were frightfully expensive—from Paris—and I hated to risk catching them on a splinter when I climbed in your window."

He grasped her ankle. "You climbed in the window." He did not look up from the imprisoned limb.

"To get into your room. I was worried you would take too much laudanum. Not an idle anxiety, as it turns out. The solution in that bottle of yours had not been properly diluted."

She had said she couldn't let him die before the ceremony, he recalled. Apparently, she dared not let him die before the marriage was consummated, either.

And he didn't want to die before then, either, rot his black soul.

"You had to save me," he said.

"I had to do something. I know nothing about

picking locks, and breaking down the door would have made a ghastly row, so I took the window route. Isn't your hand growing cold again, my lord?"

"No." He stroked her ankle. "Does it feel cold to you?"

"I couldn't tell whether it was me or you." She swallowed. "I am quite . . . warm."

He pushed the gown up higher and slid his hand over the perfectly curved limb he'd exposed. She wanted her hospital, he told himself, and she was prepared to pay the price.

And he wanted to trail his mouth over her wickedly lovely legs . . . up, all the way up to . . . His gaze shot to her hair, the wild red curls. His mind conjured a picture of what he'd find at the end of the journey, at the juncture of her thighs.

Then his gaze locked with hers, meltingly soft.

Then he was lost, rising from the water and reaching for her, lashing his arm round her narrow waist, drawing her toward him. He felt the air, cool against his back after the water's warmth, but it was her warmth he wanted.

"You will take a chill," she gasped. "Let me get you a dry towel."

"No, come to me," he said thickly.

He did not wait for her to come but swept her up in his dripping arms and held her tightly for a long, mad moment. Then he sank down with her into the scented cauldron, and as the water closed over them, his mouth found hers, and he sank deeper then, beyond saving . . . drowning in a sea of warm promises.

This was most unprofessional, Gwendolyn scolded herself as she flung her arms round her husband's neck.

It was well known that excitement of the passions exacerbated sick headaches.

Unfortunately, nowhere in the medical literature had she encountered a remedy for cases in which the physician's passions were excited. She did not know what antidote to apply when the patient's lightest touch triggered severe palpitations of the heart and a shockingly swift rise in temperature to fever point. She did not know what palliative could alleviate the coaxing pressure of a wickedly sensual mouth upon hers, or what elixir could counteract the devil's brew she tasted when her patient's tongue stole in to coil with hers.

She was aware of water lapping at her shoulders and her gown billowing up to the surface in the most brazen manner, but she could not retrieve sufficient clinical objectivity to do anything about it.

She was preoccupied with every slippery, naked inch of him, hard and warm under her hands, and she couldn't keep her hands from moving over his powerful shoulders and the taut, smooth planes of his broad chest. It wasn't quite enough. She could not resist the need to taste the smooth, water-slick skin. She eased away from his enslaving mouth and traced his wet jaw and neck with her lips while her hands continued to explore his splendid anatomy.

"Oh, the deltoid muscle . . . and pectoralis major," she murmured dizzily. "So . . . beautifully . . . developed."

She was aware of the increased urgency and boldness of his touch, and she knew her brazen behavior incited him. But his caresses were inciting her.

She felt the weight of his hands upon her breasts, a warm pressure that made her ache and push into his hand, seeking more. The sensuous mouth upon her neck simmered kisses whose heat bubbled under her skin and made her quiver with impatience. His wicked tongue teased her ear . . . maddening.

Above the water's plashing, she heard the low

animal sound he made when she shivered uncontrollably and burrowed into him, as though she could crawl into his skin. She wanted to.

She could not get close enough. The water . . . her clothes . . . everything between them . . . obstacles.

"Do something," she gasped, fumbling with her gown. She tugged at the bodice, but the soaked fabric wouldn't tear. "Get it off," she told him. "I can't bear it."

She felt his fingers struggling at her back with the tapes. "They're too wet," she said feverishly. "You can't untie them. Rip it."

"Wait. Calm down." His voice was thick.

She dragged her hand down to his belly.

He sucked in his breath. "Gwendolyn, for God's sake—"

"Hurry."

"Wait." He closed his mouth over hers and swept her lunatic rage away in an endless, soul-draining kiss.

She clung to him, her mouth locked with his while he swung her into his arms and up, out of the bath and onto the damp towels.

When he broke the drugging kiss at last, she opened her eyes to a burning gold gaze. He knelt over her, straddling her hips. His skin was slick, shimmering in the candlelight. Water streamed from his long, night-black hair.

While she watched, spellbound, he brought his hand to the neckline of her soaked gown. With one easy yank, he tore it to the waist. "Happy now, witch?" he whispered.

"*Yes.*" She reached for him and drew him down, frantic to feel his skin against hers.

Hot, hasty kisses . . . over her brow, her nose, cheeks, chin . . . and more, down over her throat to sizzle over her breasts. The scorching kisses burned the spell away, and the madness returned.

She caught her fingers in his hair to keep him

there. She needed more, though she hardly knew
what the more was. She felt his mouth close over
the taut bud of her breast, and the first light tug
shot threads of tingling electricity under her skin,
into . . . somewhere . . . a world inside her she
hadn't realized was there.

It was wild and dark, a pulsing jungle of sensation. He took her into the darkness, drawing her
deeper with his hands, his mouth, his low, ragged
voice.

The remnants of her garments fell away, along
with the last vestiges of her reason. She was lost in
his scent, so potently masculine, and in the sinful
taste of him, and in the stunning power of muscle
under taut, smooth flesh.

She wanted him to crawl inside her, under her
skin. She wanted him to be part of her. Even when
his hand settled between her legs, upon the most
private of places, it wasn't enough, and she arched
up to his touch for more.

He caressed her in secret ways that made her
moan and squirm under his hand, but it was not
enough. The tantalizing strokes slipped deeper, inside her. Spasms racked her, hot, delicious . . . but
not enough.

She trembled on a precipice, caught between
wild pleasure and an unreasoning, inescapable
craving for more, for something else.

"Dear God," she gasped, writhing like one demented, which she was. "Do it. Please."

"Soon." A rough whisper. "You're not ready. It's
your first—"

"Hurry." She could feel his shaft pulsing against
her thigh. She dug her nails into his arms. *"Hurry."*

Cursing, he pulled her fingers away. She could
not keep away. She dragged her hands down over
his belly, to the place where instinct led her. She
found the thick, hot shaft. Immense. Her hand

could not close about it. "Oh, my goodness," she whispered.

"Stop it. Christ, Gwen, don't rush me. It'll hurt and you—"

"Oh, Lord. It feels . . . so strong . . . and alive." She hardly knew what she was saying. She stroked the velvety flesh, lost in heated wonder.

She heard a strange, strangled sound above her.

Then he was caressing her intimately again, dragging her back into the frustrating madness. Her hand fell away from him as the furious pleasure swept her to the precipice.

Then it came, one swift thrust—and a stinging sensation that jerked her back to reality.

She gulped in air and blinked. "Good heavens."

He was enormous. She was not comfortable.

Yet she was not exactly uncomfortable, either. Not altogether.

"I told you it would hurt."

She heard the ache in his voice. Her fault, she reproached herself. Everyone knew it hurt the first time. She should not have let herself be taken unawares. Now he probably thought he'd done her a permanent injury.

"Only at first," she said shakily. "That is normal. You mustn't stop on my account."

"It's not going to get much better."

She looked into his glowing eyes, saw the shadows lurking there. "Then kiss me," she whispered. "I'll concentrate on that and ignore the rest."

She reached up, slid her fingers into his thick, wet mane, and drew him down.

He kissed her fiercely. The hot need she tasted ignited hers. She simmered in the devil's brew, and the pain and tightness bubbled away into nothingness.

He began to move inside her, slow strokes at first, but soon quickening. She moved with him, her body answering instinctively, gladly. In the in-

timate beat of desire, passion returned, hotter than
before. She was joined with him, and this was what
she'd needed: to be one, to take him with her to
the edge of the abyss . . . and beyond . . . into the
last, searing burst of rapture . . . and then she sank
with him, into the sweet darkness of release.

5

S ome time later, enveloped in her husband's
dressing gown, Gwendolyn sat tailor-fashion
near the foot of his bed.

She had piled a heap of pillows at his back, and
he sat with his legs stretched out in front of him—
under the bedclothes because she had insisted he
keep his feet warm.

The debauch in the bathing room had left them
famished. They had raided the larder and sneaked
up to his bedroom with a tray of thick sandwiches,
which they'd made short work of.

Though the bath, the lovemaking, and the meal
had radically improved his mood, he was not altogether tranquil.

Gwendolyn was aware of the glances he stole at
her from under his black lashes when he thought
she wasn't looking. She wished she knew what
those troubled glances signified. At present, only
one aspect of his character was truly clear to her.

Though facing a horrendous death in quicksand,
he'd tried to drive her off—because he was afraid
she'd fall in.

He had been willing to risk medical bedlam and

eventual incarceration in a madhouse, rather than subject her to marrying him.

Though informed of the deadly risks of unsupervised laudanum consumption, he had locked himself alone in his room—to spare her witnessing his miseries.

The Earl of Rawnsley, in short, had a protective streak a mile long and three miles deep.

Gwendolyn didn't think she was overestimating him. She'd had enough experience with her father, brothers, uncles, and cousins to recognize this particular ailment.

The awareness was doing nothing to restore her clinical detachment, which was in dangerous disrepair already.

Just looking at him paralyzed her intellect. When she recalled what that sensuous mouth, those strong, graceful hands, and that long muscled body had done to her, her entire brain, along with her heart and every other organ and muscle she possessed, turned to jelly.

His low voice broke into her bewildered thoughts.

"I don't think you ought to stay in here," he said gently.

She looked up from her folded hands. His carefully polite expression made her heart sink.

She could guess why he wanted her out of his sight. He'd probably spent most of the time since they'd left the bathing room devising a courteous way of telling her he'd rather not repeat the experience.

But she'd been rejected countless times before, Gwendolyn reminded herself, and it hadn't killed her yet.

"I understand," she said, her voice cool, her face hot. "I know I behaved shockingly. I scarcely know what to think of myself. I have never, *ever*, in all my life, reacted that way—to anybody."

A muscle worked in his jaw.

"Not that I've had so many beaux," she hurriedly added. "I am not a flirt, and even if I was, I hadn't much time for suitors. I didn't want to make time," she babbled on as his expression grew tauter. "But girls are obliged to make an appearance in Society, and then of course the men think one is like the others, and one feels obliged to pretend that's true. And I must admit that I was curious about what it was like to be courted and kissed. But it wasn't like anything, and not half so interesting as, say, Mr. Culpeper's *Herbal*. If it had been that way with you, I'm sure I should have behaved much more decorously downstairs. I should have fastened my mind on a medical treatise and not made a spectacle of myself. But I could not behave properly. I am truly sorry. The last thing I wanted was to make myself disagreeable to you."

With a sigh, she started to crawl from the bed.

"Gwendolyn." His voice was choked.

She paused and met his gaze.

"You are not disagreeable to me," he said tightly. "Not at all. Word of honor."

She remained where she was, kneeling near the edge of the mattress, trying to read his expression.

"How could you think I was displeased?" he demanded. "I all but ravished you."

Good grief, how could she be so stupid? He was upset with himself, not her. Because of the mile-long protective streak.

She tried to remember what Genevieve had told her about men—and the first time—but her mind was a jumble. "Oh, no, it was not like that at all," she assured him. "You were so very gentle—and I did appreciate that, truly I did. I know I should not have acted like a general: 'Do this,' 'Do that.' 'Hurry.' But I could not help myself. Something"— she gestured helplessly—"came over me."

"The something was your lusting spouse," he said grimly. "Which I should not have allowed myself to become."

"But we are wed," she argued. "It was your right, and it was a pleasure for me and—" Her face burning, she boldly added, "I am glad you lusted, my lord. I should have been very disappointed if you did not because I have wanted you to make me yours since . . ." She frowned. "Well, I'm not sure when exactly it began, but I know I wanted it after you kissed me." She crept toward him. "I wish you would not fret about me."

"This was supposed to be a business arrangement," he said. Shadows darkened his eyes. "No one would have known if the marriage had not been consummated. Your position was secure enough. I should not have touched you. You have no experience. You do not know how to protect your feelings. Your heart is too soft."

She sank back on her heels. "I see. You are alarmed that my feelings will become engaged."

"They *are* engaged," he said. "You have just told me as much. Not that I couldn't see it for myself. I wish you could see the way you look at me."

Good heavens. Was she so obvious?

But of course she was. She was not like Genevieve or Cousin Jessica. She had no subtlety, Gwendolyn was aware. But she did possess both a sense of humor and common sense, and these came to her rescue.

"Like a lovesick schoolgirl, you mean?" she asked.

"Yes."

"Well, what do you expect? You are shockingly handsome."

He leaned forward, his eyes narrowed. "I have a *brain disease*. My mind is crumbling to pieces. And in a few months I shall be a rotting corpse!"

"I know that," she said. "But you are not mad

yet, and when you become so, you will not be my first lunatic—any more than you'll be my first corpse."

"You didn't marry the others! You didn't bed them! Damnation." He flung back the bedclothes and stalked, splendidly naked, to the window. "I didn't even want to be your patient," he said as he gazed out into the darkness. "And now I am your lover. And you are besotted. It is macabre."

He would not think it macabre if he could see himself as she saw him, standing so tall and strong and beautiful in the candlelight.

"You said yourself that Providence does not grant all its creatures a pretty demise," she said. "It does not give each of us exactly what we want. It did not make me a man, so that I could become a doctor."

She left the bed and went to him. "But now I am not at all sorry I'm a woman," she told him. "You've made me very glad of it, and I am practical and selfish enough to want to enjoy the gladness for as long as I can."

He swung round, his countenance bleak. "Oh, Gwen."

She understood then that she would not have long. The stark expression, the despair in his voice, told her matters were worse than they appeared.

But that was the future, she told herself.

She laid her hand on his chest. "We have tonight," she said softly.

He'd made her glad she was a woman.

We have tonight, she'd said.

Saint Peter himself, backed by a host of martyrs and angels, could not have withstood her. He would have let the heavenly gates slam shut behind him and taken her into his arms and devoted body and soul—eternally damned though it might be—to making her happy.

And so Dorian scooped up his foolishly besotted wife in his arms and carried her to the bed and made love to her again. And he tasted, again, the rapture of being made love to, of being desired and trusted. And later, as he held his sleeping countess in his arms, he lay awake wondering whether he was dead or alive because he could not remember when his heart had felt so sweetly at peace.

Not until the first feeble light of daybreak stole into the room did something like an explanation occur to him.

Never, in all his life, had he ever done anything that was any good to anybody. He'd done no more than fantasize about rescuing his mother from a world where she didn't belong and taking her to the Continent, where she would no longer have to lie and pretend. When he'd finally got around to visiting her here, he'd missed all the hints she dropped, and gone on his merry way. If he had paid attention instead, and stayed, and helped his father care for her, they might have forestalled his grandfather and the "experts." Even at the madhouse, when it had seemed too late, it needn't have been, if Dorian had used the clever brain he'd inherited. He should have played on his grandfather's overweening pride and sense of duty, and worked him round by degrees. Mother had pulled the wool over the old tyrant's eyes for years. Dorian could have done it, should have done it.

And he should have done it later, when the ax fell, instead of storming out of Rawnsley Hall in a childish tantrum. Then he might have accomplished something. He might have used the earl's money and influence to good purpose, in scholarly pursuits, for instance, to further knowledge, or perhaps in a political endeavor.

Everyone died, some early, some late. It was nothing to whimper about. But dying with nothing but regret and if onlys was pathetic.

That, Dorian realized, was what had kept him so unsettled for these last months.

Now, though, his soul was quiet.

Because of her.

He nuzzled his wife's wayward hair. He had made her happy. He had made her forgive the Almighty for making her a woman. He smiled. He knew that was no small achievement.

She wanted to be a doctor. Equally important, she would use the Earl of Rawnsley's money and influence to good purpose.

Very well, he told her silently. *I cannot give you a medical degree, but I will give you what I can.*

And that must have been the right conclusion, because his busy mind quieted, and in a little while, he fell asleep.

After breakfast, Dorian took her out to the moors, to the place where his mother had brought him eight years earlier.

He helped Gwendolyn from her horse—treating himself to but one brief kiss in the process—then led her to a boulder at the track's edge. He took off his coat and laid it on the cold stone and asked her to sit, which she did with a bemused smile.

"Last night you said I was not your first lunatic," he began.

"Oh, not at all," she eagerly assured him. "Mr. Eversham, who took over Mr. Knightly's practice, was particularly interested in neurological maladies, and he let me assist him in several cases. Not all the patients were irrational, certainly. But Miss Ware had six different personalities at last count, and Mr. Bowes was prone to violent dementia, and Mrs. Peebles—may her troubled soul rest in peace—"

"You can tell me the details later," Dorian interrupted. "I only wanted to make sure I had heard correctly last night. I was not fully attending, I'm sorry to say. I have not listened properly since you came."

"How can you say such a thing?" she exclaimed. "You are the only man except Mr. Eversham who's ever taken me seriously. You did not laugh at my hospital idea, and you were not horrified about the dissections." She hesitated briefly. "You are rather overprotective, true, but that is your nature, and I know it is a very gentlemanly and noble inclination."

"Overprotective," he repeated. "Is that how you see it, Gwen?"

She nodded. "You want to shield me from unpleasantness. On the one hand, it is rather lovely to be coddled. Still, on the other, it is just the tiniest bit frustrating."

He understood how he'd frustrated her. She didn't like being kept in the dark about his illness. He had treated her like a silly female, as other men had done.

"I have surmised as much." He clasped his hands behind his back to keep from gathering her up and "overprotecting" her in his arms, as he very much wished to do. "Yours is a medical mind. You do not see matters as we laymen do. Illness is a subject of study to you, and sick people represent a source of knowledge. Their ailments make you no more queasy than a volume of Cicero's works does me." He paused, his face heating. "I fancied myself a scholar once, you see. Classics."

"I know." Her green gaze was soft with admiration. "You took a first, Bertie says."

"Yes, I am not merely a pretty fellow," he said with a short laugh. "I have—*had*—a brain." Embarrassed, he looked away, toward the moors. "I also had plans once, as you do. But they were not . . . well thought out, and it all ended in . . . rather a mess."

His throat tightened.

He told himself it was ridiculous to feel uneasy. He had prepared himself to tell her everything. He knew it was right. She needed to learn the facts— all of them—in order to make intelligent decisions about her future. At present, her attachment to him was probably little more than a new bride's infatuation, a response to the physical passion they'd shared. If, after he enlightened her about his past and what the future held in store, she chose to leave, she'd swiftly recover her equilibrium. If she chose to remain, she would do it with her eyes open at least, prepared for the worst. To show respect for her mind and character, as well as belief in her goals, he must give her the choice, and accept her decision, and live—and die—with the consequences.

"Dorian?"

He closed his eyes. How sweetly his name fell from her lips. He would remember that, too, no matter what happened—or he would remember, at least, for as long as his brain functioned.

He turned back to her, smiling as he shoved his windblown hair from his face.

"I know you want to hear all the fascinating details of my illness," he said. "I was only trying to decide where to begin."

She sat up straighter and her soft, adoring expression transformed into the steady green regard that had so intrigued him when they first met. "Thank you, my dear," she said, her tone thoroughly professional now. "If you don't mind, I should like you to begin with your mother."

After dinner that evening, Gwendolyn sat at a table in the library, making a list of medical texts to be sent from home. Dorian sat by the fire, perusing a volume of poetry.

She knew it had not been easy for him to talk about his past, but she was sure it had done him good. He kept too much bottled up inside him, Gwendolyn thought as her gaze strayed back to him. When people did that, matters tended to get exaggerated out of proportion, and his ignorance of medical science only made it worse.

The visual chimera he'd described, for instance, were physiological phenomena common to a number of neurological ailments, not ghastly aberrations, as he thought. Furthermore, Dorian had not quite comprehended his mother's case or the difficulties of managing lunatics. Nor had he realized that the doctors often had no way of knowing for certain until after death that the brain was physically damaged. Still, she was not sure Mr. Borson had handled the case altogether wisely.

Dorian looked up and caught her staring at him.

"You're wearing your medical frown," he said. "Am I foaming at the mouth, by any chance, without realizing?"

"I was thinking about your mother," she said. "Her hair, for instance. I'm not sure cutting it was the only option."

His face stiffened, but only for a moment. "I'm not sure what else they could have done," he said slowly. "She was tearing it out in bloody clumps, according to my father and uncle. She did not realize it was her own hair, I think. She must have believed it was the talons. The imaginary claws of the imaginary Furies."

Gwendolyn left her chair and went to him and stroked his hair back from his face.

He smiled up at her. "I give you leave to cut my hair, Gwen. I should have done it weeks ago—or at least for my wedding."

"But that is the point," she said. "I don't want to cut your hair."

"I don't wear it this way because of some mad whim you must indulge," he said. "I had practical reasons, which are no longer relevant."

"I thought you did it to spite your grandfather," she said. "If he had been my grandfather, I am sure I would have done something to vex him." She considered briefly. "Trousers. I should have worn trousers."

He laughed. "Ah, no, I was not so bold as that. When I went to London, I was concerned that someone might recognize me and tell him where I was. Then he would punish my landlady and my employers for giving aid and comfort—such as it was—to the enemy."

He'd told her about his time in London, slaving night and day. Working on the docks explained his muscles, which had puzzled her very much. One rarely saw that sort of upper body development among the nobility, though it was common enough among laborers and pugilists.

"Looking like an eccentric—and possibly dangerous—recluse keeps the curious at bay," he went on. "It discourages them from prying into one's personal affairs. Such concerns obviously applied here in Dartmoor, at least while my grandfather was alive."

"Well, I'm glad you were impractical and didn't cut your hair for the wedding," she said. "It suits your exotic features. You don't look very English. Not in the ordinary way, at any rate." She paused, struck by an idea.

She stood back to consider him . . . and grinned.

He grasped her hand and drew her toward him, and tumbled her onto his lap.

"You had better not be laughing at me, Doctor Gwendolyn," he said sternly. "We madmen don't take kindly to that."

"I was thinking of Cousin Jessica and her husband," Gwendolyn said. "Dain is not ordinary-looking either. She and I seem to have similar taste in men."

"Indeed. She likes monsters and you like lunatics."

"I like you," she said, snuggling against him.

"How can you help liking me?" he said. "I spent hours yesterday talking of little but medical symptoms and insane asylums. And you listened as though it were poetry and all but swooned at my feet. It is too bad I haven't any medical treatises about. I'm sure I need read but a paragraph or two, and you will become ravenous with lust and begin tearing off my clothes."

All he had to do was stand there—sit there—to make her ravenous with lust, she thought. She drew back. "Would you like that?"

"Your tearing off my clothes? Of course I'd like it." He bent his head and whispered in her ear, "I am mentally unbalanced, recollect."

She glanced toward the door. "What if Hoskins comes in?"

Dorian slid her hand into the opening of his shirt. "We'll tell him it's a medical treatment," he said.

She turned back to him. Behind the laughter glinting in his eyes, desire smoldered, fierce and hot.

One day, too soon, the fierceness and heat would turn dangerous—deadly, perhaps.

But she would deal with that day when it came, Gwendolyn told herself. In the meantime, she was happy to burn in his strong arms.

She lifted his hand to her breast. "Touch me," she whispered. "Make me mad, too, Dorian."

He had an attack the next day.

They had just finished breakfast when she saw him blink impatiently and brush at the air near his face.

He caught himself doing it and laughed. "I know it does no good," he said. "A reflex, I suppose."

Gwendolyn left her chair and went to him. "If you go to bed now and I give you a dose of laudanum, you'll scarcely notice when the headache starts."

He rose, and went upstairs with her, his expression preoccupied. She helped him undress, and noticed that his vision was not so impaired that he couldn't find her breasts. He fondled them while she wrestled with his neckcloth.

"You are remarkably good-humored," she said when she'd finally got him under the bedclothes. "If I didn't know better, I'd suspect my lord only wished to lure me into his bedchamber."

"I wish it were a trick," he said, blinking up at her. "But there the damned things are, winking and blinking at me. And you were right, Gwen. They are not like ghosts, after all. You described it better. 'Like colliding with a lamppost,' you said. 'First you see stars, then the pain hits.' I should like to know what it was that persuaded my brain I'd suffered a blow to the head."

She knew, all too well.

I told you he must be insulated from all sources of nervous agitation, Kneebones had said.

He was a real doctor, with decades of experience. He understood the malady, had studied Dorian's mother for months.

You saw what the news about his family did to him: three attacks in one week.

She recalled yesterday's conversation, and her conscience stabbed.

"I can see what it was," she said tightly. "Yesterday, I obliged you to relive the most painful experiences of your life. And I was not content with the general picture, was I? I pressed you for details, even about the post-mortem report on your mother. I should have realized this was too much strain for you to bear all at once. I cannot believe I did not think of that. I do wonder where I misplaced my wits."

She started to move away, to fetch the laudanum bottle, but he grabbed her hand. "I wonder where you've put them now," he said. "You've got it all backwards, Gwen. Our talk yesterday did me nothing but good. You eased my mind on a hundred different counts."

He tugged her hand. "Sit."

"I need to get your laudanum," she said.

"I don't want it," he said. "Not unless I become unmanageable. That's the only reason I took it before. I wasn't sure I could trust myself. But I can trust you. I'm not your first lunatic. You'll know when I need to be stupefied."

"I also know the pain is dreadful," she said. "I cannot let you lie there and endure it. I must do something, Dorian."

He shut his eyes then, and his face set.

"It's started, hasn't it?" It was a struggle to keep her voice low and even.

"I don't want to be stupefied," he said levelly. "I want my mind clear. If I must be incapacitated physically, I should like to use the opportunity to think, while I still can."

Gwendolyn firmly stifled her screaming conscience. Her guilt would not help him.

She had come with low expectations, she reminded herself. She had hoped to learn while ameliorating, insofar as possible, his suffering. She had never had any illusions about curing what medical science scarcely understood, let alone knew how to treat.

She had not expected to fall in love with him, almost instantly. Still, that changed only her emotions, and she would simply have to live with them. She would not, however, let them rule, and be tempted to pray for a miracle, when what she ought to be doing was listening to him and ascertaining what he needed and how best to provide it.

"You want to think," she said, frowning.

"Yes. About my mother and what you said about her. About my grandfather. The experts. The asylum." He pressed a thumb to his temple. "I do not believe I've burst a blood vessel, but I distinctly see my life passing before me." Smiling crookedly, he added, "And it is beginning to make sense."

She felt a surge of alarm, which she ruthlessly suppressed. "Very well," she said calmly. "No soporifics. We shall try a stimulant instead."

Gwendolyn gave him coffee. Very strong coffee and a good deal of it.

Two hours and countless cups later, Dorian was fully recovered and his wife was staring at him as though he'd just risen from the dead. She stood by the fire, her hands folded in front of her, her expression a comical mixture of worry and bewilderment while she watched him yank on his clothes.

"I begin to suspect you believed I *had* burst a blood vessel," he said as he fastened his trouser buttons. "Or was about to."

The comical expression vanished, succeeded by the familiar steady green regard. "I do not know what to think," she said. "Frankly, I am confounded. Two hours, from start to finish. This makes no medical sense at all."

"I told you I distinctly felt the pressure ease after the fourth cup," he said. "As though my head were being released from a vise. Perhaps the coffee washed the pressure through my system and"—he grinned—"into the chamberpot."

"It does have diuretic qualities," she said.

"Obviously."

"But you should not respond in this way." Her brow furrowed. "Perhaps I misinterpreted your account of the autopsy report, though I do not see how. Your mother's was hardly an unusual case."

"I should like to know what's troubling you," he said. "Have I been babbling incoherently without realizing it? Am I manifesting signs of mania? Is the extraordinary sense of well-being a danger signal? Because if I am at death's door, Gwendolyn, I should appreciate being informed."

She let out a shaky breath. "I don't know. I had thought the dilating blood vessels and increased blood supply—possibly augmented by leakage—triggered the aura and pain. But for the pain to stop, the vessels must contract again and diminish blood flow—and your cells and tissue are supposed to be too weak and damaged to do it so quickly and thoroughly."

He recalled what she'd told him yesterday about brain function. "I see," he said. "You fear that something has cut off blood supply too abruptly, perhaps in a dangerous and abnormal fashion—and this is a temporary and illusory surcease."

"I cannot say." Her voice was the slightest bit unsteady.

Perhaps he'd fall down dead in the next minute, Dorian thought. That did not seem possible. He had never felt more alive. Nonetheless, he wasn't going to take any chances.

He went to her and gathered her in his arms and kissed her, long and thoroughly, until she melted against him. He went on kissing her, then caressing her, and soon, carrying her to the bed.

That wasn't what he'd intended. He'd only wanted to make sure she understood how he felt about her.

But there was no stopping, once they'd begun. In a little while, the garments he'd so recently donned lay strewn about the floor, along with hers, and he was lost, drowning inside her, in the hot sea of desire.

And later, when they lay together, limbs tangled,

he found his heart was still beating and his brain was still working, and so he told her what she'd done for him.

Yesterday, he'd told her of his debauched past, expecting shock and disgust. Instead, she'd impatiently dismissed his whoring and drinking as normal male behavior.

He'd told her about his mother, the pitiable and monstrous creature she'd become, and Gwendolyn had not turned a hair. "It's like consumption," she'd said, after reducing the horrors to a logical series of physiological events. "There is no saying that her infidelities and secrets made it worse or triggered the breakdown. Her marriage was unsatisfactory. For all we know, the romantic intrigues may have reduced the emotional strain and delayed the inevitable, instead of hastening it."

If Dorian had stayed with his mother, he might have added to her agitation, Gwendolyn had theorized, because Aminta had a stronger emotional bond with him than with his father.

Moreover, the conditions at the madhouse must be put into perspective, Gwendolyn had told him. The moral faculties were often destroyed in such cases. Patients might appear calm and rational without having any more awareness or control over their thoughts and behavior than if they had been marionettes, with the damaged brain cells pulling the strings. And aware or not, patients often forgot what they were angry or sad about, just as they forgot basic hygiene, and even who they were or who they'd imagined they were minutes before.

Then he'd realized that his mother might not have endured continuous humiliation and pain, because she'd been living for the most part in a world of her own, where little could reach her.

"You have truly eased my mind," Dorian told his wife now. "Even my grandfather does not seem so monstrous. Pitiable, actually, in his ignorance, his fear of what he didn't understand, and his dependence on 'experts.' But you are not like him or his precious experts. You have a knack for making the incomprehensible make sense. You've reduced it to manageable proportions. Even this last attack seemed like little more than a damned nuisance."

She lifted herself onto one elbow and studied his face. "Perhaps, because you became less agitated, your brain did not have to work so hard," she said. "You said you needed to think, and it appears your reflections were positive. It's possible that stimulating such thought, rather than stupefying it, was the more beneficial approach."

"Lovemaking instills in me any number of positive feelings," he said. "Perhaps we must regard that as a beneficial treatment as well."

She arched one eyebrow. "I recall nothing in the medical literature recommending coitus as a course of treatment."

He slid his fingers into her wayward hair and drew her down to him. "Maybe you haven't read enough books."

6

Three weeks later, Dorian stood in the doorway of his wife's sitting room, watching her frown over a pamphlet.

Her books had arrived a fortnight ago, and he and Hoskins had helped her convert the sitting room into a study. The medical tomes stood in neat rows in a bookcase.

Her desk was not so neat. Pamphlets, notebooks, and sheets of foolscap lay in haphazard heaps.

Dorian leaned against the door frame and folded his arms and studied his preoccupied wife.

He knew what she was looking for. Not a cure, because there wasn't any, but clues to his "positive response to treatment." Though she would never admit it, Dorian knew she had hopes of prolonging his sanity, if not his life.

He had every reason to cooperate. He would be glad of an extra month, even an extra day. Yet her dogged search made his heart ache for her. She was not "practical and selfish," as she'd claimed. She cared, deeply, about her patients. She had even cared about Mr. Bowes, whose dementia made Dorian's mother's fits seem like mere sulks.

But at present it was not simply a matter of caring. Dorian feared Gwendolyn's dedication was crossing the line, from a quest for intellectual enlightenment to obsession. Last night she'd muttered in her sleep about "idiopathic inconstancy" and "lesions" and "prodromal symptoms."

He was strongly tempted to send the books back and order her to cease and desist before she developed a brain fever. Yet he couldn't deprive her of what he knew was the learning opportunity of a lifetime, or show a lack of respect for her maturity, intellect, and competence.

Fortunately, he'd been able to devise something like a solution because his mind was still functioning adequately, despite two more attacks. The last, a week ago, had continued for twenty-four hours, until he'd made her dose him with ipecac, to make him vomit. After that, he'd slept like the dead for another half a day.

Yet he'd recovered with the same sense of well-being and clarity of mind he'd experienced the two previous times. He was sure it was because she'd exorcised the demons of fear, shame, and ignorance, thus reducing emotional pressure on his damaged brain. He knew the reprieve was temporary, and he wasn't going to waste it. He had no future, but she did, and he'd spent the last week looking into hers.

"Is this a bad time to interrupt?" he asked.

Her head went up and her preoccupied gloom vanished, and the sun came out in the endless smile that could still make his heart turn over in his breast.

"There is never a bad time for you," she said. "You are the most welcome interruption in the world."

Dorian came away from the door frame, crossed to her desk, and perched on the edge. His gaze settled upon the pamphlet she'd put down when he approached: "*An Account of Acute Idiopathic Mania as Manifested . . .*"

"It is one of Mr. Eversham's studies," she said. "But your behavior does not fit his model."

He took it up and scanned the pages. "I wonder how you make anything of this gibberish." He set down the pamphlet and took up a narrow volume. "This is still worse. I should go howling mad trying to read the first sentence—and it's only three-quarters of a page long."

"They are doctors, not writers," said Gwendolyn. "You ought to see their penmanship. It is a wonder the printers are not all in Bedlam by now."

"Yours is nothing to boast of," he said with a meaningful glance at the untidy pile of foolscap covered with her even more untidy scrawl.

She wrinkled her nose. "Yes, my handwriting is horrid. Not at all like yours. I'm sure you were the finest copyist those London solicitors ever had."

"I should be happy to copy your notes legibly," he said. "In fact, I . . ." He trailed off, his mind snagging on a recollection. Something she'd said weeks ago. Something "misinterpreted."

Catching her worried look, he shrugged. "I'm all right. My mind wandered, that's all. I had interrupted for a specific reason, and the medical jargon and your ghastly handwriting distracted me." He ruffled her hair. "I came to ask if you'd like to visit Athcourt with me."

"Athcourt?" she said blankly.

"I wrote to Dain a few days ago," he explained. "I need advice on some business matters. He's now a member of the family, his place is but a few miles southeast of here, and he's an excellent manager, from all one has heard."

"Athcourt is reputed to be one of the most prosperous, well-run properties in the kingdom," Gwendolyn said, nodding. "I'm sure his business judgment is sound."

"At any rate, he's made me feel welcome." Dorian withdrew a letter from his pocket and gave it to her.

As she perused it, her mouth began to twitch. "The man is incorrigibly wicked. And what is this?" She read aloud, " 'If that nitwit Trent is still loitering about, you might as well bring him, too, since mayhem can only result if he's left to his own devices. Still, you know what will be expected of you in that case.' " She looked up. "It would appear you are better acquainted than I had guessed."

Dorian laughed. "Dain was still at Eton when Bertie first came," he explained. "About once a fortnight, Bertie would fall down the stairs or trip over something or otherwise contrive to stumble into His Lordship's path. Fortunately, I was on the spot the first time and hustled Bertie away before Dain could dispose of him by more violent means. After that, whenever your cousin strayed into the Satanic presence, His Lordship would summon me.

'Camoys,' he would say, as cool as you please. 'It's back. Make it go away.' And so I would make Bertie disappear."

"I can see Dain doing it. And you, too." She patted his arm. "It is your protective streak."

"It was my instinct for *self-preservation*," Dorian indignantly informed her. "I was scarcely twelve, and Dain, even at sixteen, was as big as a house. He had but to set one huge hand on my head to squash me like a bug." He grinned. "Still, I admired him tremendously. I should have given anything to get away with what he did."

She laughed, a delicious sound. "So should I," she said. "It was not hard to understand why Jessica was captivated with him. Or why she was so vexed about it."

"I thought you'd enjoy visiting with her while Dain and I talk business," he said.

"I should, very much." She gave the letter back. "I am glad you thought of Dain as a business advisor. A better choice than Abonville. The duc is a foreigner and of another generation."

"I knew you had reservations about him."

"He's a wonderful man, but he can be *too* paternal."

Dorian hesitated. He did not want to upset her; on the other hand, they could not spend the remaining time avoiding all mention of what lay ahead. "I trust you won't mind, then, if I end by making Dain my guardian instead," he said quietly.

There was only the briefest pause before she spoke. "If I encountered difficulties, and you were unable to assist me, there's no one I'd rather have on my side," she said. She met his gaze, her own clear and steady.

He could guess what the composure and steadiness cost her, and it distressed him. Nevertheless, they couldn't pretend they would have forever when they didn't.

He bent and lightly kissed her. "That's how I feel," he said. He drew back and grinned. "If we must choose an ally, it makes sense to pick the biggest one we can find."

A few days later, they went to Athcourt, intending to stay for two days. They wound up staying for a week.

Dain turned out to be knowledgeable—and obstinately opinionated—about a vast array of topics, and the two men were soon quarreling happily, like old friends or brothers. They raced each other over Athcourt's vast park and into the surrounding moorland. They fenced and practiced pistol shooting. One day, Dain undertook to teach Dorian some of the finer points of pugilism, and they knocked each other about in a corner of the stable yard, while their wives cheered them on.

Dain's bastard son lived at Athcourt as well. He was a wicked piece of mischief, eight years old, whom Dain proudly referred to as the Demon Seed.

Little Dominick was wary of Dorian at first, but within two days, he was inviting the Earl of Rawnsley to visit his treehouse. This, Dorian learned, was a signal honor. Until now, only the boy's adored papa had been privy to the refuge's location and initiated into its mysteries.

And so, Dorian came away from Athcourt with scraped knees and elbows, Dain's assurances that Gwendolyn's affairs would be properly looked after ... and a mad yearning for a child.

Dorian told himself it was ridiculous to long for a child he would never see born and ruthlessly focused his energies on realizing Gwendolyn's hospital dream.

Dain had agreed with him that her influential

title and wealth would not fully compensate for her being a female, and a young one at that. She would be contending with scores of men, few of whom held an enlightened view of feminine capabilities.

"I can deal with the men," Dain had said, "but I should want precise instructions. I know nothing about hospitals, even the everyday variety, and it seems that your lady has something novel in mind."

"I'm not sure she'll be as precise as one would wish, when the time comes," Dorian had answered. "Already I detect signs of emotional strain. I had thought that if I started the project now, it would make a healthy distraction. Moreover, if I am directly involved in its founding, others will take it more seriously. If the Earl of Rawnsley says the building must be a perfect hexagon, for instance, another fellow won't pipe up that it must be a perfect cube and start a row with someone who says it must be an octagon, according to the best authorities. Instead, they will all murmur, 'Yes, my lord. A hexagon. Certainly,' and write down my every word with the greatest care, as though it came direct from the throne of Heaven."

Dain had chuckled, but something in his dark gaze made Dorian edgy. "Am I overly optimistic?" he'd asked. "If you have doubts of my capabilities, Dain, I wish you—"

"I was only wondering why the devil you don't cut your hair," Dain had said. "While I doubt your coiffure would affect your credibility—you're a Camoys, after all—I should think it was a damned nuisance to look after—as though there won't be enough in organizing this project."

Dorian had smiled sheepishly. "My wife likes it."

"And you are besotted, poor fool." Dain had given him a commiserating look, then laughed. "Well, then, I collect this is as rational as you're ever going to be. Make the most of it, I say."

Dorian was determined to make the most of it.

Accordingly, on the second night of their return home, he explained to Gwendolyn his idea about getting an early start on her hospital.

She told him it was an excellent idea and she seemed very enthusiastic, but Dorian could not shake off the feeling that her mind was elsewhere: on his accursed ailment and its provoking mysteries. He was strongly tempted to lecture her. He suppressed the urge and made love to her instead.

The following afternoon, they settled down in the library to discuss the matter in detail, and she was the same. She talked enthusiastically of her ideas, and obligingly sketched out a rough plan for the building itself, and described the functions of different areas. All the same, Dorian sensed that her mind was not fully engaged.

In the following days, she went on working cheerfully with him, transforming her dreams into orderly facts and specifications, but the note of abstraction remained.

Dorian bore it patiently. He had learned from her that it was often possible to combine several treatments to combat an ailment's array of symptoms. One remedy for sick headaches, for instance, combined laudanum with ipecac—the former to dull the pain and the latter to relieve the nausea by inducing vomiting.

He had, likewise, devised a combination treatment for her. One of the "medications" arrived a week after their return from Athcourt.

Dorian slipped into her study and left the packet on her desk while she was consulting with the cook about the following day's menu. Then he left the house, to work on the next part of the remedy.

An hour later, Gwendolyn stood in the study doorway, gazing blankly at Hoskins.

"He's gone to Okehampton," the manservant said for the second time. "He had an appointment. Something to do with the hospital, he said."

"Oh. Oh, yes. With Mr. Dobbin." Gwendolyn turned away. "He reminded me at breakfast. So silly of me to forget. My wits must be wandering. Thank you, Hoskins."

She stood in the doorway, staring at the thick letter on her desk while Hoskins's footsteps faded away.

Then she shut the door and returned to her desk and took up the letter again with trembling hands.

It was from Mr. Borson, the physician in whose care Aminta Camoys had been placed. It was in response to an inquiry from Dorian. He had written to Borson a fortnight ago, it turned out, without telling her.

Dorian had attached a note to Borson's letter: "Here it is, Doctor Gwendolyn—with all the deliciously grisly details. I shall expect to find you writhing with uncontrollable lust by the time I return."

Gwendolyn read the note again, for the tenth time, and this time she could not control herself. She covered her face with her hands and wept, not because of Borson's reply, but because of what it had cost her husband to obtain it, to write and seek a favor from the man he viewed as his mother's torturer, if not her murderer.

Dorian had done it for Gwendolyn's sake, and that was what made her heart ache, unbearably, so that she wept, like the wife she was instead of the doctor she wanted to be.

Or had thought she wanted to be.

Or imagined she was capable of being.

She was not behaving very capably now, she scolded herself.

She wiped away her tears and told herself there would be plenty of time to cry later. A lifetime, if she chose to devote it to grief, and throw away the gifts God had given her, and all that her husband was trying to give her. He knew she was trying to learn, and he was trying to help her in every way he could.

She had no business weeping about it. She knew it made Dorian happy to help her. Furthermore, Borson's letter contained exceedingly valuable information. She had seen that in the first quick perusal. He had even enclosed a copy of the post mortem report, which would solve several nagging riddles . . . once she could get her mind to focus properly. And stay focused, which was not easy lately.

She kept forgetting things and missing things. She had spent a full week with Jessica before realizing her cousin was breeding. Gwendolyn had not been able to put the simplest symptoms together: physical evidence any medical student would have discerned, not to mention the uncharacteristic moodiness. Twice, while Gwendolyn had been there, Jessica—who never wept—had burst into tears for no apparent reason, and several times she had lost her temper over the most trivial matters.

Jessica had said nothing about it, and Gwendolyn had tactfully refrained from questioning her. After all, it was early days yet, and the first trimester was a notoriously uncertain . . . period.

Trimester . . . twelve weeks . . . symptoms . . .

Gwendolyn stared blindly at the autopsy report.

She had been wed for more than six weeks.

Her last menses had been two weeks before the wedding.

The report dropped from her nerveless fingers, and her gaze dropped to her belly.

"Oh, my goodness," she whispered.

*   *   *

Dorian sat in a private parlor of Okehampton's Golden Hart Inn, not with the fictional Mr. Dobbin, but with Bertie Trent, whose square face was twisted into a painful grimace.

This was because Bertie was trying to think.

"Well, Eversham do need money," Bertie said finally. "But he ain't the sort that gets on with other fellows so well, which if he was, he wouldn't be stuck in Chippenham, which even Gwen said, but he got on fine with her, and Aunt Claire liked him well enough, seeing as how he was the only one knew what to make of her spells."

"He doesn't need to get on with the other fellows," Dorian said. "He only needs to tell us what to do. Dain and I agree that we need an experienced physician on the hospital planning committee."

He also needed someone who could talk to Gwendolyn in her own language and make her listen and face facts. And take better care of herself.

But all that was explained in Dorian's letter. The thick packet lay on the table between him and Bertie, who was eyeing it dubiously, still reluctant for some reason to take it up.

"It's hospital information," Dorian said. This was partly true, although the bulk of the contents consisted of his copies of Borson's materials—so that Eversham would arrive armed with facts for his intellectual joust with Gwendolyn. "I hope he finds the proposal irresistible. If he doesn't, I am counting on you to use your unique powers of persuasion. As you did with Borson."

As soon as Dorian had realized he must write to Borson, he'd realized he'd need more than a letter. Physicians could be balky, and they did like to keep secrets, Gwendolyn had said. Also, they were often too busy with patients to attend to correspondence. Unwilling to risk a wait that could extend to months, Dorian had decided to send for Bertie.

What Trent lacked in intelligence he made up for in loyalty and stubbornness. He was loyal to Dorian, and Bertie would stubbornly persist until Borson gave him what he came for. Which Borson had done, when he realized there was no other way to get rid of him.

Dorian trusted that Bertie's loyalty and obstinacy would serve equally well with Eversham. Gwendolyn's hero had not sounded like the sort of man who would come running at the snap of a nobleman's fingers.

"Still, if it doesn't work, we can try something else," Dorian added, because Bertie was still frowning. "I realize this will be more difficult than dealing with Borson. We're asking Eversham to give up his practice and pick up and leave, which is no small matter. Even if he agrees, I realize it will take some time to settle his affairs. But you will make sure he understands I'll cover all expenses and use my influence as needed. Make sure he realizes I'm a man of my word, Bertie—that this is no madman's whim. If he has doubts, he can write to Dain."

Bertie blinked very hard. "You ain't mad, Cat. No more 'n I am—and looking well, too, better than before. She's done you good, hasn't she?"

"Of course I'm not mad," Dorian said. "And it's all thanks to Gwendolyn. She is wonderful and I am ... exceedingly happy," he added with a smile. *I want her to be happy, too,* he added silently.

The clouds vanished from Bertie's expression and a light shone in his pale blue eyes. "I knew you'd like her, Cat. I knew she'd do you good."

Dorian understood what the light signified and had no trouble guessing what Bertie wanted to believe.

But Bertie had not read Borson's account or the

post-mortem report, and even if he had, he wouldn't have grasped even the fraction Dorian had comprehended. And that was far more than he'd done the first time, seven years ago, long before Gwendolyn had explained about the brain's unique self-sufficiency, which made it so susceptible to self-destruction.

Bertie wouldn't understand that the destruction couldn't be repaired or halted, even by Gwendolyn. He didn't know that, once begun, the decay continued relentlessly ... the way it had at Rawnsley Hall, quietly moldering under the surface until the roof caved in.

Bertie believed that "good" equaled "cured," and Dorian hadn't the heart to explain the difference.

"I like her immensely, Bertie," he said. "And she has done me a world of good."

Gwendolyn wanted to build the hospital in Dartmoor.

Which meant she intended to stay here, permanently.

She stood at the library window, looking out, and Dorian gazed at her in despair.

He stood at the table, where he'd laid out several rough architectural sketches of the hospital, moments before pressing her for an answer to the question he'd asked every day for the past five days.

He had not wanted to press her.

Two weeks had passed since his clandestine meeting with Bertie, and Dorian had received no word from him. Meanwhile Gwendolyn was becoming ill. Her countenance alternated between weary pallor and a hectic flush, and she was becoming short-tempered, doubtless because she was sleeping poorly. Last night she'd bolted up from the pillows babbling about "extravavasation" of something or other.

"Gwendolyn, you can't live here," he said, his voice calm, his mind churning with troubling images of her future.

"I like it here," she said. "From the moment I came, it felt like homecoming."

"This is not a healthy climate," he said. "Even in the valleys, the damp settles in and—"

"Poor people cannot afford to transport sick relatives to coastal resorts or travel back and forth to visit them." She turned around. "The moor folk need a modern hospital. And damp is scarcely an issue. Bath is damp and cold, and people in all stages of illness and decrepitude live there while taking the waters."

"This is not a healthy place for you," he said tightly. "You've been here only two months and—" He thrust his hand through his hair. *Say it*, he commanded himself. It was time to stop pretending. She was ill, and he was making her so, and it was time to confront that, with or without Eversham.

The fellow should have been here by now, curse him, Dorian thought. Eversham would know what to do, what to say. He was an experienced, allegedly brilliant physician. He would solve the exasperating riddle for her, and make her face facts.

"You are not well," Dorian said. "You don't eat properly or sleep properly and you are tired and—and unreasonable. You sulked for two hours last night because dinner was 'boring,' you said."

"She was supposed to use the spices," Gwendolyn said stiffly. Her hands fisted at her sides. "I sent to London for them, and explained to Cook—about phlegm and congestion and reducing the pressure from excess fluid—and she went ahead and made . . . *pap*."

Dorian sighed. He had talked to Hoskins, who'd

talked to Cook, who'd said the pungent spices would give Her Ladyship indigestion, which was what kept her awake nights. Everyone knew they "raised the blood," Cook had said.

"Cook is worried about you," he said. "We are all worried about you."

She rolled her eyes. "Oh, this is lovely. I am on my way to a medical breakthrough, and no one will cooperate—because they have taken it into their heads to *worry*." She marched to the table. "If I were a man—accepted as a *scientist*—I would merely be 'preoccupied' with my work. But because I am a woman, I am taking a fit of the vapors, and my blood must be lowered. *Lowered*." She struck the table with her fist. "Of all the antiquated, *medieval* notions. It's a wonder I can think at all, with so much nonsense and anxiety clouding the atmosphere about me. As though it were not enough trouble concentrating, in this cond—" She broke off, scowled at the drawings, and moved away from the table toward the door.

"I need some fresh air," she said.

But Dorian got there before she did, and blocked the way. "Gwen, it's raining," he said. "And you . . ." The rest of the sentence faded as he took in her appearance. Her face was flushed and her bosom was rising and falling rapidly, as though she'd been running for miles, and . . . He frowned. "Your frock has shrunk."

She looked down at herself.

"It's a wonder you can breathe," he said. "It's a wonder the seams of your bodice haven't split."

She retreated a pace. "It is not a wonder," she said, her gaze averted. "This happens to all the women in my family. We are so obvious." She drew a long, shaky breath. "I'm . . . breeding."

"Oh." He sagged back against the door. "I see. Yes. Of course."

The room was dark, reeling about him, while

within, another darkness settled like a vast weight. His eyes ached, and his throat, too, and his heart was a wedge of solid pain in his chest.

"Don't!" she cried. "Don't you dare give way, Dorian. Don't even *think* about sickening now." She flung herself against him and his arms closed, reflexively, round her.

Her head pressed against his aching chest. "I am happy," she said shakily. "I want our baby. And I want you to be there."

"Oh, Gwen."

"It isn't *impossible*," she said. "Another seven months or so, that's all we need." She drew back and gave him a smile as wobbly as her voice. "If I were an elephant, it would be different. The gestation period is twenty and a half months."

He managed a shaky laugh. "Yes, let's look on the bright side. At least you are not an elephant."

"I shall look like one at the end," she said. "You wouldn't want to miss that, would you?"

He wove his fingers through her wild hair. "No, I wouldn't, sweet. You present me with an irresistible temptation."

"I hope so." She patted his chest. "The patient's motivation can have a pronounced effect on treatment, Mr. Eversham says." Her voice was nearly returned to its normal cool efficiency. "I should have told you about the baby sooner, but this is an uncertain period, and I did not want to get your hopes up for nothing. Still, perhaps I was over-cautious. It is rare for the women of my family to miscarry."

Seven more months, Dorian thought. He'd been given less than that before she came, and she'd been here for two months now.

Yet he was doing better than his mother had at this stage. The visual chimera had not worsened, blossomed into demons. His temper remained relatively even. No sudden black melancholy or inexplicable fits of gaiety or rage.

Instead, there was the fierce rapture of their lovemaking, and the moments of quiet contentment, and the joy of working with her, planning something worthwhile.

According to Borson's account, Mother had continued articulate to the last. Mad, and living in a perverse world of her own, but articulate . . . and cunning, even devious at times. Perhaps she would not have sunk into a demon-plagued world of her own if the real world had offered understanding and joy and a sense of being useful and valued and worthy of affection. Perhaps she might have lived a little longer and died more peacefully.

It was not impossible.

A few extra months, he told himself. Long enough to see their baby. That would be wonderful. And if it did turn out to be impossible, at least he would have given Gwendolyn a child, which would surely gladden her heart and banish any sentimental inclination to mourn for him.

Nevertheless, her wishing to remain here was not a good sign. She needed to start a new life, in a new place, away from sad memories. But Eversham would arrive eventually, Dorian assured himself. Her mentor would set her right.

Dorian drew his wife tightly against him. "I shall try to maintain a positive attitude," he promised softly.

"And you must speak to Cook," Gwendolyn muttered into his shirt front. "Remind her who is the doctor in this house. I ordered a curry for dinner—and it must be *hot*."

He chuckled. "Yes, crosspatch." He kissed the top of her head. "But first, let us see what Doctor Dorian can do to sweeten your temper."

7

Ten days later, Gwendolyn was recalling that conversation and the methods Dorian had employed to sweeten her temper. He had used the same techniques every day since, kissing and caressing the irritation away, drawing her out of her annoying moods and into his strong arms, to take her to heaven and back, and leave her dazed with bliss.

Now, sitting in Mr. Kneebones's surgery, she focused on those blissful sensations in order to keep her temper from taking over and leading her to do the physician a severe, possibly fatal, bodily injury.

It was hardly the first time she'd humbled herself with doctors, she told herself, and Dorian was far more important than her pride.

She treated Kneebones to an apologetic smile. "I only want to know whether those materials prove absolutely what made Mrs. Camoys's brain start breaking down."

Kneebones scowled at her, then at the autopsy report in his hand. "One cannot prove anything *absolutely* in such cases. One makes logical inferences based on observable facts and the patient's history. Mrs. Camoys did not drink to excess or indulge in opium eating, which rules out toxic insanity. She had not sustained a high fever prior to or during the decline. And if she had suffered a blow to the head, as you surmise, do you not think Mr. Budge, the family physician, would have mentioned that little detail in his account of her medical history?"

"What if he didn't know?" Gwendolyn persisted.

"Budge is a competent man. I reckon he knows a concussion when he sees one."

"But one can't, precisely, *see* them," Gwendolyn said. "She had lovers. What if one of her lovers did it? If he did as great an injury as we're talking about, she might not have even remembered." She tipped her head to one side. "Did you question her maid, by any chance? Servants often know more family secrets than the family does."

Kneebones took off his spectacles and rubbed his eyes. "I do wonder how it is that Lord Rawnsley is not in a straitwaistcoat by now," he muttered.

"That is what I am wondering, too," she said. "Otherwise I should not have come to pester you. I know there must be a logical explanation, but I cannot find it."

Kneebones set his spectacles back on his nose. "That may be due to an overactive—and highly *melodramatic*—imagination and underactive attention to observable facts."

"Tell me where I'm wrong," she said.

He pushed the autopsy report toward her. "Let us suppose your little theory is correct, Lady Rawnsley. Let us suppose Mrs. Camoys's condition arose from a blow to the head, sustained many months before the early symptoms of traumatic insanity appeared, as often happens. What difference does it make? Her son's history easily allows for physical violence, fever, alcoholism, not to mention a host of morbid conditions of the system, all of which produce similar consequences. Perhaps this has not occurred to you. Nor do you seem aware that a man may inherit character, and with it a predisposition toward an irrational, self-destructive mode of life. You fail to take into account the patient's degenerate morals, irrational behavior, and savage appearance. No matter how the initial damage began, these symptoms clearly indicate progressive deterioration."

At this, Gwendolyn's fraying patience snapped. She stood up. "My husband is not and never has been degenerate, irrational, or self-destructive," she said stiffly. "He has a powerful instinct for self-preservation—else he would never have survived a month in the London slums, let alone years." She took up the autopsy report and stuffed it into her purse. "I cannot believe you overlooked that," she said, "and I cannot believe that you, a man of science, would diagnose him as insane, simply on account of his *hair*."

She stalked out.

Lord Rawnsley did not know that his wife had been quarreling with Mr. Kneebones in Okehampton. She was supposed to be making a tour of possible hospital sites with Hoskins and quarreling with him, because his orders were to (*a*) find fault with all sites and (*b*) keep her busy until teatime.

Unaware that she was racing home at this very minute, obstinately immune to all Hoskins's delaying tactics, Dorian stood by the library fireplace. His hands were clasped tightly at his back and his gaze was fixed on a disconcertingly young and gentlemanly physician.

Eversham stood at the library table. Having finished perusing Gwendolyn's latest notes, he was now thoughtfully perusing Dorian.

"She's very near the mark with your mother's case," Eversham said. "The same theory occurred to me when I read your letter and your copies of Borson's materials." He smiled faintly. "Very handsomely written they were, my lord."

"Never mind my penmanship," Dorian said.

"You were about to tell me what you learned in Gloucestershire."

Eversham's arrival had been delayed, it turned out, on account of a detour to the Rawnsley Hall estate in pursuit of information about Aminta Camoys. He had made the detour partly because Dorian's letter had aroused his medical curiosity and partly because of Bertie Trent's tear-filled litany of Dorian's noble and heroic qualities. It had taken them several days to locate Mother's former maid.

"Shall I be delicate or brutally direct?" Eversham asked.

Dorian's heart pounded. "Brutal, if you please."

"Your mother had been having an affair with your Uncle Hugo," Eversham said dispassionately. "They were meeting secretly, in the estate's laundry house, when her maid came to warn them that your grandfather had returned unexpectedly. Your mother panicked, tripped, and hit her head on a stone sink. Since she seemed to recover almost instantly, there seemed no reason to summon the doctor—and risk discovery of the accident's circumstances."

Eversham went on to explain concussions, which could be insidiously deceptive: internal injury with no external evidence, sometimes no discernible symptoms for weeks, months, even years—by which time it would be difficult to connect the symptoms with an apparently minor accident of long before. Thus she had been misdiagnosed initially as suffering a "decline," or constitutional breakdown.

"As you may not be aware," Eversham said, "the brain functions—"

"I know how it works," Dorian cut in. "Gwendolyn explained that—and how it breaks down as well."

Eversham nodded. "It seems to break down in more or less the same way following a trauma—a blow, for instance—as it does in a number of other, quite different maladies. The point is, my lord, your mother evidently suffered a severe concussion, which it is impossible to inherit."

He took up one of the sheets containing Gwendolyn's notes. "Furthermore, Her Ladyship has detected in you none of the usual symptoms of brain degeneration. That is not surprising, since there are none to detect."

Eversham eyed Dorian assessingly. "You are remarkably fit," he added, "especially for a member of the upper classes. Your brain is in excellent working order. Both your penmanship—evidencing superior motor control—and the logical and orderly presentation of highly personal and emotionally-laden information leave that in no doubt." He returned his attention to the sheet in his hand. "She reports no lethargy or fatigue. No restlessness or sleeplessness. No difficulties with attention to detail and concentration—as your proposal for the hospital clearly demonstrates." He cleared his throat. "And it would appear that the reproductive functions are—er—functioning." He looked up, smiling. "I congratulate you, my lord. That is a pleasant event to look forward to, is it not?"

His Lordship had only just managed to digest the matter of a concussion he could not possibly have inherited. It took him a moment to catch up with the rest, during which he stared stupidly at Eversham.

It took another moment to force the words out. "What are you saying?" he asked, dazed. "Look forward to—? I have—You have—" He thrust his hair back. "Haven't you overlooked something? The things. The—the 'visual chimera'—'first you see stars, then the pain hits.' Physiological phenomena, common to a host of neurological ailments, my wife said."

Eversham nodded. "Indeed, quite common. Among others, these are classic symptoms of migraine headache. That, I collect, is what's ailing you."

"Migraine?" Dorian repeated. "As in . . . '*megrims*'?"

"Not merely headache—which is what most people mean by 'megrims'—but severe, debilitating headaches. Still, they're not fatal, for all that."

"You are telling me," Dorian ground out, "that all this time . . ." His face heated. "All these months, I have been playing bloody tragic hero—and all I've got is a bleeding, damned *headache*?"

Eversham frowned and returned the paper to the pile with the rest and straightened them, while Dorian listened to the silence stretch on and wondered what would come to fill it. Eversham had just said they were headaches. Not fatal. Why then, was he hesitating?

Gwendolyn had thought she heard Dorian's voice, but when she reached the library door, all was quiet within. She opened it for a quick peep to be sure.

At that moment, another, equally familiar masculine voice broke the silence.

"I wish I could say otherwise, my lord, but the ailment is incurable. Though it has been studied for centuries, it remains a medical enigma. I have never yet encountered two cases precisely alike. I am not sure I can even promise you relief, which I deeply regret, for I know it is murderously painful. And I cannot promise that it will not be passed on to your offspring, for there is strong evidence that it is an inherited predisposition."

A choked sob escaped her.

Two masculine heads swiveled sharply, and two gazes—one blue, one golden—shot to her before she could retreat.

"Oh," she said. "I do beg your pardon. I did not mean to interrupt." She hastily shut the door . . . and fled.

Gwendolyn ran blindly down the hall, yanked the front door open, hurtled through it and down the steps—and ran straight into Bertie.

"I say, Gwen, where are you—"

She pushed past him and hurried to his gelding, which one of the stablemen was leading away.

She snatched the reins from the groom.

Bertie hurried up to her. "I say, Gwen, what's happened?"

"Give me a lift up," she said tightly.

He bent and clasped his hands together. "Don't tell me Cat's gone and bolted again," he said as he hoisted her up. "I thought he'd get on well enough with Eversham, and I was just setting out to let Dain know, when I seen you turn into the drive and never was so astonished in all my life. You were supposed to be in—

"Gwendolyn!"

Bertie swung round. "There he is, Gwen. Ain't gone after all. What was you—"

"Let go of my foot, Bertie."

He let go, but Dorian reached them in the same moment and caught hold of the bridle. "My dear, I don't know what you—"

"I am a trifle . . . out of sorts," she choked out. "I need . . . a ride. To clear my head."

"What you need is a cup of tea," he said soothingly. "I know it was a shock to see Eversham, but I—"

"Oh, I wish he'd never come!" she cried. Her voice shook, and her eyes filled. "But that is silly, I know. It is always better to know . . . the facts. And you have made me . . . so happy—and I love you—and I shall love you always, no—no matter what h-happens." Her voice broke then, and with it the last shred of her control. She wept, helplessly, and when he reached up and grasped her waist and lifted her down, all she could do was cling to him, sobbing.

"I love you, too, sweet, with all my heart," he said gently. "But I do believe you've got this backwards."

"No, I heard," she sobbed. "I heard what Eversham said—and he knows. He's a p-proper doctor. Incurable, he said. Kneebones was right and I was wrong, and I should have known b-better."

"Backwards, indeed," Dorian said as he threaded his fingers through her hair. "The London experts, Borson, and Kneebones all got it wrong. So did I. You knew better than any of us. I feel like an utter dolt. But your Mr. Eversham says my brain is functioning and one cannot inherit concussion, and so I collect you are stuck with me—and my confounded megrims—indefinitely."

She lifted her head, and through her tears, she saw the truth glimmering in his golden eyes. "M-m-megrims?"

"Migraine, he calls it," Dorian said. "Providence has played you another joke, I'm afraid. You came all this way to nurse and comfort a dying madman in his last wretched months, and advance the cause of medical science by studying his fascinating case . . ." He smiled. "And you wound up with a perfectly healthy fellow with a boring old headache."

She reached up and stroked her husband's hair back, blinking at him through the tears that continued to fall though she no longer had anything to cry about. "Well, I love you anyway," she said.

She heard the gelding snort, and looked round to see the groom leading the horse to the stables and a worried-looking Bertie hurrying back to her and Dorian.

"By Jupiter's thunderbolts—I say—Good gad,

Cat, what's happened? What's she bawling about? I never seen Gwen do that before."

"It is perfectly normal, Bertie," Dorian answered while he gently stroked her back. "Your cousin is going to have a baby. It makes her emotional."

"Oh. Well. Oh, that is—I mean to say—Oh, yes. Jolly good. Indeed." Gingerly, Bertie patted her head. "Well done, cuz."

"And you may be godfather." Dorian drew back to peer into her face. "That's right, isn't it, sweet?"

Gwendolyn gave a watery laugh. "Oh, yes. Of course Bertie will be godfather." She let go of Dorian's lapels and wiped her eyes.

"And you shall have a lovely hospital, with a lovely new physician with modern ideas," her husband told her as he gave her his handkerchief. "And we shall make tiresome old Kneebones go away, so that he can't interfere or make obstacles or quarrel with sensible people. We shall send him as private physician to the dithering old Camoys ladies at Rawnsley Hall. If their own quacks and patent medicines haven't killed them by now, it's unlikely Kneebones can do them any harm."

She laughed again and wiped her nose—which was probably as red as her hair at present, she thought. And her hair must be a sight as well, judging by Bertie's expression.

"There, you see?" Dorian told him. "She is practically herself again."

Bertie was still eyeing her dubiously. "She's all red and splotchy."

"She simply needs time to . . . adjust," Dorian said. "It turns out, you see, that Gwen will be stuck with me for—oh, heaven only knows how long. Poor girl. She came all this way to comfort a dying madman during his last tragic days—and now—"

"And now it turns out that all Cat's got is a headache," Gwendolyn said. Her voice was still wobbly. She steadied it. "It's only megrims, Bertie."

Her cousin blinked. "Megrims?"

"Yes, dear."

"Like Aunt Claire's spells?"

"Yes, quite like my mama."

"And Uncle Frederick? And Great Uncle Mortimer?"

"Yes, dear."

"Well, then." Bertie's eyes grew very bright. He rubbed them. "But I knew it would be all right, all along, like I told you. Mean to say, Cat, it ain't all right, exactly. Very sick-making. Great Uncle Mortimer bangs his head against the wall. But megrims ain't killed any of our lot yet." He clapped Dorian on the shoulder. Then he took Dorian's hand and pumped it vigorously. Then he hugged Gwendolyn. Then, red-faced, he broke away. "By Jupiter. A baby, by gad. Godfather. Megrims. Well. I'm thirsty."

Then, frantically rubbing his eyes, Bertie hurried on to the house.

An hour later, while Bertie was recovering his emotional equilibrium in the bathing chamber, Dorian stood with his wife, watching Mr. Eversham's battered carriage lumber down the drive.

"We must get him a better carriage," Dorian said. "People judge by appearances, and young doctors have a difficult time inspiring confidence. But a handsome equipage will indicate a profitable practice. If people believe he's greatly sought after, they'll be less likely to doubt his competence."

"You think of everything," Gwendolyn said. "But it is your protective streak—which I am beginning to suspect is a throwback to the Camoys's feudal origins and the lord of the manor looking after all his people."

"Don't be silly," he said. "I'm only being practical. The man will have enough to do between doctoring and supervising the hospital construction,

without having to prove himself as well and get
involved with local rivalries and politics."

"Yes, dear," she said dutifully. "Practical."

"And you will have enough to do, without
having to leap to his defense a dozen times a day—
or bothering me about it. Pregnancy makes you
cross enough as it is. Can't have you antagonizing
all of Dartmoor."

They watched the carriage round a turning behind a hill and descend out of view. "The sun is
setting," he said. "The pixies and phantoms and
witches will be at their toilette, preparing for the
night's revelries."

His gaze returned to her. "Will you walk with
me?"

She tucked her hand into the crook of his elbow
and walked with him into the garden. He took her
to the stone bench where he'd found her quietly
waiting weeks earlier. He sat, taking her onto his
lap.

The sun hovered over a distant hill. Its glow set
fire to the clouds scattered about like goose down
pillows on a celestial bed of blue and green and
violet.

"Do you still want to build in Dartmoor?" he
asked.

She nodded. "I like it here, and so do you. And
Dain and Jessica are near."

"We'll need a larger house if we're going to raise
a family," he said. He glanced behind him at the
modest manor house. "I suppose we could add a
wing. It would not be very grand. But Rawnsley
Hall was grand and it felt like an immense tomb.
Couldn't wait to get out of there. At present, in fact,
I am strongly tempted to forget about repairs and
raze the whole confounded pile."

"You don't like it, but your heir might," she said.
"If you rebuild, you might give it to him as a wedding gift."

He lightly caressed her belly. "Are you sure you've a boy in there?"

"No, but we are bound to have one eventually."

"Even before I realized there would be an 'eventually,' I knew I should be just as happy if it were a girl," he said.

"Ah, well, you have a soft spot in your heart for females," she said. "But you also seem to have a way with little boys, and so I am not anxious either way. You will make a doting, devoted papa. Which is a good thing," she added with a little frown, "because the women of my family are rather negligent mothers. But then, they are always breeding, you see, which is distracting."

"Then I shall look after the children," he said. "Because I should like a great many, and you will have the additional distraction of hospital matters."

She stroked his hair back. "You have a gift for thinking ahead."

"I've been blessed with a great deal to look forward to," he said. "Watching the hospital rise from the ground, for instance. Discovering what modern medical ideas and principles can and cannot achieve. The possibilities. The limitations." He shook his head. "It amazes me how much I've learned about medicine in these last weeks, and how interesting it turns out to be. It even has a sort of poetry to it, and its own logic and riddles, like any intellectual pursuit. And there is the same wonderful feeling of discovery as mysteries are solved. I felt that today, when Eversham explained where your notes had led you." He kissed her forehead. "I'm so proud of you."

"You should be proud of yourself," she said. "You did not put obstacles in my way, though you wanted to—to protect me from myself. Instead, you tried every possible way to help me solve my riddle—by writing to Borson and sending for Eversham."

"Eversham is not like any other doctor I've encountered," he said. "He certainly does have his own ideas. While you were washing your face, I asked him why he had accepted you as a colleague. He told me that in olden times, women were the healers in many communities. But their arts, to ignorant folk, seemed like magic, which was associated with the Devil. And so they were reviled and persecuted as witches." He chuckled. "And so I realized I had been right from the first. I had wed a witch. And he was right, too, for you are a healer. You've healed my heart. That was the part that was ailing."

She curled her fingers round his neck. "You've healed me, too, Cat. You made the doctor part and the woman part fit together."

"Because I love both parts," he said softly. "All your parts. All of you."

She smiled, the sweet everlasting smile, and weaving her fingers into his hair, drew him down and kissed him, slowly, deeply, lingeringly.

While he lingered with her in the warm forever of that moment, the narrow red arc of the sun sank behind the glowing hill. A faint thread of light glimmered on the horizon. The night mists stole into the hollows and crevices of the moors, and the shadows swelled and lengthened, shrouding the winding byways in darkness.

The sharpening breeze made him lift his head. "A beautiful Dartmoor night," he murmured. "At moments like this, it is easy to believe in magic." He met her soft gaze. "You're magic to me, Gwen."

."Because I'm your witch, and you are my devoted familiar."

"So I am." He smiled down at her. "Let's make a spell, sorceress."

She frowned her endearing medical frown.

"Very well. But first you must help me find some eye of newt."

He laughed. Then, cradling his bride in his arms, the Earl of Rawnsley rose, and carried her into the house.

Loretta Chase

LORETTA CHASE was graduated somewhat belatedly from Clark University with a B.A. in English. In the interim, she was a jeweler's clerk, boutique sales clerk, and meter maid. Thereafter she worked at her alma mater. It was while moonlighting as a video scriptwriter that she met her husband, Walter, a video producer, who eventually seduced her into becoming an author. The recipient of several *Romantic Times* awards, she is also a Romance Writers of America RITA Award winner for *The Sandalwood Princess*, and a Golden Choice nominee for *The Lion's Daughter*. The latter was the first in a series of interconnected historical romances, followed by *Captives of the Night* and most recently *Lord of Scoundrels*, which tells Lord and Lady Dain's story. The next book of the series is in progress.

Promises

Lisa Kleypas

To Kirsten with love—
the best maid of honor ever!

1

England
January, 1820

"You're thinking about Chance again," came Elizabeth's exasperated voice. "You're letting the memory of that scoundrel ruin every opportunity of making a good match! It's time to forget him and consider your future."

Lidian Acland turned with a smile and looked into the face so similar to her own. Her mother, Lady Elizabeth Acland, was still beautiful at forty-five, although the loss of her husband a few years before had left an indelible trace of sadness in her soft brown eyes.

"I've thought about my future very carefully," Lidian replied calmly. "I intend to wait for Chance to come back to me, no matter how long it takes."

Elizabeth sighed. "Ever since Chance left a year ago, I've seen you standing alone at balls like this one, acting like a wallflower when you should be dancing and laughing with other young men."

"I don't want any of them." Lidian reached out to her mother and touched her arm placatingly.

"I don't understand your stubbornness," Elizabeth said softly. "I've always known you so well, Lidian, and this isn't like you." They had always been close, especially in the four years since Lidian's father, John, had died of a weak heart. They even looked alike, both of them small and dark-haired, with sherry-brown eyes. They shared the same temperament, practical and sensible. *But I'm not exactly the same as you, Mama,* Lidian thought silently. Even Elizabeth didn't understand the romantic core that harbored the hope, pain, and broken dreams left by Chance Spencer.

Standing together the two women watched the familiar scene before them: couples moving in a sprightly country quadrille, polite young men approaching blushing girls, dowagers and chaperons keeping a watchful eye on their charges. Once Lidian had taken part in the festivities, making eyes at handsome rakes, flirting, waltzing . . . she had loved to dance until her skirts had whirled around her ankles. And then she had met Chance, and her heart had been lost for good. He was the only man she had ever wanted.

"Mama," she murmured, "you must accept that I know what is best for me."

"But you've been buried in the country for most of your life. How can you know what is best? You're making decisions now that will affect the rest of your life. Every young man you turn away might be the one who could make you truly happy."

"I could never be happy marrying a man I didn't love."

"There are other things just as important as love. Kindness, affection, security . . . all the things I had with your father. Passion and romance fade, but friendship wears quite well over a lifetime."

"I'll have all of that when Chance returns."

"I'd like him to return," Elizabeth replied darkly, "so I could tell him what I think of him." She smiled as she spoke, so that it appeared to the other guests at the Torringtons' ball that they were having a light conversation. "Leaving you dangling by your heartstrings for years while he gallivants around the continent—"

"Mama, please . . . we've had this conversation a hundred times before."

Elizabeth reached for her hand and squeezed it. "You know I'm speaking out of concern for you, darling. I don't think you really believe Chance will come back. But you're too stubborn to admit it, even to yourself. You're afraid of being hurt again, and you've decided not to trust any man because Chance Spencer played you false. And it's all my fault that you gave your heart to a scoundrel like him."

"Your fault?" Lidian repeated in surprise.

"Yes. Ever since John died, I've depended on you to help me manage the estate and tenants. When the other girls were dancing and flirting, you sacrificed your best years, sitting behind piles of account ledgers, trying to squeeze shillings from our budget in order to make ends meet—"

"I wanted to help you." Lidian slid an arm around her mother's waist. "If you and I had lost the estate, I would never have forgiven myself. And we've managed very well, I think."

"Perhaps," Elizabeth said, looking troubled. "Unfortunately, you're more naive than most girls your age, Lidian. Forgive me for saying it, but it's true. You have such high ideals . . . you've been sheltered from experiences that might have made you more worldly-wise. Chance saw that, and he took advantage of you. What I don't understand is why you insist on remaining loyal to him."

Having no easy answer to that, Lidian sighed and glanced around the room. The ball was being hosted by the Torringtons in honor of their daughter's seventeenth birthday. Word had been spread that there would be a bountiful supply of bachelors in attendance, and so excited parents from all over Berkshire and its surrounding counties had brought their daughters. However, the Honorable Chauncey Spencer wasn't there, and as far as Lidian was concerned, he was the only man she would ever want.

Was it only a year ago that Chance had courted her so ardently, so tenderly? He had won her heart, and then he had left her. He wanted to experience more of life, he had said. Before he committed himself to the responsibilities of marriage, a wife, and children, he wanted to go on a tour of the continent—but then he would come back to her. He had asked her to understand, and Lidian had pretended that she did. He had asked her to wait for him, and she had agreed. She had been too unsure of herself, too dazzled by him, to protest.

Perhaps her mother was right. Lidian couldn't let herself believe that Chance would never return for her. The problem was, she couldn't seem to forget him, or to go on with her life. No other man had his wicked charm . . . no one else held any interest for her.

"Look over there, Lidian," came her mother's voice. "Do you see the tall gentleman by the door?"

Lidian focused on the stranger, a man in his twenties. Only an avid sportsman would have such an athletic build and sun-bronzed skin. His tawny golden hair had been neatly brushed, but it was already falling over his forehead, above a pair of bright, heavily lashed eyes. Very handsome indeed . . . but he lacked the dark allure of Chance Spencer. He stood with his hand at the waist of a young blond girl, guiding her protectively through the crowd.

"Who is he?" Lidian asked idly.

"I'm certain he is Lord Eric De Gray. I haven't seen him for years—but he's the exact image of his

father, Edgar! And the girl with him must be his
sister Dorothy." Noticing that her daughter's gaze
had fixed on the stranger, Elizabeth warmed to the
subject. "I was closely acquainted with the De
Grays while your father was still alive. We've gone
our separate ways since then, but I still hold them
in great affection. Their eldest child Edward died
not long ago in a riding accident . . . a great pity.
But my, how Eric has matured! I must find a way
to introduce you—"

"Mama, no," Lidian said firmly. "I have no interest in meeting anyone. I agreed to attend the ball
only because you insisted on it."

"But darling—"

Shaking her head, Lidian glided away to the refreshment table, keeping to an unobtrusive path
along the side of the room.

Lord Eric De Gray kept an arm around his sister
Dollie as he guided her through the crowd, deftly
fielding greetings and eager questions. They made
their way toward the refreshment table, through a
sea of smiling faces. He ignored all of them, indifferent to the glances cast in his direction.

"My goodness, Eric," his sister exclaimed breathlessly, "I had no idea you were so sought-after. I
just heard one woman say that you are the catch
of the season!"

"I wonder why," he said cynically, although
they both knew. The family had just been show-
ered with titles that had once belonged to them
decades ago. The titles—and a great deal of property—had been revoked when a De Gray ancestor
had been accused of treason in the English civil
war. Now that it had recently been proven by a
respected historian that the accused man had been
innocent, Parliament had granted the De Grays a
full restitution of all that had been taken from
them.

In the past year they had gone from being poorly landed to considerably wealthy, and reactions from everyone had been the same. The desire to marry a De Gray was at a fever pitch. If his older brother Edward were still alive, Eric would have been free to continue with a relatively normal life. But Edward had died two years ago, and now Eric was the oldest surviving son, first in line to inherit his father's title. It meant nothing to him. He would have given anything to have his brother back. All the status and attention should have been Edward's . . . and he would have handled it with his usual steady wisdom. Instead, Eric was left to assume a position of influence he had never expected or wanted.

Mothers who once dreaded that Eric might take an interest in their daughters now frantically tried to attract his interest in them. Young ladies who had rebuffed him were now all too ready to flirt and bat their lashes at him and agree to anything he wanted. Once he would have been flattered by their attention, but now he took a cynical pleasure in their ardent pursuit. He was determined not to court any of them. He wanted someone who would overlook the De Grays' newfound wealth and see only him, and he wanted the same for Dollie. To protect his sister from fortune-seekers, Eric accompanied her to balls and soirees and social engagements. He kept a watchful eye on her, lending his protection and advice whenever she required them.

"Now you can marry any woman you want," Dollie remarked.

"I have no desire to marry," Eric said. "Not for a long time."

Three young men besieged Dollie, causing her to blush to the roots of her pale blond hair. Eagerly they vied for her notice, procuring glasses of punch and plates of tidbits for her to enjoy. As Eric pulled at the edge of his cravat, which seemed to be cutting into his throat, he caught a glimpse of a girl making her way toward the refreshments. He stared at her, his attention suddenly absorbed.

Her black hair was pulled back in a smooth sweep, away from skin that seemed impossibly pure and polished. Her figure was slim, with half-bared shoulders that gleamed enticingly in the light of the chandeliers. It was a pity she wore such a vacuous look, her face as lifeless as a mask. Pretty as she was, no man would approach a girl who seemed so utterly disinterested in the scene around her. He had met women like her before, beautiful shells with nothing inside. But this one was so striking, with her porcelain skin and glowing dark hair, that he didn't want to believe she was like the others.

"De Gray!" came the voice of his old friend George Seaforth. A short man with cropped red curls and abundant freckles, George had attended school with him when they were boys. Following the path of Eric's gaze, George saw the dark-haired girl and shook his head. "That's Miss Lidian Acland," he said. "Daughter of the late Sir John Acland. Don't waste your time with her, De Gray."

"Why not?"

"She's pining after someone. Apparently she has been for a long time. The rumor is, she's in love with a good-for-naught named Chance Spencer, and she has no interest in any other man. Besides that, she has no dowry to speak of. Since the father died, the family coffers have been dry."

Eric showed no reaction to the statement, aside from an ironic smile. Two years before, the same thing had been said about him. He had been the second son, with only modest prospects. He would certainly be the last to reject a woman based on the size of her dowry. His gaze returned to Miss Lidian Acland, and he wondered what was behind her beautiful, secretive face.

* * *

Just as Lidian reached the refreshment table, she
became aware of a disturbance nearby. A slender
blond—Lady De Gray, if she wasn't mistaken—
had been jostled while holding her punch. The
strawberry-colored liquid had splashed on her
white silk gown. Close to tears, the girl gazed helplessly at the stain, while the three men around her
burst into effusive apologies.

Immediately Lidian moved past the dismayed
men and pulled the girl to a corner, away from
everyone's view. She blotted the stain with a clean
napkin. "It's just a little splash," she said cheerfully, smiling into the girl's distraught face. "Don't
worry, we'll cover it with something. No one will
notice."

The girl was scarlet with embarrassment. "They
was pressing so close—my elbow was jarred—"

"It happens to everyone," Lidian replied com-
fortingly. "I've seen it dozens of times. Once I
dropped a bit of iced cake on my front and left a
smear right on my—well, you can just imagine."
She reached for the pink orchid pinned to her own
bodice, the only ornament she had been able to afford for herself. Carefully she pinned it to the girl's
waist, concealing the punch stain. "There, the
flower looks perfect."

"But your gown is so plain without it," the girl
exclaimed, and then flushed even deeper. "Oh, I
didn't mean—"

"It's all right," Lidian said, stifling a laugh. "Really. My name is Lidian, by the way. Lidian Acland."

The girl gestured to herself. "Dorothy De Gray.
But you must call me Dollie, as my family and
friends do." Managing to recover from her acute
embarrassment, Dollie smiled back at her. "You're
very kind."

"Not at all—" Lidian began, but her words

caught in her throat as a man approached them.
Eric De Gray, merely handsome from a distance,
was awe-inspiring up close. Except for a small scar
on the side of his chin, his features were perfect.
Lidian was mesmerized by his eyes, the cool green-
gray of a Scottish lake. The irises were rimmed
with charcoal, the dark edge distinct against the
bright, smoke-touched green. His gaze made her
uncomfortable. She looked away with great effort,
feeling hot color rise from her throat.

Eric stared at the wary young woman before
him. The remote mask had settled back on her
face . . . but it was too late. He had seen the way
she had smiled at Dollie, a flash of unexpected and
dazzling warmth. She had given away her only ornament to save his sister embarrassment—and she
could ill afford the loss. Without the orchid, there
were no distractions from the fact that her gown
was cheaply made and slightly yellowed with age.
She intrigued him as no woman had in a long time.
He wanted her to smile again . . . he wanted to hold
her and pull her dark hair loose from its pins.

Dollie introduced them with practiced ease, and
Eric bowed politely. "It appears that you've come
to my sister's rescue, Miss Acland."

She began to edge away, making it clear she had
no wish to converse with him. "It was no trouble
at all, my lord. If you will excuse me—"

He gestured to the crowded floor. "Is this dance
taken, Miss Acland?"

She hesitated and made a show of fumbling with
her dance card, separating the thin silver covers to
examine the translucent ivory pages. They were all
blank. "Actually no, but I don't—"

"Please do me the honor." He extended an arm
in a gesture too insistent to refuse.

Smiling in delight, Dollie took the soiled napkin
from Lidian. "Go on," she urged. "You'll enjoy
waltzing with my brother—he's very good." She

winked at De Gray. "I'll go make conversation with the dowagers in the corner."

In the face of their gentle bullying, Lidian could find no way to refuse. Reluctantly she settled her gloved fingers on De Gray's hard, solid arm, and he guided her into the whirl of dancing couples. There was authority in his hands, one of them steady at the small of her back, the other clasped lightly around her fingers. He pulled her into a waltz so swift and smooth that she felt as if her toes were barely grazing the floor.

De Gray's voice was deep and quiet, containing a pleasant trace of raspiness. "There's no need to be skittish."

Realizing she was as stiff as a board, Lidian forced her muscles to loosen. As they danced, many people in the crowd watched them closely. Women snapped open their silk fans and whispered behind them. Acutely aware of the attention they were receiving, Lidian frowned in discomfort.

"Don't you like to dance, Miss Acland?" De Gray asked.

"You would have done better to ask someone else," she said bluntly.

He stared at her quizzically, one brow arching. "Why is that?"

"Because I'm promised to someone."

"You're betrothed?"

"Not formally. But I've given my heart to him." She looked into his eyes and added meaningfully, "He's my one true love."

Rather than looking chagrined, De Gray seemed amused. "Where is this true love of yours, Miss Acland?"

"He's touring the continent at present. But he's coming for me soon."

"Of course," he said in a patronizing tone. "In the meantime—"

"In the meantime I'll wait for him."

"For how long?"

"Forever, if necessary."

"He must be quite a man to merit such devotion."

"Yes, he . . ." Lidian forgot what she had meant to say, as she stared into his green-gray eyes. He had a peculiar effect on her, making her feel slightly off balance. She had never thought to be stirred by someone so unlike Chance. De Gray had none of Chance's boyishly naughty charm, none of his roguish flair. Instead he was self-assured and intimidating. She tried to imagine what De Gray would be like if he were in love. He would be overwhelming. He would have the power to put a woman through hell if he chose. A chill went down her spine at the thought. Thank heaven he didn't have such power over her!

"Tell me about him," De Gray said.

Lidian wrinkled her brow as she tried to find the right words to describe Chance. "He's handsome . . . full of life . . . elusive. He doesn't like to stay in one place for long. He craves excitement and adventure, and he sweeps everyone along with him."

Eric was fascinated by the way her shyness had dropped away for one brief moment, letting him glimpse the romantic soul beneath. She was inexperienced with men—and it was clear what her misguided loyalty to her errant lover would cost her. "When was the last time you were with him?" he asked. When she averted her gaze and refused to answer, he prodded her insistently. "A year? More?"

"One year," she said crisply.

"Does he write to you?"

She refused to show any sign of temper. Her face became as closed and blank as before. "I don't wish to talk about him."

"Certainly, Miss Acland."

Although his tone was polite, Lidian knew very well what he was thinking—that she was a fool, and Chance would never come for her. She wished impatiently for the waltz to end. Arrogant man! He didn't know anything about Chance. He didn't understand the magic that bound Chance to her, and her to him. What they had shared was far out of the ordinary: the sweet, dizzying kisses, the way Chance teased her, the way she had never seemed to stop smiling when he was near. Chance seemed to have walked out from the pages of the romantic novels she had read so avidly, or the poems of passionate longing and love. She wanted nothing less than that.

The music ended with a flourish, and Lord De Gray escorted Lidian to the side of the room, where her mother waited. Elizabeth was calm as she exchanged a few words with De Gray, but underneath Lidian could see that her mother was filled with excitement.

"My lord," Elizabeth said with a smile, "I'm certain you don't remember me. The last time I saw you, you were still a small boy—"

"I recall a little, Lady Acland," De Gray said. "You used to visit and paint watercolors with my mother."

"Yes, that's exactly right! Please tell the duchess I remember her most fondly."

"I hope you'll grace our parlor again soon, Lady Acland. I'll convey your good wishes to my mother." He bent over Elizabeth's hand and kissed it respectfully, then turned to Lidian. There was a teasing glint in his greenish eyes. "Thank you for the dance, Miss Acland."

Lidian gave him a perfunctory curtsy, still smarting from his prying questions and condescending attitude. She turned her back on De Gray as he left them, and sighed with relief that the episode was over.

To her dismay, she saw that her mother's eyes were filled with the eager light of matchmaking. "He's as charming as he is handsome," Elizabeth exclaimed. "And when you danced, you looked so wonderful together—"

"Nothing will come of this, Mama," Lidian said flatly. "He is besieged with hopeful women. And I told him I wasn't interested in marriage."

"You told him *what?*" Elizabeth's excitement began to deflate rapidly. "Lidian, say you're only teasing—"

"It's true. I made him understand that I'm waiting for another man."

"Oh." Elizabeth's forehead was wreathed in disappointment. "All I can say is, I hope you're aware of what you're doing, Lidian. Turning away a man like De Gray, while you pin your hopes on that blackguard Chance Spencer . . ." She shook her head and firmed her jaw. "I've been meaning to tell you about a decision I've made recently."

Lidian shot her mother a wary glance, waiting for her to continue.

"The other day I saw an advertisement for a small house to be let for the season—it's in a good location, a little south of St. James. It will suit us quite well."

"There's absolutely no need for us to lease a London house," Lidian said in bewilderment. "We can barely afford to keep the roof over our heads as it is. Mama, you can't be suggesting that we waste money staying in London in order to find a husband for me!"

"It's not a waste," Elizabeth countered stubbornly. "It's an investment in your future. You only think you love Chance because you've never truly associated with any other men. After some exposure in the city, you'll see how much more life has to offer."

"Mama, this is the most ridiculous notion you've ever had—"

"I've made up my mind."

"We'll be ruined!"

"Perhaps. But at least you'll have had a decent chance at a husband. And if John were alive, I know he would agree with me completely." She walked away toward an empty chair while Lidian scowled after her.

2

Lidian sat in Acland Hall's small library, in the chair her father had once occupied. Painstakingly she totaled the most recent entries in her account books. In the meantime Elizabeth supervised their small staff—two maids and a cook—as they went about their daily tasks of cleaning and mending. Since they could not afford more help, Elizabeth was always busy with tasks that other women of her station were seldom required to do. John Acland had left his family with a tiny inheritance, and an annual income from the estate that barely covered their meager expenses.

Lidian was diligent in her role as estate manager, attending to the tenants' needs as well as those of the Acland family and servants. It was a tiresome responsibility, always scrimping and economizing, never climbing out of debt. The house was beginning to reflect their hard circumstances, but it hadn't yet lost its charm. Acland Hall and all its furnishings were old and worn but lovingly tended. The wood panels were brightly polished, and the faded carpets and upholsteries were kept immaculate.

If only they could restore the house to its former beauty someday! Lidian felt guilty for not having married someone who could make that possible. Her mother deserved an easy, comfortable life. Lidian knew she was being selfish, thinking of her own desires instead of what was best for her family and its dependents. But she couldn't help loving Chance and dreaming of a life with him. And she couldn't bear the idea of a cold, practical arranged marriage.

As she stared at the long list of numbers, written in her own tidy hand, Lidian heard a muffled knock at the front door. One of the maids answered it, and soon afterward came an exclamation of delight from Elizabeth. Curiously Lidian set down her pen and left the library. She went to the entrance hall and stopped in amazement. Her mother and a housemaid were struggling to hoist an enormous flower arrangement onto the mahogany table in the center of the hall.

"How beautiful," Lidian said, her eyes wide with surprise.

Elizabeth rushed to her with a small card clutched in her fingers. "It was just delivered for you. Here, you must read this at once!"

Smiling at her mother's enthusiasm, Lidian opened the card.

With thanks for your gracious gift to Dollie —
Lord De Gray

The arrangement consisted of pink orchids, exactly like the one she had pinned on Dollie's gown last night. Lidian stared in shock at the profusion of costly flowers. No one had ever made such a grand gesture to her before. Slowly she gave the card to Elizabeth and reached for one of the blossoms, pulling it from the arrangement and stroking its delicately arched petals.

"He intends to call on us soon," Elizabeth said triumphantly. "I would stake my life on it."

Lidian hardly knew what to think. "I suppose I would have no objection to that, although I don't see why—"

"Lord De Gray has taken an interest in you, Lidian!" In a flash Elizabeth's mind turned to practical considerations. "We must rearrange the furniture in the parlor and exchange that worn needlepoint chair with the good one upstairs—oh, and the cook must have some cakes and biscuits prepared for when he arrives . . ." She hastened to the kitchen while Lidian stared at the flowers in bewilderment.

Contrary to Elizabeth's excited expectations, Lord De Gray did not come to call. Although Lidian was relieved for her own sake, she became more and more annoyed with Lord De Gray as she saw her mother's hopes deflate day after day. Unfortunately, the episode seemed to have made Elizabeth all the more determined to lease a house in London for the rest of the season. So far Lidian had managed to dissuade her, but she knew her mother hadn't yet given up hope.

Busily Elizabeth sorted through the handful of invitations they received for the next month's events and insisted that Lidian accompany her to a private ball given by friends in London. "We never miss the Willoughbys' annual dance," Elizabeth said emphatically, "and this year it is especially important that we attend."

"Why this year?" Lidian asked dryly.

"Because Lady Willoughby mentioned in her letter to me that several prominent unmarried gentlemen have been invited—including Lord De Gray."

"I have no interest in Lord De Gray or any other man except for—"

"Don't mention his name," Elizabeth pleaded, clapping her hands over her ears. "Promise you'll attend, Lidian. For my sake. *Please*."

The Willoughbys' London town house was elegantly furnished in the French style, with delicate chairs and tables poised against a lush backdrop of paintings and silk-covered walls. The ballroom floor had been polished to a brilliant gleam, while the air was richly scented with beeswax and flowers.

The luxury of the scene made Lidian glad that she had worn her only new dress for the season, a white sarcenet silk overlaid with mint-green gauze. The bodice was cut in the newest fashion, with the waist set at least two inches below last year's style. It emphasized the roundness of her breasts and draped over her hips in gentle folds. She had curled her dark hair with hot tongs and pulled it all up on the crown of her head. An extra number of hairpins had gone into her coiffure in an attempt to secure the mass of silky black curls, most of it too soft and fine to stay confined for long.

Dutifully Lidian exchanged greetings with the Willoughbys and accompanied her mother to the refreshment room. They chatted with friends and ate delicacies from small china plates while music from the adjoining ballroom drifted around them.

Lured by the intoxicating melody, Lidian edged to the doorway and peeked into the ballroom. Couples whirled in time to the music, smiling at each other as they moved in graceful arcs across the floor. She remembered the first time she had ever danced with Chance, at a ball just like this one. He had taken her into his arms without even being introduced, ignoring her startled laughter. "Wh-who are you?" she had spluttered, automatically following his lead. He had been wicked, dark, dashing, unlike the other polite young men who had approached her that evening.

"My name isn't important," he had replied, smiling down at her. "And neither is yours."

"I beg your pardon?" She had been amazed by his audacity.

"All that matters is that we're meant for each other."

"You don't even know me!" she had exclaimed.

"I know that you're the most beautiful girl I've ever seen. You can tell me the rest later."

Chance had swept into her life and stolen her heart with a seductive charm that would be impossible for anyone else to equal. He had made her feel beautiful, desirable, special. Wistfully Lidian watched the dancers, her mind consumed with the past. "Come back to me, Chance," she whispered. "Come back—"

"Miss Acland." A quiet voice startled her from her thoughts. She looked up with a start and saw Lord Eric De Gray standing before her. He was as handsome as she remembered, with aquiline features and a gaze that seemed to read her every thought. His dark golden hair was brushed back from his face, but a lock threatened to fall over his forehead. He was striking and elegant in a dark blue coat, a stiff white cravat, and beige pantaloons. Even in his relaxed stillness, there was a sense of force and energy about him that made her want to step back.

"Still pining after your absent lover?" he asked.

"I'm not pining," she said with great dignity. "I'm waiting."

"Can you be so certain he's not with someone else, Miss Acland? There might be another woman in his arms this very moment."

She responded to his taunt with a frosty look. "I'm beginning to find your conversation offensive,

Lord De Gray." She paused and added reluctantly, "But thank you for the flowers."

He smiled, extending his hand to her. "Favor me with a dance, Miss Acland."

"I can't. I'm sorry." She looked away from him, clutching the small silver dance card in her fist.

Rather than argue, he shrugged. "Very well. My regards to you and your mother."

"Thank you," she murmured, and watched him walk away. She experienced a moment of regret, knowing that one dance wouldn't have signified anything. Perhaps she might even have enjoyed it. But she didn't want to encourage De Gray or give her mother false hopes.

"Lidian?" Her mother appeared at her side. "I saw you speaking with Lord De Gray! What did he say?"

"Nothing, Mama. He merely wished to convey his regards."

There were ripples of feminine excitement across the room as De Gray approached a group of young women and their chaperons. His sister Dollie was there, taking his arm and drawing him into a conversation with some of her companions. After a few minutes, he escorted an attractive blond to the center of the room, bowed perfunctorily, and took her in his arms for a waltz. De Gray was an exceptionally good dancer, showing off his partner to advantage.

Lidian tore her gaze from the sight and struggled with doubt and an unreasonable twinge of jealousy. For some reason she was suddenly angry with Chance and Lord De Gray and all men in general. She didn't want to watch all these animated girls angling to catch matrimonial prizes—she wanted to be somewhere peaceful and private, away from the music and small talk.

She waited until her mother's attention was centered on a discussion with some old friends, and

then she left the room. Having been acquainted
with the Willoughbys' home for many years, she
had an idea of where she wanted to go. Slipping
by the ballroom, the card room where the old people were fond of congregating, and the hunting
room where the men liked to smoke, she headed
to a set of receiving rooms on the other side of the
house.

Finding an unoccupied parlor, Lidian closed the
door behind her with a sigh of relief. The room was
quiet and dim, except for a burning log on the grate
contained behind the firescreen. She removed her
long white gloves and tossed them carelessly to the
floor, then stretched her bare hands toward the fire.
For a few minutes at least, she would have some
peace.

The door was opened so quietly that she didn't
hear it. All at once the sound of a man's voice startled her, and she whirled around with wide eyes.

"It's not proper for you to be here alone, Miss
Acland."

Lord De Gray came into the room and closed the
door. Dapples of red and gold firelight played
across his features as he approached her, making
the shadows and angles of his face more pronounced. His gaze swept over her figure, sheathed
in white silk with the diaphanous overlay of pale
green gauze.

Trying to recover from her surprise, Lidian answered with a touch of sarcasm. "Neither is it
proper for you to be here with me, my lord. I
would appreciate it if you would leave. I have no
desire for your company."

"There are only two possible reasons for that.
One is that you find me unattractive—and I don't
believe that."

Lidian was both amused and affronted. "You
have quite a high opinion of yourself, don't you?"

"The other is that you think you're in love with another man."

"I *am* in love with another man."

"And no one could make you forget him?"

"Not for a minute."

"No doubt he's the only man you've ever kissed."

"I've kissed dozens of men," she lied coolly.

Sudden laughter gleamed in his eyes. "I wish I'd been one of them."

She wrapped her arms around herself and frowned up at him. "Please leave, my lord."

De Gray reached out to straighten a tiny fold of the green gauze at her bodice. The touch was light but intimate, making her heart quicken uncontrollably. "I hope you're not afraid of me."

"Certainly not," she managed to say, yearning to move away from him but determined to stand her ground. "I'm angry with you."

The touch of playful laughter remained in his eyes. "You'll be even angrier in a moment."

"Why—" She was astonished as she was suddenly caught in his steely arms, her hands trapped between their bodies. Inhaling sharply, she began to cry out, but his mouth was on hers in a hot crush of sensation. She twisted and struggled, but his hold was inescapable. Her head bent back, and a silken lock of her hair slid from the upsweep of curls, falling over her face. A hairpin or two dropped to the carpeted floor. De Gray paused, loosening the pressure of his arms, and he brushed the curl back behind her ear. Lidian stared up at him in shock. "Let me go," she whispered.

His face was suddenly austere, his green eyes veiled by gold lashes. His hand slid behind her neck and gripped tightly while his mouth returned to hers. A chord of denial shot through her—*no*, she belonged to Chance, she would feel nothing for anyone else—but there were no more thoughts as she became a willing prisoner while he possessed her mouth with gently devouring kisses. When he finally lifted his head, she was barely able to stand on her own.

The last man to kiss her had been Chance, and now this stranger had erased that sweet memory. She stared at him while the breath rushed hard in her lungs and her legs trembled beneath her. Although she expected to see insolent triumph on his face, there was nothing except a flash of confusion that seemed to mirror her own.

"Miss Acland—"

Lidian lashed out and felt her palm connect with his cheek. Had she the strength, she would have slapped him harder. The blow caused her hand to sting. She turned away in an effort to flee, but De Gray reached out and caught her wrist. Slowly he brought her stiff hand to his face, and he pressed his mouth to her reddened palm. His lips were hot against her skin.

Stunned by the gesture, Lidian stood there with her hand held stiff in his grip. It was now a secret that bound them, this kiss . . . a memory that must be put away and ignored. The feelings it had aroused would be denied for the rest of her life. She had betrayed Chance, responding this way to a stranger. She was both astonished and ashamed by her own behavior.

His clear eyes held hers as he spoke quietly. "You will forget him, Miss Acland. I'll make certain of that."

Lidian wrenched free of him and stumbled slightly in her haste to leave the room. A quick fumble at the door handle, and then the paneled door swung open, allowing her to escape.

A few days later, the memory of the kiss at the Willoughbys' ball still tormented Lidian. She couldn't stop thinking about Lord De Gray, his mouth on hers, the way he had crushed her against his body. She dreamed about him kissing her again and again while she struggled against him in pleasure and shame. Even worse, her dreams of Chance had faded until she could scarcely remember what he looked like. The image of Chance's dark eyes had been replaced by gray-green ones, and his charming quips were supplanted by the memory of how De Gray had kissed her hand after she had slapped him.

Naturally she hadn't told her mother what had happened—she was too ashamed of herself. Proper young women didn't behave this way, allowing a man she barely knew to take liberties with her. Besides, it would only fuel Elizabeth's determination to find a match for her. Elizabeth was busy making arrangements for them to live in London for the rest of the season, in spite of her daughter's objections.

Chance, you've stayed away too long, Lidian thought wretchedly, laying her head on the cluttered surface of her desk. *Why did you ask me to wait, and then disappear? You must come for me soon.* She didn't know if she could be strong in the face of her mother's insistence and her own weakness. She was lonely and all too vulnerable to temptation.

"Lidian!" Elizabeth burst into the library, her face flushed and her breathing alarmingly rapid. She raised a letter clutched in her fist and gestured with it in a jerky movement. "You won't believe it—read for yourself—"

"What is it?" Lidian asked in concern, rushing to her. "Bad news?"

"No, no, quite the opposite!" Wildly excited, Elizabeth thrust the letter into her hands.

Lidian took the paper and bent over it, reading rapidly. After the first paragraph, she stopped and looked at her mother dazedly. "It's from the Countess De Gray."

"Yes, it's a reply to a letter I sent last week. Go on, read it!"

Dearest Lizzie,

I would like to spare you the trouble of letting a house in London. It is hardly necessary when there are so many extra rooms at De Gray House. I hope you and your daughter will do me the very great favor of coming to stay with my family. It is my conviction that Dollie will greatly enjoy Lidian's companionship, and hopefully the reverse will be true as well!

The household consists of Edgar and myself, Dollie, and Edgar's brother Garrett, who has stayed with us for the past two years, ever since his wife died. I believe it would benefit him, as well as the rest of us, to have two new faces to enliven our situation. I confess, I am also asking for my own selfish reasons. I would dearly love the comfort of a cherished friend who could reminisce with me about earlier, happier days, when your dear husband and my beloved son Edward were still alive. They are still young and vibrant in our memories, aren't they? Please say you'll come Lizzie . . .

Lidian stopped reading and set aside the letter. She spoke in a firm voice. "I can't, Mama. You must do what you think is best, but I won't go."

"Yes, you will," Elizabeth said, turning steely. "I won't have you buried out here when there is an opportunity to go to all the finest balls and parties of the season, and meet every eligible man in London—"

"And what better way to become acquainted with Lord De Gray than to stay with his parents and sister?" Lidian asked sarcastically. "I have no interest in him, Mama!"

"Then choose someone else—take Chance Spencer if he ever returns. But in the meantime, you will accompany me to the De Grays' house and spend the rest of the season there."

"Who will take care of the estate affairs while we're gone?"

"You can do it from London. We'll find a way."

"Mama, this is impractical, inconvenient—"

"For once I want you to be young and irresponsible," Elizabeth said in determination. "You've been robbed of so many precious years! For a few months I want you to have what you should have had, if only your father wasn't—"

"Please don't talk about Papa," Lidian said, her obstinacy fading. Dispiritedly she sat in the chair before the desk and surveyed the piles of work there. "Let's not argue about this, Mama. Won't you just accept that I don't want anyone if I can't have Chance?"

"Accept that my only daughter will have no husband, no children, no home of her own, all because of a scoundrel who made false promises to her? Never!" She went to Lidian and stood over her, staring at her with love and purpose. "Come with me to the De Grays' estate. I'll never ask another thing of you, darling. Do it for my sake, to ease my worry over you. Please don't refuse me, Lidian."

De Gray House was located on Upper Grosvenor Street, bordering Hyde Park in a thick grove of plane trees. The classically designed house was fronted with towering Doric columns and rows of Palladian windows that made every room airy and bright. Inside, the main hall contained a sweeping double staircase that led to the second and third floors. White and ice-blue walls were adorned with burned-gold swags and moldings, and sumptuous paintings in ornate frames. Before Lidian could fully absorb the grandeur of the place, the Countess De Gray appeared to welcome them.

The countess embraced Elizabeth first while Lidian stood back shyly and watched them. Julia, as Elizabeth called her, was a slender and beautiful woman with the same silvery-blond hair as Dollie. "My goodness, Lizzie," she exclaimed, "you haven't changed a bit in the last ten years!"

"Oh, I've changed," Elizabeth replied wryly, surveying her own voluptuous figure. "But you, dear Julia . . . you're as willowy as ever. How can I ever forgive you?"

Julia laughed and turned to face Lidian. "Lizzie, what a beauty your daughter is! She favors you, but I can see a little of John in her as well." She walked forward and put her arms around Lidian, hugging her in a flurry of silk and delicate perfume. "I'm so pleased you've come to stay with us, my dear," she murmured. "Both of my children have taken such a liking to you."

Lidian flushed, not knowing how to reply.

"Lidian!" Suddenly Dollie appeared in a flurry of golden curls, her delicate face glowing. "You're finally here! Come, I'll tour you around the house while the maids unpack your things."

Just then someone else appeared, a tall man with dark hair, who seemed to be in his mid-forties. He came from the first floor hallway, pausing on his way to the grand staircase as he saw them. There were liberal touches of silver at his temples and a scowl on his lean face. He would have been a handsome man, if not for the bracket of lines around his mouth that betrayed a keen cynicism and disappointment with life. "Who the hell are you?" he muttered upon seeing the new arrivals.

Flushing in embarrassment, Julia hastened to smooth over the awkward moment. "Garrett," she said lightly, "these are the guests I mentioned to you before—my dear friend Lady Acland and her daughter Lidian."

His gaze swept over them without much interest, lingering for an extra moment on Elizabeth. Then he grumbled a surly greeting and continued on his way.

Julia winced slightly. "You must forgive my brother-in-law Garrett," she remarked once he was out of hearing. "He's usually more civil than that."

"I should hope so," Elizabeth said crisply, shaking her head in disapproval.

Dollie giggled and led Lidian upstairs while Julia took Elizabeth into the parlor. "I must apologize for Garrett," Julia confided, as they seated themselves on French chairs with delicate curved legs. "He was always charming and agreeable until two years ago, when his wife Audrey died of an unexpected fever. He loved her quite desperately. Losing her was a devastating blow. After the funeral, Edgar and I invited him to stay with us for as long as he wants. He seems to take some small comfort in being with his family, but he's an intensely private man. Much of the time we hardly know he's here." She shrugged gracefully, her mouth touched with sadness. "I doubt Garrett will remarry. Since Audrey's passing he's shown no interest in women—respectable ones, that is."

"Are there any children?"

Julia shook her head. "I'm afraid they were never blessed with children. But Garrett never seemed to care about that as long as he had Audrey. Now he has no one."

Elizabeth felt slightly more sympathetic toward the man, despite his incivility. "It is difficult to grow old without a life's companion," she remarked. "At least I have the comfort of my daughter."

"Will you ever remarry, Lizzie?"

"Heavens, no!" Elizabeth smiled at the notion.

"John was quite irreplaceable. If only I could see Lidian happily married, I would be content to spend the rest of my life with my grandchildren about me."

"But you're still youthful and attractive!" Julia exclaimed. "You could easily find another husband. I know some distinguished men of suitable age and situations—"

"No, no," Elizabeth said with a laugh. "All I want is to find a husband for Lidian. I have no intention of seeking any suitors for myself."

"You sound as stubborn as Garrett! It appears I must focus all my matchmaking efforts on Lidian."

As Lidian and Dollie ascended the stairs, Lidian glanced at their surroundings with a touch of uneasiness, half-afraid that Eric De Gray might suddenly appear. "Dollie," she asked warily, "does your brother live here with the rest of the family?"

"Eric? No, he resides in a town house near Pall Mall." Dollie smiled slyly as she added, "Now that you're staying with us, I suspect he'll visit more frequently."

A frown crossed Lidian's face. "Oh."

Dollie threw her a perplexed glance. "You seem dismayed. Well, I thought every woman in the world had aspirations to catch my brother!"

"Your brother is attractive," Lidian admitted, in the most objective tone possible. "However, I'm already in love with someone."

"Are you?" Dollie made a face. "That's too bad. I would like Eric to marry a girl like you someday. Someone kind and natural and unstuffy. Most women put on such airs around him." Dollie paused and added proudly, "He's the catch of the season, you know."

After a long, enjoyable talk with Julia, Elizabeth went to change from her traveling clothes into a blue day dress. It was a relief to stay at the home of an old friend, gaining a brief respite from the daily worries that she and Lidian usually faced. And this visit would be good for Lidian, if only to broaden her experience and show her some of the possibilities life could offer.

Elizabeth went toward the great staircase that led downstairs, but stopped at a large gold-framed mirror that adorned the end of the hall. Seeing that a few wisps of her hair had escaped their pins, she reached up to smooth them. She preferred everything about her appearance to be neat and controlled, never a hair out of a place or a spot on her clothes. The sound of footsteps was muffled by the Aubusson carpet, and she didn't hear a man approaching until he had almost reached her.

Embarrassed at having been caught primping, Elizabeth turned to face him with a guilty smile. However, her smile faded rapidly as she saw that the intruder was Garrett De Gray. His black eyes simmered with discontent, and his mouth had a hard, sullen cast. He looked untidy, as if he had just arisen from bed and dressed too hastily. She could detect the smell of brandy about him—and it was only the middle of the day!

"Lord De Gray," she said crisply, drawing herself up to her full height of five feet, three inches.

"Lady Acland," he said thickly. "If houseguests must be tolerated, I suppose you'll do."

"I beg your pardon?" Elizabeth said in astonishment. She would have felt sympathy for any other man in his situation, but this insolent creature hardly merited such kind regard.

He responded with a shameless glance up and down her body. "As plump and tidy as a little hen. Widowed in your prime . . . truly a waste. You may visit me at my rooms in the east wing if you're in need of companionship."

"Why, you rude man!" Elizabeth exclaimed, flushing in surprise. "No one has ever addressed

me so disrespectfully—and coming from Edgar's
brother—"

"Edgar and I are nothing alike, thank God. He's
burdened with the proprieties and standards I
never bothered living up to."

"You would do well to imitate him," she said
frostily, and continued past him toward the stairs.

"Would I?" Garrett asked, and laughed nastily
while she hurried away from him. "The east wing,
madam. Don't forget."

3

Eric tapped a restless rhythm on the inside wall
of his carriage. Suddenly his fingertips stilled
on the embossed leather, and his hand clenched
into a tight fist. He was exasperated with himself
for not being able to stop thinking about Lidian
Acland. Perhaps it was because she had shown
such determined indifference to him—he had
never been able to resist a challenge. The memory
of the kiss at the Willoughbys' ball still haunted
him. Her mouth had been so soft beneath his,
yielding sweetly to his urgent pressure. He wanted
more, had wanted it every minute since that night
three weeks ago.

After considering various plans to see Lidian
again, he had asked his mother to invite the Aclands for an extended visit. She had complied without hesitation and had written to him that the
Aclands were now comfortably settled at De Gray
House. *Such a lovely girl,* his mother had written in

her elegant script. *Lidian is shy but very sweet. I am tempted to offer her some of my gowns, or Dollie's, as it appears that she and Elizabeth have brought painfully few clothes and possessions with them. However, they are both proud, and I wouldn't dare risk offending either of them. Call on us soon, my dear . . .*

Eric intended to. He wanted to find out if the attraction between him and Lidian was as strong as he remembered. And if so . . . there was the problem of cutting through the illusions that made her cling so stubbornly to her past love. No man worthy of her would have left her, had there been any choice. To find out more about Spencer, Eric had decided to pay a visit to Craven's, the gambling club on St. James Street.

As a member of the club, Eric occasionally enjoyed trying his hand at the gaming tables and socializing with friends . . . but that wasn't his purpose tonight. Craven's was the best place he knew of to obtain information. The proprietor, Derek Craven, was acquainted with everyone of significance in England and Europe, no mean accomplishment for a cockney who had been born in the gutter. Craven had established the finest gambling club in the world, and he knew exactly how to supply what his patrons wanted. It was rumored that he had every man of means in London investigated, so that he knew all about their inheritances, bank accounts, and property holdings.

Eric's carriage stopped in front of the building, a marble structure fronted with massive columns and pediments. It was part Grecian temple, part bawdy house. There were several forms of entertainment offered at Craven's, including exquisite French cuisine, fine wine and liquor, billiards and cigars, lively music and beautiful house wenches. All of this was intended to stimulate the appetite of the patrons for one thing: gambling. Unimaginable amounts of money were spent nightly at the hazard tables and in the card rooms.

Ascending the wide steps and nodding to the butler, Eric entered the club. Foreign diplomats, aristocrats, politicians, and businessmen all mingled in the famed central gaming room, lined in gilded columns and swaths of dark blue velvet. The room was octagonally shaped and topped with a domed ceiling. Seeing Derek Craven's slim, dark form at the central hazard table, Eric went to join him. Craven greeted him with a friendliness reserved for his wealthy patrons and motioned for an employee to bring Eric a drink.

"Good evening, milord," Craven said in his cockney-accented English. He was a dark-haired man with a hard face and cold green eyes. His white teeth were slightly snaggled, giving his smile a snarling quality. "In for a bit o' play this evening?"

"Perhaps," Eric replied, watching the roll of dice across the green felt of the hazard table. He accepted the snifter of brandy a waiter brought him, and warmed the glass in his hands. "Craven," he said abruptly, "there's something I'd like to ask you."

Craven's black brows rose in silent inquiry.

Eric spoke quietly, not wanting the other men around the table to overhear. "I'm interested in finding out what you know about a certain Lord Chauncey Spencer. He's touring the Continent right now, but I expect he'll return soon."

Craven gave him an assessing glance. "May I ask what your interest is, milord? Owes you some money, does he?"

Eric shook his head and took a sip of brandy. "It involves a woman."

"Ah." Craven's smile appeared again. "She must be a fine bit o' fluff, to please a gentleman so particular as you. Does she belong to Viscount Spencer?"

"In a way."

"I know a little somefing about 'im," Craven admitted. "For almost a month, 'e's come to the club almost ewery night."

"He's back in England?" Eric asked with a touch of surprise.

Craven nodded, his face turning hard. "Spencer plays deep and doesn't pay 'is bills. At this rate, I'll refuse credit to him soon. E's no better than flash-gentry, in spite ow 'is fancy title. Family's well-heeled but not rich. They won't leave much for 'im to inherit."

"Is Spencer here tonight?" Eric asked.

" 'E's in one o' the card rooms right now. Would you like me to show you, milord?"

At Eric's nod, Craven casually disengaged himself from the hazard table and motioned for him to follow. Eric swallowed the remainder of his brandy and gave the glass to a passing waiter. Together he and Craven walked through the octagonal room, past the dining and buffet areas, and approached the long row of card rooms. "The lady you want . . ." Craven remarked idly, "is she Spencer's mistress?"

"No. She believes herself to be in love with him."

"A pretty wench, is she?" Craven asked, seeming to be interested despite himself.

Eric gave him a speaking glance. "Beautiful. With black hair and skin the color of new milk."

Craven made an admiring sound. "Rum goods, it sounds like. I would wish you luck, De Gray, but I don't believe in luck. Only the kind a man makes for 'imself."

"An interesting statement, coming from the proprietor of a gambling club."

Craven smiled and gestured to their opulent surroundings." 'T'isn't luck what brought me all this, milord."

They stopped at one of the card rooms, where blue velvet drapes were parted to reveal a small group of men seated at a round table piled with gambling chips, cards, and refreshments. One of the players boasted loudly as he gathered in an armful of chips. Eric had no doubt that the man was Chance Spencer.

"This is nothing compared to the streak of luck I had on the Continent," Spencer was saying, his cheeks flushed with excitement and strong drink. He was a handsome man with slick black hair and a dark, sculptured face. "Everything I touched turned to gold. There were crowds of women around me, watching each turn of the card . . . they find it very erotic, you know, watching a man gamble—" He stopped as he saw Craven standing at the doorway, and a smug expression settled on his face. "Craven," he said heartily. "I see you've come to witness my success."

"Good evening, gentlemen," Craven murmured, his gaze sweeping the room. "Shall I send fresh cards to the table? More wine, per'aps?"

The five men at the table assured him of their comfort. Eric exchanged greetings with them, recognizing them from the club or from recent society events. One of them stood respectfully to shake his hand. "Lord De Gray," he murmured with a smile, "please convey my regards to your lovely sister."

"I will indeed," Eric replied.

Taking notice of Eric, Spencer stared at him intently. "We haven't met before."

Craven introduced them, and Spencer favored Eric with a charismatic smile. "Would you care to join us, De Gray? I've emptied the pockets of everyone else here."

Eric shook his head. "I'm on my way to the dining room."

"Afraid of losing your money?" Spencer taunted.

Derek Craven grinned at the question and gestured toward Eric. "Our Lord De Gray 'as money to burn. But what 'e wants, 'e can't buy."

"Everything worth having can be bought," Spencer countered. "Even people."

"Except for a few," Eric replied, finding it difficult to believe that this was the man Lidian Acland had given her heart to. Spencer's sort existed everywhere—self-important parasites who survived on the merest fringe of respectability. With a polite nod, Eric made his departure from the card room, wondering grimly why he was so fascinated with a woman who was in love with the likes of Spencer.

Derek Craven followed Eric casually. "Well, now you've met Lord Spencer. No woman in 'er right mind would choose a crowing bantam like Spencer over a gentleman such as yourself."

"Women," Eric said darkly. "Who can understand how they think?"

Craven snorted with amusement. "True, milord. But thank God for 'em, all the same."

Staying at De Gray house promised to be more enjoyable than Lidian had expected. She had never slept in such beautiful surroundings: a bedroom decorated in pale pink damask and delicate scrollwork panels, with satinwood furniture polished to a high gloss. The rest of the house was just as lovely, its elegant rooms kept spotlessly clean and bright.

Although Lidian never forgot her concern with the Acland estate affairs, she found herself putting it to the back of her mind as she and her mother spent a great deal of time with Julia and Dollie. Together they went on shopping trips in London and carriage drives in the park, while at home they made plans and pored over invitations for upcoming society events.

In the past few years there had been no time for Lidian to cultivate friendships with other young women, and she found herself liking Dollie very much. The girl was intelligent and kindhearted, possessing the disarming ability to laugh at her own faults. "I'm too romantic and impulsive for my own good," Dollie laughingly admitted to Lidian. "I seem to fall in love with a new gentleman every week."

"And what becomes of all these infatuations?" Lidian asked with a smile.

"They fade quickly. I haven't yet found the man I'm destined for."

"How will you know when you've found him?"

Dollie chewed her lip thoughtfully. "I'll know when I look into his eyes or when he kisses me. It will be pure magic! Do you feel like that with the man you love, Lidian?"

Lidian hesitated for a long moment. Whatever magic she had felt with Chance had faded long ago. A year of waiting and wondering had taken its toll on her emotions. There was so much that was still unresolved between her and Chance. "I think I did," she said quietly. "But being in love is not all magic, Dollie. And it's not something I'd care to experience again."

Dollie looked intrigued and sympathetic. "Uncle Garrett says the same thing. Now that his wife is gone, there's not enough of his heart left to give to anyone."

"Your poor uncle," Lidian murmured sincerely. Although he could be surly and short-tempered at times, she rather liked the man. There was a softness beneath his gruff facade that she had discovered a few days ago, when he had accidentally intruded on her while she was reading by herself in the library. Embarrassed to be caught with a

novel entitled *Love Lost Forever*, she had jumped
slightly and set the book aside.

Usually Garrett was indifferent to her, but there
was an amused gleam in his dark eyes, and the
lines on his face had relaxed a little. "What are you
reading, child?"

Lidian had flushed guiltily. "A romantic novel,"
she had confessed. It was one of her favorites—she
had read it many times and brought it with her
from Acland Hall. "You must think I'm very silly,
my lord, indulging in idle fancies."

"No," he had interrupted quietly. "Such fancies
can make life very pleasant." He went to pour himself a drink. "Continue with your reading, child.
I'll be gone in a moment."

"Lord De Gray . . . you won't tell anyone, will
you?" She couldn't bear it if anyone else found out
that she had been reading love stories, and teased
her about it. She could only imagine how Eric De
Gray would mock her.

"Certainly not." He had actually smiled. "If you
prefer, you may call me Uncle Garrett, as Dollie
does."

Since she already referred to the earl and countess as Uncle Edgar and Aunt Julia, Lidian had nodded in agreement. "Thank you. However . . . I'm
not certain my mother would approve." It was
clear to everyone that Elizabeth did not hold Garrett in the same high regard she had for the other
De Grays. Elizabeth frequently directed small barbs
at him, criticizing his drinking, his smoking and
gambling, and his habit of coming and going at all
hours.

"Yes," Garrett had said dryly, "your mother and
I don't seem to be on the best of terms."

"I think that is a pity."

"Oh?"

Lidian chose her words carefully, knowing that
Garrett had never seen the side of her mother that

was loving, charming, and vulnerable. All he had seen was the reserved, disapproving facade that Elizabeth adopted whenever he was near. "I know my mother seems to be prim and proper, and rather critical . . . but underneath she is a warm and delightful person. She misses my father terribly, and she's had so much responsibility since he died. If only you . . ." Lidian stopped, having said more than she had intended.

Garrett's expression had been unfathomable, but for a moment there had been a curious look in his eyes. "If only?" he prompted.

"If only you would try talking to her some time," Lidian said earnestly, "I think you would like her very much."

He had responded with a sardonic snort, nodding to her as he departed with his drink in hand. Lidian had wondered if he would follow her suggestion. She soon concluded that he wouldn't.

One evening Garrett brought a guest to share supper with the De Grays, a beautiful woman with white-blond hair, pouting ruby lips, and a lazy, melted-sugar voice. Although she was clad in a dark, high-necked gown, the woman, whom Garrett introduced as Lady Hewet, seemed barely respectable. At supper she slid Garrett long looks through the black fringe of her lashes and told amusing—if shocking—stories about the latest scandals in London.

"Have you heard that Lady Montbain has recently given birth to her fifth child?" Lady Hewet asked with a catlike smile. "A dear little boy with curly black hair."

"How wonderful," Julia replied sincerely. "Lord Montbain must be terribly proud."

"He would be," Lady Hewet said with a throaty giggle, "if the baby resembled him. Unfortunately the child bears a striking likeness to his best friend, Lord Lambert!"

Garrett smiled slightly. Dollie and Edgar looked down at their plates with severe concentration while Lidian felt her face turn pink. She darted a quick glance at her mother, whose lips were compressed so tightly that they appeared to have been sewn shut.

Mama, please don't say anything, Lidian thought, but Elizabeth spoke in a crisp, controlled tone. "Lady Hewet, I fear that such conversation is not suitable for the ears of impressionable girls."

Lady Hewit's red lips curved in a droll smile. "They must learn about life sometime, dear."

"Perhaps," Elizabeth replied. "But not now . . . and not from you."

Lady Hewit's smile disappeared with a twitch, and she turned to Garrett, whispering slyly in his ear, while Julia hastened to find a new topic of conversation.

Later that night, Elizabeth aired her feelings to Lidian as she unpinned her hair at the dressing table. "Garrett De Gray is offensive in too many ways to count," Elizabeth exclaimed, dropping the pins in a heedless scatter. She picked up a silver-backed brush and dragged it through her dark hair in swift strokes. "I can't think why Edgar and Julia allow him to stay here with all of his carryings-on, bringing women of questionable reputation to supper . . . how such a refined family could produce such an abrasive creature is impossible to fathom! Did you see the way he allowed that woman to rub every part of her anatomy against him? And in front of *everyone!*"

Lidian repressed a smile, suspecting that Elizabeth would rather die than admit that she was jealous of Garrett De Gray. "He's not completely objectionable," she said lightly. "You must admit, he is rather attractive for a man in his late forties."

"Is he? I've never been able to see him clearly

through the cloud of cigar smoke swirling constantly around his head."

Lidian laughed. "Poor man. He wants reforming badly, doesn't he?"

"There's not a woman alive with the strength and patience to do it," Elizabeth said darkly, and set the brush on the table. "Certainly not Lady Hewet!"

"Perhaps Uncle Garrett needs the influence of a woman like *you*, Mama," Lidian dared to say, watching her mother's face in the vanity mirror.

Elizabeth seemed astounded by the remark. "Me? . . . I would prefer to have as little exposure as possible to that ill-natured man!"

"I think his bad behavior may be a result of loneliness," Lidian remarked. "It's very difficult to love someone for so long and then lose her—or him—unexpectedly. You of all people can understand that, Mama."

"I would rather not discuss him anymore," Elizabeth said in a no-nonsense tone, and Lidian agreed dutifully.

Seated at one of the mahogany desks in the De Gray library, Lidian added stacks of figures from an account book that had been delivered to her by the temporary estate manager at Acland Hall. She concentrated on the numbers, unaware that someone had entered the room until she heard a familiar voice.

"Miss Acland. What a pleasant surprise."

Lidian rose from her chair with such haste that she nearly knocked over the inkwell on the desk. She stared at Eric De Gray, lean and powerful in his riding clothes. Although she had tried to prepare herself for when they would meet again, she was aware of a breathlessness she couldn't quite control. His self-assurance was formidable as he stood there with a casual smile playing on his lips.

All at once she remembered the way he had kissed her, the warmth of his mouth, the light grip of his hand on the back of her neck. A blush covered her face, and she tried in vain to recover her wits.

"I'm sure it's no surprise to you," she finally said. "You must have known that my mother and I were staying with your family."

"Do the accommodations please you, Miss Acland?" He spoke with such excessive politeness that it almost seemed like mockery.

Lidian nodded cautiously. "De Gray House is magnificent, and everyone has been very kind."

"A fortunate coincidence, that our mothers have renewed their acquaintance."

"Fortunate for whom?" she parried, backing away as De Gray came farther into the room.

His glance encompassed her from head to toe, taking in every detail of her brown-wool-and-corded-silk gown. Was it her imagination, or did his gaze linger at her breasts? The high-necked gown had fit perfectly three years ago, but as she had matured, the bodice had become a little too snug. Unfortunately there hadn't been enough money to have more than one or two new gowns made every season. Lidian stared at De Gray defensively, resisting the urge to cross her arms over her chest.

"You're more beautiful each time I see you," he murmured.

"Lord De Gray . . . I want to make something clear," Lidian said uneasily, ignoring the compliment. "I have come here against my better judgment because my mother was adamant about it. I certainly hope you don't think I have any designs on you merely because I'm staying at your parents' home."

De Gray stared at her speculatively and reached into his pocket. "I happened to find these at the

Willoughbys' ball after you left me. They belong to you, don't they?"

Lidian blushed fiercely as she stared at the pair of white gloves in his hand. They were the ones she had left in the parlor when she had rushed away after he had kissed her. She must have them back, or he could use them to tarnish her reputation. "My lord . . . you wouldn't tell anyone about that night, would you? You must keep your silence—"

"Of course."

"Thank you," she said in relief, holding out her hand for the gloves.

De Gray came closer and touched her chin with his forefinger, nudging it upward until she met his gaze directly. "However, there is a price to pay for my silence."

"A price?" she repeated in confusion, withdrawing her hand.

"Another kiss . . . and this time no slap afterward."

Lidian jerked back from him in outrage. "You are the most shameless, petty, unprincipled—"

"Do you want these back?" he interrupted, dangling the gloves before her temptingly. "Or shall I return them to you at a family supper some night and let you make the explanations?"

Lidian made a grab for them, but he held them high over her head and smiled maddeningly. "What shall it be, Miss Acland?"

Her mind whirled. The thought of letting him kiss her, after all the nights of remembering . . . made her weak with anxiety. But perhaps it wouldn't be the same. She might feel nothing this time. Oh, how she would love to show him that he didn't affect her! She answered in a burst of frustration. "Oh, do it! Do it quickly, and then leave me alone!" She closed her eyes and waited, her lips clamped shut, her nostrils flaring with her rapid breath.

Eric prolonged the moment, enjoying the sight of her upturned face, her fine black brows drawn together in a frown. He cupped her cheeks in his hands, his thumbs smoothing over the downy surface of her skin, his fingertips meeting the silky edge of her hairline. It was exquisite pleasure to hold her again. She flinched at his touch, as if the heat of his hands had startled her, and he felt the pulse in her throat against the heels of his hands.

Lowering his mouth to hers, he kissed her gently, warming her lips until they parted in hesitant welcome. He explored her mouth leisurely, teasing, tasting, until his heart thumped and his body ached with desire. He felt her reach for the lapels of his riding coat, her fingers clutching tightly to compensate for a sudden loss of balance. Breaking the kiss, he stared into her eyes, feeling as if he could drown in the soft darkness.

Somehow Lidian found the strength to pull away from him. "I hope you enjoyed that," she said, striving for a cool tone, as if the kiss hadn't affected her in the least . . . as if she weren't bewildered and shattered by the sensation of their breath and lips and heat mingling.

De Gray smiled and handed her the gloves. "Chauncey Spencer is a lucky man."

"How did you find out his name?" she asked unsteadily.

De Gray spoke in a cool, amused voice. "Miss Acland, the torch you're carrying for Spencer is hardly a secret. A friend told me about it the night of the Torringtons' ball."

For a moment Lidian's mind was blank with surprise. Then anger swept over her. How dare he imply that she was an object of amusement or pity! She twisted the gloves until they were a long rope in her hands. It didn't matter what De Gray and his fashionable friends gossiped about. Let them mock her for having loved Chance—she didn't care what anyone thought of her. She turned back to the account books on the desk. "I have work to do," she said shortly.

But De Gray wasn't ready to leave. "As a matter of fact, Miss Acland, I saw Spencer last night."

It took Lidian several moments to comprehend what he had said. She spun to face him, her mouth open in astonishment. "What?"

"It seems the Honorable Chauncey Spencer has returned from the Continent. I happened to meet him at Craven's last evening. He was playing cards and relating the experiences of his 'grand tour'—"

"You're lying!"

His gaze locked on her face, taking in every nuance of her expression. There was a sudden hard gleam in his eyes, which could have been anger. "No," he said softly. "Your true love is in London, and apparently he hasn't yet taken the time to seek you out."

Lidian felt as if she had been hit in the stomach. "I don't believe you."

"He spends most of his evenings gambling at Craven's—"

"Don't you dare say a word against him," Lidian hissed, "or I'll hate you forever!"

He stared at her in the highly charged silence, his gaze piercing.

"Eric?" came a light feminine voice, and suddenly Dollie appeared in the doorway. "I thought I heard voices in here. So you've finally come to visit! Well, I certainly hope you intend to stay for supper . . ." Her smile faded as she looked from Lidian's defensive posture to Eric's hard face.

Immediately De Gray's expression was wiped clean, and he gave his sister an easy smile. He walked over to her and brushed a kiss on her cheek. "Little sister," he murmured, "I wouldn't dream of missing supper. I want to hear about your latest conquests."

Dollie laughed and pushed at his arm. "Save your charm for Mama and Lady Elizabeth. They're taking tea in the parlor." She threw a hopeful glance at Lidian. "Won't you come, too?"

Lidian shook her head and blindly made her way to the desk. "I must see to these account books."

Dollie's face registered her disappointment. "Oh, dear. I do hope you'll finish soon, Lidian." Slipping her arm through her brother's, she left the room with Eric, who didn't spare Lidian a backward glance. "She has an astonishing head for numbers," Dollie's voice came floating back. "She's as intelligent as she is pretty, Eric . . ."

"Really." De Gray's voice was dry.

After they were gone, Lidian sat down at the desk and stared at nothing in particular. Her mind was swimming with questions. Chance was here, in London. She remembered the way he had told her good-bye, promising that he would return soon, that he would miss her and think of her every day . . . How could he seem so sincere and then *ignore* her upon his return? There must be some misunderstanding, either on her part or his. She had to see him and find out what had happened.

Craven's . . . De Gray had said that Chance gambled there every night. Perhaps he would be there this evening. Some of her anxiety faded, replaced by determination. If Chance was at Craven's tonight, she would find him, and she wouldn't rest until she had gotten an explanation from him.

During supper, Lidian sat quietly at the De Grays' long linen-covered dining table and studiously avoided glancing at Eric. She didn't speak to him except when politeness required. He responded with the same indifference, focusing his attention on his family. Lidian could see that her mother was surprised by her unusual reticence, not to mention the De Grays, who clearly adored Eric. The group laughed and talked animatedly as they discussed the latest social and political events in London. Lidian felt isolated from all of them, unable to think about anything except the fact that Chance was somewhere in the city at this very moment . . . and she would see him soon.

After supper she expressed a desire to retire early to her room, pleading a headache in order to avoid socializing with the De Grays. Dollie followed her, wearing a pucker of concern on her forehead. Together they paused in the central hallway. "Lidian . . . are you all right?"

"I'll be fine after a long night's rest."

"You don't like my brother very much, do you?" Dollie asked sadly.

Lidian hesitated. "I really have no feelings for him one way or the other." She smiled warmly at Dollie. "However, I adore you and your parents."

"We feel the same way about you. Perhaps you would regard Eric in a different light if you spent more time with him."

"Perhaps," Lidian said doubtfully, and hugged her briefly. "Good night, Dollie."

The girl smiled at her and went back to join the others while Lidian ascended the great curving staircase.

Late that night, when De Gray's carriage was gone and the household was asleep, Lidian donned a hooded cloak made of heavy gray wool and slipped out of her room. Her heart pounded as she crept carefully to the servants' stairs and made her way to the first floor. Crossing through the kitchen and the servants' hall, she left through the entrance at the back of the house.

The February air was cold and biting, but the sky was unusually clear with only a few streamers of cloud winding through the star-dotted sky. Lidian shivered and pulled the hood of the cloak over her face as she hurried through the courtyard of De Gray House and out to the street. After a few minutes of walking, she saw the dark outline of a hackney cab rattling toward her. She hurried toward the vehicle, waving her arm. "Here," she called, "over here!"

The hackney came to a stop, and she caught a glimpse of the driver, a wizened little old man wearing a dark knitted cap. "Take me to St. James Street," she said. "To Craven's."

"Aye, milady." He waited until she had climbed into the carriage, and clicked to the horse.

As the hackney traveled toward the south of London, Lidian smoothed her hands over the velvet pouch of her reticule, feeling the shape of coins and rustling bank notes. She had scraped the money together shilling by shilling for emergencies such as this. Glancing at the scenery they passed, she saw dark shapes scuttling in and out of the shadows, pickpockets and prostitutes emerging to mingle with the gentlemen who would devote themselves to an evening's revelry.

" 'T'isn't safe for a pretty young girl to be alone out at night," the driver remarked, turning onto St. James and passing the endless line of carriages stopped in front of the gambling club. The hackney came to a halt.

"I'll be all right," Lidian said, handing him some coins and descending from the vehicle. "Good evening, sir."

"Sir," he repeated with a croak of a laugh, as if no one had ever called him that, and he waited until she crossed the street before the carriage rattled away.

She was intimidated by the palatial white building, the light pouring from the windows, the thoroughly masculine atmosphere. Patrons entered the club in a steady stream, under the watchful eye of a butler at the door. Clutching her reticule, Lidian made her way up the steps. Many curious stares were directed at the sight of an unaccompanied woman approaching the doorway.

"Miss?" The butler regarded her with an imperturbable expression.

Lidian summoned a smile, trying to appear confident. "I believe Lord Spencer is one of the members of your club. Would you see if he is here tonight? It is urgent that I speak with him."

The butler shook his head. "Miss, it is not club policy—"

"Please, ask him to come out here and see me. I don't think he'll mind."

The butler regarded her dubiously, glancing at her hopeful face and her respectable but well-worn cloak. Lidian could almost see his inner debate taking place. He wanted to refuse her, and yet something made him hesitate. She held her breath, hoping desperately that he wouldn't turn her away.

All at once the dilemma was solved by the appearance of a second man. He was small and bespectacled, with an air that revealed him to be an employee with high-standing authority. He seemed mildly surprised to see her on the doorstep and turned to the butler. "Is there a problem?" he asked.

The butler lowered his head and murmured to him, while the smaller man stared at Lidian through his spectacles. Finally the smaller man identified himself as the club factotum and spoke to her briskly. "No women allowed in the club, miss. That is a rule Mr. Craven holds fast to."

"I don't wish to come inside. All I want is for someone to notify Lord Spencer that I wish to speak to him." The thought of being refused made her eyes sting and glisten with unshed tears. "Please, sir."

Both men looked rather alarmed at her expression. "Don't cry, miss," the factotum said hastily. "I'm sure there's no need for that. I will inquire if Lord Spencer is at the club tonight. Your name, if you please?"

Lidian answered in a rush of relief. "I'd rather not say. Just tell him that an old friend is asking for him." She had a feeling Chance was here; she knew it in her bones.

"Very well. If you wouldn't mind waiting here, miss?"

"Certainly," she whispered gratefully.

The factotum disappeared into the club, while Lidian stood back and watched as the butler admitted more members. In a few minutes she saw a man's tall shape in the doorway. Hesitantly she pushed back the hood of her cloak and stepped forward. She heard Chance's familiar voice, overlaid with bewilderment. "What in God's name . . . Lidian? My God, I can't believe you're here!"

He was so handsome, so familiar, with his black hair and striking face. After a year of waiting and dreaming, Lidian couldn't help throwing herself into his arms. She laid her cheek against his shoulder, tears slipping from beneath her lashes. "Chance," she said in aching relief. "Chance, it's really you." Slowly his arms closed around her, and she gave a faint sob at the feeling of being held by him.

When he finally spoke, the smell of wine was strong on his breath. "Good God, I never expected this." A quiver of amusement touched his voice.

"When did you return from the Continent?" Lidian asked, still pressing close against him.

"Just a few weeks ago."

"Why didn't you come for me? There was no word from you, nothing—"

"How is it that you're here?"

Lidian stared at him intently. Was it her imagination, or was Chance slightly less dashing than before? She had remembered him as larger than life, taking her breath away with his masculine beauty . . . but now he didn't seem quite so extraordinary. Yet she still wanted him. Chance was her first and only love, and she could hardly blame him for assuming more human proportions instead of the godlike ones her memory had bestowed on him.

"I'm staying at De Gray house," she told him. "You must call on me, Chance. We have to talk. I've missed you, waited for you—"

"The De Grays," he interrupted, his interest caught. "How has this association come about?"

"My mother and the countess are old friends. Will you come, Chance?"

"Yes, I'll try . . ."

"When?" Lidian was suddenly angry and ashamed that she was pleading with him, her pride in shreds.

"I don't know exactly when. I'm a busy man, darling. Soon, I promise." He smiled down at her and kissed her forehead. "Be a good girl, Lidian, and go now. This is no place for you."

"Perhaps . . ." Lidian began, wanting him to take her home, but he had already turned away. How could he dismiss her so abruptly, so nonchalantly? He went inside the club, leaving her on the doorstep. "You won't come," she whispered. "You have no intention of calling."

Lidian heard the butler's voice as if it were far away, asking if she required him to procure a hackney cab for her. She shook her head and descended the steps. Numbly she approached the street, wanting only to be away from the bright lights of the gambling club. There was a peculiar thunderous sound in her ears as she tried to comprehend that she had seen Chance, spoken to him, and it had been nothing like the dreams she had nurtured for so long. He didn't love her. What they had shared was far less important to him than it had been to her. Confusion, anger, bitterness rushed over her in a blinding tide. The thunder grew louder, and she shook her head impatiently as she walked forward.

All at once there was an angry shout, and she was caught in a viciously painful grip, jerked backward until her balance was lost and she was dragged to the side of the street. Before her stunned eyes, a large carriage with several outriders hurtled by at an astonishing speed. Many wealthy people preferred to travel at such a pace, signifying their own importance with the thunder of many horses and riders. Such a spectacle was certainly impressive, although it was hazardous to anyone unlucky enough to be caught in their path. She had nearly been flattened by them—she had been in too much of a daze to notice their approach.

Turning away instinctively from the sight, she found herself crushed against a man's hard chest. He smelled of shaving soap and linen, and a trace of brandy. For a second she thought it was Chance—he had followed and pulled her out of harm's way—but then she lifted her head and looked at him. "Lord De Gray," she said in astonishment.

Eric De Gray's face was taut and pale, his eyes gleaming with cold fury. He looked as though he were ready to commit murder. "You little fool," he said savagely, giving her a shake that jarred her entire body. "What the hell were you thinking?"

"Lord De Gray," she gasped, her hands coming up to his steely wrists. "You're hurting me—"

"You were walking straight into the path of that carriage," he snarled. "You could have been killed, and hurt several others while you were at it."

"I wasn't thinking," she managed, setting her teeth as he shook her once more. Tears came to her eyes. "Don't, Eric ... please ..." She didn't know why she had used his first name—it had never even appeared in her thoughts. But it seemed to have a miraculous effect on him, calming him instantly. He became very still, staring down at her as he continued to grip her upper arms.

It was a long time before he spoke. "You're all right." It was neither a statement nor a question but something in between.

"Yes." Lidian lowered her face and struggled to keep her tears at bay. "Let me go."

His grip loosened, but he didn't release her. "I happened to be visiting the club tonight. Derek Craven came to me a few minutes ago. Apparently his factotum had told him there was a dark-haired girl at the front entrance asking for Lord Spencer. I knew it couldn't be you, but I decided to have a look, just in case. Why in God's name are you here?"

"Because you told me that Chance was here almost every night."

"Of all the idiotic, reckless ... I didn't think you'd be fool enough to come here alone!"

"Well, I was," she retorted, gazing up at him through a wet blur. "And Chance turned me away. Now I know that all his promises to me were false. I hope you're very h—" The word *happy* wouldn't seem to come out, and she bit her lip hard to keep from breaking into sobs.

Lidian expected him to sneer then and continue telling her what a fool she was ... but instead she felt the light brush of his hand on her hair, and she heard the *ping* of a hairpin dropping to the street.

"Your hair always seems to be coming loose," he murmured, toying with the shiny dark lock that had come free. His touch moved to her cheek, his knuckles drifting over the smooth curve. "You have the power to twist Spencer, or any other man of your choosing, around your little finger. Don't you know that?"

"Oh, of course," she said bitterly, thinking that he was mocking her.

Her dazed misery began to abate, her heartbeat returning to its normal pace. She began to feel more like herself. Pulling away from De Gray, she adjusted her bodice and rumpled skirts. As she reached up to her hair, she discovered that most of her hairpins were falling out. She jabbed them back in tightly, welcoming the tiny needles of pain in her scalp.

"My driver and carriage are waiting nearby," De Gray said as he watched her. "I'll take you back to De Gray House."

Lidian winced. She didn't want to face the coming hours of tossing and turning in her bed, tormented with memories, regrets, and unwanted emotions. "I'll never be able to sleep tonight," she murmured.

There was a long moment of silence, and then De Gray replied casually, "If that's the case, you may as well stay with me."

She glanced at him suspiciously. "What do you mean?"

A calm, slightly mocking expression had settled on his face, as if he were contemplating a proposal he fully expected her to refuse. "Would you like to have an adventure tonight, Miss Acland?"

No one had ever said anything like that to her before. She readied herself for an insult, an offensive proposition—but she couldn't stop herself from asking, "What kind of adventure?"

"Just a small one."

She knew she should refuse immediately . . . yet the temptation to agree was strong. The thought of going back to De Gray house right now, fresh from such crushing defeat, was none too appealing. "What if my mother discovers that I'm gone?"

"You were willing to risk that for Spencer, weren't you?"

"Yes, but . . ." Lidian fell silent, unable to believe that she was hesitating. *Tell him to take you straight home*, she thought. *After all that's happened, you should know what comes of trusting men, no matter how appealing they seem.* She was caught in the position of being unwilling to say no and unable to say yes. She settled for looking up at him helplessly, her brows quirking in a frown.

Suddenly De Gray laughed and straightened her cloak, drawing the hood protectively around her face. "Come with me," he said, making the decision for her.

"Where are we going?"

"The pleasure gardens at Vauxhall."

"I've heard of that place. Aren't there prostitutes there? And thieves?"

"Every kind of person you can imagine," he said, walking her toward the long line of private carriages waiting outside the club.

Lidian was at once worried and intrigued, wondering how she had come to this turn in her life, going to Vauxhall with a man she barely knew, in the middle of the night. "Why are they called 'pleasure gardens'?"

"Perhaps you'll find out," he said in a tantalizing tone.

"Before I agree to go with you, you must promise that you'll be a gentleman."

He grinned and signaled for his carriage. "Unlike the other men of your acquaintance, Miss Acland, I never make promises I can't keep."

4

With all the whispers of decadence and scandal that accompanied the mention of Vauxhall, Lidian had never actually been quite certain what it was. She quickly discovered that an evening at Vauxhall, an area located north of Kensington Lane, was exactly like attending a party—the most amazing party she could ever imagine. She had never been exposed to a large group of such uninhibited people: aristocrats, dandies, ladies, and prostitutes. Music from a large orchestra filled the air while food vendors sold ice cream, cheesecakes, and biscuits. Lines formed at a lottery booth where tickets were sold for a chance to win colorful trinkets.

Lord De Gray paid the extravagant sum of two guineas apiece for them to enter the gardens. Lidian took care not to meet anyone's gaze and stayed close by De Gray's side. However, curiosity soon got the better of her, and she stared at her surroundings with wonder. The gardens were laid out in a pattern of five walkways, some of them covered with awnings and bordered with trees, with gravel or brick underfoot. A cold night breeze whipped around her, and she shivered, glad for the warmth of her thick wool cloak.

De Gray stopped and purchased a narrow black felt mask for her, similar to those many other peo-

ple were wearing. "No proper young lady would
be caught without one," he assured her dryly, "as
well as husbands spending a night away from their
wives, or young bloods who wish to appear dashing—"

"Are you going to wear one?" she asked, letting
him tie the strip of felt behind her head.

He turned her around to face him, adjusting the
mask until she could see through the eyeholes. "It's
no scandal for me to be here, Miss Acland. You, on
the other hand, would be ruined." Noticing that
Lidian's gaze had strayed to a man walking by
with a tray of biscuits, he smiled slightly. "You
must be hungry. You barely touched your supper
earlier."

"I was too nervous to eat. I kept thinking
about . . ." Her voice trailed away as she recalled
how eager she had been to see Chance.

"Forget about that," he said abruptly, and drew
her toward the Grove, where more than a hundred
supper boxes were located. They were filled with
couples enjoying plates of ham, tongue, and
chicken while listening to the orchestra. The music
was loud and invigorating, causing all thoughts of
Chance to fade from Lidian's mind. De Gray seated
her at a supper box, its interior painted with a
country scene by the artist Francis Hayman. The
crowd hummed and sang along as the orchestra
played a popular tune.

At De Gray's gesture, a waiter brought them
plates piled with miniature roast chickens, paper-
thin slices of ham, pastry, and cake filled with layers of cream and berry jam. Lidian applied herself
to the food hungrily, pausing in surprise as De
Gray handed her a glass of wine.

"I'm not allowed to drink wine," she said, hesitating.

De Gray lowered his mouth to her ear. "I won't
tell," he said conspiratorially, his low voice causing
a pleasurable prickling along her spine. She smiled

and accepted the glass, taking a sip of the rich red
vintage. De Gray urged more delicacies on her and
teased her until she couldn't help laughing at his
nonsense. She leaned into the warmth of his side
with increasing trust. The novelty of being in such
a place and receiving the flattering attentions of a
handsome man worked a peculiar spell on her. She
wanted the night never to end. . . . She was in the
middle of an enchanting dream. Fireworks were set
off at the conclusion of the musical performance,
spinning rocket wheels that shot into the sky and
bursts of colored light that unfolded into brilliant
blossoms. Lidian watched in delight while the
crowd cheered at each new display.

Afterward De Gray escorted her from the supper
box and strolled with her toward the Grove. "I
wish I could feel this way forever," Lidian said,
still glowing from the wine and entertainment.

"What way?" he asked, smiling at her excitement.

"As if I had wings!" She sighed suddenly. "Of
course, tomorrow I'll have to come back down to
earth."

De Gray stared at her with dark gray-green eyes,
and for a moment there was a strange touch of
yearning in them. Lidian had the feeling he wanted
to say something to her, make her understand
something important—and yet something held him
back.

Finally he replied in a neutral tone, breaking the
spell. "Tonight isn't over yet." Stopping at the lottery booth, he paid a few shillings for her to draw
a prize. At his urging, Lidian plunged her hand
into a bowl of paper tickets and curled her fingers
around one. She pulled it out and handed it to the
man in the booth.

"A prize for the lady!" the man exclaimed, examining the number on the ticket. He reached behind the counter and retrieved a small object for

her. It was a painted tin whistle strung on a blue
ribbon.

Lidian hung it around her neck and blew it until
she produced a shrill sound. Without ceremony De
Gray removed the whistle from her puckered lips
and tucked it inside her cloak.

"Now, whenever I whistle, you must obey my
summons," Lidian said with a laugh.

De Gray smiled and made a slight bow. "Any-
time, my lady."

She regarded him dubiously. "You won't forget
your promise, will you?"

He stared down at her and stroked aside a tiny
wisp of hair that had caught on the edge of her
mask. "Never."

Lidian didn't protest as he slid his arm familiarly
around her back. They strolled along some of the
walkways, where couples promenaded back and
forth and randy young men ogled the women who
passed. As they neared the end of the Hermit's
Walk, Lidian caught a glimpse of two entwined figures, a man and woman kissing passionately in the
shadows. She blushed and glanced up at De Gray,
who had also seen them. Lidian wondered how
many other women De Gray had brought here, and
if he had ever seduced a girl into forgetting her
inhibitions along one of these shadowed walkways.

"Have you ever been in love?" Lidian asked
shyly, gazing at his austere profile.

"I've felt something close to it, a time or two."

"Perhaps someday you'll know what it's like,"
she said in her most mature tone.

She heard the catch of a laugh in his throat. His
voice was brushed with irony. "I certainly hope
so." They stopped at the most narrow path Lidian
had seen so far. It looked dark and quiet, a tunnel
of shadows and rustling leaves. "That is known as
Lovers' Walk," De Gray said. "Any young woman
foolish enough to venture there is practically beg-

ging for a scandal." He turned to her, one brow
arched mockingly, and gestured to the path. "Shall
we?"

"I don't know," Lidian said, wondering what he
wanted from her. Perhaps he was trying to make
her look foolish, painting her as a timid, silly creature. But she couldn't possibly go in such a place
with him. It was bad enough to be at Vauxhall,
away from the protection of her mother, drinking
wine . . . She should put a stop to it now. She had
no idea what had come over her, behaving so ir-
responsibly.

"Are you afraid?" he asked softly.

"Certainly not!" Lidian tried to reason with herself. What was the worst that could happen? He
might try to make an advance to her . . . and then
she would reprove him, and that would be the end
of it.

Recklessly she started down the path, and he fell
into step beside her. Soon they passed another couple, whispering and exchanging kisses, and Lidian
averted her gaze. She began to feel increasingly
nervous as they were plunged into thicker darkness, the trees blocking all but a few gleams of the
sky overhead.

"It's very late," she commented. "It must be past
midnight."

"Two o'clock, I'd guess."

She tried to think of another topic of conversation. "Will you be attending the Brimworthys' ball
on Friday?"

"I hadn't considered it."

The path became narrower, more intimate, another world away from the bustling, busy city of
London. Unnerved by the silence, Lidian asked
abruptly, "Lord De Gray, are you planning to
make an advance?"

He laughed, stopping and turning her to face
him. "Would you like me to?"

"No, it's just that . . . if you are, I would rather have done with it right away, instead of worrying about it!"

His voice was soft and amused. "You have the least patience of any female I've ever encountered, Miss Acland."

"I'm a very patient person. Just not where you're concerned."

"Why is that?"

"You make me so . . . so . . ." She floundered for the right word and finally settled for *"annoyed."*

"Really." She saw the flash of his white teeth in the darkness. "Well, in the future I'll try to be more agreeable. And since you seem to be so eager for my advances . . ." He bent down to her and brushed a kiss on her lips, as light and soft as the touch of a butterfly's wing. Drawing back, he smiled at her. "Now your adventure is complete."

Lidian laughed, reassured by his casual gesture. "Thank you," she said, meaning it sincerely. He had accomplished the impossible, turning one of the worst nights of her life into something quite enjoyable. Tomorrow she would pick herself up and go on with her life. And from now on she wouldn't be naive. She would never let a man take advantage of her again.

De Gray stared into her upturned face and lightly fingered a lock of hair that dangled at her temple. "I'll take you home now."

After he brought her back to De Gray House in his carriage, Lidian reached her room the same way she had left, through the servants' door and up the back stairs. It wouldn't be long until dawn. She knew she would be exhausted for the approaching day, but she didn't care. She undressed and slipped into bed, pulling the covers high beneath her chin. Later she would think about Chance, about how he had looked and all he had said, but for now her thoughts were filled with fireworks and mu-

sic . . . and the memory of Eric De Gray's arms
around her. "I'll see you soon," Eric had said with
a teasing glint in his eyes as they had parted tonight. "Just to make certain you're recovering."

She knew he was referring to her unpleasant experience at Craven's tonight and her feelings about
Chance. "I intend to recover very quickly," she had
assured him. "I have no illusions left about men. I
won't ever make such mistakes again."

"So cynical," he had mocked, and left her with
a grin.

During the next month there was no word from
Chance, nor did Lidian expect there to be. She
would have preferred to have a great deal of time
alone, to reflect on her past and why she had been
so vulnerable to a man like Chance, but the De
Grays kept her constantly busy with parties and
musical evenings, afternoon calls, and carriage
rides through Hyde Park. She was becoming acquainted with the circles of Julia's and Dollie's
friends, most of them likable and accomplished
women. Her mother seemed happier than she had
been in a long time, and Lidian realized how much
Elizabeth had missed all the social activities they
had enjoyed so many years ago.

Eric De Gray came to visit every few days, and
in spite of her efforts to remain indifferent, Lidian
found herself looking forward to his arrivals. Her
heart beat faster every time she heard his deep
voice in the entrance hall, and when she went to
greet him, she was aware of the insolent but flattering glances he cast down the length of her body.
His manner with her was friendly and teasing, similar to his relationship with Dollie.

On one of De Gray's visits, he lounged in the
parlor with Dollie and Lidian, reminiscing with his
sister about their childhood escapades, particularly
the time they had stolen the gardener's clippers

and applied their budding artistic talents to re-sculpting the hedges in the formal garden. "Poor Edward," Dollie exclaimed, laughing, "he was punished along with the two of us."

"Even though he had nothing to do with it?" Lidian asked in surprise.

"Our parents never discriminated among their children," Dollie replied. "If one was naughty, the others were spanked as well."

"Edward never complained, though." An absent smile crossed De Gray's face. "He was the responsible one, always helping to pull us out of our scrapes, sharing our beatings for things he didn't do."

"What a dear he was," Dollie exclaimed, smiling as she brushed a sudden tear from her eye. "I miss him. Do you still think of him often, Eric?"

De Gray's smile faded, and he picked a stray thread from the soft wool of his trousers. "Always." He kept his face averted and changed the subject. "Would the two of you care to join me in a ride through Hyde Park tomorrow morning?"

"Oh, yes," Dollie said instantly.

Lidian hesitated. She considered any number of excuses but finally settled for the truth. "Thank you, but I'd rather not. I don't ride very well." It had been years since she had ridden a thorough-bred, and certainly nothing comparable to the quality of the mounts in the De Gray stables.

"We'll find a gentle horse for you," De Gray said. "There's a five-year-old in the stables named Lady." His eyes twinkled as he added, "A quieter and more responsive female I have yet to meet."

Dollie laughed and pretended to pummel him for his remark while Lidian shook her head. "My riding habit is old and sadly out of style, and be-sides—"

"Oh, do borrow one of mine!" Dollie exclaimed. "But I can't—"

"No arguments," De Gray said softly.

Before Lidian could reply, Dollie left the room, saying, "I have just the thing, a black habit, form-fitting, with a blue scarf. I'll go see about it now!"

"Wait," Lidian called after her, but the girl didn't seem to hear. Nonplussed, Lidian gave De Gray a wry smile. "Well, it seems I'm going to ride with you tomorrow."

"You'll enjoy it."

A silence fell over them. It was their first opportunity to talk privately since the night at Vauxhall. "What did your brother look like?" Lidian asked suddenly. "I've never seen a portrait of him."

"I have one that was painted of the three of us—Edward, Dollie, and me—when we were much younger. It was my mother's favorite. She had it taken down five years ago when he died. She said she couldn't bear to look at it. It's at my town house now."

"I'd like to see it someday," Lidian said without thinking, and then colored. It sounded as if she were angling for an invitation.

He laughed at her discomfort. "That could be arranged."

She hesitated and asked quietly, "How did it happen?"

Eric understood that she was referring to Edward's death. "A riding accident. He fell during a jump he never should have tried." He stood and walked about the room, pausing to examine the figurines on the fireplace mantel. He glanced at Lidian swiftly. It wasn't easy talking about Edward, but something in her warm brown eyes encouraged him to continue. "I've thought about him every day since. He and I were nearly inseparable. God knows I never wanted to step into his shoes. At times I—" He stopped and closed his hand around one of the figurines, his fingers gentle on the fragile porcelain. "I wonder if I'll spend the rest of my life being a poor imitation of Edward."

"Surely no one's asked you to," she murmured.

Eric shrugged. "Edward was meant to be the next earl and to manage the family's affairs and produce the heirs my father wants. He was born for it, not I. While Edward always made the highest marks at school and conducted himself honorably, I spent my time playing pranks and chasing after barmaids. . . . And now I find myself trying to live up to the damnably high standards my brother set." Eric smiled crookedly. "One of my former friends actually called it a 'stroke of luck,' losing Edward. I've never given a damn about the family fortune or the title. I feel as if I've stolen it all from him somehow." Eric set down the figurine while a wash of uncomfortable heat built beneath his cravat. He hadn't meant to say so much . . . he'd never talked so freely about Edward to anyone. Sensing Lidian's small presence nearby, he turned and discovered that she was standing just behind him.

Her face was soft with compassion. "If Edward couldn't be the one to take care of the family, I'm sure he would want you to. And I know without a doubt that you'll do very well at it."

Eric stared at her wordlessly. Lidian Acland wasn't like any of the shallow, giggling young flirts he had met or like the coolly sophisticated society lionesses his friends had married. She was honest, caring, sincere—and so beautiful that he almost hurt with wanting her. Admittedly she had faults, most notably her stubbornness, but that was fitting justice. Things had always come too easily to him. He had never had to wait for anyone or anything in his life, and now he was finally having to learn patience. *God grant me the strength*, he thought wryly, longing to cup the smooth curves of her cheeks in his hands and kiss her.

Instead, he flicked the tip of her chin with his

finger in a careless gesture. "Have you heard from Spencer?" he murmured, much as he might have asked Dollie about one of her admirers.

Her thick black lashes lowered. "No. I've spoken to my mother about him, though. I told her I'd heard through the grapevine that Chance had returned. I said I had no further interest in him. . . . She was relieved, of course, and said that I deserved better than Chance." Her gaze fell to her hands, her fingers twisting together. "Do you still see him at your club?"

"Occasionally." Eric refrained from telling her that Chance had established himself as an arrogant young ass. Apparently he was earning a reputation as a dashing blade about town. There were frequent rumors concerning his affairs, gambling debts, and even a duel over some aristocrat's wife. As far as Eric knew, few men claimed to respect or even like Chance Spencer, although there always seemed to be a few dandies and wastrels hanging about him. "Is it true, what you said to your mother?" he asked. "Do you have any further interest in him?"

Lidian was spared from having to reply by Dollie's timely interruption, announcing that she had found the perfect riding habit and that Lidian must come try it on at once.

In London society there was no more eagerly awaited harbinger of spring than Lord and Lady Blasedale's annual ball. "They always stage a treasure hunt," Dollie informed Lidian breathlessly, "and all the guests are given the same clue. Last year the prize was a ruby necklace, and the year before a diamond brooch! This is the first year I'll be allowed to participate. Wouldn't it be exciting if either of us was to find the treasure?"

Lidian smiled at the thought. "Yes, it would—

although I rather doubt I would be the one to discover it."

"One never knows," Dollie said, and spent all afternoon speculating on what the treasure could be.

The Blasedales' huge, ungainly mansion seemed to occupy half of Upper Brook Street with its stalwart granite-and-marble facade of carved cherubim and seraphim. Its many fountains were filled with statues of dolphins, winged horses, and other fantastical figures, while each wall was covered with scenes of mythology and history.

Lidian was dressed in her best gown, the green-and-white satin. A strand of pearls borrowed from Lady De Gray had been twined through her dark hair. Her mother and the De Grays had praised her appearance tonight, saying she had never looked so beautiful. But it was Eric De Gray's opinion she was looking forward to the most. "I'm positive he'll be there," Dollie had assured her earlier in the day, and Lidian had crossed her fingers hopefully. She couldn't explain exactly why she wanted to see him so much, but she was giddy with anticipation.

Just before the De Grays had left for the ball, a pristine white box had arrived for Lidian, containing a perfect pink-and-white orchid. There was no message on the enclosed card, only the engraved name of Lord Eric De Gray. Under the smiling regard of the entire family, Lidian had flushed in pleasure and fastened the orchid to her bodice.

Occasionally she touched the fragile petals of the flower as she talked with the other guests at the ball. They were congregating in the ballroom, awaiting an announcement from Lady Blasedale. Lidian's gaze swept the room in search of De Gray, but to no avail. Just as she began to think he might have decided not to attend, he appeared at her side. He was dressed in buff-colored pantaloons, a well-tailored black coat, and a crisp white cravat. "Miss

Acland," he said, his eyes gleaming warmly, and he raised her gloved hand to his lips.

"Thank you for the orchid," Lidian said softly. "It's beautiful."

"It doesn't do you justice." His gaze moved over her in a quick, almost proprietary sweep.

She gave him a shy smile. "Your family seems to think you have taken an interest in me."

"What do you think, Miss Acland?"

She hesitated and said softly, "I'm not certain."

Before he could reply, Lady Blasedale appeared before the assembled guests. The black plumes fastened in her gray hair bobbed merrily as she nodded her thanks for their applause. "Welcome, dear guests, to our annual ball! Tonight we will share a delightful repast, and later I hope the young people will dance until their slippers are worn, but for now—our treasure hunt." She paused as many guests, especially the females, cheered their approval. "The treasure this year is an emerald bracelet." She smiled as she heard the rustle of pleased murmurs. "I have but one clue to offer you as to its location. As you search through the mansion, bear in mind the number *four*." She held up four pudgy fingers to emphasize the point and beamed at them. "Good luck to you all, and if anyone tires of the hunt, please join us for refreshments as we await the outcome. We shall alert you when the bracelet has been found by ringing this bell." She indicated a large silver bell and pulled a silk cord, sending a loud musical peal throughout the room. "The treasure hunt has begun!"

The guests scattered immediately, one man pausing to examine the fourth spindle on the staircase, someone else heading for the fourth picture in the art gallery, and others going to investigate such objects as the fourth pot in the kitchen and the fourth room in a particular hallway. Dollie came to Lidian, her eyes bright with excitement. "Come, let's hurry!" she exclaimed. "I have some ideas about where it could be."

Lidian glanced up at Eric. "Will you join us in the treasure hunt, my lord?"

He laughed and shook his head. "I have every confidence that you and Dollie will find the bracelet. I'll pass the time in the billiards room with friends—"

"And come out reeking of smoke and brandy," Dollie interjected, shaking her head disapprovingly.

Eric gave her an innocent look, as if unjustly accused, and headed toward the billiards room.

Eagerly Dollie tugged Lidian out of the ballroom. "Let's go upstairs," she said. "I happen to know a thing or two about Lady Blasedale. She loves to do needlework, and she has a special sewing room for it. The bracelet could be hidden there or perhaps in the nursery. The Blasedales dote on their children and grandchildren."

"I'll investigate the sewing room," Lidian said.

"I'll locate the nursery, then."

Sharing Dollie's enthusiasm, Lidian hurried to match her pace as they ascended the long staircase. They split apart at the top of the stairs and went on their individual missions.

Just as Eric reached the billiards room, a sixth sense prompted him to glance over his shoulder. A dark figure moved in his field of vision, a man walking through the entrance hall.

"Come in for a drink, De Gray," someone from inside the billiards room called. It was his friend George Seaforth, his face flushed to a shade of red that clashed with his ruddy hair. Eric threw an absent smile in Seaforth's direction. "Later. I believe I'll join the treasure hunt after all."

"I'll wager he's searching for something other than the bracelet," Seaforth remarked, and there was a scattering of laughter as Eric departed. He made his way to the entrance hall and stared at the man, who had already reached the top of the stairs. Eric couldn't be positive of his identity, but he had a fair idea. "Spencer," he muttered, his jaw tightening.

Having found Lady Blasedale's sewing room, Lidian ventured inside and scrutinized the small wooden table and the covered embroidery hoops arranged in a row. Each piece of work was in a varying stage of completion. She checked beneath the fourth hoop from the left and the fourth from the right, finding nothing beneath them. Next she searched through the baskets of colored silk thread that were neatly piled on chairs and footstools. To her disappointment, the bracelet wasn't there. As she prowled around the room, trying to think of anything she had left unchecked, she became aware that someone was standing in the doorway. She turned toward the intruder with an inquiring smile . . . until she heard his voice.

"The only treasure worth finding in this place is you."

Her face turned stiff, and she suddenly felt cold. "What do you want, Chance?"

5

Chance gave her a wicked smile, the one he had always employed to charm his way into getting whatever he wanted. His striking presence, so elegantly dark, seemed to fill the room. "I want to talk with you."

"It's too late for that," she said in a low voice. "Once I might have been interested in what you have to say—but no longer."

He laughed gently. "Don't be angry with me, darling. You have every right to be upset about my past behavior, but I deserve a chance to explain—"

"You deserve nothing," she said fiercely. "And I don't give a fig for your explanations."

"Don't you?" He smiled again, his gaze seeming to take in the disturbed quickness of her breath, the rising flush on her face. "You're not indifferent to me, Lidian, although you're trying hard to convince yourself of it."

"You're right," she said, her eyes glittering. "I'm not indifferent. I hate you because of what you've taken from me."

He appeared momentarily startled. "What have I taken, pray tell?"

She shook her head, refusing to explain. "Just stay away from me. I wish never to see you again."

"How can you say that? Don't you remember what we shared? We were in love with each other, Lidian."

"I thought so," she said, wiping a hot tear that had suddenly trickled down her cheek. "But apparently we were both in love with *you*."

He made a soft sound and moved forward, intending to comfort her. Lidian stepped back, nearly stumbling over a large basket of spools. "Stay away!"

"Let me remind you how it was between us, and then we'll talk. Come into my arms, darling." He paused, however, as he saw the change in her face and realized that she was staring over his shoulder at someone else who had just arrived.

Were she not so upset, Lidian might have laughed at the way Chance spun around to see Eric

De Gray standing there. Ineffectually Chance tried to dismiss him. "De Gray," he said in a pleasant, man-to-man tone, "as you can see, you've stumbled onto a private scene. If you wouldn't mind leaving—"

"Get out," Eric said, his face as hard as a blade.

Chance's mouth fell open in shock. "You don't understand—"

"Out," Eric repeated, staring at him without blinking.

Completely unnerved, Chance began another faltering protest and cast a bewildered glance at Lidian. She turned away from him, wiping her wet cheeks. She heard him leave, the click of the latch as the door was closed. She had never felt quite so defeated, so weary. Perhaps later she would be embarrassed to recall that Eric De Gray had witnessed the humiliating scene, but for now she was numb. With an unsteady sigh, she looked up at Eric. "Thank you," she whispered. "If you don't mind, I'd like to be alone for a few minutes."

Strangely, he seemed angry with her. "You little fool," he said roughly, ignoring her request. "You know he's a worthless bastard. Why can't you let go of him?"

Lidian stared at him through a screen of wet lashes. "Chance came to me at the time I was most vulnerable. He spun all sorts of beautiful dreams, and made me believe in them. And when he abandoned me, everything withered away, and I was left with much less than I had before. Now I don't trust my own judgment." She tried to set her trembling jaw and failed. "I don't know what love is anymore. . . . I thought I did, and I was wrong. All I'm certain of is that I don't want to be hurt again."

"Everyone is hurt, sooner or later. You can't be so damned fragile that you let one man destroy all your trust." As Lidian turned away from him, Eric stopped her. He was close enough that his warm breath touched her temple, and she sensed his tremendous power held tightly in check. "You don't know how much I want to seduce you," he said, his tone quiet and fierce. "I could make you feel things you've never dreamed of. . . . I could make you forget everything except the pleasure you feel in my arms. But I'm not going to take advantage of you. That would make me no better than Spencer. You'll have to come to me, Lidian, when you finally let go of your illusions and decide what you want."

She jerked back in annoyance. "There's no need to speak to me as if I were a child!"

"You are still a child, in many ways. But that doesn't stop me from loving you."

Her mind went blank, and her lips parted in wordless amazement.

Eric stared into her uncomprehending face. "I have from the moment we met. I love you for your beauty and intelligence, your stubbornness, the way you've taken care of your mother and the estate and shouldered responsibilities that any other girl would have walked away from. I love you for all those reasons—and for a thousand more I have yet to discover." His mouth twisted in self-derision. "I'll be damned if I stand by and watch you wring your hands over the likes of Spencer. He's no good—and you know it better than anyone. It's time to be honest with yourself, and with me."

Confused and defensive, Lidian struggled to reply, but Eric reached out and touched her lips with his fingers. The gesture might have been tender, except that his face was dark with impatience. "I can't stay here alone with you," he muttered. "My self-restraint has its limits."

"Wait," she whispered, but he was already heading to the door.

All at once Dollie burst into the room. "Lidian, what has taken you so long? I've just come from the nursery, and—" She stopped suddenly at the unexpected sight of her brother. "Eric, why are you here? Have you decided to join us . . ." Her voice faded as her brother turned away abruptly and raked his hands through his hair. "Oh, dear," Dollie murmured, apparently sensing the tension between them. "I do hope you haven't been quarreling."

Lidian forced herself to smile, although her face felt stiff with the effort. "I'd rather call it a 'spirited discussion.' Shall we continue to search for the emerald bracelet?"

"That won't be necessary," Dollie replied. "The treasure hunt is over."

"Have they rung the silver bell yet?"

"No . . . but they will." Triumphantly Dollie held up her wrist, which glittered richly. The emerald bracelet, far too ornate for a girl of Dollie's age, was clasped around it. "I found it in the nursery, around the fourth little doll in the crib." She paused and asked hopefully, "Do you think Mama will let me wear it?"

Eric glanced at the bracelet. "Perhaps when you're twenty-five," he said dryly.

"Let's go downstairs and announce my victory," Dollie exclaimed, taking Eric's arm. "Come, Lidian!"

Lidian shook her head. "I'll join you later. I would like a moment of privacy to settle my thoughts."

Dollie began to argue, but Eric steered her from the room without a backward glance. "What is the matter . . ." came the faint sound of Dollie's voice, fading as they left.

Lidian reached out and caught the edge of the door, shutting it carefully. She wandered aimlessly around the small room, her mind in a turmoil. Eric

De Gray had said he loved her. She felt a touch of exhilaration, but it was quickly overwhelmed by fear.

She had been afraid ever since Chance had left her—afraid that he didn't love her and that perhaps she wasn't worthy of being loved. To risk her heart again and face the possibility of more pain and rejection . . . the thought made her feel as if she were poised on the edge of a cliff, ready to fall into the endless void below. For the first time she recognized that her professed love for Chance had really been an excuse all this time to protect herself against more heartbreak. But she couldn't let that fear cripple her forever.

Lidian sat at a small sewing table and picked up an empty spool, rolling the cylinder of wood between her hands. When Eric had held her a few minutes ago, he had been a hairbreadth away from crushing her in his arms. The back of her neck prickled in excitement. She had wanted him to kiss her, to claim and possess her with the passion she remembered from before. The wood grew moist between her palms, and she exhaled slowly, realizing she had been holding her breath. It was natural that she should feel such an attraction to him. He was a disarmingly handsome man. But her feelings for him went far deeper than that.

She had seen how protective and loving he was with his family and how they all relied on him. He was not a man to take responsibility lightly, and he was fiercely devoted to the people he loved. She remembered the way he had rescued her the night she had gone to Craven's, and how he had turned the dismal experience into a sparkling adventure. *I never make promises I can't keep,* he had told her, and she knew in her heart that it was true. Lidian's fists clenched around the spool as a feeling of urgency swept over her. She shouldn't have let him go just now. She wanted to be with him, and tell him . . . tell him what?

She lifted a hand to her hair and smoothed it in a distracted gesture, tucking a stray lock behind her ear. All at once everything was clear, as if she had been staring at the rippled surface of a pond that had suddenly become still and smooth. She wanted to tell Eric the truth: that she dreamed about him at night, that lately thoughts of him had occupied her every waking moment. She wanted to know all his secrets and tell him hers in return. Her eyes widened, and the spool dropped from her hand. She *loved* him—and it made everything she had once felt for Chance seem as dim and fleeting as a shadow. How could she not have seen it before?

She stood up in a flurry, desperate to find Eric and make him understand how she felt. "Please, don't let him have left already," she whispered in a brief prayer, hurrying from the room.

The emerald bracelet was displayed for everyone to admire, and Dollie's cleverness was praised until she had turned red with pleased embarrassment. Music from the orchestra in the ballroom began to fill the air, and the Blasedales proceeded with a sedate waltz, inviting their guests to join them. Having seen no sign of Lidian, Eric decided grimly that he may as well take his leave. He had no desire to put up a facade for the rest of the evening, while Lidian did her utmost to avoid him.

Eric sent a servant for his hat and overcoat, and another for his carriage. In short order he conveyed his good wishes to Lord and Lady Blasedale, telling them that he had another engagement to attend. They reacted with disappointment, trying to persuade him to stay, but he refused with a regretful smile. He went to the entrance hall, settled a dark hat on his head, and shrugged into his overcoat.

The cold wind struck him in the face as the butler

opened the heavy front door. Eric stepped outside and thought he heard a soft voice behind him.

"My lord."

He was amazed to discover that Lidian had followed him, dressed only in her silk gown. She bid the butler to close the door, and wrapped her arms around herself as she stared at Eric. Her dark eyes were brilliant in her pale face. She seemed troubled and breathless, as if it took all her will to hold back a flood of words.

"What is it?" he asked, moving toward her.

"I must talk with you right away." She laid a hand on his arm, her fingers digging into his coat. "Please, take me with you."

The idea was unthinkable. Her reputation would be in tatters before the night was through. She had to be desperate to make such a suggestion. "I'll call on you tomorrow at De Gray House," he said, trying to urge her back inside.

Lidian resisted, shaking her head and shivering as a gust of wind bit through her gown. "Our families will be there—they won't let us talk alone."

Eric considered his chances of finding another private place inside the Blasedale mansion and realized it would be almost impossible.

"Your carriage," Lidian suggested while he removed his overcoat and placed it around her shoulders.

"No. If anyone sees you getting into a carriage with me—"

"I don't care." Her tone was quiet but stubborn.

He swore silently. The longer they stood out here debating, the greater their chance of being discovered. "Five minutes," he finally said. "Then you'll go back inside and join the others."

She nodded, her teeth chattering, and he ushered her swiftly down the flight of steps and into the dark interior of his carriage. The footman's expression was impassive as he closed the small door behind them. It was cold in the vehicle, but at least they were shielded from the outside breezes.

"Now," he muttered, sitting opposite her, "what is so damned urgent that you're willing to risk your reputation?"

"You were right about Chance," she said softly. "He is a scoundrel, and I should never have put my trust in him. After I lost my father and then Chance, I felt as if every man I ever loved would slip away from me somehow. I didn't want to lose anyone ever again, and so I tried to protect myself. But I have no choice now—I must take another risk or else lose you." She paused, gathering her courage to tell him the truth. "The first time we met, I began to love you. I didn't want to admit it . . . and I didn't realize how deeply I cared until tonight." Her eyes glittered, and her mouth trembled. "I love you," she repeated. "You're everything I've ever wanted."

Eric longed to believe her, but pride and caution held him back. "You can't be certain of that. At the moment you don't know what's real and what isn't."

She slid into the space next to him, one small, gloved hand curving around the hard edge of his jaw. She leaned close, her soft, seeking lips pressing against his. "Is this real?" she whispered.

Eric closed his eyes, fighting for self-control. Being alone with her in this small, private space was a dangerous proposition. He put his hands on her waist, intending to ease her away. All at once the overcoat fell to the floor with a heavy thud, and her slim, silk-clad body was in his arms. The sight of her bare shoulders and throat was his undoing. His breath caught, and his blood began to thunder in his ears.

"I love you," Lidian repeated, her arms sliding around his neck. "I'll make you believe me . . . Eric . . ." Something wild and pagan rose in-

side her: the need to possess him and match his
will with her own. As if in a dream, she found
herself pushing the hat from his head until it
dropped to the floor. She kissed his forehead, the
bridge of his nose, the lean surface of his cheek,
until he made a smothered sound and turned to
seize her mouth with his own. He kissed her feverishly, his mouth hard and demanding, his large
body tense beneath hers.

His lips slid to her neck, savoring the downy,
tender skin and the swift flutter of her pulse. His
fingers delved beneath the neckline of her bodice,
cupping the round, naked weight of her breast until her soft nipple rose tightly into his palm. He
seemed to relish the small cry that came from her
throat, and he brought his mouth back to hers, his
tongue meeting hers in a hot slide of sensation.

Lidian gasped as he adjusted her against his hard
loins, until the masculine pressure fitted intimately
to her body. The piercing pleasure climbed rapidly,
and she shivered and molded herself tightly
against him, until Eric groaned and tore his mouth
from hers. "Lidian," he said with an effort, even as
his hands moved over her back and hips, "I can't
take any more of this."

Gazing up at him, she dared to brush back a few
locks of hair that had fallen onto his forehead. His
face was taut, his eyes dark and bright with desire.
"You must believe me now," she said, her voice
sounding a shade deeper than normal.

His mouth twisted wryly. "I'm beginning to," he
admitted.

She rested her head on his chest, listening to the
heavy, regular thump of his heart. "Are you planning to propose to me, my lord?"

"Not this evening."

"I would accept, if you did."

Eric laughed suddenly and kissed the soft hollow

beneath her ear. "Impatient wench. You can't accept before I propose."

"When?" she persisted.

He lifted her chin and stared into her flushed face, his eyes gleaming with amusement. "When I'm convinced that you're certain of what you want."

"I told you—"

He silenced her with a brief kiss and reached down to pull the coat back over her body. "You have to return to the ball," he murmured. "With any luck, they won't have noticed that you're missing."

Elizabeth Acland was filled with pleasant speculation as she, Lidian, and the De Grays returned home after the Blasedales' ball. When Elizabeth had first noticed the odious presence of Chance Spencer at the gathering, she had been sick with dread, expecting that he would attach himself to Lidian and monopolize her attention for the entire evening. But Lidian had seemed completely disinterested in him, and they hadn't shared even one dance together. Perhaps Lidian was finally through with Chance and had matured enough not to be deceived by his oily charm. And if that was the case, then perhaps Lidian would view Eric De Gray in a new light.

Too excited and restless to sleep, Elizabeth went downstairs after everyone else had retired. She decided to have a sherry by herself and reflect privately on the changes she had seen in her daughter. It was her greatest wish that Lidian would find a good man to marry and have her own family someday. Cautiously she went into the library and was pleased to discover that a few coals were burning brightly on the grate.

Approaching the sideboard, she poured a small glass of sherry and went to warm herself at the fireplace. Sighing with pleasure and loneliness, she looked upward and raised her glass in a toast. "I have a feeling that everything will be all right, John," she said quietly. "Lidian is maturing into a beautiful and sensible young woman. You would be proud, my dear."

"He would indeed." A voice from the darkness startled her out of her wits. Elizabeth turned quickly, the sherry sloshing from the glass onto the carpet. She saw the figure of Garrett De Gray seated in the high-backed armchair. He held a brandy snifter in his hand and was sipping from it slowly.

Elizabeth turned hot with embarrassment. "How dare you spy on me!"

"As any member of the family can tell you, I come here every evening to finish the day with a brandy."

"You drink far too much."

"Yes, I do," he said evenly, and rose from his chair to take the glass from her nerveless fingers. "Allow me to replenish your drink, Lady Acland. Sherry, is it?"

"There's no need."

He ignored her, going to the sideboard and pouring sherry from a crystal decanter. "Now that we're to be part of the same family," he remarked, "it seems a truce is in order. Please sit with me and enjoy the fire."

"I have no wish to disrupt your private ritual, Lord De Gray."

"It would please me to share your company, madam. In spite of your sharp tongue, you do enliven the scenery somewhat."

"How can I resist such flattery?" Elizabeth asked dryly, and accepted the sherry from him. She occupied the chair next to his, primly arranging every fold of her dress until it was perfect.

Garrett sat watching her, his expression unreadable. "Do you often talk to your late husband, madam?"

"No, not often." She shot him a defiant glance. "However, I sometimes find it comforting."

"Perhaps I should try talking to my wife, Audrey." He smiled slightly. "Although if she's been observing me from heaven for the past two years, I suspect she'd like to give me a good scolding."

"She died of a fever, I understand?"

Garrett nodded and drank deeply of his brandy. "And your husband?"

"His heart." She paused and added hesitantly, "I had thought to grow old with him. I never expected to lose him at such an early age."

"Yes." For the first time they shared a glance of understanding, and Elizabeth realized that Garrett De Gray had remarkable eyes, the rich, dark shade of coffee. "Now that your daughter will be taken care of," he said slowly, "what do you envision for your future, madam?"

"To spend the rest of my life in peace, in the country."

"Exciting," he commented dryly, swirling the brandy in his snifter.

"And what do *you* intend, my lord? To reside in your brother's house for the rest of your days?"

He looked both amused and annoyed. "No, my wasp-tongued little friend. I'll take a house when I'm ready. For now I desire the company of Edgar's family."

Immediately Elizabeth was sorry for her sharp comment. "I don't blame you," she said. "I'm sure it is very difficult to live alone—and they are wonderful people, each in his or her own way."

He smiled at her conciliatory statement. "I would like to offer you an invitation, madam."

Elizabeth tensed, wondering if his invitation would resemble the insulting proposition he had made when she had first arrived at De Gray House.

"Any time you please," he continued, "you may join me here for a nightcap."

Elizabeth inclined her head in acknowledgment and stared at him demurely over the edge of her crystal glass. "Perhaps I will some evening . . . if you endeavor to be agreeable."

"I can do that," he said, and smiled at her—not in the insolent way he usually did but with a friendly twinkle in his eyes.

Elizabeth surprised herself by accepting Garrett De Gray's offer, not once but several times, until it became a habit to join him every evening. The rest of the family knew nothing about their clandestine meetings, and by tacit agreement they kept their budding friendship a secret. Somehow their conversations turned from reminiscences about their marriages to Audrey and John, into far more intimate discussions about their childhoods, their personal feelings, their likes and dislikes.

In the quiet darkness, lit only by the small fire on the grate, it had become easy for Elizabeth to reveal things about herself that she never would have confessed in the daytime. Garrett was similarly forthcoming, allowing her to know the private side of himself that few were privileged to see. He was very different from her husband. John had been a gentleman at all times, quiet and refined, with the gentlest of natures. Garrett, by comparison, told her stories of his past that were colorful and occasionally ribald. He possessed a quality of earthy masculinity that intrigued her as much as it shocked her.

Elizabeth found herself enjoying these private interludes far too much. Two nights ago, however, she had decided that their intimacy had progressed too far. She had become so enthused by his description of Paris, a city she had always dreamed of vis-

iting, that she had exclaimed without thinking,
"Oh, how I would love to see it!"

"Someday I'll show it to you," he had replied,
as nonchalantly as if it were a place to be found at
the end of the street, instead of in a foreign country.
All night after they had parted, Elizabeth had wondered what he had meant. Had he been implying
that they would journey there together? Could he
possibly be assuming that she was in the same cat-
egory as one of his lightskirted female friends? A
love-starved widow—that was probably what he
thought of her. Well, she couldn't allow such a mis-
apprehension to continue. Last evening she had
stayed in her room instead of joining him for their
nightly conversation, and for hours she had waited
miserably to fall asleep.

In the morning she happened to meet Garrett as
they were both heading toward the grand staircase
at breakfast-time. She stopped as soon as she saw
him, feeling terribly awkward.

"Lady Acland," he said with an unfathomable
expression. "You didn't join me downstairs last
night."

Elizabeth stood in the middle of the hallway and
replied uncomfortably. "Yes, I . . . I feel our conversations of late have become entirely too personal. I have decided to put a stop to our evenings
alone."

He frowned and stared at her for a long moment.
"I see."

Elizabeth felt the need to explain further. "I do
enjoy our discussions, my lord. In fact, I look forward to them every night, however . . ." She
paused, wondering how to explain.

He stepped closer, startling her by reaching for
her hand. His large, warm fingers enfolded hers in
a strangely thrilling clasp. "Lady Acland," he said
quietly, "please tell me if I have offended you in
some way."

"No, indeed," Elizabeth replied, suddenly short of breath. Now that he was next to her, his scent drifted to her nostrils, the subtle mix of sandalwood and cigars that had become pleasantly familiar to her.

He stared down at her hand, her skin pale against the darker tone of his. His voice was unusually gentle, and he seemed to choose his words with great care. "Let me assure you, madam, that I hold you in the highest regard. I value all your confidences, as I hope you value mine."

"Of course," Elizabeth managed to say, lifting her gaze to his.

The depths of his eyes were dark and warm. "Don't deprive me of your company, madam. I would sorely miss the sight of your face at the end of each day."

Elizabeth blushed like a girl just out of the schoolroom. She gave him a small nod of assent and took his arm as he offered to escort her to breakfast. A thought flashed through her mind— would John have objected to her associating with such a man? No, she decided, glancing up at Garrett De Gray's strong profile. John might even have liked him. Garrett was a good man, if a trifle blunt and outspoken. Inside he was kind and honorable: it was loneliness that had made him so abrasive.

Soon after the Blásedales' ball, Lidian, Dollie, and the rest of the De Grays attended a day of boating and picnicking on the Thames, hosted by friends of the family. It was a clear spring day, the cool breeze blowing over the water and causing the bright flags on the boats to snap merrily. The women dined on thinly sliced roasts and an array of salads while many of the men filled the various boats on the water.

"Where are Eric, Uncle Garrett, and Papa?" Dollie asked idly, wandering with Lidian past a line of festively colored tents. "Are they on one of the boats yet?"

Lidian shook her head. "I believe they're still on shore, in the midst of that large group conducting a political discussion."

Dollie made a scoffing sound. "Eric once told me that when men are pretending to have political discussions, they are usually talking about women."

Lidian smiled. "I wouldn't be surprised." She caught sight of an archery range beyond the tents, and watched as some of the women expertly shot arrows into the hay-stuffed targets.

"Would you like to try?" Dollie asked, noticing her interest. "It isn't as difficult as it appears."

For the next half hour or so, Dollie tried to teach Lidian the skill of archery while both of them couldn't help laughing at her wildly flying arrows. After missing the target as many times as she had hit it, Lidian handed the bow to Dollie with a wry smile. "I'd better stop now, before I accidentally skewer someone." She lifted a hand to the painted tin whistle she had decided to wear around her neck that day. "I wore this for luck, but I'm afraid it hasn't worked very well. Thank heaven archery isn't a skill one needs in everyday life."

"It's fun, though." Dollie fitted an arrow to the bow and took careful aim. Just then a handsome young gentleman approached her, and Dollie saw him from the corner of her eye. She let the arrow fly, deliberately sending it wide of the target. "Lord Bolton," she said shyly, "perhaps you would care to help with my aim? I can't seem to get the knack of this."

Lidian wanted to laugh. Dollie was extremely proficient at archery and could hit the center of the target whenever she chose. "I believe I'll go keep company with my mother," Lidian said, smiling as she left.

Crossing behind a tent, she enjoyed the cool

breeze that blew on her face and throat. She was dressed in a blue wool gown and a light cape, her dark hair twisted and pinned to the nape of her neck.

"Lidian."

She turned at the sound of a man's voice. To her astonishment, she saw Chance Spencer standing there. He was dressed in dark clothes and a black silk cravat with an ornate gold and diamond pin. His pantaloons were tailored much too tightly, displaying the mound of his manhood just like a male peacock showing its plumage.

Lidian's brows drew together. "What are you doing here?"

"I came to see you," he said easily.

A scornful smile touched her lips, and she started to walk past him without a word. He caught her wrist in a tight grip. "You can't really mean to walk away from me," he said. "Not when every woman in London wants me."

She shook her head in amazement at his conceit and pulled at her wrist.

He refused to release her. "That's quite an accomplishment," he remarked, "landing a De Gray. All the wealth and social standing a woman could desire. Does he know you were mine first, darling?"

"I was never yours."

"That can be remedied," he replied. Before she could react, he clamped his hand over her mouth and locked an arm around her waist. He jerked her forward with astonishing swiftness while she fought to free herself. Chance pulled her past a line of trees, out of view of the boating party. There was a hackney carriage waiting on the road nearby. Dimly Lidian thought she might have heard Dollie calling her name, but it might have only been the echo of her wildly thundering heart.

Without ceremony Chance shoved her into the hackney and signaled to the driver. The vehicle started with a lurch and moved swiftly along the street, taking her away from her family and friends. Collapsing on the seat opposite Chance, Lidian gasped with outrage and fear. "Why are you doing this?"

Chance was maddeningly smug. "Simple, darling," he replied calmly. "I want a duel with De Gray."

She stared at him in bewilderment. "Wh-why?"

"You must have heard of the name I'm making for myself in London. Everyone of importance has heard of me, but I still don't receive the respect I deserve. Men like De Gray look down their noses at me and sneer that I'm not fit company for them. Well, I've come up with a plan to remedy that."

"By abducting me?"

"Exactly. When it becomes generally known that I've dishonored you, De Gray will challenge me to a duel. I've become quite accomplished with the sword, you know. I've studied under the greatest fencing masters on the Continent. I've already killed one man in a duel this year, a petty little squire who felt moved to defend his wife's honor." A boastful smile crossed his face. "When I best someone as wealthy and respected as De Gray, everyone will fear and admire me—and I'll be one of the most acclaimed men in London."

Lidian stared at him as if he had gone insane. "You would ruin me, and either wound or kill the man I love, simply to enhance your reputation? My God, this isn't a game, Chance!"

"All of life is a game," he said lightly.

"You're not a man at all," Lidian said through her teeth. "You're nothing but a cowardly peacock. Attacking a woman you once claimed to love is the lowest, most base—"

"I did love you." He chuckled and shook his head, as if she were a child. "Lidian, don't you understand anything about the nature of men? I meant everything I said to you."

"Then why did you make promises you never kept? Why claim you wanted me and then never come back for me?"

Chance shrugged. "Time passed . . . and I forgot what an enchanting creature you are. But I did care for you, in my own fashion."

"In your own fashion?" Lidian repeated blankly. A brittle laugh erupted from her throat. "God, I was such a fool!" She stared at him with such cold fury that Chance's smile faded, and he shifted uncomfortably. "Take me back," she said.

"I'm afraid I can't do that."

Lidian's voice was very soft. "If you harm Lord De Gray in any way, I'll make certain you pay for it. And if you do provoke him to duel, and he doesn't kill you . . . I will. I swear it on my own life."

Chance stared at her in amazement, and he then laughed. "What a bloodthirsty little wench! I never suspected there was such passion in you. This promises to be quite an enjoyable interlude indeed."

Lidian settled back in her seat, praying silently that Dollie might have caught a glimpse of Chance forcing her into the carriage.

6

Talking with a circle of friends, Elizabeth was surprised when Dollie De Gray approached her with a pale, tense face and drew her aside. "Aunt Elizabeth," she murmured urgently, "something's wrong. It's Lidian . . . I think she is in trouble."

Elizabeth went cold, wrenched with sudden concern. "What is it? Tell me quickly, Dollie!"

"A minute ago I saw her leaving the boating party with someone."

"With whom? Your brother?"

The girl shook her head, looking troubled. "A dark-haired man. I think it may have been Lord Spencer. He rushed her into his hackney carriage, and they ignored me as I called out to them."

"Dear God," Elizabeth said, turning white. It was clear that Spencer would place Lidian in some compromising situation. The matter must be handled quickly and discreetly. "Dollie, you must find your brother for me and tell him immediately."

"Yes, Aunt Elizabeth." Dollie sped away.

Elizabeth stood as still as a statue, frozen with fear for her daughter, unable to believe that such a disaster had taken place. After a minute or two had passed, she was aware of a man approaching her. She glanced upward and made an inarticulate sound as she saw Garrett De Gray's unreadable face. "Lord Spencer has taken Lidian," she began in a faltering voice, and he took her hand in a hard, reassuring grip.

"I was with Eric when Dollie told him," he said quietly. They walked to a small grove of trees, where they could talk without being easily observed. "Everything will be all right, Lizzie. Eric has gone after them, and he'll take care of her."

"If Chance Spencer has ruined my daughter, I'll . . . I'll shoot him," she whispered.

"I'll shoot him for you," Garrett said without amusement.

He was so strong, so capable and concerned, that Elizabeth nearly lost the tight hold on her emotions. "I thought Lord Spencer was finally out of our lives."

Garrett frowned. "I never would have expected Lidian to have the bad judgment to go off with a man like Spencer."

"She's a good girl!" Elizabeth said in a burst of defensive anger. "I brought her up with the highest morals, and she has always behaved with honesty and unselfishness." Tears slipped down her cheeks. "And if you don't believe that, then you and your entire family be damned."

Garrett pulled her into his arms, holding her against his broad chest. "I believe you," he said, in a soft voice he might have used to comfort a frightened child. "Hush, Lizzie. You did a splendid job with her—she's nearly as perfect as you are. Hush, don't cry."

But Elizabeth made no effort to stop her tears. For the first time in the many years since her husband died, she was letting a man hold her, soothe her . . . and it felt strangely right. "You're trying to make a fool of me," she said miserably. "You certainly don't think I'm perfect."

He brushed his knuckle over her wet cheek, catching a tear or two. "Later I'll tell you exactly what I think, Lizzie. After your daughter is safely returned, you and I have a long discussion ahead of us."

"Concerning what?"

"This, among other things."

Before Elizabeth could react, Garrett bent and possessed her mouth with a devastating kiss. When he lifted his head, she was so astonished she could hardly speak.

"Y-you," she stuttered, "are the most insulting, sh-shameless man I've ever . . . to bring this up at such a time . . ."

"Yes, I know." He reached in his coat for a handkerchief. "Take this and blow your nose."

She obeyed, staring at him with eyes as round as

buttons. "You're disgraceful, Garrett," she said, her voice muffled through the square of linen. "My daughter was right—you want reforming badly."

"Only from you," he said, and held her close. "Don't worry," he murmured, "Eric will reach her in time."

"Get away from the window," Chance said as Lidian stared outside. "There's nothing to see . . . and no one will help you."

Lidian ignored him, leaning out the window of the enclosed carriage and gazing at the traffic behind them. Her heart skipped a beat as she saw a horse and rider approaching them at a headlong gallop, the distance closing rapidly between them. It had to be Eric, she thought, and cried out, waving her arm frantically to attract his attention. Suddenly she felt Chance's grip on her arm, yanking her back inside the hackney. Lidian tumbled to her seat and stared at him with satisfaction. "You're wrong," she said breathlessly. "He's coming for me—and he'll make you pay."

Realizing that he was going to be deprived of the opportunity to force himself on her, Chance pounded angrily on the roof to alert the driver. "Don't stop the carriage for any reason," he shouted.

But in less than a minute, there was the sound of shouting outside, and the thunder of the horses' hooves and carriage wheels began to slow. Lidian tried to look through the window once more, but Chance shoved her back to her seat. "Don't move!" he snapped.

The hackney stopped and swayed, and soon the carriage door was wrenched open violently. Lidian scrambled to leave, launching herself at the man who reached inside for her. She gasped with relief as she felt Eric's hard grip at her waist, swinging her down to the road.

"Thank God," she said tearfully, throwing her arms around him. He held her in a brief, crushing grip, and released her, his gaze raking over her. "I'm all right," she said, smiling up at him. She lifted her hand to his face, trying to assure herself that he was real. It was Eric . . . but he wore an expression she had never seen before, so cold and murderous that she flinched. His green-gray eyes were as hard as ice as he watched Chance descend from the carriage.

Lidian's smile vanished, and she broke the silence in a faltering voice. "He . . . wants to duel with you."

Chance tried to summon a cocky smile. "I'd say there was sufficient provocation for that, wouldn't you, De Gray?"

"No duel," Eric said softly. "Although I'd take pleasure in slicing you to ribbons, I won't have her name ruined."

"Then how shall this be settled—"

Before the sentence was finished, Eric reached Chance in one swift stride. His fists landed in a hard, pummeling rhythm while Chance howled in protest and tried to defend himself. The two of them locked in combat and fell to the side of the street, swearing and brawling. Eric slammed Chance's head to the ground and continued to hit him mercilessly, not pausing even when Chance began to lose consciousness.

Lidian rushed to him, urgently calling his name. "Eric, please . . . you must stop!"

Eric paused, breathing heavily as he stared down at Chance's battered face. "Don't ever come near her again," he said thickly, "or I'll finish what I started tonight."

"Never," Chance croaked, his eyes slitting open.

Eric wiped his blood-smeared fists on Chance's

coat and stood up. Slowly Chance eased to a sitting position, groaning as he gingerly touched his face.

"I knew you'd come for me," Lidian said with a wavering smile. Eric glanced at her with no expression and led her to the hackney. She obeyed his prompting to enter the carriage, and wondered why he looked so grim.

"I'm not returning to the boating party," he said. "You'll have to go back alone."

"Wh-what?" Lidian was utterly confused. "You . . . you seem angry with me. Eric, you don't think this is my fault, do you? You can't possibly believe that I went with him willingly!"

"I don't know what to believe," he said coolly.

"I love *you*, not Chance!"

"Not long ago you would have given anything to be with him."

"But everything's different now. I thought you understood." She clambered out of the hackney as he strode toward the chestnut gelding he had ridden. "Where are you going?"

"I don't know," he said over his shoulder. "At the moment I don't care."

Hurt, afraid, anxious, Lidian tried to think of how to convince him to stay with her. He must be made to understand how much she loved him, wanted him, enough that she would *never* have gone anywhere willingly with Chance Spencer. "You must listen to me—"

"I'm in no mood to talk now."

She watched in disbelief as he took the gelding's reins in hand and swung easily onto the horse. "Eric!" she called, but he didn't seem to hear. All at once she remembered the whistle around her neck. He had once promised to come to her whenever she used it. She fumbled with the small object and managed to bring it to her lips. Using all her strength, she blew until it produced a shrill, piercing blast.

Eric stopped at the sound. Slowly he turned his head, and their gazes locked. Lidian didn't dare breathe as he approached her. Eric stared at her with frustration, anger, and an odd flicker of amusement. "What the hell do you want?"

"To be alone with you."

Tension built in the silence that followed. "Later," Eric finally said.

"Now," she insisted softly.

He contemplated her for a moment. Finally he reached a hand down, and she grasped his taut wrist. His fingers closed around her arm, and he pulled her up to the saddle in front of him.

Lidian was filled with relief as she felt his arm close around her, holding her steady as he signaled the horse with the pressure of his thighs. They did not speak for the next few minutes, each of them lost in private thoughts and questions. At the end of the short journey, Eric reined in the horse in front of an elegant town house with an ivory Palladian-fronted facade.

"Is this yours?" Lidian asked.

He nodded, dismounting the gelding and helping her down. A servant appeared to take the horse while Eric escorted Lidian inside with a firm hand on her elbow. The interior of the house was cool and refreshing, the walls tinted cream and pale yellow, with French furniture and hangings of burgundy and gold. Lidian had a brief impression of an imperturbable butler and a pair of servants who politely went about their work and hid any trace of surprise that their master had brought an unchaperoned girl there.

Eric took her to his private suite, a receiving room decorated in cream and slate blue, with a bedchamber visible through the doorway.

"Well?" He slanted her a questioning glance, arching one brow as he waited for her to speak. But his expectant, slightly mocking expression was

wiped clean as Lidian removed her cloak and unfastened the top button of her bodice. Nervousness
made her fingers slightly clumsy, but she progressed to the second button and then the next. She
paused to see if he was watching her and discovered that she had gained his complete attention.

"Chance forced me to go with him," she said,
unfastening yet another button. "It happened so
quickly that I had no opportunity to alert anyone.
I had no choice in the matter." The bodice of her
gown began to sag from her white shoulders. Carefully she removed the blue ribbon from her neck,
and dropped the whistle to the floor. "Chance is a
vain, cruel, shallow man, and I was a fool for ever
thinking I loved him. You're the only one I
want . . . the only man I trust and love and desire."
She eased her arms from the bodice, her upper
body clad only in a thin chemise that revealed the
shadow of her cleavage and the pointed tips of her
breasts. Eric's gaze was riveted on her.

Noticing that he seemed to be having difficulty
breathing, Lidian was encouraged enough to pull
the pins from her hair. It fell in a black silken river
over her shoulders, rippling down to her waist. "I
want to show you exactly how I feel about you,"
she said. "After today there will be no more
doubts."

Eric crossed the room and took her small form
in his arms, crushing the softness and silk of her
against his taut, aroused body. He ducked his head
to her shoulder and pressed his lips to the smooth
white curve. "Lidian," he said hoarsely, "my sweet
love . . . you don't have to do this."

"Do you finally believe me?"

"Yes." He let out a long sigh and smoothed his
hand over her shining hair. "You don't have to
prove anything." He paused and added reluctantly, "We can wait until we're married."

"If that's a proposal, I accept," she whispered,

kissing his ear. Boldly she urged his hand to her breast, beneath the thin covering of her chemise.

Eric made a soft sound and fondled the round weight, his touch gentle and ardent. His mouth twisted in a self-mocking smile. "To hell with waiting," he muttered, pulling her gown the rest of the way down her body and stripping the chemise from her. Lidian trembled with a peculiar excitement as she stood naked before him, a blush spreading from her head to her toes. Eric sealed his mouth over hers while his hands searched over the pale curves of her breasts and hips.

Impatiently he shed his own clothes, tossing them to the floor and lifting Lidian in his arms. Carrying her into the bedchamber, he lowered her to the velvet counterpane and stretched his long body over hers. He covered her breasts with kisses, pausing to bite gently at the sensitive tips and pull them deep into his mouth. Shivering with pleasure, she traced the hard muscles of his back and pressed herself close to him, astonished by the beauty and power of his body. He murmured endearments and praise as he made love to her, fighting to restrain his passion. "I've wanted you for so long, Lidian . . . tried so hard to be patient . . ."

"You don't have to be patient now," she whispered, touching his chest. It was as hard and smooth as marble, warming beneath her small palms. She felt the pounding of his heart and was amazed that she could affect him so deeply. His hand moved over her stomach to the softness between her thighs, and her breath caught as she felt the intimate stroke of his fingers there. His eyes were clear gray-green pools of light, holding her gaze as he touched her in ways she had never imagined. He pushed her thighs apart and lowered his hips to hers, beginning to enter her. There was a hard, moist probing at her very core, and then a deep, startling thrust. She arched in pain and surprise, but he murmured and kissed her, soothing her until she relaxed beneath him.

They were joined completely, their bodies and hearts pressed so close that they seemed like one being instead of two. Lidian wrapped her arms around his neck, surrendering herself completely to him.

He stared into her small face and smoothed back her hair with an unsteady hand. Pushing deeper inside her, he began a rhythm that made her lips part in soundless wonder. She clung to him, twisting beneath him in rising demand, opening herself wider to him, until all at once the tension broke in a climax of vibrant power.

A long time later, she stirred in his arms and said drowsily, "Our families will be worried. We must leave . . ."

Eric pressed his lips against her forehead. "I've compromised you."

"Hopelessly," Lidian agreed, tracing an idle pattern on his chest. Her lips curved with a smile. "I hope you're finally convinced of how much I love you."

"Convince me again," he whispered, and pulled her close.

"You look beautiful," Elizabeth said, dabbing at her eyes with a lace handkerchief. They waited together in a small room at the back of the church while the wedding guests were being seated. Lidian smoothed the skirts of her wedding gown, made of layers of delicate white silk and silver trim. The scooped neckline and puffed sleeves were finished with gleaming touches of silver, and the veil was a simple layer of transparent silk fastened to her hair with white roses.

"I suspect you'll be doing this soon with Uncle Garrett," Lidian said.

"That remains to be seen," Elizabeth replied primly.

Lidian laughed. "Everyone knows the two of you adore each other, Mama. I hope you don't make him wait too long."

Elizabeth returned her smile. "We do seem to get on well together," she admitted. "And I am pleased that you asked him to walk you down the aisle in place of your father, Lidian."

There was a knock on the door, and Elizabeth went to open it a crack. She widened it enough to admit Garrett De Gray, who looked exceedingly handsome in a dark formal coat and butter-colored pantaloons.

Garrett smiled at the sight of Lidian in her wedding finery. "My nephew will be so awestruck by your beauty that he'll hardly be able to speak."

"He had better speak," Lidian said with a mock frown. "At least long enough to say his vows."

"Eric asked me to bring this to you." Garrett handed her a small velvet box.

Lidian took the gift with surprise. Nothing could have pleased her more than the wedding present he had already given to her: his promise to have her family estate restored to all its former splendor. Overwhelmed, she had thrown herself into his arms. "If only you knew how I've dreamed of seeing Acland Hall as it once was," she had said, scattering kisses over his face. "It's the most wonderful thing I could ever ask for ... well, the second-most."

"What's the first?" he had asked softly.

"You," she had replied with a smile, staring up at him with glistening eyes.

As Lidian opened the velvet box, Garrett glanced at Elizabeth with obvious admiration. His gaze traveled over her trim form, clad in a peach silk gown. "I can scarcely tell the two of you apart," he murmured.

Elizabeth rolled her eyes. "Your eyesight must be failing."

Lidian looked inside the box and lifted out a solid gold whistle, covered in diamonds and strung on a long gold chain. She smiled, understanding its meaning, and kissed it impulsively.

"What an unusual little ornament," Elizabeth said, staring quizzically at the whistle. "But you certainly can't wear it with your wedding gown, dear."

"I'll carry it along with my flowers for luck." Lidian picked up her flowers and slipped her arm through Garrett's. "I'm ready," she said, and her mother embraced her before leaving to join the congregation.

Waiting with Garrett at the back of the church, Lidian spoke to him quietly. "I hope you have honorable intentions toward my mother, Uncle Garrett."

"I'm afraid I do," he confided. "The De Gray men seem to have quite a fascination for Acland women."

"Thank heaven for that," she said with a smile, and walked with him to the altar, where Eric stood waiting.

Lisa Kleypas

After graduating from Wellesley College with a political science degree, LISA KLEYPAS decided to make writing her full-time career. She is a former Miss Massachusetts and competed in the 1985 Miss America Pageant. Lisa's bestselling novels with Avon are *Only in Your Arms, Only With Your Love, Then Came You, Dreaming of You, Midnight Angel,* and *Prince of Dreams*. Recently married to an environmental scientist, Lisa and her husband live in Houston, Texas.

The Kiss

Kathleen E. Woodiwiss

The milliner's face glowed with cheerful enthusiasm as she handed a large, ribbon-bedecked hatbox to the tall, dark-haired man. "I hope Miss Heather will be pleased with her new bonnet, Mr. Jeffrey. I'm convinced it's one of my finest creations."

"You've certainly outdone yourself this time, Mrs. Brewster," Jeff Birmingham agreed. " 'Tis nigh impossible for me to imagine my sister-in-law looking less than radiant in any gift of clothing I buy her, but you always create something exceptional for me to give her for her birthday. I'm indebted to you."

"As I should be to you, Mr. Jeffrey, for what you and your lovely family have done for me. Miss Heather looks so exquisite in my bonnets, every time she's seen wearing one of them in public, my shop overflows with women wanting something just as fetching. Why, since you've been buying gifts for Miss Heather here, my hats have been selling faster than Mrs. Thompson's peach pies."

Jeff laughed with an amiable ease that was contagious. "I'm delighted to have been of some ben-

efit, Mrs. Brewster, though there's no question in
my mind that your talent is the real reason for your
success. I wouldn't be here today if I hadn't been
tempted by the display of beautiful hats in your
shop window so long ago."

Thelma Brewster vividly recalled the day two
years past when he had come into her shop, looking for all the world like the handsomest man who
had ever been born. He had been on much the
same quest then and, after carefully perusing her
available stock, had described exactly the kind of
bonnet he had been looking for, an intricately em-
bellished piece he had seen in a Parisian fashion
plate. Though she had advised him of the cost involved, certainly more than she had once considered realistic for the area, he had nevertheless
ordered the hat. She had dared more extravagant
designs after that, and as a result, her struggling
business began to thrive. In spite of his refusal to
take any credit for her success, she gave it anyway,
knowing she would never have risked venturing
beyond her humdrum efforts without having first
been challenged by the man.

Since then, she had learned much about Jeff Birmingham, his fine tastes, and his fondness for his
family. She was perceptive enough to realize that
anyone who doted on his sister-in-law as much as
he did would likely coddle his wife as well. That
is, if the handsome rake could ever settle his sights
on a young lady he wanted to marry. No doubt her
business would receive an even greater boost if the
future Mrs. Jeffrey Birmingham happened to be as
winsome as the present mistress of Harthaven,
which seemed a far-fetched feat indeed.

Mrs. Brewster bustled along behind as Jeff made
his way toward the door. "You know, Mr. Jeffrey,
sometimes I think Miss Heather makes it terribly
difficult for you, her being so beautiful and all."

Pausing short of the portal, Jeff turned and raised

a dubious brow, somewhat taken aback by her statement. "Your pardon, Mrs. Brewster. I don't think I quite follow you."

The woman lifted her plump shoulders in an innocent shrug. "You're the handsomest bachelor left in these parts, Mr. Jeffrey." She politely refrained from adding, "And also the richest." "So you must be aware of the tizzy you've created, keeping the whole countryside on tenterhooks. People are simply abuzz with conjecture, trying to guess which one of our fair young ladies you'll eventually be choosing for a bride. Personally, I think you'll have a tall order, finding one as rare and as beautiful as Miss Heather. She and Mr. Brandon are a sight to behold when they come into town, and now, with Miss Heather carrying their second child, you'll have absolutely no chance to catch up with your brother, even if you could find a wife to compare."

Jeff smiled in relief, thankful the woman hadn't started to imagine that he was coveting his brother's wife. A few gossips had been rude enough to insinuate such a thing, and he never failed to be appalled by the suggestion that his love for Heather went beyond the boundaries of a deep brotherly affection. "I'm in no hurry, Mrs. Brewster, and believe me, I'm not trying to surpass my brother. In fact," he lowered his tone as if confiding a well-kept secret, prompting the woman to lean forward in anticipation, "I've been far too busy of late to even think of settling down with a wife, much less lend any consideration to starting a family."

Mrs. Brewster was horrified at the thought of the man remaining unattached. "Oh, Mr. Jeffrey, you just can't let Oakley Plantation go without a mistress now that you've finished refurbishing it," she protested. "Your warehouses and lumber mills will grow mighty tiresome in time if you don't have something better to come home to than a big, ol' empty house."

"I'll consider your advice, Mrs. Brewster," Jeff responded, smiling jauntily as he settled a tall beaver hat over his black, neatly cropped hair. Holding the large hatbox aside, he pulled open the door of the millinery shop and winked at the woman as he paused on the threshold. "But I'm afraid I've come to accept my lot as a confirmed bachelor."

"Oh, tish!" Mrs. Brewster waved away his remark. "I'll believe that, you handsome young devil, when I see you laid in your grave with no widow to mourn your passing. Now, I'll bid a good day to you, sir, before I set my sights on you myself, lonely widow that I am."

Tipping his hat in a debonair manner, Jeff gave her a rakish grin as he stepped back to the boardwalk. "And what a tempting wife you'd mak— *Oooff*!"

His last words were jolted from him as a slender, raggedly clad form crashed into him, nearly knocking him back upon his heels and sending his hat and the milliner's box flying helter-skelter. A frightened screech, definitely of a feminine origin, squelched his startled oath as he struggled to regain his balance and, at the same time, assist the young woman who was teetering precariously toward him on her toes. He straightened to his full height, clasped her narrow waist, and stood her safely upright as he mentally prepared a tactful apology. Then he found himself staring down into the widest, most vivid blue-green eyes he had ever seen in his entire life. A copious wealth of deep auburn hair tumbled in unrestrained confusion around a tear-stained, dirt-streaked face, the sublime beauty of which Mrs. Brewster had just been doubting the existence of.

He was momentarily awestruck as an old famil-

iar dream came winging back to him, one wherein
he found himself running across a rolling meadow,
chasing the love of his life. Though he had often
been haunted by that recurring fantasy, he had
never glimpsed the woman's face ... until now. It
was as if he stood once again on the very brink of
that same illusion and looked down upon a visage
he had both desired and cherished for at least half
a lifetime.

"I beg your pardon, Miss ... ?" He waited ex-
pectantly, hoping she would supply her name, for
he was certain it had to be something superlative
to do justice to the bearer of it, but his words seemingly fell on deaf ears as the girl tossed an anxious
glance over her shoulder. Her eyes widened even
more as a giant of a man rounded a distant corner
at a run and spied them.

"Hold that girl!" the man bellowed, raising an
arm to command their attention. "She's a run-
away!"

The girl bolted past Jeff, putting wings to her feet
as she leaped over the hatbox and raced into the
street, oblivious of an oncoming four-in-hand as
she looked back at the man.

Mrs. Brewster screamed and quickly clasped her
hands over her eyes to keep from seeing the girl
trodden beneath the horses' hooves, but Jeff was
already on the run, sprinting behind the fleeing female and, with his long legs, overtaking her.

The girl's breath left her abruptly in surprise as
two very capable arms swept her upward against
a male form and bore her at a breakneck run toward the far side of the thoroughfare. For a fleeting
moment, the din of thundering hooves drowned
her outraged protests, but she was determined to
berate the man soundly for his improper advances
just as soon as she could be heard. Then she
glanced over a wide, manly shoulder and gulped
as she focused her gaze on a swiftly passing coach

and the four horses racing ahead of it. The convey-
ance was so close, the breeze from its passage flung
dust and grit in her astounded face. She immediately decided she was very fortunate to be alive.

"My goodness!" she murmured breathlessly in
awe. "You saved my life!"

The tall gentleman set her to her feet once again,
commanding her full attention as he grinned down
at her. It was the most dazzling smile she had envisioned since she had given up childish reveries
of knights in shining armor.

"I was reluctant to lose you so soon after I found
you," Jeff answered glibly, convinced that she had
stepped out of his dreams. "What were you running away from in such a panic?"

"*From Me!*"

The shout completely disrupted the girl's tenuous composure, and she would have whirled and
fled if not for a large, thick-fingered hand reaching
out to seize her upper arm in an unyielding vise.

"Ye're not goin' anywhere, Raelynn Barrett!" the
huge man roared ominously. His voice was naturally deep, and though he softened his tone a meager degree as he continued, it still seemed to rock
them with its volume. "*Not after I've promised ye to
another!*"

"Unhand that girl, you ruffian!" Thelma Brewster demanded as she marched up to them. "This
is Charleston, for heaven's sake! No man in his
right senses would ever think of accosting a young
lady on these streets without fear of being taken to
task by our menfolk. You, *sir*, must be a stranger
here to be so vile."

Jeff placed a hand upon the elder woman's arm
and cocked a warning brow at her, bidding her to
hold her silence. He had no idea what kin the man
was to the girl, but if the fellow had authority to
arrange her life, Jeff could only conclude that he
was her father or guardian.

"Perhaps you'd like to step over to Mrs. Brewster's shop and discuss this matter privately," Jeff suggested, briefly indicating the place across the way. His goal was to first try and calm the man with the hope that he would be more reasonable with the girl. A handful of patrons had already gathered from nearby shops, and more were hurrying toward them from across the street and along the boardwalk. "We seem to be *attracting* a lot of attention here on the street."

"I don't give a blasted hoot who hears me! The little wench is comin' wit' me!"

"Oh, please!" Raelynn sobbed, trying to pry his beefy fingers from her arm. "Please don't sell me to that brute! I've done you no hurt! And you swore on my mother's deathbed that you'd watch over me until I was properly wed. Is this how you keep your promises?"

"Gustav said he'd wed ye when he got around ta it," the man rumbled. "An' that's good enough for me."

"You sold me!" Raelynn railed in a panic. "As soon as our ship touched shore, you went out and sold me to the first buffoon with money enough to suit your purposes." Her voice lowered to a rasping snarl. "I curse the day you came into our lives claiming to be my mother's long lost brother! You took what little wealth we had remaining after my father's death and squandered it buying passage on the first ship sailing from England. You might as well have killed my mother yourself! Instead, you let her die of starvation and disease in that rat-infested hold, all for your love of money and gain." Her ire strengthened. "Well, a pox on you, Cooper Frye! I won't be sold to the likes of Gustav Fridrich for two hundred—or even *two thousand* Yankee dollars!"

"Ye've no choice in the matter, missy," Cooper stated emphatically, drawing the girl relentlessly toward him. "Ye're comin' wit' me right now!"

Jeff had felt his hackles rise even before Mrs. Brewster nudged him sharply in the ribs. He laid a restraining hand upon the other man's wrist and stepped between him and the girl. "Wait a minute, will you?"

"Stay outa this!" Cooper flung the words with enough venom to make Mrs. Brewster stumble back in sudden consternation, but Jeff never wavered before the other's menacing glare. " 'Tain't none o' yer affair! This is me niece, an' no other but me own bloomin' self will be decidin' what'll happen to her."

"Well, I'm making it my business . . ." Jeff said almost pleasantly.

Cooper issued a loud, derisive snort and stepped closer threateningly, pushing his bewhiskered face forward until his broad nose nearly met the thinner, much more noble one. "Per'aps, stranger, ye'd like to taste me fist in yer mouth."

Jeff refused to retreat before the glowering red eyes that bore into him at very close range, or the foul breath that reeked of a fetid stench like that of one who had passed the night swilling strong rum. They were the same height, Cooper Frye easily outweighing him twice over, but Jeff knew how to handle himself in a fight if it came to that. "You'd be wise to listen to my proposal, Mr. Frye," he cautioned. "If you truly want to sell the girl, then I am offering to buy her."

Mrs. Brewster's startled gasp came a fraction of an instant before Raelynn Barrett caught her own breath in surprise. It remained frozen in her chest as she stared in amazement at the tall, splendidly garbed man who had come into her life only a few moments ago. Why would he want to buy her? With his good looks and polished manners he had no need to lay out coins for a woman, and certainly

not such a sorry-looking one as herself. What could
he possibly see in her?

A calculating gleam began to shine in Cooper
Frye's gray eyes as he considered the expensively
garbed man. The dark blue frock coat and gray
breeches had obviously been tailored by one of superior reputation in the trade, for the cut was crisp
and impeccable. The tall, fashionable riding boots
sported turn-down cuffs of gray above polished
black leather and, like the smooth-fitting breeches,
seemed to mold the lean, muscular shape of the
long legs. Cooper was doubtful that he had ever
seen such costly clothes before, even on the streets
of London.

"Why would ye be wantin' ta buy the wench?"
For once, Cooper's voice was mellow enough to be
tolerable. "Ye got an itch ta 'ide her away from yer
wife an' take yer ease wit' her when ye've got
nothin' better to do?"

"For shame, you cod-faced lout!" Mrs. Brewster
exclaimed in outrage. "Mr. Birmingham would
never dream of doing such a thing!"

Jeff had no wish to destroy the woman's unswerving confidence in him by admitting that he
was extremely interested in the girl, at least enough
to want to rescue her from this oaf and to see her
gowned in clothes as fine as those that Brandon
was wont to buy for Heather. The dull brown,
threadbare dress Raelynn presently wore did little
justice to her uncommon beauty.

"What is the price you'll take for her?" Jeff asked
tersely. "Name it, and let this matter be done. The
whole town is here to observe this event."

Cooper Frye scratched his bristly chin reflec-
tively and flicked a glance across the wall of faces
that was pressing in close around them. "Well
now," he drawled, wondering if his intended lie
was too extravagant for the other's purse. He decided to leave some room for haggling. "Gustav

Fridrich was willing ta pay a bloody five hundred o' yer Yankee dollars ta have her. I've got to have at least that much and maybe a hundred more ta be able ta face that ornery German and tell him I've sold the chit ta someone else."

Jeff made sure his offer was far more generous than the stranger could have expected. "Seven hundred fifty should give you enough courage to do the deed."

Cooper's mottled tongue flicked across his wide, gaping mouth as he gawked at the other man. "Seven hundred fifty?" he repeated, staggered by the thought of such an extravagant sum. "For the girl here?"

"We have witnesses." Jeff stated the obvious, nodding toward the ever-growing crowd. "Most of these people know me and can attest that my word is true."

"I can vouch for his integrity better than anyone here," a nearby clothier heartily declared, pushing his tall, broad-shouldered bulk through the mass of onlookers until he faced Cooper Frye. "In fact, if Mr. Birmingham isn't presently carrying such a sum on his person, I'd be only too happy to send one of the clerks into my shop here and fetch it for him. So if I were you, Cooper Frye, I'd listen carefully to what my friend has to say. He has other friends in this crowd who are equally loyal and who'll be glad to report this event to any interested parties."

"Thank you, Farrell," Jeff murmured. He accepted the man's offer of a temporary loan and, after receiving a leather pouch filled with gold coins from his friend, returned his attention to Cooper Frye and counted out the necessary amount. "Now, Mr. Frye, I'd advise you to heed my words carefully. Before receiving this pouch, you must sign a bill of receipt pledging that you'll never interfere with me or the girl again. If you should do so, then you'll forfeit what you get here today, either by returning it to the last coin or, if you cannot pay, hiring yourself out to me as a servant until the sum is repaid in full. Do you understand?"

"Where's the receipt?" Cooper inquired bluntly.

Jeff accepted a quill from Farrell, who had been astute enough to foresee the need, and quickly rewrote a lading bill to conform to the requirements of the contract. "Sign at the bottom if you're able to write your name," he instructed Cooper. "Otherwise, make your mark."

"I can write me name," the huge man boasted, swaggering a bit before the crowd, but when he applied the quill to the parchment, he bent over the top of a nearby cask and painstakingly scratched out his name in simple letters.

Rolling up the contract, he handed it back to Jeff, who scanned it quickly, then delivered the bag of coins.

"Remember what you've promised," Jeff cautioned. "If you bother us, you'll forfeit the money."

"I heard ye the first time," Cooper answered sharply. Then, with a leering smirk, he faced Raelynn, who stood in stoic silence before him. "Now that ye'll be takin' yerself a rich lover, I don't suppose I'll be seein' ye 'round where I'll be."

Raelynn's eyes flared with fiery rage at his affront; then, as she took command of her temper, they narrowed into cold, icy shards that pierced him where he stood. " 'Twill gratify my most fervent wish, Cooper Fyre, if I never, *ever* see you again as long as I may live."

"What's this now?" Cooper queried in feigned surprise. "Ye'll not be showin' ol' Uncle Coop a bit o' fondness afore we part? After all I've done for ye?"

"Be on your way," Jeff advised the man curtly. "If Raelynn hasn't had enough of your antics, then I certainly have."

"I'm goin'! I'm goin'!" Cooper assured him. Chortling to himself, he turned and, tossing the bag of coins in his hand, strolled back across the street from whence he had come.

Raelynn breathed a sigh of relief at his going, but her feeling of contentment was brief, to say the least. Though she was not necessarily averse to the idea of being owned by Mr. Birmingham, she was certainly not blind to the dangers of such a relationship. His unparalleled good looks and easy charm could pose a dire threat to a virtuous maid who had no knowledge of men. Whether they were roués or gallant gentlemen, her experience with them was seriously lacking. For that reason she could not be content with the current situation. Despite what Cooper Frye thought, she was not made of ice.

Stepping beside Jeff, she gazed up at his lean profile as he watched the departing figure of Cooper Frye, and mentally affirmed her admiration of all that she saw. Her heart fluttered unnaturally as the elusive, manly scent of his cologne wafted through her senses, making her realize just how crucial it was for her to establish a code of conduct between them before they were ever alone together. He affected her so strongly that she could not be sure she would be able to stand steadfast and stoically deny him that which he might ask of her.

"Mr. Birmingham"—her voice quavered oddly as she spoke—" 'tis most urgent that I speak with you in private."

Any satisfaction Jeff derived from seeing the last of Cooper Frye dwindled rapidly as he looked down into the smudged and troubled face of Raelynn Barrett. That was when the full import of his actions hit him broadside. Had he taken her to an inn and shared a room with her for all the world to see, he could not have done more to destroy her reputation than what he had just accomplished by buying her. If the thought hadn't taken root on its own, then Cooper's taunt had certainly set the seed in fertile soil. Before nightfall, word would spread throughout the area that he had bought himself a young woman, one who was likely destined to become his mistress. How could he have been so blind as not to see what crime he was committing against her? Usually he was far more perceptive than that. What could he possibly do now to restore her honor?

Coming to himself, he realized that Mrs. Brewster was offering the use of her shop. "And perhaps you'd like some tea while you talk."

The milliner hurried back to her shop, scooping up the hatbox and Jeff's beaver as she went. Ushering them in, she led the way to her small apartment in the back, where she made tea as the couple settled at her small table and faced each other rather apprehensively across its surface. Raelynn waited for the woman to excuse herself, but in her haste to set out her best teapot, cups, and a variety of sweetcakes on porcelain plates, Thelma completely forgot the girl's request for privacy.

Jeff also felt the need to talk with Raelynn alone and drew Thelma aside to ask a favor of her, having settled his mind on the only option open to him. "As you can see for yourself, Mrs. Brewster, the girl is in desperate need of some clothes to wear. Would it be too much of an imposition if I asked you to go back to Farrell's and see what he has available in the way of women's clothing that would fit Raelynn—perhaps some gowns and other essentials that were ordered but never picked up?"

"I'd be delighted to, Mr. Jeffrey, but how shall I know what you want to spend for her? Farrell's seamstresses are the best in the area, and I know some of their gowns can be quite elaborate and costly."

"If you're unsure about anything, ask Farrell to help you. He knows me well enough to be able to lend you whatever advice you might need. Otherwise, Mrs. Brewster, I will entrust the decisions to you and your excellent taste."

"Should I bring the clothes back here, then?"

"I rode my stallion into town today, so ask Farrell to have the packages loaded in a hired livery, then send the driver here to await our departure to Oakley."

Jeff escorted the milliner to the front door and watched as she scurried across the street. Then he made his way once more to her private quarters. In his brief absence, Raelynn had washed her face and smoothed her hair, presenting a neater demeanor as she poured him a cup of tea. Watching him from beneath long silky lashes, she daintily sipped from her own cup.

"You're no doubt curious about what I have in mind," Jeff began forthrightly.

Raelynn inclined her head in a slow nod. "I have no idea whether you are married or single, Mr. Birmingham, so you can perhaps understand that I am completely bemused as to what I should expect. Will your wife be my mistress? Or are you my one and only master?"

"I do not consider myself your master, Raelynn," he said with a smile. "And you'll have no mistress, either. I am a bachelor."

"I hope you'll understand, sir, if I tell you that that fact gives me cause to worry," Raelynn admitted candidly. "I have only just met you, and yet suddenly I find myself your solitary possession. I dare not allow myself to think what your intentions may be. To be sure, sir, though you are neatly attired and handsome beyond a mere girl's dreams, I am no more disposed toward becoming your plaything than I was willing to accept Gustav Fridrich's plans for me."

"'Tis difficult to tell you what has been on my mind since I first saw you," Jeff replied haltingly. "Perhaps I was too intrigued by your beauty to realize that I was acting irrationally, inadvertently doing you more harm than good. I fear you might think me a fool, Raelynn, but I feel as if I've known you the whole of my adult life...."

Raelynn eyed him curiously. "I would never think you a fool, Mr. Birmingham."

"I'm a man in my early thirties, and I've come this far through life never having been tempted to ask for a lady's hand. You may think my proposal completely outrageous, especially since we've just met, but I can think of no better solution to disarm the gossips who'll be wont to talk about this incident for weeks or even months to come."

Though perplexed, Raelynn grew increasingly more attentive as the moments sped by. "I am listening, sir."

"You have need of a protector, Raelynn, and I am in want of a wife to still the wagging tongues that have given me no peace for several years now. They are set to clacking without provocation, even going so far as to spread the sordid rumor that I yearn after my brother's wife. 'Tis a lie I've longed to serve quick death to, but not at the cost of squandering my freedom by taking to wife some woman I cannot tolerate. I know you are young..."

"Ten and nine, to be exact, sir," she stated softly.

"Very young," he mumbled pensively behind his cup as he raised it to take a sip.

Raelynn was hanging onto his every word and did not allow his reply to pass without acknowledgment. "That depends, sir, on what you have in mind. I'm far too old to be considered a child, and if 'tis your desire to become my guardian, I would then advise you to consider the gossips and their wagging tongues. In England, I knew several ladies younger than I who had wed doddering ancients, but they were soon widowed and, much to their delight, bequeathed enough wealth to marry whom they would. A pair of them selected young, handsome pups who had to be mothered like children, and my friends soon became exasperated with them. As for me, sir, I would rather wed one who is mature enough to know his own mind and yet young enough to give me a brood of children and be with me 'til I am ancient, too.''

It was Jeff's turn to stare at her in awe. "Raelynn, do you truly comprehend what I am suggesting?"

She was reluctant to answer for fear she might be wrong. "And what is that, sir? Tell me outright, so I may not be mistaken."

"I am proposing that we be married posthaste," he said simply.

A smile softly curved her lips. "Then I was not mistaken, sir. And though we've only just met, I am willing to accept your offer of marriage . . . if you might lend some thought that we are, after all, strangers and need some time to come to know each other ere we share a bed together as man and wife."

It was some hours later when Jeff Birmingham and his bride-to-be arrived at Oakley. It seemed he had not long to wait before a carriage came smartly up the lane, and a moment later, Kingston, the butler, showed his brother and sister-in-law into the drawing room where Jeff was awaiting them. Considering all the townspeople who'd witnessed his purchase of Raelynn, he'd known the news would reach Brandon at the lumber mill before traveling on to Harthaven and Heather, and that there would be no need to send a request for their presence, for they'd be concerned enough to come at once. During the long ride home, he had assured

Raelynn of his honorable intentions, but upon seeing Heather's face, he wondered if he might have to repeat them to her as well.

His housekeeper, Cora, had answered his summons and now stood in the doorway, awaiting his instructions. Her wide grin told him that the black woman was taking everything in and enjoying the whole affair.

Raelynn had retreated several steps to stand near Jeff, as if for protection, and watched the two newcomers hesitantly. It was not hard for Raelynn to discern that this was the sister-in-law whom the gossips had avowed Jeff was in love with, for she was beautiful beyond belief. Still, the fact that Heather was at least six months along with child should have deterred such talk.

Heather's heart went out to the young woman who, in spite of her shabby garments, held herself with a subdued and natural grace. She seemed wary of them, as if doubtful of being graciously received, which Heather could totally understand, having experienced similar qualms when Brandon brought her home from England to meet his friends and family.

The expression of curiosity that Brandon bestowed upon his brother motivated Jeff to lend his immediate attention to Raelynn, giving the elder no opportunity to take sweet revenge for all the needling Jeff had once done. When he had learned that Brandon had been forced to marry Heather after mistaking her for a woman of the streets, Jeff had been unrelenting in his efforts to get his sibling to realize what a great treasure he had unwittingly stumbled onto in Heather. The greatest obstacle had been Brandon's pride, but since he had already fallen head over heels in love with his wife, it had only been a matter of time before Brandon came around to conceding that she was the best thing that had ever happened to him.

Jeff hurried on with the introductions. "Raelynn, this is my brother, Brandon, and his wife, Heather. Brandon . . . Heather . . . this is Raelynn Barrett."

"Your pardon," Raelynn murmured demurely, sensing the other woman's discomfiture. "My presence here must confound you. I would have stayed in Charleston, but Mr. Birmingham insisted that I come with him and meet his family. No doubt you have much to discuss and need some privacy."

"I think we do," Heather responded gently, greatly heartened by the softly spoken and refined eloquence of the young woman. At least Jeff had not been taken in by some unschooled hoyden, though that possibility had seemed remote.

Jeff gestured to Cora. "Show our guest to the blue room upstairs and help her bathe and dress for dinner. Kingston has already taken several packages upstairs, and you'll find everything she'll need in them. Another guest will be arriving shortly, and he'll want to meet her as soon as possible."

The black woman gave him a toothy grin. "Yo' means yo' want her back here lickety-split, Mr. Jeff?"

"Faster than that, Cora," he urged with more truth than humor, drawing a gleeful cackle from the servant.

Beckoning for Raelynn to follow, Cora hurried into the hall, chattering all the while as she led the Englishwoman upstairs. "Mr. Jeff's done turned this big ol' house into a showplace. Jes' wait 'til yo' see this here bedroom I'm takin' yo' to."

In the absence of Raelynn, the three family members faced one another in indecision. Feeling a need to mentally organize his planned announcement before airing it, Jeff crossed the room and, taking a decanter and a crystal snifter from an imported cabinet, poured a small draught of brandy into the glass. Joining the couple again, he handed the snifter to Brandon.

"News of my purchase traveled fast," Jeff commented. "I was sure I'd have to wait at least another half hour before I saw your face."

Brandon savored a tiny sip of the brew as he returned his brother's grin. "I was at the lumber mill when I heard about the incident in town. I thought it best to return to Harthaven before someone took a notion to ride out and tell Heather."

Heather was, in fact, near tears as she settled onto the settee. "Jeff, how could you take advantage of that poor girl's dilemma and buy her like a slave off a block? Raelynn will not be able to hold up her head for all the slander that is bound to be said about her. Despite your good intentions in saving her from her uncle's greedy plans, you've become as much a culprit by bringing her into your house without a proper chaperon."

Jeff came and squatted down in front of her. Gathering her slender hands in his, he spoke as gently as he could. "My dearest Tory," he murmured, using his pet name for her, "will you trust me enough to believe that I would not knowingly bring shame to any lady or any member of my family?"

"Jeff, you've always been so sensible," she assured him through the threat of new tears, "but I'm afraid in this case you've not thought of the consequences your gallantry may have invited."

"Actually, I've considered a great number of things since my confrontation with Raelynn's uncle," Jeff stated slowly, as if allowing her time to digest his words, "and I've also come to some conclusions. The only way I can be certain that Cooper Frye can never interfere . . ."

Hoofbeats sounded in the lane outside the house, drawing Jeff's immediate attention. In a rush now, he quickly gave his excuses, disappeared into the hallway, and after a muted exchange with Kingston, leaped up the stairs two at a time, leaving the servant to answer the door. A moment later Kingston led Reverend Parsons into the drawing room.

Heather exchanged a quick, worried glance with her husband, who responded with an almost imperceptible shrug before he strode quickly forward to clasp the other man's hand in greeting.

"So good to see you, Reverend," he said affably. "We missed you while you were away."

" 'Tis good to be back with my flock and reassure myself of their good health. You and Heather are certainly looking well." He paused as he glanced around in search of his host. "But where is Jeffrey?"

"I think he took flight when he heard you coming," Brandon quipped, then tried to curb his grin as his young wife looked around, seeming completely disconcerted by his statement.

"Aye," the reverend answered wryly. "I heard about the commotion in Charleston. It makes me wonder if some of my flock have taken on different coats in my absence, although I can't imagine Jeffrey being a wolf in sheep's clothing."

Brandon smiled with droll humor. "Whatever the precise cut of his coat, Jeff certainly has a way of calling attention to himself."

Heather rolled her eyes heavenward in disbelief, wondering how her husband could make light of this dreadful situation with Reverend Parsons present.

"Jeff was just being chivalrous, Reverend Parsons," she assured him, ready to defend her brother-in-law with unswerving loyalty.

Reverend Parsons chortled as he accepted a glass of lemonade from Kingston. "Now, Heather, don't get your pretty feathers ruffled. Jeff and I are old friends. Why, I've known him about as long as anybody has, excepting Brandon here. His gallantry is unquestionable . . . uh . . . for the most part, that is."

While the two men exchanged amused glances, Heather took up a lacy handkerchief and began to fan her flushed face. She wished fervently that she would suddenly awake and find that this whole incident had been nothing more than a bad dream.

Eyeing his agitated wife closely, Brandon acquiesced and came to sit beside her on the settee. A fleeting moment of cherished intimacy passed between them as he lifted her slender fingers to his lips and looked at her with warmly glowing green eyes, winning a soft and loving smile from her lips in response.

Reverend Parson settled into a chair across from them. "What does your son think about his parents acquiring a new baby? Is he hoping for a sister or perhaps a brother to play with?"

"Our black housekeeper swears we'll be having a little girl this time." Heather smiled as Brandon threaded his fingers through hers. "Hatti deciphers the signs so well, we've considered telling Beau that he'll be getting a new sister named Suzanne Elizabeth in the next couple of months."

"And if it turns out to be a boy?" the reverend inquired.

Brandon chuckled. "We'll just have to tell him Hatti made a mistake and let her explain it away."

Manly footsteps were heard accompanying those of a more delicate tread, and all eyes became riveted on the parlor entrance as the footfalls approached the drawing room. Then Jeff slid back the panel doors and, holding Raelynn's hand, led her into view, prompting the two gentleman guests to rise in appreciation of her stirring beauty. Her rich auburn hair had been swept high on her head and intricately woven with a corded ribbon that matched her gown of silver blue satin. Elegantly coifed and regally gowned, Raelynn Barrett was lovelier than any cherished dream.

An aura of warmth swept Heather as she stared at the couple, and it came to her that she had never seen Jeff looking quite so proud or handsome. His shirt and stock of flawless white seemed to gleam beneath his meticulously cut black silk frockcoat. Narrow breeches, waistcoat, silk stockings and low shoes, all of the same hue, completed the sleek, manly costume.

"Gentlemen." Jeff dipped his head forward slightly as he gave verbal recognition to the men. Then he clicked his heels in a crisp, shallow bow as he faced Heather. "My lady." He swept a hand to acknowledge the splendid beauty who stood beside him. "I would like to present Raelynn Barrett, the woman who is to become my bride."

For a moment the occupants of the room could only stare in amazement. Heather felt her heart swell with unbelievable gladness. Confident now that all was well in the family, she slipped her hand into Brandon's, which clasped and held it lovingly. Together they turned as Reverend Parsons beckoned the couple into the center of the room. Raelynn accepted Jeff's proffered arm and seemed to glide effortlessly beside him.

"Is the lady consenting?" Reverend Parsons queried with careful concern.

Raelynn lifted her gaze to Jeff and smiled as she gazed into his shining green eyes. "I could not have hoped for a more chivalrous champion had I spent the last ten years of my life searching for him. In the short time I've known him, I've come to realize that he's incredibly kind and tender, and I am honored that he has asked me to become his wife."

Jeff faced the man and lent further insight behind their motivation. "We've discussed the matter at some length," Jeff avouched. "Raelynn is in desperate need of a protector, and marriage is the only way we can strip Cooper Frye of his claims as her only kin. I sent for you tonight, Reverend, so you could perform the ceremony for us here in the privacy of my home. Are *you* consenting?"

The man looked to Brandon as the elder Birmingham. "You know your brother better than anyone. Can you name a reason why I should delay the nuptials?"

Brandon spoke with unswerving confidence. "Jeff has always been clear about what he wants out of life, Reverend. He's acted with a great deal more certainty than I've been able to lay claim to at certain times. If he says this marriage should take place, then I am one to believe him."

Reverend Parsons nodded as he accepted Brandon's vote of approval; then he peered questioningly at Heather. "Have you anything to say, my dear?"

"Only to lend my heartfelt endorsement," she murmured with a radiant smile.

The reverend slid a small black book from inside his coat and began to leaf through the pages. "When I was summoned here by Jeffrey's servant, the man advised me to come prepared to perform a wedding ceremony. Little did I know then that it would be for my host." He smiled at the couple. "Now if you will stand before me, Raelynn and Jeffrey, I will speak the words to unite you in marriage."

The moments sped past as the muted voices melded in a ritual nearly as old as time itself. Jeff drew a simple gold band from his pocket and slipped it on Raelynn's finger as he repeated the words:

"With this ring I thee wed. . . . "

His voice was strong and steady, attesting to his unwavering confidence in the decision he had made. When Reverend Parsons spoke the final words of the ceremony unifying the couple, Jeff

faced Raelynn and was amazed to see her translucent eyes awash in mistiness.

"You may kiss the bride," the reverend invited.

Raelynn blushed as she lifted her face to accommodate the tall stranger whom she had just married,
feeling rather forward doing so. A peck on the cheek
was certainly all that she was expecting since Jeff had
agreed to give her time to get acquainted with him
before pressing her to become his wife in actuality.
When she felt the first light brush of his mouth on
hers, she was startled by the warm, sweetly moist
contact and was hardly aware of her own lips opening in surprise. Her breath stilled in waiting suspense
of her first kiss. Then, as lightly as thistledown being
borne along on a gentle breeze, his lips moved upon
hers, parting ever so slightly to conform to the sup-
pleness of hers.

When Jeff finally drew back, Raelynn swayed
weakly against him, realizing with some astonishment that his kiss had sapped the strength from
her limbs and been far more potent than she had
ever imagined anything could be. Considering that
mere minutes ago she had asked for separate
rooms, how could she now tell him that she
yearned for more of that blissfully sweet nectar?

Jeff laid his arm across the small of her back and
drew her closer still, lending her needed support
as he whispered, "Are you all right?"

Raelynn nodded slowly as she sought to calm the
frantic pounding of her heart and dull her senses
to the breathtaking reality that she was in the arms
of this tall, handsome man and he was her husband. She was entranced by his nearness and vividly aware of the casual pressure of his manly
form. Had she been able to command her wishes
into existence, she entertained no doubt that Jeff
Birmingham would have been exactly where he
was at that precise moment in her life.

Gathering some remnant of her scattered poise,

Raelynn managed to face the other occupants of the room. "I beg your forgiveness for my faintness. 'Tis been some time since I last took food."

Heather was there immediately to give her an affectionate hug. "I'm so happy for you both. I'm sure that if Jeff had searched the wide world over, he could not have made a better choice for a bride. And whether you know it or not, my dear, your husband ranks among the best."

Reverend Parsons took his leave shortly after bestowing his blessings and good wishes on the couple. Having other visits to make before retiring to home and to bed, he declined their invitation to stay and partake of the wedding supper. Instead, waving farewell, he rode away, leaving the small clan of Birminghams to gather in the main dining room.

The elegant table was long enough to sit twelve or more easily, but no rigid formality was on display tonight. Jeff had long ago pooh-poohed the idea of the master and mistress of the house sitting at opposite ends of a long table unless they were entertaining a large crowd. Tonight the settings were cozily arranged near one end. A place had been provided on Jeff's right for his young bride and, close on his left, one for Heather, leaving Brandon to take the chair beside his wife.

"All I can say, brother," Brandon commented with puckish humor as he considered the table setting, "is that you're true to your mold. You haven't changed a whit since I first brought Heather home to Harthaven."

"Nary a mite," Jeff agreed. " 'Tis certain I'm still the friendlier of us two and have no penchant for isolating myself, as you have been known to do."

Brandon sought to shrug away his brother's waggish gibe with a chuckle, but for a moment his humor was poorly contrived. Because of his own stubborn arrogance, he had once endured the torturous separation of not only a long, formal table between himself and his young wife but different bedrooms as well. In retrospect, he mentally likened the pain of his lengthy abstinence to that which a roué might have suffered had he been imprisoned in a cell right across from a woman whose beauty and form he could see but not touch. Though Heather had come into his house as his wife and been close under his hand, he had found himself beset in much the same way. Even now, the memory of his own foolishness made Brandon squirm uncomfortably in his chair.

"No one's infallible where pride is concerned, Jeff," he replied, having learned that truth the hard way. "In fact, you might be surprised to realize where you are susceptible."

Laughter twinkled in Jeff's green eyes. "I've tried to learn from your example, brother, and refrain from making any rash vows that I'll later regret."

Heather sensed Jeff's pointed glance as the two men made subtle reference to the torment Brandon had suffered while trying to hold her at arm's length. Reaching out, she squeezed her husband's hand reassuringly and conveyed her loving devotion with a warm, gentle smile. "We should all be willing to learn from other's mistakes, Jeff," she responded gaily, glancing toward her brother-in-law, "but sometimes when we make them ourselves, we're better able to grasp the full import of the lesson."

Jeff leaned back in his chair and sipped his wine. He thought of his own recent pledge to wait before claiming his conjugal rights with Raelynn and hoped he could be as strong-willed as his brother had been in controlling his manly desires, yet perhaps not quite as stubborn so that he could quickly discern a warming in his wife. " 'Tis strange how similar circumstances seem to follow in a family,"

Jeff said. "I may find the pigeons coming home to roost after all."

Brandon elevated a brow in curious question, then glanced at Raelynn as he began to understand Jeff's quandary. In view of the fact that they had wed in haste, he could imagine his brother being gallant enough to agree to a gentlemanly wait before reaping the pleasures of a marriage bed.

Raelynn seemed confused by the brothers' repartee. "Is something amiss?"

Heather dispelled the very idea. "Oh, you needn't fret that it's anything serious, Raelynn. The Birmingham men take great pleasure in sharpening their wit on each other's hide. They're about as tough-skinned as a pair of ol' mules, and it's always a challenge for them to see which one gets the last word in. Still, I've never known two who are closer friends."

It was some time later when Raelynn and Jeff stood on the portico of Oakley and bade farewell to the other couple. The night was still and warm with the faint scent of jasmine in the air. The kind of evening made for lovers, Jeff mused as his young wife strolled along the porch and looked out on the moonlit grounds and huge trees that raised their lofty canopied heads into the belly of the starlit sky.

"There were recent times in England when I yearned to look out and see something besides the squalor of London," Raelynn reminisced in a soft, murmuring tone. "You see, my father, who was once a wealthy lord, was falsely accused of treason against the crown. Everything was taken from him except for a wee bit of money he managed to hide for us. Later, he died in prison, though he claimed his innocence with his last breath. When my uncle found my mother a few months ago, he said we could start a new life here in the Carolinas where no one would lay the title of traitor to our name. During the voyage, my mother discovered that my uncle had spent the last of our money. She died during the crossing, and upon landing my uncle set about providing for himself. He brought Gustav Fridrich to look me over, and the man promised him a purse once Cooper Frye delivered me to his house, but on the way I managed to escape. Now all that seems an eternity ago and a whole continent away. Little did I dream when I woke this morning that I would be married before the evening was over and living amid such splendor. It seems, Jeffrey, that I owe you much more than my life. Indeed, I cannot imagine how I can ever repay you for saving me from a miserable existence and bringing me to this safe, beautiful haven."

"No payment is required beyond the vows we exchanged, Raelynn." Jeff's gaze was nourished by his wife's fluid grace as she came across the porch toward him. When she stood close, he gazed down into her shadowed face and lifted his lean knuckles to lightly brush a loose tendril from her cheek. "And I am patient."

Raelynn sighed as her eyes searched his. "Do you mean that?"

"We have certainly done this whole thing wrong-about, Raelynn. We have put the sail abaft the mast or, if you will, the cart before the horse, but I would have you consider this, madam. The most serious vow was given first, and now we must take into account all the rest." He cupped her chin and stared into her liquid eyes. When he continued, his voice was soft and husky. "It seems I've known you for a thousand years and have only awaited your coming, yet with trembling breath I shall tarry even longer 'til you know the full extent of my honor, as well as my failings, and choose to come to me of your own free will."

"We are strangers. . . . " she whispered breathlessly.

"We are married," Jeff countered gently. "And

you are everything I desire. I knew that the moment I saw you."

"Please take me in, Jeff," Raelynn pleaded faintly.

"Your wish is my command, my lady." He took her arm and gallantly complied, then accompanied her upstairs in silence as she made a slow, measured ascent. Escorting her to the entrance of the bedroom adjoining his, he reached out to push the door open and waited for her to leave him. She did not.

Blushing lightly, Raelynn faced her handsome husband. "Would you think me forward, Jeffrey, if I asked to be kissed?"

He stepped close, and she reached parted lips up toward his in anticipation, eager to receive his gently questing kiss. Her senses quivered crazily as Jeff's arms tightened about her and pulled her fully against his long frame. His eyes flamed as he searched her face, seeming to stare into her very soul, demanding answers she was too embarrassed to give.

Jeff was rather amazed that she did not pull away, for the sensual pleasure of holding her against him had affected him in ways he was sure his young wife could not ignore. But instead of pulling back, Raelynn yielded completely to him, leaning into him and raising on tiptoe to accommodate his height.

Desiring her more than he had any woman, Jeff was bold enough to forge ahead, though a part of him waited apprehensively for that moment when she might show some resistance. Lowering his head, he seized her lips with a greedy fervor that made Raelynn catch her breath in delight, and she clung to him with a fevered passion she had not even known she was capable of.

No denials came, and Jeff bent to sweep Raelynn in his arms. He bore her to the bed, pausing only to thrust the door shut with his heel.

Kathleen E. Woodiwiss

KATHLEEN E. WOODIWISS is America's pre-eminent author of historical fiction. She has written eight novels, all of which have become multimillion-copy bestsellers. Her novels have been translated into fifteen languages. Ms. Woodiwiss lives in Louisiana, where she is currently at work on a new novel.